NOTHING
CAN
ERASE
YOU

NOTHING CAN ERASE YOU

A THRILLER

TRANSLATED BY SAM TAYLOR

MICHEL BUSSI

AMAZON **CROSSING**

Published by Amazon Crossing, Seattle

www.apub.com

Amazon, the Amazon logo, and Amazon Crossing are trademarks of Amazon.com,
Inc., or its affiliates.

ISBN-13: 9781662509049 (paperback)
ISBN-13: 9781662509056 (digital)

Cover design by Mumtaz Mustafa
Cover illustration by Mariachiara Di Giorgio © Les Presses de la Cité

Printed in the United States of America

For Isabelle and Marie-Claude
and our memories of Auvergne

If I had cut his wings
He would be mine
And he would not have left.
Yes, but then . . .
He would no longer be a bird.
And for me,
It was the bird that I loved.

"Txoria Txori" (The bird is a bird) by Joxean Artze,

translated from Michel Bussi's French translation of the
Basque original

"Professor Ian Stevenson, of the University of Virginia, studied thousands of cases from all over the world of children who claimed to remember memories that appeared to be evidence of reincarnation. His work at the institution's Division of Perceptual Studies enabled him to create the 'Stevenson model,' which noted certain surprising recurrent themes: changes of gender were rare, less than five percent; the child began giving information on their previous life from around two years old and generally stopped around ten; their death in the previous life had often been violent and premature; physical, somatic, and mental anomalies such as unexplained scars, birthmarks, phobias, and abilities were quite common."

"And is he serious, this Professor Stevenson? I mean, is he a scientist? Does he have a laboratory? Is it just a bunch of hot air, or can we believe it?"

"What exactly are you referring to when you say, 'Can we believe it?'"

"The stuff he's talking about. Those testimonies—are they true or not?"

"In your opinion, what enables someone to determine whether something is true or not?"

"I . . . I don't know . . . I guess if most people think something, it must be more true than false."

"So if we include Hindus, Buddhists, one-fourth of Europeans, and almost a third of Americans, then a majority of people on this earth believe in reincarnation. They are convinced that our body is merely a form of clothing . . . and that our soul survives it."

"And so you change clothes when the old ones wear out; is that right? Is that what reincarnation is? The soul is like a flea, jumping from person to person, or from a person to a dog, from a dog to a cat, from a cat to a rat . . . Is it as simple as that?"

"No, it's not that simple. On the contrary, it is a long journey. A journey of which we remember nothing, under normal circumstances. Except when it goes wrong . . ."

"What do you mean, 'when it goes wrong'?"

First Age

The Infant Soul

"Let me explain, Maddi. It's not that complicated. Infant souls are souls at the beginning of their journey. They discover life, and death. At that point, their only goal is to learn to survive."

I

Disappearance

Esteban

1

I am a rational person. Fiercely independent. Profoundly free. Sufficiently wealthy.

That is how Esteban sees me, I hope, through his eyes of a ten-year-old. It is also, I suppose, the image I project to my patients. *Dr. Maddi Libéri, family physician, 28 Boulevard Thiers, Saint-Jean-de-Luz.* Strong, reliable, straightforward. Nobody knows my faults, my doubts, or my inner life. Least of all my son.

My apartment, on the third floor of Rue Etchegaray in this old port city, possesses one of the most beautiful views of the Grande Plage, 150 meters away as the turnstone flies (the turnstone being a bird local to the Basque coast), and a forty-five-second walk.

And why wouldn't we walk it?

It is our morning ritual. Every day—before my first consultation, before Esteban goes to school, even before we eat breakfast together—the two of us dress in whatever we find on the floor of our bedrooms and run down to the beach. And once winter is over and the water temperature is above sixty-five degrees Fahrenheit, we also go swimming in the sea. All the streets in Saint-Jean-de-Luz lead to the ocean, as if the town were built with the express intention of providing every balcony with a glimpse of waves.

It has just turned eight o'clock. The beach at Saint-Jean-de-Luz is practically deserted. I can count fewer than twenty tourists scattered along the sandy crescent, from the Chevaux seawall to the Port seawall.

In front of the terrace of Toki Goxoa, a restaurant with a commanding view and a bar constructed from multicolored tiles, Esteban unties the red beach towel that he has been wearing as a Superman-style cape around his neck and drops it onto the sand. Then he pulls his Biarritz rugby shirt over his head and kicks off his green espadrilles.

"Let's go swimming, Mom."

"Just a second, honey."

I always observe first before taking a plunge; call it a doctor's instinct. I begin by looking at Esteban himself. His skinny little body, with the bones showing under the skin: collarbones that look like a strong wind might break them, tibias poking out from his long, baggy indigo swim shorts (the same color as the Basque sky that morning) decorated with a small white print of a whale on the left leg. Esteban is of average size for his age. I weigh and measure him every Saturday after my last consultation. Another of our rituals.

"Come on, Mom!"

Esteban waits impatiently while I undress. Before leaving the apartment, I put on a simple net dress over my fuchsia-and-lilac bikini. I love the feel of the mesh against my skin, the light threads imprisoning my belly and freeing my legs halfway down my thighs. I love still feeling that I'm desirable at almost forty—and not only in the eyes of the retirees who walk their poodles on Quai de l'Infante.

I examine the ocean. In the distance, out toward Hendaye and Socoa beach, surfers in black wet suits are lined up like a colony of ants as they prepare to brave the waves. Behind us, the Basque flags that line the pier snap and billow in the Atlantic wind.

"No, not today, honey. It's too rough."

"Huh?"

Esteban stares incredulously at the sea. The waves are several meters high. He's not dumb—he knows it would be impossible to go swimming in these conditions. Not that this stops his complaining.

"But it's my birthday!"

"I know that. So? You think I'm going to let you drown just because it's been ten years since I gave birth to you?"

Esteban gives me one of those irresistible Little Prince smiles that could break the will of any mother. There's a tiny gleam of sadness in his pale blue eyes. I run my hands through his blond hair to console him, and because I like the way he looks when his hair is a little tousled. How sweet he is, my Little Prince, half daydreamer and half rebel. Every night, when Esteban is sleeping like a baby, I stand on my balcony and bless the asteroid from which he fell.

"We'll go swimming tomorrow, honey. Or this evening, if I get off work early enough . . ."

He pretends to believe me.

"Okay, Mom."

He knows I'm not the kind of doctor who ever rushes her patients. My son and I understand each other intuitively, without having to spell everything out. A single look is enough to seal our mutual trust, our closeness. No man could ever come between us. I must always keep the other side of my bed empty, so that Esteban can join me there at dawn. No lover could ever wake me in the morning with an "I love you" so innocent and sweet.

I quickly rummage through my purse and hand Esteban a one-euro coin.

"Will you get us a baguette?"

Yet another of our rituals. This one began when Esteban turned nine. Always after our morning swim, he would dry off, put on his shirt, and run to the bakery all on his own — one minute thirty-five seconds at a sprint—while I returned home. As I finished my shower, he'd return and set the kitchen table: black cherry jam, sheep-milk yogurt, fruit juice freshly squeezed the day before. We would eat breakfast together; then he would take his shower while I put on my makeup, and then we'd go out together, hand in hand, I to my surgery and Esteban to school.

Esteban closes his hand around the coin.

9

From the distance of time, I wonder now: Why was I in such a rush to get home that morning? We had plenty of time, given that we hadn't gone swimming. Why did I merely brush off a few grains of sand blown onto his shoulder and automatically glance down at the top of his low-slung shorts, hanging down enough to show the birthmark on his abdomen, before walking away? Why didn't I turn around after I'd begun walking? Why didn't I make sure he had picked up his towel? That he'd put on his rugby shirt? That he was heading in the direction of the bakery, along Rue de la Corderie?

Perhaps because that is what rituals are for. To reassure us. To verify that all is well. To convince us no accident can occur. Because we believe that we are safe if we follow the same path every day.

In reality, we are constantly letting our guard down. Relaxing our vigilance, out of laziness. Shirking our responsibility.

◆ ◆ ◆

"Esteban?"

I stick my head out of the shower while the hot water continues to pour down my back. The bathroom wall—essentially a mirror three meters wide and two meters high, surrounded by turquoise zellige tiles—reflects my own body back to me, tanned from our first spring adventures: our walk to the summit of Larrun, white-water rafting on the Nive, your clumsy first attempts at paddleboard on the Lac de Saint-Pée, at surfing in Guéthary, at Basque pelota on the court in Arcangues. We have our whole life, Esteban, to become champions.

"Esteban?"

My hand gropes for the faucet, and I manage to turn it off without splashing water everywhere. I wrap my body in a towel, facing away from the mirror. I will leave the inspection of my imperfections for another time.

"Esteban, are you home?"

The only answer I receive comes from Patrick Cohen. It is 8:30 a.m. on France Inter, and the radio presenter begins his report by announcing that the French national soccer team, currently at the World Cup in South Africa, has refused to get off the bus to take part in training. Is there really nothing more important happening anywhere in the world? Anyway, what is Patrick Cohen doing in my living room?

"Esteban?"

Many mornings, as soon as he gets home from the bakery, Esteban takes advantage of the fact that I'm in the shower to change the radio station to something loud and trendy like Fun or Sky. Even more often, he'll turn off the radio, pick up his guitar, and improvise a few chords. Sometimes he writes his arrangements down in composition books for sheet music. Esteban is gifted. I feel certain he has perfect pitch, even if I've never taken the time to have him tested.

I come out of the bathroom, and my feet soak the poplar floorboards. Poplar—the one wood that must never get wet, because even a single drop can leave a permanent stain. But I don't care about that now. A vague fear has me by the throat. I take another step into the open-plan kitchen before freezing.

My footprints will be imprinted forever on the untreated wood. I can't move. All I can do is stare at the empty kitchen table. At the guitar hanging where I left it, on its rack.

Esteban has not come home.

I do not cry out. I tell myself he must be playing a prank on me. One by one, I open the doors to our bedrooms, our cupboards, the bathroom. I lean down to peer under the beds. I climb onto a stool to look on top of the wardrobe. I almost fall, but who cares. Once more, I open the doors to each cupboard, to the refrigerator, the oven. I'm starting to breathe fast. My heart feels like it's about to explode. I feel like I'm on the verge of a panic attack.

Where could Esteban be? On today of all days. His . . .

Suddenly, I have an idea.

I rush back into the bathroom. I don't know how he might have managed it, but Esteban is smart; he could have waited until I got out of the shower before going in there to hide. Or, even more likely, to seek out what I've hidden in there. I hold my breath and crouch down, then open the cupboard under the sink.

It's there.

His birthday present. A unique lyre-guitar with the look of an ancient instrument and the sound and wiring of an electric guitar. Esteban has gazed at it dreamily so many times in front of the display window at Atlantic Guitar. He could never have dared hope that his mother would . . .

I tear myself from these fond thoughts.

Esteban is not here.

He hasn't come to the bathroom to find his gift. Esteban is not in the apartment at all. He did not come home.

This has never happened before.

I check my watch through tear-blurred eyes. I have to hold my wrist to stop its trembling. I left him more than twenty-five minutes ago. It takes him less than three minutes to go to the bakery, pay for the bread, and come home.

I drop my towel and put on underwear and the first piece of clothing I find—a long T-shirt hanging on the end of the bed—and I hurtle downstairs. I cross Rue Etchegaray, then Rue Saint-Jacques. Most of the stores are closed, and only a few elderly couples are walking along the pedestrianized streets. I am past them before they have time to turn their heads.

I shove open the glass door of Le Fournil de Lamia and grab it just before it smashes against the inside wall.

"Have you seen my son?"

I don't bother looking to see if they have any other customers. The baker stares at my frightened, ghostlike face.

"No . . . no, not this morning, Madame Libéri. But—"

I leave before he can finish his sentence. The beach is less than a minute away. Forty seconds if I sprint. In front of me, a grandmother pulls her dog aside; a grandfather withdraws his walking stick. I arrive, breathless, outside Toki Goxoa. Tourists are sitting at tables, eating breakfast on the large wooden terrace that overlooks the beach. I keep going, staring at a small red dot straight ahead.

My target. My hope.

I run as fast as I can. With every stride, clouds of sand are sent flying at passing tourists.

At last I come to a halt.

The Superman towel is there where we left it on the beach, as crumpled as it was when Esteban dropped it to the ground almost half an hour ago. The Biarritz rugby shirt lies beside it. Esteban never put it back on.

I quickly scan the entire beach, the entire ocean, from the Chevaux seawall to the battlements of Fort Socoa; then my eyes search for footprints in the sand in front of me, below my feet, but all I see are a few little hills of sand. The wind has erased all trace of Esteban.

Prevented by the wall from crashing onto the town itself, enormous waves crash onto the beach ahead of me. I don't want to believe it. I don't want to look at the waves. I want to turn to the white facades of the houses behind me, with their blood-colored half-timbering, the window boxes full of flowers, the rows of specialty stores, the rich tourists; I want to go look for a dog that Esteban might have started playing with, a girl or a boy his own age, a sandcastle somewhere, a buoy on the beach, but my eyes are magnetized by the ocean.

The waves are more than three meters high now.

I hear again the words I spoke to my son that morning: *No, not today, honey. It's too rough.*

They will echo inside my head for the rest of my life.

I can't believe it. Esteban would never have disobeyed me.

2

"So your son is wearing swim shorts, is that correct?"

The two policemen stand behind the counter at the police station. The first one fixes me with his sepia-colored eyes, like painted marbles. They seem hardly to blink at all. I don't know what color eyes the other man has, because he hasn't looked up at me since I came in. He began taking notes, the keyboard making a noise like a machine gun, as soon as I opened my mouth. This is the second time I've gone over the facts with these men.

"Yes. Just a pair of trunks. His shirt and his towel were still on the beach."

The lieutenant's eyes still do not blink. Beside him, the typist's fingertips continue rattling the computer keys.

"Blue shorts, right?" asks the lieutenant, whose name is Lazarbal.

I try to be as brief and precise as possible. At that moment, emergency search teams are already combing the beach—called into action as soon as I explained to a police officer on the street what had happened. Three Zodiac boats are patrolling the coast, despite the howling wind, the roaring waves.

"Indigo."

"Indigo?"

The keyboard clatter abruptly falls silent. I guess that the typist is doing a Google search for the color indigo. What a waste of time! I've already described the color of Esteban's shorts to at least five different uniformed men.

"Yes, indigo!" I almost shout. "It's not that difficult, is it? Midway between blue and purple."

Lazarbal blinks three times, no doubt a sign of extreme agitation, before staring glassily at me again.

"Okay, Madame Libéri. Indigo shorts. So, apart from the color, is there another detail that could help us find him?"

I have to keep calm. I swore I would. More than twenty searchers including lifeguards are out looking for Esteban. These men are doing their best. I have to believe that. I have to help them. Answer their questions, again and again. Rinse, repeat, hope.

"There's a logo on the left leg of his shorts—a little white whale."

The typist's keyboard starts clattering again. Lazarbal's eyes seem to come alive for the first time, the eyelids blinking fast then slow, fast then slow. Maybe he's somehow sending a message in Morse code to those looking for Esteban? Or perhaps the message is for me, a subliminal form of reassurance.

"Don't worry, Madame Libéri. The search teams have a photograph of your son. They're good at their job. Now let's try to think calmly. So tell me again: Your son is . . . ten years old?"

"Yes. Today is his birthday."

Lazarbal's eyes turn to glass again.

"Exactly ten years old, then."

I don't like the way he emphasizes *exactly*. What is that supposed to imply? That he's surprised by the coincidence? What connection could there be between Esteban's disappearance and his birthday?

"Ten years old," the lieutenant repeats. "Excuse me, Madame Libéri, but isn't he a little young to be left alone on the beach?"

I have to shout my answer, to be heard above the typist's tap-dancing fingertips.

"I live on Rue Etchegaray, a hundred meters from the beach. All the streets are pedestrianized. Esteban is used to it. He's a mature kid for his age. Very calm and responsible."

Lazarbal's eyes are vacant. Is he even listening to me? Is he really there to help me, or is he already preparing to prosecute me for criminal negligence?

"Is your son a strong swimmer?"

Does he think I can't see what he's getting at? I'm not going to fall for this trap. The typist will note down everything I say. I speak in a manner that will require capital letters.

"ESTEBAN DID NOT GO SWIMMING. I TOLD HIM HE WAS NOT ALLOWED. MY SON DID NOT DROWN. HE WAS . . . HE WAS KIDNAPPED!"

Lazarbal's dead eyes do not contradict me. So that's one thing in their favor.

"The possibility that your son has drowned is only a theory, Madame Libéri. For now, we must keep an open mind. Even if . . ."

Even if what? screams a voice in my head.

"Even if the beach wasn't exactly deserted this morning. We have more than thirty potential witnesses. Not to mention the tourists on the terrace of the Toki Goxoa. You have just informed me that your son is intelligent and followed your advice. He could not have been abducted by a stranger without putting up a fight. And if he did put up a fight, someone would have seen him, or heard him."

Someone would have seen him . . . or heard him. I repeat the lieutenant's irrefutable logic inside my head. My skull feels as vacant as his glassy gaze.

"We have questioned every tourist on the beach," the policeman insists. "Nobody saw your son leaving the area, with or without another person."

"Nobody saw him go swimming either!"

Lazarbal responds with more Morse code: three brief flutters of his eyelids, then two longer blinks. His eyes dart toward the typist's computer screen before fixing me once again.

"That's true. The first witnesses were more than a hundred meters away and had no reason to keep watch over your son. In fact, nobody remembers him even being there. We only have your testimony."

Bastard!

"What about his towel? And his shirt?"

Lazarbal raises his hand slightly, like a cop by the roadside asking an agitated driver to calm down.

"Nobody doubts your word, Madame Libéri. Quite the contrary, in fact. It's true; we found his towel and his rugby shirt, in the exact spot where you left him. So everything does seem to indicate that he . . ." At last Lazarbal's eyes betray a quiver of anxiety. "That he disobeyed you. That . . . that as soon as your back was turned, he ran straight into the ocean."

"NO!"

Capital letters again.

I repeat myself, even louder this time:

"NO! I'm certain that's not true! I know Esteban. Today is his birthday. He couldn't wait to get home, to unwrap his present. He would never have disobeyed me, least of all today. Something must have happened to him."

I am exasperated by Lazarbal's blank gaze. In a fleeting thought, a stupid professional reflex, I wonder if perhaps he has tunnel vision, a condition that involves the loss of peripheral eyesight. That would explain why he's stuck in an office instead of being out in the field, searching for my son along with most of his colleagues.

"If we accept for a moment your theory, Madame Libéri, that your son was abducted, then he must have known his kidnapper. It could only have been someone he was willing to follow. Do you have any idea who that might be? A close friend? A relative? His . . . his father?"

"Esteban has no father! I am a single mother. And for your information, Lieutenant, that is by choice."

At least those vacant eyes do not seem to judge me. Or perhaps he simply doesn't care how I've chosen to raise my son. His hand reaches out to a stack of paper beside him while his eyes remain fixed on me. Perhaps it's not tunnel vision that he has, but the opposite: the overdeveloped peripheral vision common to all of nature's predators . . .

"Who could it have been, then?"

"I have no idea."

He spreads out some pictures on the desk before me—prints of images taken on cell phones.

"We will check. We will search. We already have collected a dozen photos from this morning, most taken by customers at the Toki Goxoa. You are in many of them. Almost all were taken when you came back to search for your son."

My gaze glides over the photos—my too-short T-shirt, my bare thighs. The clerk can't help turning his head to look, but Lazarbal immediately picks up the photographs and files them away.

"We'll have enlargements made," says the policeman, "and we'll ask you to examine them, to see if you recognize anyone. We also have a few shots of the beach taken just before you came back, but Esteban isn't in any of them. Nobody saw him in the streets of town either. So, in the absence of any evidence to the contrary, I'm afraid the most likely scenario is that—"

The typist will have to smash those keys when he transcribes this:

"ESTEBAN DID NOT DROWN! How many times do I have to tell you? Go ahead; look at your blown-up photos. You'll see that Esteban left his towel, his shirt, but not his espadrilles. So where are those espadrilles? You're not telling me Esteban wore them to go swimming?"

I cling to that hope. I'll cling to any hope, as long as I don't have to imagine my child's body swept away by the ocean.

"I'm sorry, Madame Libéri. I know it must seem horrible of me to imagine the worst, but it's possible your son walked to the edge of the sea in his espadrilles, took them off to go swimming, and that the waves carried them off. Or someone could have picked them up . . ."

"But this someone left the shirt and the towel?"

"It's possible. Or his espadrilles might be buried in the sand somewhere. We'll search for them."

The keyboard ceased clattering a long time ago, as if the typist had lost interest in my opinions. I do have one last line of argument, though. It's the only thought that prevents me from running straight into the ocean and letting the current sweep me away too.

"The Biarritz rugby shirt—it doesn't have any pockets."

"Sorry?"

"And his swim shorts—they don't have pockets either."

For the first time, Lazarbal looks wide awake. His eyelids are fluttering like frightened bees.

"Yes . . . ?"

"I gave Esteban a one-euro coin, as I do every morning, so that he could buy bread from Le Fournil de Lamia. If he'd gone swimming, he must have left the money on the beach. Nobody goes swimming with a coin in their fist. I didn't find the coin on the towel, nor in the sand, nor anywhere around it."

"We'll look for that, too, Madame Libéri. We'll comb the whole beach; I promise."

"I already searched, Lieutenant. And I'll keep searching."

While praying desperately that I don't find it. Because if I never find it, that means Esteban didn't go swimming. It means he is still holding that one-euro coin, wherever he may be.

To find that coin would be to sentence him to death. To search for it is to hope.

I searched for it, through all those years.

I hoped, through all those years.

I never found either of them.

I never found the coin.

And I never found Esteban.

3

Ten years later

The sand on the beach at Saint-Jean-de-Luz, almost white from the sun, slides between my toes. I take a step forward and stop. I try to choose a landmark—the Chevaux seawall, the Toki Goxoa bar—and I sink my foot as deep as possible into the sand before pulling it up, causing a tiny landslide of pale grains. Another step, and I start again.

What am I searching for after all these years?

What am I hoping for?

Esteban disappeared so long ago. Ten years, to be exact.

"This is pointless," says Gabriel's voice behind me.

I don't bother turning around to smile at him.

Esteban would have turned twenty today.

"Look," says Gabriel. "We've only just arrived, and the wind is already erasing our footprints."

He's right, as always. Nothing has changed in ten years. The same wind sweeps the beach at Saint-Jean-de-Luz; the same flags snap and billow on the pier; surfers defy the same waves; the same waiters serve customers in the same cafés; and tourists enjoy the same beach. And yet, none of it is identical to that day. No wave is the perfect twin of its predecessor; no cloud stops for a moment in its race across the sky.

Gabriel comes up behind me, throws his arm around my waist. I watch our shadows stretch over the sand, glued together, like a couple embracing in an old black-and-white movie.

I free myself from his arm.

I'm sorry, Gabriel. I promise there will be other mornings, more magical than this one.

Esteban would have turned twenty today.

Esteban would have been a brilliant student. Esteban would have passed his baccalaureate with flying colors, and we would have celebrated, the two of us, in the best restaurant on the Basque coast—Les Jardins de Bakea, perhaps. Esteban would have been a swimming champion; the years would have sculpted his body into something sleek and athletic. Esteban would have kept playing guitar, would have let his blond hair grow long. Esteban would have held my hand, on this beach, on his birthday, and I would have been so proud.

You're the one holding my hand now, Gabriel. And I don't let go.

This is the first time I have been back to the Grande Plage.

I needed to leave ten years ago, after the police gave up their search one month after Esteban's disappearance. I went far, far away. I opened a new surgery overlooking another, colder, calmer sea, between two cliffs in Etretat, Normandy.

I needed to rebuild my life. Gabriel has been with me almost all that time.

Gabriel's hand is strong, warm, solid . . . and essentially empty. What it holds is merely a dead branch—my five wooden fingers.

I remember now everything that I thought about that morning— June 21, 2010—before leaving Esteban alone on the beach. *No man could ever come between us. I must always keep the other side of my bed empty, so that Esteban can join me there at dawn. No lover could ever wake me in the morning with an "I love you" so innocent and sweet.*

Never again will Esteban join me at dawn. It is Gabriel, now, who occupies the empty space in my bed, but none of his morning "I love yous" have the same power as Esteban's.

Gabriel is the one who kisses me these days—and he does so now.

But his kisses do not have the power of Esteban's either, even if they do make me feel a little better this morning.

I asked Gabriel to come with me to Saint-Jean-de-Luz for a week, making no attempt to hide from him what I was searching for. He agreed right away. I booked a room at the Hôtel la Caravelle, close to my old apartment. I chose the best room, the honeymoon suite, to make Gabriel happy. I can afford it: I make plenty of money, and I have very few desires.

I continue dragging my feet through the sand, stupidly searching, as if I imagine that, ten years later, I could discover a one-euro coin. The one that Esteban must have dropped before running into the ocean and drowning. As if I hope to finally put an end to the mystery—all its unanswered questions, its unsolved equations.

What happened on this beach, the morning of June 21, 2010?

Gabriel continues to hold my hand, and we walk like that, side by side, down the sand.

It's a long beach, more than a kilometer from end to end, and we walk slowly. Gabriel keeps stopping to give me a kiss. I am happy to let him, to try not to appear too distant, to force myself to admire his bewitching dark eyes, his brown hair, his skin that never loses its tan even through the Norman winter.

No man could ever come between us.

I never would have believed that anyone could replace Esteban. Not that Gabriel has replaced him. He is content to occupy the empty space. He has accepted it all—my sadness; my moods; my tears; my fears; my never seeing any friends, only a psychiatrist; my silences; my therapy sessions. He has prevented me from going crazy. He has never complained, never asked questions. He is content with the little tenderness, the few caresses, I've been able to give him the past few days.

We walk randomly. I stare at the battlements of Fort Socoa at the end of the bay: its high round tower, the colorful boats lapping at its base. From where I stand, it looks more like a Lego castle than an impregnable fortress.

The few people who know us, Gaby and me, think that I am the strong one. I am Dr. Maddi Libéri, after all, widely admired for the way she rebuilt her life, whereas Gabriel seems more of a dreamer: poetic, whimsical, a little lazy.

The truth is quite the opposite. People have no idea. All these years, it has been Gabriel who has supported me.

◆　◆　◆

I see him from a distance.

At first, all I can make out is a vague stain of color against the sun-dazzled beach. It's still early; there aren't many tourists around. Maybe fifty altogether: a few couples, a few joggers, a few dog walkers, a few families.

I move closer, dragging Gabriel along with me. Meter after meter, the stain grows clearer, the color more precise.

Indigo swim shorts.

At first, I just feel a small tingle. For the past ten years, every time I've set foot on a beach, whether sand or pebble, every time I've skirted around the spread-out towels, evaded the flying beach balls and splashes of water, the laughter of children running toward the sea, my heart has twisted with the same ache. I can't stop myself following the figures of ten-year-old boys, so skinny in their baggy swim shorts, nor prevent my heart from racing whenever one of them is wearing blue trunks. That pain has struck me a dozen times, a hundred, on the beaches of Etretat, Deauville, Cabourg, Honfleur.

I let go of Gabriel's hand.

I head for the Port seawall. A group of young adults is playing volleyball. The boys are muscular, the girls slender, all of them talented. The ball never touches the ground.

Gabriel stays to watch them. I keep walking.

I have a clear view of the child in the indigo trunks now, even if he is facing away from me. He's about ten years old. He's put his towel down next to his mother, a blond woman in her thirties, very slim, with narrow hips and a flat chest.

My thoughts thrash like the wings of a frightened bird. I try to reason with myself. Indigo trunks, worn by a ten-year-old boy. I've encountered this same sight before and will again in the future. Even so, a skeptical voice inside my head remains unsatisfied.

It's true, of course, that such trunks can be bought anywhere, but to find exactly that pair, on this of all days?

The boy is sitting on his towel. I still can't see his face, but I can observe his legs, folded under him, and the logo on the swim shorts he wears . . .

Printed on indigo cloth, on the left leg.

A small white whale.

The trunks that boy is wearing are the same ones Esteban wore ten years ago.

What are the chances of such a thing happening, here, now? I try to think rationally, to stop myself falling into the chasm that's opening before me. Obviously, there must be hundreds, even thousands of swim shorts precisely identical to that pair, being worn by hundreds, even thousands of boys.

But here? Today?

Gabriel is behind me, still watching the volleyball girls. Let him do what he wants. Besides, it's better that he isn't here. I won't have to explain why I want to move closer to that boy and his mother, even if I fear my legs won't carry me that far.

I don't want him to see my hands as they tense. I don't want him to see my eyes grow hypnotized by the boy's tousled blond hair, by his skinny legs, his bony body.

I'm close enough now—less than ten meters behind them—to hear what they're saying.

"Mom, are we going swimming?"

His mother says nothing, just opens a magazine.

What happens next takes place in slow motion. The boy turns to his mother, to beg her.

He doesn't notice me. For him, I do not exist.

But he is all I see.

I recognize every contour of his face, every crease around his smile, every blue spark in his iris, every curve from his forehead to his chin, every dimple, every eyelash, every momentary expression.

It's *him*.

It's not just some kid who resembles him; it's not some doppelganger.

It's my Little Prince.

It's Esteban.

What does it matter that this makes no sense, that he ought to be twenty years old now, that believing this is pure folly?

I know it's him.

◆ ◆ ◆

Every morning, the boy in the indigo trunks goes down to the beach at Saint-Jean-de-Luz. He and his mother lay their towels in the same place each time: between the Port seawall and the terrace of Toki Goxoa.

I am now sitting eight meters behind them. I scoot toward them gradually, meter by meter, as patient as someone attempting to tame a bird.

Neither of them has noticed me. The mother is always reading a book or a newspaper, and whenever the boy's gaze reaches me, it seems to pass straight through, as if I'm transparent, as if I were made not of flesh and blood, but of dust. As if the hourglass of my life has been upturned, my Little Prince has come back to life, and now I'm the one who's the ghost.

I am not a ghost. I am solid and alive, I know I am, and every indifferent look he gives me is like a sword in my guts.

25

I have not said anything to Gabriel.

How could he possibly believe me?

He is waiting for me now, asleep in bed, in our hotel room. He likes to stay up late at night with his screens, and to wake late the next morning. He hates the idea of a morning swim.

Inwardly, I thank him for this.

Every morning since our arrival, I have been able to spy on the boy and his mother without having to explain myself. Just for an hour, before they leave the beach and I return to the hotel to see Gabriel.

The boy's name is Tom.

He is a calm, obedient boy. He seems a little sad at times.

He's bored, I think. He often goes swimming.

He's a very strong swimmer, just like Esteban was.

His mother doesn't swim. She barely even watches him. She just shouts the occasional piece of advice, without looking up from her books. Don't go too far. Don't get sunburned. Dry your hair. Tom keeps asking his mother if she will play with him. She pays him attention for a few minutes, then leaves him alone with his boredom.

Tom's voice is not exactly like Esteban's. His skin is a little lighter too. But these tiny differences pale beside their similarities. If Tom and Esteban stood next to each other, it would be almost impossible to tell them apart.

Identical twins?

For three days, I have been trying to reason with myself. I am a scientist. I studied medicine. I do not believe in any kind of god or afterlife. Esteban would be twenty years old now, while Tom is only ten. It's impossible, even if Tom smiles like Esteban, laughs like Esteban, swims like Esteban, wears the same trunks as Esteban . . .

Tom cannot be Esteban.

So I cling to the possibility of negative proof, the one thing that could still convince me that I am not falling into a bottomless void of suppositions, that could prevent me from believing in such an absurd illusion.

Esteban's angioma. His birthmark, which had been clearly visible above the top of his swim shorts whenever they slipped low on his hips.

Every time Tom stands up, undresses, and dresses, I watch him. In the rare moments when his mother brushes sand off his body, I watch. I stare at his lower abdomen, torn between two emotions: my mind's reasonable hope that I won't glimpse any blemish on his skin, so I can dismiss this as a strange coincidence, and my heart's crazy, obsessive desire to see that birthmark on the right side of his lower abdomen—proof that Esteban really is there, alive, in front of me.

What does it matter that he hasn't aged a day in ten years? That he doesn't remember me, that he answers to a different name and has another mother? What does it matter where he went, what he did, for all those years?

What matters is this: he is back.

Despite all my vigilance, I haven't succeeded in seeing Tom's bare lower abdomen. He wraps himself in a towel whenever he takes off his trunks. I haven't managed to catch a glimpse of that area when he comes out of the sea either, in that moment when his heavy, waterlogged swim shorts slip a little lower around his hips. I curse his mother, who in three days at the beach has not once rubbed sunscreen on her son's body. Tom's pale skin was red by the end of the first morning. He never complains, but the sunburn makes it even harder to distinguish any dark mark on his skin.

It's almost as if his mother wanted to hide it by letting him get burned . . .

"Mommy, are you coming?"

Tom is in the water. The waves only come up to his waist, but a few meters farther out to sea some of them are much bigger. It would take just one strong wave to knock him over. I resist the urge to yell at him, to tell him to get out, to insult his careless mother. She looks up reluctantly from her book.

"Come on, Mommy," Tom pleads. "You don't have to swim, just take my picture. Look!"

He jumps as high as he can whenever a wave threatens to crash over his back, falling back into the foam and spitting out salty water, laughing, before regaining his balance and waiting for the next wave.

Esteban loved playing like that too. But when he did it, I was with him.
"Mommy!"

To my surprise, his mother gets to her feet. She grabs her cell phone and walks toward the ocean.

I am less than seven meters from his towel. Now's my chance.

I watch his mother as she holds the phone in front of her eyes, continuing to move toward the water. I may never get another opportunity. There's no one around, except for an elderly couple, who look like they're dozing, and their grandchildren, who are digging a pool.

I crawl over, taking my time. With a confident gesture, I grab Tom's mother's beach bag. Her purse is in there, along with a disordered mass of books, pens, keys, and various bottles that I don't have time to examine.

I glance up at the sea: Tom's mother is still facing away from me.

My fingers close around the purse. I open it, pushing away the swarm of dark thoughts this action provokes: *I'm going crazy, searching through a stranger's private belongings. If I get caught, I . . .*

I extract her ID card. I must memorize it as quickly as possible. I have only a second; after that, I must put everything back, move away, become invisible again.

My fingers tremble. The plastic card slips from my grip, onto the sand. Shit!

I stare imploringly at the ocean. Tom is still in the water. His mother stands there filming him, waiting for him to stop acting like a dolphin.

I pick up the card, sweep the sand away with the back of my pinkie, and read.

Amandine Fontaine

La Souille

Hameau de Froidefond

63790 Murol

4

The décor in Dr. Wayan Balik Kuning's office is a mix of sobriety (a marker of seriousness for Le Havre's upmarket clientele) and exoticism (offering a peaceful atmosphere, conducive to relaxation and the sharing of confidences). The color scheme is a range of yellows: saffron canvases on the walls, topaz rugs on the floor, corn-colored leather sofa and armchair, untreated wooden furniture, decorated with a few small copper knickknacks—a clock, two lamps, a few discreet sculptures of Balinese divinities.

While I lie on the couch, Wayan Balik Kuning lights an incense stick. He takes his time pressing play on the Dictaphone and sits down in the rubberwood chair. Across from me.

I prefer it this way.

During our first therapy sessions, he sat behind me. I hated not being able to see him, hated feeling like I was talking to a wall, not being able to tell if he fell asleep or played *Candy Crush* on his Samsung. Also, Wayan Balik Kuning is not exactly unpleasant to look at. He is the refined product of a Balinese-French marriage. Warm brown complexion, jet-black hair with flecks of silver. Sad eyes, and the honed body of a rugby player.

"Let me see if I understand you, Maddi: you're saying that this child, Tom Fontaine, resembles Esteban?"

"No, Wayan, that is not what I said. Let us be precise: *resemble* is not sufficient. I told you . . . It was him!"

Wayan sinks more deeply into his seat, holding on to the carved armrests. He must suspect that this is going to be a complicated session. He has no idea how complicated . . .

"Maddi, you know as well as I do that that's impossible. Esteban would be twenty now. That fact puts an end to all speculation, all possible illusions about identity theft or whatever. Tom is not Esteban."

I am about to react, but Wayan raises his hand, ordering me not to interrupt.

"So we must consider the problem from a different angle, and the first question we must ask ourselves is this: Why are you convinced that this boy, about whom you know nothing, bears such a strong resemblance to your son? We will not be able to answer that without asking other, more difficult questions, beginning with why you wanted to return to Saint-Jean-de-Luz ten years after your son's disappearance. You must understand, Maddi: it isn't what you found on that beach that matters, but what you went there in search of."

I force myself to remain lying on the corn-colored leather couch. I slow my breathing so I can express myself as calmly as possible.

"Not this time, Wayan. What you're saying was true, I admit, the other times: when I thought I'd recognized Esteban in Cabourg, in Deauville, or in Honfleur. That was my brain refusing to let my wounds heal. They were merely instances of resemblance—I admitted that. You convinced me of that. But it's different this time. It's really him!"

Wayan speaks with even greater composure than I do. From his tone, I understand that he will simply refuse to accept any irrational explanation into his course of therapy.

"If that is what you believe, then we have a great deal of work ahead of us, Maddi. I hope you realize that?"

"Yes, I'm sure I've more work to do. However, I'm going to have to stop seeing you."

I raise my head a little, to observe his reaction. Wayan's handsome face appears frozen.

"I'm sorry? Maddi, please tell me I've misunderstood . . ."

I force myself to smile as I gaze at the pictures of temples in Angkor, Borobudur, and Wat Saket fixed to the walls, the posters of Mount Batur and rice fields.

"I'll miss you, Wayan. You've helped me so much during these years, truly. But . . ."

Wayan Balik Kuning, the emperor of self-control, is barely able to conceal his panic.

"Have I disappointed you? Was I insensitive? If it's a question of money, I could—"

"No, not at all. It's just that . . . I'm going to move."

There is a silence. A sandalwood-scented cloud spreads from the incense stick throughout the room. The question-mark trunk of a Ganesha sculpted from a lava stone appears to be holding back a sneeze.

"But . . . why . . . ? Where . . . where are you going?"

"To Auvergne," I say. "There's a little village in that region, just five hundred people, and they've been looking for a new doctor for almost three years. They'll welcome me as if I were the greatest healer in the Hindu pantheon."

I've never seen Wayan look so sad before. He is irresistible, looking at me with those handsome, glistening eyes. How many of his patients have fallen in love with him?

"And does Tom Fontaine happen to live in that area too?"

He's smart too.

"Yes. I'm sorry, Wayan. I have to . . . find out for sure."

"And how will you do that? By looking for his birthmark? Esteban's angioma? And what else? Do you plan to make friends with Tom Fontaine's mother? Insinuate your way into their family while concealing your own past? Are you hoping to replace her? Just because this boy looks like the son you lost?"

"I didn't lose him! He was stolen from me."

For a second, my voice sounds shrill, demented. But I force myself to be calm again. I don't want my last session with Wayan to end on a confrontational note.

"I . . . I'm sorry, Wayan. I have to go there. I've already made the decision. I've handed in my notice at the surgery in Etretat. The people of Murol are expecting me."

Wayan stands up. This normally never happens during a session.

"Do you mind if I smoke?"

I smile. "It's your office."

He pulls a long, thin cigarette from a drawer and lights it. I suppose his next patient won't be able to smell these few puffs of smoke, beneath the heavy sandalwood scent of incense.

"You've rebuilt your life here, Maddi. You don't live alone." He hesitates for a long time. I've never seen him so uncertain over which words to choose. "Are you sure that your . . . that Gabriel will be okay giving up everything to go with you?"

I smile again.

"I haven't spoken to him about it yet, but he would follow me anywhere . . . as long as that place has an internet connection."

A hurt expression briefly crosses Wayan's handsome face. I know he isn't insensible to my beauty, my energy, or to the many tears that I've shed in front of him over the years. Unless it's the opposite, and I have, without knowing it, fallen in love with him? But even if that were true, what would it change?

"I have one last thing to ask you, Wayan. Can I get back all the recordings of our sessions? I'd like to listen to them. I know you're not supposed to share recorded sessions with your patients. But I hope you'll make an exception for me, as a favor to a grieving mother."

He takes a long drag on his clove-scented cigarette. The smell pervades the room now. He's going to have to burn a lot more incense if he wants to cover it up.

"Are you sure that's a good idea?"

"I'm not sure of anything, to be honest. That's why I'd like to take them with me."

Wayan shuffles slowly toward his desk.

"If you insist. I'll copy them onto a USB key. Do you want only yours, the ones from this office? Or do you also want the ones . . . from before?"

"All of them, Wayan. Please."

I hear his fingertips tapping at the keyboard.

"When are you leaving?"

"In six months. I'll spend one last Christmas here, and I'll go in February. The volcanoes should be covered in snow by the time I arrive."

"Surely you can continue therapy until then?"

"I'm sorry, Wayan. You've helped me, truly. But I need a break . . . some distance from my current life. Even from therapy."

He stares at the screen, as our past sessions flash up one by one. His eyes are soft with melancholy.

"Maddi, can I ask you a favor?"

His eyes remain trained on the screen as he squeezes every one of our eighty-three meetings into a single folder.

"Once you've left this office, you'll no longer be my patient. We will, so to speak, become colleagues once again. How would you feel about going for a drink with me before you leave? Or going out for a meal one evening . . ."

He takes one last drag on his cigarette. I gaze tenderly at him.

"As you said earlier, Wayan, I don't live alone. I have Gabriel."

"But you are a free woman."

"True. But you're not a free man."

"What do you mean? I have no wife, no child, no . . ."

I interrupt him, as gently as I can. "Even so, you're not free enough to give up everything, to sacrifice everything. I don't think I could live with a man who wasn't capable of that. I'm selfish, aren't I? You are a very attractive man with many wonderful qualities, believe me, but you are not the kind of person who can leave everything behind. You couldn't abandon it all to follow the woman you love."

Second Age

The Child Soul

"The soul's second age, Maddi, is where one comes to understand that one does not live only for oneself. That others matter, are important. The soul must learn to transcend—or at least to control—its urges to trick, play, cheat, seduce. To love."

II

Arrival

Welcome to Murol

5

Six months later

I open the shutters of my surgery to reveal a view of the Puys mountain range, the Château de Murol perched on the nearest hill, and the ridge of the Puy de Sancy that cuts off the horizon. With the shutters open, sunlight pours into the room, as if seeking the cool shelter of the old granite stones.

This was not the view I had been expecting.

For six months before moving to Auvergne, I had been preparing myself for grayness, low skies, snowy roads, dripping gutters, cold stone houses and smoking chimneys, deserted streets, scarves and hats, draft-proofed lives . . . Since I got here, however, it has been the complete opposite.

None of the locals can recall a winter so mild. Sixty degrees Fahrenheit in the middle of February. Temperatures in the upper seventies on the volcanoes' sunny slopes. My windshield barely manages to freeze overnight.

My surgery is located in the center of Murol, close to the lava bridge that spans the waters of the Couze Chambon. The streets here are not as lively as the Rue Gambetta in Saint-Jean-de-Luz, admittedly, but it's hardly a ghost town either, what with the ski-starved tourists who come in search of something to do, the neat processions of hikers, the noisy kids coming out of school and waking the old people, as sun-numbed as sleeping cats behind their lace curtains.

I moved to Murol three weeks ago, and I have no regrets at all. These poor people have spent three years waiting for a doctor! I was welcomed like a returning king. Everyone came to see me: the mayor, the schoolteacher, the plumber, the butcher, the caretaker of the little museum. They all reassured me: there are people here all year round. They all congratulated me when they saw how hardworking I was. They all offered to help me—invitations I'm not afraid to take them up on. They told me: if a person opens their door here, or knocks at someone else's, they won't be alone for long.

Thank you, my friends, but I am not alone.

I turn on my computer. I check the day's schedule on Planyo, the appointment-booking app. Everything is done online these days; even in Auvergne, there's no need for a secretary. I squint into the dazzle of sunlight reflecting from the screen as I read distractedly through my list of patients.

Suddenly, my eyes open wide.

I force myself to control my excitement, to take deep breaths.

I knew it would happen eventually. I am, after all, the only doctor in a ten-kilometer radius. I just had to be patient, wait for him to come to me. Everything I have undertaken in the past six months—leaving Normandy, moving to the other side of the country, settling in at the Moulin de Chaudefour, opening this surgery—has been done with only one goal in mind: making this meeting happen.

That does not prevent me from shaking with surprise.

Mélanie Pelat: 9:00 a.m.

Gérard Fraisse: 9:15 a.m.

Yvette Mory: 9:30 a.m.

Tom Fontaine: 9:45 a.m.

◆ ◆ ◆

"You're next, madame."

It is 9:55 a.m. A reasonable delay, designed to give the impression that I haven't been rushing through my previous patients. But for me, those ten extra minutes were unbearable.

"Please, come in."

In the waiting room, Amandine Fontaine puts an organic-living magazine down on the coffee table, rises to her feet, and walks toward my surgery with Tom.

I close the door behind them, enclosing the three of us in the privacy of my office. As Tom walks past, I fight the temptation to ruffle his blond hair, to put my hand on his shoulder, to stroke his cheek. I haven't seen him since June last year. He is wearing an old pair of jeans, a cream wool sweater with frayed sleeves. His clothes are too big for him, crumpled-looking; a far cry from Esteban's designer outfits. Even so, Tom has never looked so much like him as he does now.

I have prepared for this, rehearsing the consultation in my head more than a hundred times. I must not show the emotion I feel.

We're separated by a desk. Tom glances sideways at the candy jar. Rewards for brave little girls and boys. I turn to face him, as if Amandine did not exist. This is not a stratagem: I always act this way with my younger patients. I prefer to first hear them describe their symptoms in their own words, before their parents get involved.

"So, what's going on, Tom?"

Tom gazes at me with his sea-blue eyes, surprised to be asked a question.

Those eyes, my God . . .

But it's Amandine who answers. "Nothing, he's fine now. Tom missed three days of school. He was coughing too much to go. Sore throat, runny nose . . . and he doesn't know how to blow his nose, of course. Well, you get the idea. But it's over now."

So why see a doctor if the child is no longer sick? I am about to ask this, but Amandine doesn't give me time to speak.

"I just need a doctor's note. For school. Otherwise, they make a big fuss about absences, you know. And today is the last day before the February holidays."

There is something abnormal about the way Amandine stares at me. I flash a professional smile. Is it possible she recognizes me? I had my hair cut before coming to Murol. I wear glasses when I work, and she's never seen me with glasses before. How could she possibly make the connection between the new village doctor and some woman glimpsed on a beach in Saint-Jean-de-Luz six months before, over a period of three days? Three days when she barely even looked up from her magazines?

"I'm just going to come out and say it," Amandine continues. "I'm not really into doctors or medicines or vaccines or all that stuff. I'd rather look after Tom myself. You understand? I believe in prevention, common sense, natural methods."

I breathe out, relieved. It is not me she's suspicious of, but the medical system in general. I'm used to this: it's increasingly common, especially among young mothers. They read a few books, visit a website, participate in a forum or two, and they feel like they've been to medical school.

"Well, thank you for being honest."

Amandine smiles back at me. She's already preparing to get up and leave. As soon as she gets her piece of paper, she'll be out of there.

"But I must be honest too . . ."

Amandine Fontaine's smile curdles instantly. Tom is still eyeing the candy jar.

"I can't give you a doctor's note without examining your son first. I'm sorry; that's nonnegotiable."

I tried to find the right mix of friendliness and firmness. Amandine frowns, hesitates. Surely she's not going to just walk out of here with Tom? I decide to talk directly to him again.

"I'm not going to hurt you, Tom. I just need to check everything's working as it should."

Without waiting for the mother's permission, I stand up and move toward him. Amandine still looks uncertain. Is it just her maternal instinct, the desire to protect her son, or does she have something to hide? I fear that she's not going to let me touch Tom, that she will get up and stand between us, but suddenly she grimaces, pinned to her chair by an intense stomach pain. What if it's the mother, rather than the son, who needs a doctor?

"Tom never gets sick," she manages to say, struggling to conceal her discomfort. "It's been two years since he saw a doctor."

"Well, we can catch up on lost time. Come on, Tom. Climb onto the table, and let me take a look at you."

He obeys, in thrall to my enthusiasm and determination. I begin by examining Tom's ears, nose, and throat. I confirm his mother's diagnosis: he has all the symptoms of benign laryngitis. The inflammation has practically disappeared. So Amandine was right about that, at least: her son doesn't need any medicine.

"Everything looks perfect, Tom. You can even go to school this afternoon if you like."

Tom's face lights up with a broad smile. It's Esteban's smile. Oh, my Little Prince . . . I realize that every time I lay eyes on this child, every time I touch his skin, examine his throat, listen to his chest, I will descend a little further into a hell from which I may never emerge.

I feel as if I were touching Esteban's skin, breathing Esteban's scent . . .

And yet I have no choice. I must keep sinking deeper into the underworld. If my son is down there, I must search for him.

"Please stay where you are, Tom. I'm not quite done. Could you take off your sweater and your T-shirt for me?"

Tom obeys. Amandine says nothing. Is it because she's in too much pain? Or has my authoritative tone subdued her? Or perhaps she simply has no real reason to refuse an examination.

I palpate Tom's shoulder blades, his ribs, his stomach, his knees, his elbows, his wrists. I feel as if my fingers are going to catch fire. An irreconcilable conflict arises in my mind, between reasonable Dr. Maddi Libéri and Esteban's inconsolable mom. The doctor in me tries to think rationally: I have examined hundreds of ten-year-olds, and I know that the vast majority of them are roughly the same weight and height (to within a few kilos and centimeters), have the same skinny body shape, the same thin limbs, the same flat biceps. And yet, Esteban's mom refuses to let go of belief: my hands' memory does not lie; I recognize my own child's body when I touch it.

"Wonderful, Tom. Now lie down, please. Don't worry; I'd like you to just lower the top of your pants a little."

Tom unfastens the buckle of his belt.

This time, Amandine reacts.

"What are you doing?"

"Nothing out of the ordinary. Just checking him for signs of pubescence."

"He's ten!"

"Well, exactly."

Amandine doesn't dare argue with me. She must be thinking about the medical websites she's visited that have cited instances of premature puberty. Her hesitation allows me to keep the exam going.

Tom unbuttons the top of his jeans and drags his blue boxer shorts down a few centimeters.

I freeze.

It's impossible. Logically, medically, it cannot be.

And yet I knew even before I examined Tom that it would be there.

The proof, hidden away but impossible to erase. The angioma is in the shape of a teardrop, a chocolate-colored stain on the right side of his lower abdomen. Exactly like Esteban's.

His birthmark.

Impossible to falsify.

Tom is still lying down. I haven't yet told him he can get up, get dressed again . . .

Everything I'd once thought real has been overturned. I could accept a physical resemblance. I could accept, very nearly, the fact of those same swim shorts, even the coincidence of him wearing them on the same beach. But this mark? How could I possibly believe that its presence there is random, with no other cause than the great lottery of genetics?

Am I going crazy? Am I hallucinating?

My fingers delicately touch the brown mark. Amandine stands next to me, waiting for the exam to end. I force myself not to bombard her with questions. Who is Tom's father? Why was he wearing those indigo trunks in Saint-Jean-de-Luz? Why did she go there for her vacation? There has to be an explanation . . .

As soon as Amandine comes closer—presumably to tell me that she's had enough, that she's taking her son home now—I stammer the only question I can think to ask without betraying myself.

"This angioma—this birthmark, if you prefer—when did it first appear?"

"When do you think? It's a birthmark, right?"

Amandine glares suspiciously at me. She has the upper hand again. Why did I ask such a ridiculous question? I need to play for time, to examine the mark in more detail. I have to think of another question. I touch the dark stain again and frown as if worried. Inspecting it more closely, I'm forced to acknowledge that it's not identical to Esteban's. It's slightly paler, less developed. But that proves nothing; I also know that angiomas change over time, particularly during childhood, and that in 80 percent of cases they disappear completely.

Tom's skin feels warm against my fingertips. He doesn't move. He's just as calm as Esteban was. Observing the world around him, analyzing it, without revealing his own thoughts.

It's not impossible that this dark stain was caused by a burn, years before, but why would anyone have mutilated the child in that precise spot? My wild supposition at least provides me with the idea for another question.

"This mark . . . Are you certain that Tom never burned himself?"

Amandine raises her voice. "You don't think I would remember that? What exactly are you insinuating? That my son had an accident and I didn't even realize?"

She steps forward and pushes me out of the way.

"You can get dressed now, Tom," she tells her son.

Apparently, this movement was too much for her. She holds her stomach again now, as if someone just punched her. She holds on to the edge of the table, trying to catch her breath.

"Are you all right, Madame Fontaine?"

She doesn't answer me. Whether out of anger, embarrassment, or pain, I can't tell. Perhaps a mix of all three. I take advantage of her silence to address Tom.

"Tom, what about you? What do you think of that mark?"

The boy's eyes waver between my face and his mother's.

"I . . . I've always had it."

"You don't have any memory of an accident? A burn, something that would have hurt, maybe when you were very young?"

"No. No . . ."

Amandine, having caught her breath, barks at me. "What is your problem, Doctor? You should be careful: people around here don't like it when strangers start poking around in their private lives. Tom and I have learned to deal with things on our own. I don't need any advice, especially where it concerns my health or my son's. I bet I've read more medical magazines than you have. So you see . . ."

Yes, I see.

Tom refastens his pants and climbs off the table. As he walks past me, I ruffle his blond hair. I can't resist: the impulse is like a wave of emotion, like mainlining heroin, like that sensation of naturalness, that instant of happiness I felt whenever Esteban would come up to me in search of affection.

"See you soon, young man."

Amandine glowers at me.

"How much do I owe you, Doctor?"

Once again, her face twists in pain, and she clutches her stomach. Even her pride can't make her cover up what's happening this time. She sits down even as she takes out her purse.

"Doctor?"

It's Tom who says this, in a small, shy voice.

"Doctor, could I go to the swimming pool during the holidays?"

I had almost forgotten the beach at Saint-Jean-de-Luz. Tom is an excellent swimmer, as good as Esteban was. Esteban used to spend all his winter holidays at the pool, and his summers at the beach.

"Yes, Tom. You're fine now, no problem."

I turn to his mother, just as she hands me some cash.

"You, on the other hand, are not fine, Madame Fontaine. Please let me examine you. It won't cost anything extra, and . . ."

"Doctor, with all due respect, keep your nose out of my business!"

A heavy silence blankets the office while I count out the woman's change. Tom is still eyeing the candy jar on my desk. Surely his mother won't object to me giving him a reward . . .

"Would you like some honey candy?"

Tom immediately withdraws his hand and steps back, seeking refuge in his mother's arms, as if I'd offered snake venom. He looks terrified, like someone in the grip of an uncontrollable phobia.

What is Tom so afraid of?

Honey candy?

Horrific memories fill my head.

They have the sweet, treacherous taste of summer.

Is it possible that Tom and Esteban were both terrorized by the same enemies?

6

Savine Laroche parks her 4x4 Renault Koleos outside the mayor's office in Murol. The social worker's car is easily recognizable. Bright orange. A 2008 model, its rust spots concealed by bumper stickers advertising the Vulcania amusement park and the Michelin Man. Despite being thirteen years old, the car still works perfectly, climbing the hills of Auvergne with the pep of a race car. Savine Laroche knows nothing about engines, but the mechanic in Murol looks after her old Koleos with the tenderness of a lover. He's a nice guy, Gilles Tazenat, even if he did charge her three hundred euros for snow tires she probably won't use all winter.

Before going into the mayor's office, Savine takes a moment to admire her surroundings. The village is curled in on itself, the houses huddled together, tall and fragile, protected by their slate roofs and supported by the granite beams of their doors and windows. The Couze Chambon runs through the town, whose streets and bridges are built up like battlements—presumably to preserve Murol when the river is in spate. The mayor's office is high and solid, constructed from black lava stones.

Savine knows this village by heart, this high landscape with its softened curves, and yet every morning she loves it anew, with the same intense passion. She would hate to live on a plain, just as she would hate to live up in the mountains. The only landscape she loves is this kind of rolling countryside, the horizon like a series of waves over the peaks of the hills, folded over one another as if God had been creating origami. She is devoted to her job, and she knows all too well the poverty of rural life, the secrets festering in farmhouses, in the silences of hamlets, behind closed shutters and crumbling facades. She has a huge amount of work to do here. But though she finds poverty within every village that clings to the slopes of these volcanoes, she can't help thinking that life is never quite as bleak out here in the open air.

◆ ◆ ◆

"Hello, everyone!" she calls out, opening the door to the mayor's office. "Have you seen this sun? It's like springtime."

In fact, only one of her fellow employees is there, left behind while the others have gone out to lunch.

"Has everyone else abandoned you, Nectaire? I bet they've gone to swim in the Chambon, haven't they?"

Nectaire Paturin is the secretary at the mayor's office, responsible for all the stamps, forms, and photocopies. It's said that he used to be a policeman in Clermont, before ending up here. Savine likes Nectaire, even if he is her exact opposite—sluggish, slow, pessimistic. He must be slightly older than she is, late forties, but in many ways, they are in the same position—single, graying, known by all to be dreaming of retirement.

"I'd rather they went ice-skating," grumbles Nectaire. "It's not normal, temperatures like these in winter."

"I know; it's true. There are no seasons anymore. But it's not all bad. Look . . ." Like a magician, Savine produces a bouquet of daffodils from behind her back. "Ta-da! First of the year. Make a wish. I picked them near the Chiloza waterfall."

The secretary gazes in consternation at these February daffodils. He couldn't look more panic-stricken if he learned that the volcanoes were spewing fire.

"And that's not even the best part! There's already fruit on the trees."

49

The secretary almost falls off his swivel chair. This time, Savine conjures a kilo of mandarins, each one wrapped in paper.

"Were they picked near the Chiloza waterfall too?" asks Nectaire.

"Of course! At least that's what old Chaumeil at the Besse market told me."

Savine's desk faces Nectaire's, and she puts the mandarins she bought in the neighboring village on it, set between an orange plastic dinosaur, an orange plush stuffed toy, and an orange New York Knicks mug. Savine's favorite color is not a mystery.

Nectaire is still fixated on the mandarins like a fortune teller gazing into a crystal ball.

"You see," the secretary says, "it's true. There really are two kinds of people in the world."

Aaah . . . this is Nectaire Paturin's favorite phrase. Even the simplest gesture, he believes, is symbolic of some greater truth and reveals the schisms that undermine society. Nectaire is not just sluggish, slow, and pessimistic. He's also a philosopher.

"There are those who buy mandarins wrapped in paper, and those who buy them without paper."

Savine's eyes widen. "Wow, that's deep!"

Nectaire runs his hand through his woolly, unkempt hair. He gazes vacantly through the window, giving himself time for further inspiration to strike. The Auvergne sky is perfectly blue, as if the mountains were too rounded for a single cloud to cling to them. Nectaire is not one of those men spurred to greater action by the thought of time running out—he's more of a plodding workhorse—but he possesses a pair of irresistibly childlike eyes that seek to understand every mystery of the universe that surrounds him.

"The ones who buy mandarins in paper," he goes on, "are naturally trusting. They feel no need to check beneath the fruit's wrapping to see if it might be damaged. They consider the risk to be minimal, or at least not sufficiently important to warrant their vigilance. They don't even wonder why some fruit is wrapped up like that and some fruit is not.

In fact, they tend to think that the wrapped fruit is prettier. They like it when the world is fancy and unpredictable; they see in that a respect for their own desire for freedom. In short, these people are optimists. Like you, Savine."

Savine gratifies him with a charming smile. "And the others?"

"The others are pragmatic. They trust only their own judgment. They view the world only through the filter of their reason. Or their system of values, if you prefer. They are pessimists, suspicious of life. Like me, Savine! They are . . . What's the word? Cautious."

Savine gives a whistle of admiration, then unwraps one of the mandarins with great excitement.

"You don't know what you're missing! Among life's many surprises, the best are found under wrapping paper."

She stands up and hands the fruit to the secretary.

"You can check for yourself that it's not rotten. Or would you like me to peel it for you too?"

"No, that's fine, thank you."

Savine and Nectaire exchange a complicit smile, but they don't say anything. Like two lovers attracted by their polar opposite. The social worker finally breaks the silence before it grows too intense.

"Will you return the favor and make me a cup of tea? You can put whatever you want in it. I won't check to see whether you're trying to poison me!"

◆ ◆ ◆

Nectaire has taken more than a dozen sachets from his desk drawer. Each one bears a handwritten label that includes the day and place its contents were harvested. *Lemon Balm, Wild Rose, Juniper, Hawthorn, Pine Bud, Yarrow.* The drinking of Nectaire's infusions is a local tradition. He concocts these mélanges himself, based on obscure criteria such as the weather, his moods, how tired or excited he feels, and the current state of his digestive process.

His face blank with concentration, hands equipped with a hollow measuring spoon, he is about to create the perfect decoction, when the door to the mayor's office suddenly opens. A strong gust of wind sends the powders of dried plants flying so they mingle in a deliciously fragrant cloud.

Nectaire coughs and almost chokes as a small, wiry man in his sixties, with muscles as knotted as an olive tree, enters the room.

"Hello, everyone. I'm just passing through." He takes off his cycling helmet and turns to face Savine. "I . . . I need to talk to you."

"Go ahead, Martin."

"Um . . . in private."

Savine looks intrigued. Martin Sainfoin is the village's only policeman. A few years before, he would have been called a country warden. He himself would have preferred a more grand-sounding title, like *captain of volcanoes*, *Auvergne ranger*, or *mountain guard* . . . Oh well. For the past forty years, he has patrolled the roads, paths, and mountain passes on two wheels, using his Pinarello racing bike for the roads and his Orbea mountain bike for the rockier tracks. Martin Sainfoin is a minor local celebrity, champion of multiple seniors' cycling races between Limoges and Clermont-Ferrand. For the past seven weeks, he has been training for the national championships by riding a hundred kilometers per day.

"In private?" Savine asks, sounding surprised.

Nectaire, behind his desk, makes himself invisible, devoting himself to the precise measuring of every ingredient in his infusion.

Martin lowers his voice and says, "It's about Amandine Fontaine. And Tom. Kind of a strange story."

"What's happened?" Savine sounds anxious.

Amandine and Tom are under the social worker's protection, along with a few other vulnerable families in the village.

"I'm not sure yet. I need to check a few things. Can you meet me tonight? At La Poterne?"

La Poterne is a bar in Besse, the neighboring village, where most of the area's inhabitants congregate in the evenings to read the local pages of *La Montagne* and talk about the news.

"Sure, if you want."

"You have time to sit down and have a cup of tea with us, don't you?" asks Nectaire, behind them.

"Another time. I'm supposed to ride four mountain passes in a row this afternoon. An elevation of two thousand meters and—"

He is interrupted by the whistling of the kettle.

"Come on," says Nectaire. "I've made a Paturin special infusion. Unless you're worried about being caught doping?"

Martin Sainfoin hesitates a little too long. The door opens again, and three other employees come inside: Alain Suchet (a.k.a. Souche), the gardener; Géraldine Jume, the accountant; and Oudard Benslimane, the cultural activity leader.

"Ah, Martin, just the man I was hoping to see," says Oudard. "The young people of Besse, bored by the lack of snow, have got it into their heads to organize rave parties on the Puy de Sancy. I'm afraid we're going to spend our February holidays playing hide-and-seek."

Savine has already brought out five cups, and Géraldine has taken a *flougnarde*, an apple-and-rum tart, out of the fridge. Martin Sainfoin, feeling trapped, glances at his watch. If he wants to ride all the way to the Col de la Croix-Saint-Robert, take the time to check out the Amandine story, and be at La Poterne by seven o'clock, he's going to have to pedal faster than he's ever pedaled before.

7

12:45 p.m.

My car is parked in the small lot near my surgery. There are four empty spaces. No one is shopping now; most of the village stores close during lunchtime.

Once I'm inside the car, I face the view of the Château de Murol's keep; the castle tower sticks out above the wave of fir trees like a cork in a wine bottle. I slide the key into the ignition of my Alfa Romeo MiTo. All I have to do is turn it and drive back up the Couze Chambon valley—six kilometers of winding road—and I'll be home, at the Moulin.

I close my eyes.

Instantly, I see the birthmark again. A dark stain on pale skin. The image is imprinted on my retina, as if I stared at the sun for too long. Is it Tom's mark I'm seeing in my mind? Esteban's? Impossible to be sure. The two blend together in my memory.

What was I hoping for when I decided to move here? When I spent all that time waiting for Tom and his mother to come to visit me? When I imagined, for days on end, that moment when I would ask the boy to undress?

I'd been hoping for proof. Why not admit it? I'd expected a confirmation. I had been following the thread of my intuition.

No, their resemblance is not merely a resemblance.

These coincidences cannot simply be coincidences.

There's something more going on here . . . Even if Esteban would be twenty now, even if Tom wasn't born yet when Esteban disappeared, even if. . .

I bend down and retrieve my Samsung from my handbag: 4G, three bars.

I type frantically.

Birthmark.

I skim through the search results. Birthmarks have been called many things over the years, in different places, according to their color and their shape: mongoloid stain, coffee stain, red wine stain . . . The specialists seem to be in agreement on several points. These marks aren't rare: they occur in more than one child in ten. And their origin is almost always unknown. For a long time, the accepted theory was that they were hereditary, but now we know that, most of the time, there's no genetic explanation for these marks. The way they evolve is still a mystery too. In the majority of cases, they disappear when the child grows older, without leaving any trace at all.

Like a vanishing memory.

I continue to hesitate. Gabriel is waiting for me at the Moulin; I told him I would be home for lunch. And yet I know I can't just leave my research here. I have to keep going. Like a traveler on the stone bridge ahead of me, I have to pass over to the other side, where other ways of thinking will be revealed.

My hand shaking, I type into my phone:

Birthmark . . . reincarnation.

For an instant, as my request goes soaring over the volcanoes, I hope there will be no hits, no options other than a few websites run by cranks and some crackpot discussion forums.

Who am I kidding?

Dozens of results suddenly appear on the screen. I have, I know, entered a new world, one whose existence I had only guessed at, a world that none of my professors at med school ever mentioned.

I click on one option and read the synopsis of a book, *Where Reincarnation and Biology Intersect*. The author, a certain Ian Stevenson, notes that the medical establishment, unable to offer a rational explanation for these marks that appear at birth and disappear by the end of childhood, has come up with no better answer than that tired old phrase "pure random chance."

But human beings don't like random chance. People want the events and elements of their lives to be imbued with significance. In his work, Stevenson demonstrates that, in many cultures—Hindu, Buddhist, animist—these marks hold a precise and long-accepted meaning: they are evidence of previous lives.

My throat tightens. I look up for a moment. The parking lot is still as empty as it was before. I feel as if I were alone, in a ghost village.

I look down at the screen of my phone again. I know I shouldn't keep reading. Why consult all these articles about something in which I don't believe? Why torture myself this way?

But I do read them. The articles list dozens of examples of children with birthmarks. These are not simple testimonies, easily disbelieved, but genuine biological analyses with photographic evidence. The cases all show stains, marks, defects . . . and in almost every one, the article claims, the doctors working with the children arrive at a single conclusion.

I bite my lips, incapable of tearing my eyes away from what I will learn next, the terrible truth.

Each mark corresponds to the position of an old wound.

It indicates something important about the person who has been reincarnated.

It is a sign that the person died a violent death.

I arrive at the Moulin de Chaudefour. I didn't pass anyone on my drive from Murol. I followed the road's curves, my fingers tensed around the steering wheel of my MiTo, clinging on tightly as I negotiated the bends of life, shaken, overwhelmed, but determined.

I refuse to believe these stories.

Even if I can't deny that I saw the same mark on Tom's body as I saw on Esteban's.

I park in the Moulin's vast parking lot, most of it overrun by weeds. *I don't want to believe these stories.*

Because to believe them would be to admit the horror—the unbearable truth that I've spent all these years forcing myself to push away.

I walk toward the Moulin. My gait is unsteady, as if my legs refuse to walk straight and are seeking to follow any other path. I look up.

The enormous Moulin de Chaudefour lies in front of me. Two hundred and fifty meters long, with a huge dining room and an uninterrupted view through its glass doors of the slopes of Mont-Dore and the Chaudefour Valley.

The Moulin is one of five hotels that opened in this location in the 1970s, back when the Chambon-des-Neiges ski resort was still one of the most popular in Auvergne, with its ten ski lifts and its twenty kilometers of runs. Climate change spelled the resort's end, however, despite the installation of snow cannons and the creation of high-altitude runs. It closed twenty years ago. What remains of it is like a ghost town, or the set of a Western, one of those settlements deserted after the gold rush: an oversized parking lot, pylons rusting in the middle of the forest, wide deforested tracks.

I was able to buy the Moulin de Chaudefour, which at one point could host more than fifty guests, for a third of its list price. Too far from working ski slopes, too far from stores, too far from everything. Yet I had immediately fallen for this former hotel, with its stone walls thick enough to withstand a nuclear explosion, its elegant glass-lined hall, its dining room warmed by an immense fireplace, its pine corridors upstairs with their rows of rooms.

A veritable palace.

A fairy-tale chalet.

Way too big for me.

◆ ◆ ◆

"Gabriel? Hey, are you home?"

The door to the Moulin is not locked. Gabriel would never have gone out without locking it.

"Gabriel?"

He has to be here, somewhere, headphones over his ears, probably in our suite of rooms—the Bois-Joli—the ones with the best view of the Chaudefour Valley, the Cascade de la Biche waterfall, and the Dent de la Rancune dike.

"Gaby, I'm back!"

I head toward the kitchen. There's a glass in the sink, a knife on the drainer. On the table I find half a baguette, some bread crumbs, and a newspaper, *La Montagne*, open to the TV guide.

I sigh as I fold the newspaper, put the baguette in the bread bin, then sweep the crumbs into the palm of my hand. Loneliness can submerge me when I least expect it. Despite myself, I think back to Wayan's last words, six months before, at his office in Le Havre.

Are you sure that Gabriel will be fine with giving up everything to go with you?

I wonder, as I've wondered so many times before, if I would be happier alone. Probably better not to think about that.

I climb the pale pine stairs. The walls are still hung with photographs of the snow-covered ski resort; of people dressed in anoraks in faded colors, jacquard sweaters and salopettes, ski masks, snow boots; of drag lifts, wooden sleds, and snowball fights.

"Gabriel? Are you in the bedroom?"

Gabriel had agreed to my plans for Auvergne. Unhesitatingly. Meekly. He'd even joked about it: *Well, the weather can't be any worse than it is here in Normandy!* I was surprised that he didn't debate the issue more, that he accepted the move so easily. Did he simply not care? Saint-Jean-de-Luz,

Etretat, or Murol . . . What did it matter to him where we went, as long as he was free to do what he wanted? In other words, to spend all his time staring at screens. He claims he's broadening his skill set when he's on his devices, consolidating his knowledge, assessing his needs, finding his path, and so on. I don't argue the point. It isn't that I'm worried that he isn't being productive; I'm productive enough for both of us, and he knows that. I just need . . . what? Company?

I open the bedroom door. Gabriel is asleep in bed.

You don't criticize a cat for sleeping all day; you don't ask him to work; you're just happy that he's there when you get home, purring contentedly, smiling and joking, glad that you're back . . . because he was bored without you.

My feet make the floorboards creak, loud enough to wake him. Gabriel's dark eyes open; he stretches, kicks away the sheets. He wears no shirt. I can see his hairless chest, his flat stomach; the rest of his body is hidden under a pair of sweatpants.

"Are you coming back to bed?" he asks sleepily.

"Didn't you get up at all this morning?"

"I . . . I don't feel too good. Can you take a look?"

A quick diagnosis. Hand to the forehead. He has a slight fever. Stuffed-up nose. Chesty cough. The mountain air doesn't seem to suit him . . . He's been catching colds and chest infections ever since we got here. His nightstand has become a medicine cabinet. I give him precise instructions on what to take, and when I get home, I check to see that he's followed them. He's such a momma's boy . . .

As I lean down toward him, he tries to pull me onto the bed.

"Come on, five minutes. Just a quick cuddle."

"I really don't have time, sorry. I only have forty-five minutes to eat; then I need to get back to work."

Gabriel pretends to pout. "I'll eat lunch later," he says. "I had a late breakfast."

On his nightstand, between the packets of Doliprane, Exomuc, and Humex, I see that his tablet is plugged in. Gabriel must have spent the morning playing some stupid game again, or looking at one of those websites that claim to teach you how to become a trader in a few clicks.

I sigh, then kiss his cheek. I'm already preparing to leave. I don't want to get mad at him. Not today. I've got bigger fish to fry. *Make no promises. Don't ask for any either.* Gabriel acts like a teenager. But maybe I don't want him to grow up, to become serious, boring, predictable, self-assured, independent, sad, squashed flat, like all those men crushed by the weight of their responsibilities. I prefer to keep my fragile little bird at home with me, even if the inhabitants of Murol will soon start to believe I'm alone here, so little do they see of Gabriel. They'll think I'm some old maid. I'll have all the gigolos in the valley at my door . . .

"You're not leaving already, are you?" Gabriel groans.

"Sorry, and I have appointments until late . . . Call me if there's a problem, okay?"

"Okay, have a good day."

Gabriel is already falling asleep, without bothering to cover himself with the sheets.

I go downstairs.

I lied, just now.

My next appointment isn't until 1:45 p.m. And I'm not hungry either.

I park my MiTo in one of the parking lots at the old Chambon-des-Neiges resort, at the location that was once the foot of the chairlift for Puy Jumel. All that remains there now is a field of wild grass dotted with snowdrops: hundreds of white flowers, as if nature were teasing the former ski resort with the illusion of snowflakes. The hamlet of Froidefond lies three kilometers below as the crow flies, but the drive, which follows the winding D36 road, is much longer.

I get out of the car and walk along the path beside the Couze Chambon, advancing through shady undergrowth, avoiding the nettles and brambles by holding on to the branches nearest the riverbank. The water level is quite low; it's possible to jump from rock to rock across the river without getting wet. The river must have been orphaned by the snowy mountain peaks that would normally feed it until the end of winter. It looks like a baby river; a few rocks lined up together would be enough to dam it.

And yet the stone bridge that spans the river at the entrance of Froidefond is wide. A single, majestic arch, its large size disproportional to that of the hamlet, which consists of ten houses with black granite facades and closed shutters, a wash house, a fountain, and—a little farther below—two farms, one on either side of the road.

La Souille is the second farm. Or it used to be, anyway. All that remains of it are a two-story house with cob walls; a barn with a broken roof that no longer contains any animal feed; a plastic tarp intended to shelter the barn but which, poorly tied down, floats in the wind, half-torn; a few rusty plowshares; a filled-in well; a stone bench with a bicycle leaning on it; and some chicken wire twisted between four stakes to protect a small vegetable garden. Hens run amok, watched by skinny cats sitting on windowsills.

This is the first time, since moving to Murol, that I haven't merely driven through the hamlet without stopping, only glancing at the farm before stepping on the gas again. I didn't want to come before now; I wanted Amandine Fontaine to make the first move. She was bound to do that at some point, since I'm the only doctor in the valley. I wanted that excuse before approaching her again. To become her family doctor . . . someone who would be able to visit on the spur of the moment. To go in without knocking. Able to ask questions, examine, probe, simply because she is concerned.

However suspicious Amandine is of me, she came to me first. She is caught in my trap now.

◆ ◆ ◆

1:15 p.m.

I've walked to the fountain on the outskirts of Froidefond. Nobody saw me, or at least I hope they didn't, though I suppose anyone could be spying on me from behind a loose plank or an attic dormer. It's hard to tell whether Froidefond is an abandoned hamlet or a place full of carefully renovated second homes whose owners come here only in the summer.

If I lean down a little, the fountain is tall enough to hide me. The water that pours from the copper pipe and fills the basin has a strange reddish tint. This isn't uncommon, in areas of volcanic earth. The spring water must be ferruginous, slightly spicy; good for the digestion, so they say. I look with faint disgust at the oxidized walls of the granite cistern, the stagnant water inside. No doubt it's a long-held local tradition to drink from it, but that won't stop me prescribing Spasfon to my patients.

From where I stand, I have a clear view of the farm's courtyard, the hens, the cats, and the front door. I have to wait only a few minutes before I see the door open. Amandine comes out. I watch her take a few steps forward, lift up one of the plastic tarps covering the vegetable garden, bend down to pick a handful of herbs, then grimace in pain as she stands upright. She's holding her belly again, as she did at our appointment. This time, though, her pain is accompanied by a dry cough. Amandine rushes back inside without closing the door behind her.

The courtyard is empty but for the hens once again.

I keep waiting. I feel stupid, spying on poultry like this. Stupid and embarrassed. Anyone in the hamlet could spot me here. I can always claim I've come to visit Amandine and Tom, that I was concerned about my patient, but . . .

Just then, I hear the four chords. The same ones in a row, repeating.

E, G, D, A, E, G, D, A.

It sounds pretty awful.

The refrain increases in volume as if the player were coming closer, but not in quality. Quite the opposite, in fact. At last, I see Tom appear. He's the one playing those chords. He heads toward the bench in the middle of the courtyard. It is, first and foremost, his solitude that strikes me, that strange anxiety in his gaze, as if he fell into that courtyard from a moon or a rocket, and every aspect of his surroundings frightens him. Esteban had the same look in his eyes sometimes: an absence, a distance, that window open on a planet where only true artists can lose themselves. But Esteban was loved, listened to. I was attentive to his every need and ability. Tom, on the other hand, appears neglected.

I watch as he pushes the bicycle out of the way and sits down on the stone bench, surrounded by clucking hens. I tell myself not to jump to conclusions. There is no reason to believe that Tom is being mistreated, or that Amandine doesn't love him. The fact that he lives in a run-down farmhouse, or that his mother relies on her own herbal remedies to keep him healthy, does not in itself mean he is in danger.

E, G, D, A, E, G, D, A.

Finally, I recognize the opening chords to "Wonderwall."

Tom's musicianship leaves a great deal to be desired. At least he and Esteban don't share the same talent. For a second, I feel reassured, before telling myself that Tom has probably never had a music teacher. He has probably never even owned a guitar, or any stringed instrument at all.

I squint. The mist from the fountain's red water is irritating my face. Or at least that's how it feels—like a person leaning too long over the embers of a fire they mistakenly thought had gone out.

At last, I manage to see the instrument Tom is trying to play. He has taken a supple branch and tied a rope between its two ends, like an arch twisted into the shape of a U. Then he has attached six strings in a row between the rope and the wood.

A homemade guitar. Or maybe a harp. Or . . . could it be . . .

A lyre?

I cough. The iron vapors are setting fire to my throat.

A lyre.

Is it my imagination, or could that scrap of twisted wood and its strings truly be an attempt to replicate the gods' ancient instrument? Or do I only think that because Esteban loved the lyre?

I remember that birthday present, which he never received. A lyre-guitar. Am I losing my mind? Will everything that Tom does and says always remind me inexorably of Esteban?

All boys play a guitar at some point in their lives, don't they?

A guitar, yes. But a lyre?

"Time to go!" a voice calls through the open front door.

Amandine comes out, holding a book.

Tom puts his instrument on the bench and straddles his bike.

His mother doesn't say goodbye, or tell him to have a good day. She doesn't even look at him. She just smiles as she sees Tom ride away, as if she's relieved to be rid of him.

I know I shouldn't think this way. That it is impossible to interpret a smile, a look, a gesture, and even less so the absence of any of these things.

◆ ◆ ◆

1:25 p.m.

I catch sight of Tom, already three bends in the road below me. It will take him less than five minutes to reach the school in Murol. Less time than it will take me to walk back to my MiTo, drive to work, and park. My schedule for the afternoon is packed with appointments. But I have arranged them to ensure that I'll be free when Tom's classes end. His school is less than a hundred meters from my office.

The door to La Souille has just banged shut. Amandine did not spot me. I stare out one last time over the valley, watching the final curves before the village as Tom's bicycle approaches them and then disappears.

8

Martin Sainfoin decides to shift into the highest gear. It has been years since he did that. His speedometer wavers between forty-eight and fifty-one kilometers per hour. The Domaine campsite is on a slight uphill, so this is no mean feat. Quite a few of the youngsters at the Arverne Cycling Club would struggle to keep up with this pace, he knows. He accelerates even more.

Fifty-three kilometers per hour.

He is focused, head lowered, eyes fixed on the white lines that run along the ribbon of asphalt. His body shape is aerodynamic, like a high-speed train, and the wind glides over him, seeming almost to carry him forward.

Martin stands on his pedals and speeds up again. He has to reach maximum momentum before facing the ultimate challenge: the Col de la Croix-Saint-Robert. The fourth and final ascent of the day.

He's already conquered the peaks and passes of the Banne d'Ordanche, the Rocher de l'Aigle, and the Croix-Morand: a total of about twenty kilometers spent climbing, with an elevation gain close to fifteen hundred meters. But the best is yet to come: the highest mountain pass in Auvergne—1,451 meters—a finale experienced in howling wind, with not a single tree to shelter him. Granted, it's not the Ventoux mountain or the Tourmalet, but the repeated ascensions of the Puys are just as tough. He loves these steep, rapid climbs, with long, curving descents in between peaks that allow him to enter another valley right away and then attack yet another ascent.

He loves them today especially. His legs are like pistons. Could it be the rum flougnarde, or Nectaire's infusion giving him extra strength? If he can keep this pace up all the way to the summit, he'll ask the secretary at the mayor's office to brew him a whole barrel of the stuff before he competes in the national championships.

Okay, here we go. A ten-kilometer climb, with forty-three bends to negotiate.

How many times has he ridden this route? He knows he shouldn't start off too fast; the first few kilometers are the steepest. He remembers Bernard Hinault, who in 1978 signed young Martin's helmet in Besse, at the start of the Tour de France's fourteenth stage. The champion cyclist, known as the Badger, had unraveled here in volcano country, losing the stage to that asshole Joop Zoetemelk. Who could have imagined, seeing Hinault struggling up those mountainsides, watched by curious cows, that he would win his first Tour de France a few days later in the Alps?

It's true: the mountains of Auvergne aren't as celebrated as the Pyrenees or the Alps. But they still are a tough beast to tame.

Martin shifts to a lower gear, but doesn't stand on his pedals. Not yet. The slope is steep but steady for another kilometer. Better to save energy for the bends.

His heart rate accelerates. He's now going twenty-nine kilometers per hour. He's never taken this part of the route so fast before, and he has the impression that he could go even faster. That he could catch even the greatest cyclists in the world if they were on the road in front of him. He glances up to admire the ridgeline, pure green, uncluttered by rocks or glaciers.

He lets his thoughts take flight. He is eight years old, and cycling is all he cares about. All summer long, he has been listening to the Tour de France on the radio, but today the racers will ride by his home. He is there, on that famous day—July 12, 1964—along one of the Auvergne's giant bends; he sees the man, and he will never forget what he sees. He watches as Raymond Poulidor leaves the great Jacques Anquetil behind him on the climb, gaining meter after meter. The Norman champion Anquetil, would, at the end, hold on to his yellow jersey by a slender fourteen seconds, finishing on the verge of total collapse. But that day, Martin knew beyond any doubt: when he grew up, he wanted to be not Anquetil, but Poulidor.

First bend, first acceleration: only for twenty meters, to keep up the tempo.

But life had had other ideas for Martin. Fate. He would become not Poulidor, but a Sunday rider, waiting for retirement and for the day when he could ride on Mondays, Tuesdays, Wednesdays, Thursdays, Fridays, and Saturdays too.

The Mont-Dore mountain range lies stretched out ahead of him, beyond the knolls of the bare volcanoes that he must skirt around. This is the first time he's ever attempted the Col de la Croix-Saint-Robert in winter. Never in his life has he seen the pass with so little snow. In other years, it would have been impossible to make this ride in winter, unless he had snow chains on his wheels.

Martin unzips his collar. It feels like midsummer.

Two years ago, he nearly had his moment of glory. He might have won the national seniors' championship, if only he hadn't let those two Bordeaux riders pass. Back then, he hadn't trained enough. But now . . . The time has come to give everything, starting at the sixth bend. The slope plateaus at 5.7 percent; if he gets his timing right, he could stay above twenty-five kilometers per hour for the whole ride. Maybe even twenty-eight. His legs have never felt so powerful.

What the hell did Nectaire put in that tea?

Martin almost laughs, watching himself eat up the kilometers like this. He knows he will never be a great cyclist, only an amateur, but that doesn't stop him dreaming of achieving a little glory of his own, a victory, arms raised at least once at the summit of a mountain, a bouquet with his name on it . . .

Martin takes one last look at the summit of the Puy de Dôme before attacking the last ten curves. He will never be Bernard Hinault or Thibaut Pinot, but he might at least be Pierre Matignon, a largely forgotten racer who finished last in the 1969 Tour de France, a tortoise that one of the fastest hares of all, Eddie Merckx, had been unable to catch before the cyclists reached the summit of the highest volcano on the day of the Puy de Dôme stage that year.

The greatest story in the Tour's history.

Only eight bends left. The hardest ones.

An icy headwind. No houses anymore to shield him, not even a cow.

Martin zips up his top.

And yet he still feels he can go faster. Normally, this close to the summit, his legs are weakened by lactic acid, from his thighs down to his calves. This time, they keep going like clockwork, even though his heart is having to beat harder and harder.

Only three hundred meters to the summit. He'll have the whole descent to get his breath back, to let his heartbeat slow down.

A stabbing pain in his chest. The first warning.

Martin looks around. Not a soul. It would be ridiculous to stop now. He just slows down a little, shifts into an easier gear, then grimaces with regret. He's riding at less than ten kilometers per hour now. If this were a race, the peloton would come speeding past, just before the top of the hill, and he would watch them vanish over the edge.

One hundred meters.

Another knife to his heart. The pain is so intense, Martin almost falls off his bike. By some miracle, he keeps his balance and keeps riding, weaving from side to side, unable to grasp what is happening to him. He's barely moving forward now, just enough to stay upright. He forces himself to breathe more slowly, more deeply. Once he's over the top, he'll be able to glide down the other side.

One meter.

The third blade stabs him. Instantly, all the communication circuits inside his body are cut. His fingers can no longer grip the handlebars.

The bicycle falls sideways. Martin doesn't even have enough strength to remove his toe clips. His helmet and the carbon frame crash against the asphalt with a metallic clatter.

Not that Martin hears it. He can't hear anything, can't speak, can't get up, can't even reach the cell phone in his pannier. He knows that nobody will ever come to rescue him here, at the top of the mountain.

He knows he will die.

His heart stalls, in violent jerks, followed by long seconds without breathing.

What the hell was in that damn tea?

Followed by *Would I have won the national championships that day if I hadn't let those Bordeaux riders pass?*

That is his last thought.

Would he have been given his bouquet at the summit? His little cross of flowers, bearing a few words. His epitaph . . .

Martin Sainfoin. He was no Poulidor.

III

Apparition

Honey and Oats

9

Afternoon sunlight floods the paved square outside the mayor's office. The heat clings to the lava rocks, making the terrace feel like a giant fireplace. A little warmer and you could unfold deck chairs, open parasols. Savine, having stepped outside to smoke a cigarette, savors the view of the Saint-Ferréol church bell tower, the ruins of the Château de Murol, and the school playground. She breathes in the intoxicating scents of pine sap and honeysuckle, and listens serenely to the few sounds that break the stillness—a woodpecker hidden in a nearby tree, the hum of a chain saw in a distant forest, a radio playing music from behind a window—before it's all swept away. The torpor, the sweetness, the slow drip-feed of hours. First, a bell rings, midway between a fire truck alarm and a church bell. Then the cavalry charges: fifty galloping creatures burst out of the playground, satchels on backs, coats hanging half-off, scarves flying, laughter trailing.

School's out.

This is the village's daily adrenaline shot: kids hurtling along streets, cars parked on sidewalks, bicycles zigzagging between open car doors.

"Nectaire, come and look."

Savine left the front door open. The school is less than fifty meters away. All the children, in small and noisy groups, pass by on their way down Rue de Jassaguet.

"What?"

"Forget your stamps and come here. Quick!"

The secretary hesitates. He is terrified of drafts. He is focused on the most delicate task of the day: using a damp sponge to remove the stamps from the envelopes he has received, capturing them with tweezers, and arranging them in a laminated folder. Particularly since he has just received some rare ones from Pico do Fogo, Kverkfjöll, and Almolonga. Excellent additions to his private collection, his pride and joy, which he will bequeath to the Murol mayor's office when he retires: ten albums completely filled with stamps representing volcanoes all over the world. Nectaire Paturin has compiled a list of villages located on the mountainsides of volcanoes that are still more or less active. He writes to each in turn, then waits to receive their response . . . and a stamp.

"I can't. It'll all go flying."

"Just hurry up!"

The vulcatelophile—a rare species among the many branches of the great family tree of philatelists—covers his treasure with a thick sheet of blotting paper, then places the block of basalt he uses as a paperweight on top, to hold it all down. Savine groans inwardly: Why is this guy always so slow?

At last, Nectaire Paturin goes outside.

"Shhh," the social worker says. "Don't move. Just watch."

The secretary observes the groups of children going their separate ways. He knows almost all of them. Nathan, the butcher's son; Jade, Ambre, and Enzo, distant cousins; Eliot and Adam, little criminals-in-waiting. Yanis, who nearly drowned in Lac Chambon last summer . . .

"What am I supposed to see?"

"The parking lot of the medical center over there. Look."

Nectaire squints. All he sees is a parked car. Burgundy colored. A rather classy vehicle, he thinks, even if he knows nothing about cars, about the size of a Renault Clio or a Peugeot 208. He deciphers the brand name.

MiTo. Alfa Romeo.

"Isn't that Dr. Libéri's car?"

"You're a genius! Now lean down and look inside."

Nectaire twists his wiry body as far as he can. Yep, no doubt about it—that's the doctor sitting behind the wheel.

"Okay, so she's in her car. So what?"

"Shouldn't she be in her office?"

"Well, no, not necessarily. Maybe she needs some time alone to send a text to a lover? The only strange thing, in my opinion, is that she came to live in this place. She's still a beautiful woman for her age."

"How tactful of you, Nectaire. Thank you."

The secretary blushes, starts to make excuses. That was not what he meant. "Of course, there are pretty women in Murol too; that's not the point. So . . . what was your question again? The doctor sitting in her car as the kids come out of school?"

"She can do what she wants, can't she?" the secretary concludes, eager to get back to his Filipino stamps.

"I've been watching her for a while," the social worker explains. "She's been staring into her rearview mirror the whole time. I was wondering what she could be looking at . . . and now I know."

"So who does she have her eye on? Yanis's father? Or Eliot and Nolan's? Is she hot for lifeguards and ski instructors? I bet she's surprised that there are actually some handsome men living around here . . ."

"Don't be an idiot. She's been spying on that kid ever since he came out of school. The only one who's all alone. Amandine Fontaine's son, Tom."

"Well, you'd better watch out—I think she's getting out of her Lamborghini."

Nectaire is right. He and Savine have just enough time to withdraw to the corner of the wall, leaving behind nothing but a faint cloud of smoke. Maddi Libéri opens her car door and appears to hide behind the vehicle. Tom is the only child who hasn't yet left the school playground. He's standing next to his bike, his eyes perpetually moving, lips half-open, making jerky little movements, as though having a conversation with some invisible children.

"What do you think of that?" asks Savine, her eyes glued to the scene.

"Well, little Tom has always been a little odd. I get the impression there are several people living inside his head. He's a nice kid, though. I like him . . ."

"I'm not talking about Tom! I mean the doctor."

Nectaire leans his head around the corner of the building.

"Oh . . . Well, she's watching Tom . . . Yes, I would say that she likes him too."

Savine drags him back into hiding.

"She likes him?" she asks irritably. "Are you joking? Did you see her eyes? She's looking at that kid like he's her own son!"

The secretary, moving at the speed of a snail that wants to explore every crack in the wall, eventually looks around the corner again.

"Okay, I see what you mean. She looks . . . hypnotized. But so what? She's hardly going to kidnap him. She's a doctor. Maybe she's noticed something off about Tom. I know Amandine is your little protégée, but all the same, she's not very . . . What's the word?"

"What?"

"Not very . . . maternal."

"Oh, and you'd know all about that, I suppose? Being maternal."

Just as the conversation between Nectaire and Savine threatens to become a row, a minivan roars the wrong way up Rue de l'Hôtel-de-Ville, the driver ignoring the fact that it's a one-way street and going well over the 30 kmph speed limit. It's a blue Kangoo, the official vehicle of the local gendarmerie. The van stops in the middle of the street, outside the mayor's office, blocking Dr. Libéri's view of Tom. Three gendarmes rush out. Lieutenant Lespinasse, from the Besse brigade, is the only one who speaks.

"Savine, Nectaire, go back inside and round up the other employees."

Soon the three gendarmes are inside the mayor's office, address-ing not only Savine and Nectaire, but their colleagues Alain Suchet,

Géraldine Jume, and Oudard Benslimane, plus two town councilors also returned from lunch, Jacques Mercœur and Sandrine Gouly.

The gendarmes don't bother closing the door behind them.

"It's Martin. Martin Sainfoin. He was found at the top of Croix-Saint-Robert. Next to his bike. Heart attack."

Lieutenant Lespinasse, noticing that the front door is still open and wishing to keep his announcement private, slams it shut.

An eruption of volcanic stamps goes flying into the air, before fluttering down like butterflies.

10

"Gabriel, don't interrupt. I just need you to listen to me."

I have just arrived at the Moulin de Chaudefour. I parked my MiTo outside the door, straddling the sidewalk, despite the empty parking lot beside the house. I toss my handbag and coat onto the nearest chair. I pour myself a glass of Bénédictine—a souvenir of Normandy—and collapse onto the sofa.

It's eight o'clock in the evening, but dinner can wait.

Gabriel sits facing away from me, eyes glued to his computer screen. He told me he was planning to work hard the whole afternoon. To take a self-assessment in English: a series of tests to measure which language skills he has acquired, partially acquired, or exceeded. According to Gabriel, English is indispensable in today's market. The less a person comes out from under their duvet, the greater their need to speak a language understood all over the globe. Telework, which combines a concern for the planet with a concern for privacy, is the future. "Look at telemedicine," he likes to say. "Even you will be doing this soon."

If you say so, Gabriel.

He is clearly exhausted from his English classes, but not to the point that he's ready to leave his computer. He's on *MTW-1—My Tidy World One*—a cooperative ecological game in which the players inhabit a virtual world without pollution, where they can teleport from place to place at the cost of zero energy, build cabins using trees that grow back overnight, light their homes with fireflies, even grow blue carrots if that's what they desire.

"Listen to me, Gabriel. Listen to me tonight, at least.

"It all began in Saint-Jean-de-Luz. You were there too, Gabriel. It began with those indigo trunks, the ones with the little whale design on them. That can't have been a coincidence. At best, I might believe it was a trap someone had set for me, though who that someone might be or why they might have done it, I have no idea. Anyway, it's one possible theory, and it makes some sense. Lots of people knew about those trunks: they were mentioned in the newspapers ten years ago, and in the posters—with Esteban's photograph—plastered all over town.

"But how does that explain what happened next? Above all, how does it explain the astonishing physical resemblance between Esteban and Tom? A doppelganger? But that someone would have had to go through hundreds of thousands of children, trying to find the one who looked most like Esteban, then make him put on a pair of identical swim trunks. What sense does that make? And what about all the other stuff? That birthmark, for instance. Do you think this hypothetical plotter put a small ad in the newspaper: *Seeking a ten-year-old boy with a brown birthmark on his abdomen, who looks exactly like this photograph?* It's ridiculous, impossible. And yet it's reality. Oh, and, of course, the ad should also mention that the kid has to like music, and preferably play the lyre and . . . and hate honey.

"Am I dreaming, Gabriel? Am I hallucinating this whole thing?
"Gabriel?
"Gabriel?"

Only now do I notice the flesh-colored wireless earbuds he's wearing, so elegant and discreet. Gaby hasn't heard a word I've said. He doesn't even know I've come home. Am I living with a ghost at home too? Or am I the one getting everything mixed up? Am *I* the ghost? I only talk with the disappeared these days, after all; nobody else listens to me.

I tiptoe out of the room. I open the front door. It's warm out. The quarter moon illuminates the eroded mountain peaks, revealing, like a stone mirror, a crescent-shaped crater. Somewhere in the night, a cricket chirps out of season, forgetting that it's still winter.

I know what I must do: call the only living person capable of listening to me. Even if he's not going to like what I have to ask him.

I take out my phone. One last hesitation, which I cut short by thinking about Gabriel's selfishness. *Sorry, Gaby, but the handsome Dr. Wayan Balik Kuning is everything you're not. Hardworking, attentive, understanding. That doesn't detract from all the love and affection I feel for you, of course, but . . . I need him.*

◆　◆　◆

"Hello, Doctor."

"Maddi? What a surprise! You don't call me Wayan anymore?"

"I do, Wayan, I do."

"So . . . how's Auvergne, and your new life?"

"Later, Wayan. I'll write to you about it; I promise. But . . . I need to ask you for something. Some specific information."

"Go ahead," he says with a hint of irony. "I assume you're not calling Wayan the man, but rather Wayan the shrink."

Is Wayan still in love with me, or is he only joking? Surely he's found some other pretty woman to replace me since I left Normandy.

"You're going to think I'm crazy, Wayan, but . . . I need you to tell me about . . . reincarnation."

There is only silence at the end of the line.

"Not that I believe in it. Of course not. I'd just like to get a handle on the basic idea. And I figured you would know about it. Since you're . . ."

"Of Balinese origin? Is that what you were going to say?"

I can tell that he's annoyed.

"So, since I'm Balinese, I must be a Hindu? Is that what you think? And if I'm a Hindu, I must believe in karma, dharma, and nirvana . . . That's a rather simplistic line of logic, Maddi; don't you think?"

"I just need to know the main principles. It's important."

"All right, if you insist. But for the record, you're speaking to the man, not the shrink. Okay? Part of the reason I left Bali to become a psychiatrist was to get away from those beliefs. To follow a different path than the one I was supposedly brought up to walk."

"I understand, Wayan."

"*Wayan*," the psychiatrist repeats. "Yes, let's start there. Do you know what that name means?"

I hesitate, considering different possibilities. Wise? Serious? Kind? Intelligent? Handsome? In love?

Before I have time to make a choice, he continues. "All Balinese men, almost six million people on this earth, have one of only five first names. *Wayan*—or *Putu*—meaning eldest, is given to the family's first son. The second is called *Kadek*. The third, *Nyoman*, and the fourth, *Ketut*."

"So I'm assuming you were the firstborn?"

"Actually, I wasn't. In families with more than four sons, the parents start again at the beginning, and the fifth son is also called *Wayan*. Or, to be more precise, *Wayan Balik*, which can be translated as *Return to Wayan*, and so on . . . And, since I'm evidently confiding in you, I can also tell you that my eldest brother, Wayan, died three years before I was born. Consequently, in my parents' eyes, I am both myself . . . and him. From a Western point of view, I'm sure such a conflation of personality must be difficult to understand."

"No . . . I think I understand . . ."

Wayan is silent for a moment before continuing. "So, to return to your question, Maddi . . . yes, reincarnation is part of daily life for Balinese people, as it is for all Hindus and, more generally, the vast majority of men and women who live in Asia. Every child that is born carries the burden of its previous lives. To give you an example, when I came into the world, my parents consulted a medium to find out which of my ancestors I resembled. We don't have surnames in Bali: the parents choose names based on their children's previous lives, which inform our tastes, our talents, our future occupations. So, not only do I share my first name with a dead older brother; one of my distant uncles died of jaundice two days before I was born. *Kuning*, in Balinese, means yellow."

I burst out laughing, unable to stop myself at the memory of the color scheme in Wayan's office: saffron paintings, topaz rugs, corn-colored sofa.

"I'm sorry."

"Don't be. I would rather you laughed at such superstitions than believed in them. Not that I'm critical of those beliefs; they help billions of people accept death. And there is absolutely nothing to prove that they are false. Just as there is absolutely nothing to prove they are true."

I think again about the articles I read on birthmarks. Two days ago, I would have considered reincarnation no more likely than unicorns or the fountain of eternal youth.

"What do you think, Maddi?" he asks. "Should something be proven to exist before you believe in it? Or should everything be considered possible until it's proven impossible?"

"I don't think anything. I'm like all Europeans . . . Reincarnation just seems a rather . . . distant concept."

"So you think! Polls suggest that more than one European in four believes in reincarnation. And perhaps that's not so surprising, given that the idea first took root in Europe. I bet you didn't know that, did you?"

No, Wayan, I didn't. Until yesterday, I fell very much in the camp of the skeptical.

"The theory of reincarnation developed in ancient Greece, at the same time as the concepts of democracy and the republic . . . Plato, Pythagoras, and many others believed in it. The Greeks were buried with thin strips of gold bearing directions so that their souls wouldn't become lost between two lives. That religion is known as Orphism, a reference to the myth of Orpheus."

"Orpheus? Isn't he the one who played—"

"The lyre, yes! Or the guitar of the gods, if you prefer. It was the instrument used to charm the guardian of Hades, to bring back loved ones to a new life."

A lyre!

Tom had played a sort of lyre in the courtyard of the farm. Esteban had asked me for a lyre-guitar for his birthday. Had he known what it meant in the old legends? Who could have told him about it? Why would he . . .

"Maddi? Are you still there? Don't hesitate to ask, if you want me to come to Auvergne. I may be six hundred kilometers away from you in Le Havre, but you know perfectly well that there's nothing and nobody to keep me here. Just say the word, and I'll be there!"

11

Three days later

The cemetery in Murol is hidden away, sheltered from the heat, between a cool mountain stream and the shade of the pines. The surrounding fields are covered with primroses. The cows have already been led out to pasture, but they hang back, a polite distance from the ceremony. The village appears as though it's come together to celebrate the coming of spring—the rebirth of flowers, the return of insects and swallows—rather than to attend a funeral.

Nearly everyone is here. Everyone in Murol knew Martin Sainfoin. The mayor—a woman who runs the biggest dairy cooperative in the region—explained to me that, as the village doctor, it was important that I be there for the burial. It was a question of give-and-take, she said. When I first arrived in Murol, she'd offered the assistance of several of her employees to help me renovate my office, and they'd all come to introduce themselves: Alain Suchet to prune the trees outside my window; Oudard Benslimane to give me a rundown of the current cultural calendar; Savine Laroche to brief me on the most worrying social cases; Nectaire Paturin to offer help with any paperwork stamping or the selection of plants for infusions; and, of course, Martin Sainfoin, who gave me an overview of the area's problems: drugs, alcohol, domestic violence, and so on.

Nobody has a bad word to say about Martin. Is that why Mother Nature has blessed his funeral with such glorious weather? Even the cemetery itself is full of colors and flowers.

All the riders of the Arverne Cycling Club are present, wearing their blue-and-gold uniforms. They have placed two wreaths by his gravestone, where a pair of granite handlebars emerge from a marble plaque. I suppose we should be grateful they didn't bury him in a yellow jersey. Martin Sainfoin would not have minded in the least, but the priest refused. Martin had a sense of humor, and a very big heart . . . even if his heart was the very thing that failed him in the end.

The priest, escorted by two children from the choir, leads the prayer recital. One of the children holds the bucket of holy water, the other the basket for the collection. Their names are Yanis and Enzo; I know them. Yanis is asthmatic, Enzo diabetic. Not that they are bitter about these gifts from God.

The crowd gathers more tightly around the coffin. I remain at a distance. I can tell from the looks they give me that I'm still considered a stranger. Gabriel holds my hand. We have reconciled since my phone call to Wayan Balik Kuning. Gabriel listened to me as I told him the whole story, and he reassured me about all of it—the lyre, the birthmark, the physical resemblance to Esteban, and all the rest. "There has to be an explanation," he told me. "We just need to give it some thought, do some research." He promised to help me. He even agreed to leave his lair for the afternoon and put on a black jacket, a pair of dark jeans, and a tie, so I wouldn't be alone at the cemetery. Thank you, Gabriel. I know how much it pains you to wear that particular disguise.

Four cyclists—the youngest about twenty and the eldest not far shy of a hundred—have stood up together to carry the coffin. I recognize Maximilien, the handsome lifeguard; Lucas, the currently unemployed ski instructor; Jules, the retired farmer; and Baptiste, the baker's apprentice.

The faithful line up behind them, reaching for their wallets. The choristers have put the bucket and the basket in front of the open grave:

holy water for the hereafter, and a few euros for the here and now. I'm able to identify almost all the villagers: in three weeks, they've all been to see me, and it's possible that I know more of their secrets than most people who were born and bred in Murol.

Is that why they keep staring at me? For the past few days, I've had the impression that the locals are spying on me. In particular, the two gray-haired employees at the mayor's office, the energetic social worker and the overstressed secretary.

I could have sworn that the secretary was unmarried, since he acts like such an old bachelor, but apparently, I was wrong. He has linked arms with a woman who looks as eccentric as he is normal. She must be about his age, early fifties, but she dresses as though she's closer to thirty. An ethnic tunic, multicolored pantyhose, an elegant straw hat, Buddhist wheel earrings, and a strange copper pendant in the shape of twisted spirals.

I spot Amandine, opposite her, dressed in contrasting dark sobriety. She stands apart from the rest of the group: Is that because she's shy, or because she's in such pain that she can't stand on her own for very long and has to lean against the cemetery wall? Noticing the grimace of fatigue that distorts her face, I think the latter explanation more likely. She has come without Tom. Presumably she thinks a funeral is no place for a ten-year-old boy. I would have thought the same, before. I remember that I didn't want to take Esteban to my father's funeral, in Hendaye. He was only eight at the time. I tried to explain to him that everyone would be sad, crying, that he might find it scary, but that he could draw a picture for Grandpa instead, or write him a letter.

The aspergillum, the holy water sprinkler, is passed from hand to hand. Some people make the sign of the cross; others murmur inaudibly. The big strong men in their blue cycling shirts cry like babies. Losing a friend is like losing one's illusion of immortality.

Will Grandpa be able to read the letter?

It's strange how memories resurface sometimes. I haven't thought about that conversation with Esteban even once in the past twelve years. Not until this ceremony, this cemetery . . . this mystery.

I hope so . . .

I had been sitting at the foot of Esteban's bed, waiting for him to fall asleep.

So Grandpa's not dead, then? It's just that his body was too old. But his head is still alive. He just needs to find a new body. Why don't you have a baby, Mommy? That way, it could be a nice new body for Grandpa.

I think I smiled at that. Or maybe I explained that I didn't plan to have another baby, or that things didn't work that way—the body and the soul—that each baby had its own personality. Or maybe I didn't answer him at all, just kissed him good night and turned off the light. I honestly have no idea. I wasn't really focusing on what he'd said. It just struck me as a little boy's sweet whim, perhaps influenced by a cartoon he'd seen on TV, or a conversation that had happened during recess. Why had that memory not come back to me before? Because it hadn't had any meaning for me up to this point, any resonance. But now . . .

Amandine moves closer, at the last minute, so she won't have to wait in line before the coffin. She walks carefully, like a doll with dying batteries that might topple over if it meets the slightest obstacle. It's the gait of an alcoholic, but Amandine has no other symptoms of that addiction. Maybe it's just the gait of a very tired person. I've had time to study her, from the fountain above her farm, from the Froidefond bridge, and from the two or three other observation posts I've found in this little hamlet.

I am aware that I might come across like a voyeur. I prefer to think of my behavior as surveillance, or even a form of vigilance. It's almost my duty as a doctor.

It's become an obsession, anyway.

Watching Tom. Following Tom. Protecting Tom.

I know I can't keep doing this much longer. I need to find another plan. Amandine will spot me eventually. Well, either she or the village social worker, Savine Laroche. That woman has been glaring at me ever since she walked into the cemetery.

She has nothing to worry about, though. I don't want to harm Tom. Quite the opposite, in fact.

I wish I could reassure all of them, tell them I'm not crazy. I came here to heal them, to do my job to the best of my ability. But I can feel their eyes on me like a heavy weight. Suddenly I feel fragile and lost. I need help. I can't deal with this on my own. The first face that comes to mind is Dr. Wayan Balik Kuning's, though I don't really understand why.

I try to erase him as I squeeze Gabriel's hand.

12

The cemetery slowly empties, like a cracked hourglass laid on its side. Some of the villagers have parked their cars by the roadside, but most of them walk back to the village, in small groups. It's easier going downhill than it was coming up, as if, now that the funeral's over, they already feel lighter.

Savine picks up her pace, looking up at the church bell tower and the French flags hanging from the windows of the mayor's office. She's just exchanged a few words with the mayor and with Alain, the gardener. Nectaire, still holding the arm of the woman in the hat and the multicolored tights, took advantage of Savine's conversation to get a hundred-meter head start, but at the pace she's going, she'll soon catch them up.

"Aster, do you mind if I borrow Nectaire?"

The two are clinging to each other as they descend the slope, like a couple of old people out on their daily walk, afraid of getting lost even though they always follow the same route.

"If you like."

The woman lets go of Nectaire's arm and invites Savine to take her place.

"Usain Bolt is all yours. I have to go open the store anyway."

Savine obediently links arms with the secretary, who accepts his new partner without batting an eyelash.

"See you tonight, Brother," Aster says as she walks away, her Mary Poppins boots slapping against the asphalt.

Aster Paturin runs a store in Besse that sells local organic produce. It's named La Galipote. She also sells the kind of stuff tourists find exotic: there are entire aisles filled with healing lava rocks, creams and soaps to make a person more youthful, vials of spring water that cure rheumatism, ointments for snake bites, and alcohol made from salamanders, while above the customers' heads hang dozens of dream catchers woven from the wool of five-legged sheep, witches riding broomsticks, and puppets carved from tree bark found in enchanted forests. The customers love all that stuff, particularly since Aster seems to genuinely believe in what she's selling. Nectaire lives with her, in an apartment above the store. They aren't quite twins, but they might as well be—they were born about nine months apart.

Aster disappears into the village along with most of the other mourners. Nectaire and Savine are left alone amid the fields. Walking, for Nectaire, is a sort of yogic, almost mystical activity, in which every movement, every effort, should be savored and appreciated.

"Could we speed up a little, Nicky? It'd be nice to get back to work before midnight, you know. Because if you keep pausing before every step to make sure you're not going to crush an ant . . ."

Nectaire doesn't get annoyed by this comment. In fact, he never gets annoyed. He observes Savine for a moment. She's dressed in her taupe wool jacket and her peasant dress, her slender legs ending in a pair of chunky walking shoes. He's always loved that mountaineering look of hers.

"Go ahead if you like. You don't have to wait for me."

"No, I need you. I . . . There's a favor I have to ask you." Savine hesitates, almost forcing Nectaire to a halt. "How would you feel about doing your old job again?"

"My old job?"

"You used to be a cop, right?"

Nectaire stops. He stares intensely at a brown cow in the next field. The creature has sad, brown eyes, and she leans her neck over the barbed-wire fence as if she were listening to their conversation.

"What exactly did you have in mind?" he asks.

"I want you to investigate something."

"There are gendarmes for that . . . But there would have to be a crime—a theft, or a murder—before they came here to investigate it."

"Precisely! The gendarmes won't come here, so I need my own Sherlock Holmes to solve the mystery."

"As a proud Francophone, I would rather be Hercule Poirot."

The social worker smiles at this little joke. She can sense Nectaire's interest.

"I just want you to find out certain information. You must still have some friends at the police station in Clermont, right?"

"Maybe . . . But what kind of information?"

"I bet you can guess."

"Dr. Libéri? Surely you're not still convinced she's about to kidnap Tom Fontaine! If she imagines Amandine can afford to pay a ransom, she really is deluded."

Nectaire begins slowly walking again. Savine still holds on to his arm.

"I've found her several times recently hiding behind that fountain near their farm, or beside the river. It's like she's prowling around La Souille, spying on Amandine and Tom."

"She does live at the Moulin de Chaudefour," says Nectaire. "Froidefond is on the way."

"Sure, but it's a bit strange that she stops there every time, don't you think? It's not like there's anything interesting to do in Froidefond!" She squeezes the secretary's arm. "You've got to believe me, Nectaire— there's something really fishy about all this. You can see it in her eyes. Sometimes she seems perfectly normal, just a respectable doctor, but other times it's like she's trying to hide this strange madness. Come on; I'm not asking for much. Just dig into her past a little bit. I mean, we hardly know anything about her. And I have an instinct for this kind of thing."

"An instinct. Hmm . . ."

Nectaire stops again to examine some grass on the roadside. They've advanced about fifty meters since the start of their conversation. The Murol sign is still two hundred meters away.

"You should beware of your instincts," he advises her, pulling up a fragrant stalk of couch grass and putting it to his lips. "Would you like to know a secret? Instinct is the reason I resigned from the police force . . . and why I don't want to do any more investigating."

"What do you mean?"

"When I was a cop, I relied totally on my instincts. I was like Columbo, always following a hunch, gathering evidence in my own way. I imagined that I had a gift, that I could solve a mystery before all those by-the-book cops got anywhere near it."

The cows in the next field have moved away, as if giving up hope of ever seeing the humans walk all the way past them.

"A gift. Yes, I see."

"And I was wrong every time! Innocent people were arrested because of my stupid instincts. I was like one of those detectives in a novel who thinks the culprit is always the person nobody suspects. I never went where the evidence pointed; in fact, I was suspicious of it, imagining red herrings and complicated conspiracies. But the truth is often mind-numbingly simple. The culprit is the one that all the evidence points to, and the cop's job is just to handcuff him and type up a report. In Clermont, my nickname was Inspector Clouseau. As soon as I suspected someone, they would immediately cross him off their list of suspects."

"So you were useful after all!" Savine jokes. "I'm sure they won't mind answering a few of your questions. Anyway, instinct is a female thing. Leave that part to me. All I want you to do is find out about Maddi Libéri. Does she have a criminal record? That kind of thing. Oh, and I'd like you to find out more about Martin Sainfoin's death as well."

They have almost reached the Murol sign. The mayor's office isn't far now. At the entrance to the village, some children are playing Frisbee with a hat they've taken from Yanis, the only child who has dressed too warmly.

"Martin?" Nectaire asks, surprised. "What does he have to do with all this?"

"Don't you remember, the day when you gave him that tea, he wanted to see me, that evening, in private? He said he wanted to talk about Amandine Fontaine."

"I still don't see the connection. Martin had a heart attack."

Savine hesitates. She watches as Yanis runs in pursuit of his hat.

"I know, but . . . don't you think that's strange? The key witness who dies before he can talk . . ."

"Oh, come on! Surely you're not saying Martin was murdered?"

"You don't believe it?"

"Not for a second."

"Well, I must be on the right track, then, mustn't I, Inspector Clouseau?"

"Ha ha, very funny."

They pass the group of laughing, jeering children. Yanis's hat has ended up stuck in the gutter that runs along the roof of the real estate agency.

"According to Souche," says Savine, "Lieutenant Lespinasse asked for an autopsy before the funeral. So they must have thought there was something strange about that coronary too. Martin had been examined by a doctor a couple of weeks before, and he had a certificate declaring that he had no heart problems at all."

"And who signed that certificate?"

"If you took your nose out of your teas and your stamps for a minute, you'd already know the answer to that! Everyone knows, except you. Didn't you notice the way everyone was staring at her? How many doctors are there in the village? The person who examined Martin Sainfoin and told him his heart was in perfect condition was Maddi Libéri."

Nectaire Paturin appears to process this news. Is his brain already searching for hidden clues? Or is he still refusing to investigate anything?

The mayor's office is just across the road, but Nectaire tries to usher Savine a little farther on, toward the pedestrian crossing. The social worker finally lets go of his arm and steps onto the road.

"Don't tell me you're afraid to jaywalk too?"

The secretary keeps going until he reaches the crossing.

"We get about three cars per day on this road!" Savine says.

Nectaire stops, turns, and smiles. "Well, you see, there are two kinds of people in the world—those who cross roads using the crossings and those who cross them wherever they feel like it. You understand? Those who wait for the little green man to light up and those who rush across as soon as the cars start to brake."

Savine is already on the other side of the street.

"Yes, I get it. And I am definitely in the second camp. Is it serious, Doctor?"

"Oh yes. Deadly serious. It means that you plan your life like a race against the clock, that every minute counts, that every second you fall behind is like a piece of your life you'll never get back. It means, in short, that you are afraid of dying."

Savine watches Nectaire start across the quiet Rue de Jassaguet as if it were Boulevard Haussmann in Paris.

"Oh, and you're not?"

"Of course I am. So let's say that the world can be divided between those who think they have only one life and those who believe, even subconsciously, that they have already lived many previous lives and that they will live many other lives after this one."

"And that's true for you, is it? Lots of previous lives? Is that why you take your time?"

"I don't know; it's just a theory. But how else do you explain the fact that some people have an unquenchable wanderlust while others, like me, are only happy when they're at home? Maybe it's because I've already been on dozens of family vacations to Australia, Lapland, and

Easter Island in my previous lives," he adds sarcastically. "So now I've lost some of my motivation to strap on a backpack and explore."

Savine enters the courtyard of the mayor's office, deep in thought, just as five teenagers hurtle down the road on skateboards, Rollerblades, and a scooter, speeding past Nectaire—still midstreet—as if he were merely a road cone. She recognizes three of them: Eliot, Nolan, and Adam.

Nectaire stands there shaking for several long seconds after the youngsters have disappeared in the direction of the bridge over the Couze Chambon.

"Why aren't those little jerks at school?" the secretary demands.

"It's the winter holidays!" She observes the green, empty slopes of the Massif du Sancy in the distance. "And with weather like this, where else can they go to get their thrills?"

"If only they'd broken a leg or two in another life," Nectaire grumbles.

He starts crossing the road again, more cautiously than a hedgehog in the rain, staring in turn at the mayor's office, the closed school gates, and the empty parking lot of the doctor's office.

"One thing's for sure anyway," he adds. "If it's the holidays, that doctor of yours can't spy on Tom coming out of school anymore."

Savine climbs the three steps that lead up to the terrace of the mayor's office. Her smile disappears in an instant.

"This isn't a joke, Nectaire! I'm serious. I really do believe that kid's in danger. And I'm worried that Amandine isn't strong enough to protect him. You could see how exhausted she was at the cemetery. It's my job to worry about the welfare of local kids! Just like your job is . . . um, cutting out stamps and making tea."

Nectaire has finally reached the other side of the road.

"Well, then, you'd better get your swimsuit and your life preserver. You know as well as I do that Tom isn't a skier or a skateboarder. What he loves is swimming. In summer, the kid is always at the lake. And in winter? He's at the Super-Besse pool."

13

Tom has just swum two hundred meters in the lap pool of the Hermines water park at Super-Besse. Fifty meters each of butterfly, backstroke, breaststroke, and crawl. He looks up at the big clock above the foot-bath, waves at Maximilien the lifeguard, who is sitting up on his tennis umpire's chair, and heads for the showers.

Tom is relieved. He had been worried that the pool would be full of bored tourists, since the ski lifts aren't working, but it's practically empty. Maybe all those Parisians are out hiking instead.

Tom stands under the hot shower for a long time. He could just shower when he gets home, of course, after cycling the seven-kilometer uphill between the pool and Froidefond, a half-hour ride that will inevitably leave him covered in sweat. But he prefers the showers at the pool. At home, the showerhead is rusty and the water a tepid trickle. That's another reason why he loves the Hermines pool. Because everything here is so clean: the windows, the glazed blue tiles on the walls, the pale tiles underfoot. Even when it's raining outside, when everything is muddy, when the Couze Chambon overflows its banks and the streets are transformed into open-air sewers. The swimming pool is his refuge. Once he's through the turnstile, once he's left his sneakers in the locker at the entrance, nothing bad can happen to him.

This is what Tom thinks as he watches the boy walk into the showers. He's about the same age as Tom. The same height and body shape, too, with the same long swimmer's arms. But it's the boy's swim shorts that he notices first. They're indigo, just like his.

The boy goes straight to the shower, like Tom did fifteen seconds earlier. He stands under the jet of water nearest Tom's, separated only by a glass divider, which is so transparent Tom could almost believe he's looking into a mirror.

"Hi."

"Hi," repeats the mirror.

Not a mirror, then. Mirrors don't talk. Tom wants to go through the glass. The boy on the other side, he sees now, doesn't really look like him. Their eyes aren't exactly the same color; the boy in the mirror has slightly darker irises, darker hair, too, and his face is longer. But he does move in the same way. He rubs every part of his body with shower gel, just like Tom does, and he picks up his bottle of shampoo the same way Tom picks up his own.

"Have you been swimming long?" Tom asks. "I've never seen you at the pool before."

"It's the first time I've come here," replies the strange mirror.

Tom's hand reaches out and touches the glass divider.

"Do you . . . really exist?"

The mirror boy makes the same gesture. Their hands touch without touching.

"What do you think?" replies his reflection. "Your questions are nuts."

"Why do you say that?"

"I mean, you can see me, can't you? And I'm talking to you! That proves I exist."

"Not necessarily," Tom says, without moving his hand away. A thin film of condensation forms around his fingers, as if he's wearing a glove of mist too big for him. "I could have invented you. So you'd just be in my head, you know, like a ghost . . ."

The strange reflection slicks his hair back.

"Oh, that's nice! So you're calling me a ghost?"

"Don't get annoyed!" Tom says. "I was just thinking out loud. I'm not used to talking to people. I don't have many friends around here. Actually, the other kids here say *I'm* a ghost. That's my nickname: Phan-TOM. Because my name is Tom, you see."

The reflection smiles at him.

"I don't have many friends either."

"No kidding!"

The reflection's smile freezes. He pretends to be annoyed and sprays foamy shampoo onto his hair. "So you still think I'm a ghost?"

"No . . . I mean, I don't know. It's more complicated than that. You know what I think, really? I think you're a memory of my past. You're *my* ghost, but you're from one of my previous lives."

The white foam flows over the reflection's face, whitening everything but his two big eyes.

"Whoa! Seriously? I'm from one of your previous lives? I must be really old." The reflection moves closer to the glass divider, facing Tom, whose face is also covered with foam. "I don't look old, though."

The two boys stare at each other's white faces.

"If I explain it to you," says Tom, "you won't tell anyone, will you? It's a secret."

"How could I repeat it if I'm a ghost?"

It is Tom's turn to smile.

"That's true! Okay, I'm going to try not to annoy you, but you need to know the truth. As far as I can tell, you died when you were ten."

The foam is stinging the mirror boy's eyes, so he sweeps it away. "I'm about to turn ten. Does that mean I'm going to die?"

"No, no, you don't understand . . . You're already dead! You died ten years ago. In fact, you died at more or less the exact moment when I was born. And your soul, or your mind at least—your thoughts, all that stuff—came to live in my little baby body. That's why I can see you and talk to you: you're like a memory of my past. It's like I'm seeing myself in a mirror, ten years later. But with a different face and a different body."

"We look alike, though," the reflection says.

"A little bit, yeah . . . and we're wearing the same trunks. That's how I knew you were my ghost."

Foam bubbles trickle from the reflection's hair down to the end of his nose, and he blows them away. They fly through the air before sticking to the misted-over glass. He stares at Tom for a long time.

"You're nuts! But I like hearing your crazy ideas."

This time, Tom feels genuinely upset.

"You don't believe me? All right, then; here's a test. Tell me what sorts of things you like."

"Apart from hearing your crazy ideas, you mean?"

Tom sighs. He's starting to realize that taming his ghost won't be easy.

"Yes, idiot, apart from that."

"Well, swimming, obviously . . . I love music too."

"Just like me! You see?"

The reflection has now rinsed off all the shampoo.

"No, not really. I mean, all kids our age love music, don't they?" He bends down to pick up his shampoo bottle. "I have to go. Sorry, Tom. See you another time. It was great chatting with you, learning that I was dead and all that . . ."

"Okay, go ahead. But don't worry; you'll see me again. All I have to do is close my eyes and you'll reappear wherever and whenever I want . . . seeing as you're just a figment of my imagination."

The reflection freezes.

"You're a total wacko. Seriously, can't you see that I'm actually alive? Look . . ."

He flattens his hand against the glass divider, then suddenly starts banging it. Several times, as hard as he can. The glass shakes, and the sound echoes through the locker room. Barely ten seconds later, Maximilien appears in the doorway. He doesn't look too keen on getting his flip-flops wet, so he yells at them from the other side of the footbath: "Hey! What's going on?"

"Um . . . nothing, Max," Tom stammers.

But the lifeguard is already on his way back to his high chair.

"See?" says the reflection.

"What am I supposed to see?" Tom asks. "Don't you realize that I'm making all this up? You're like a doll who thinks she's a real girl, or like a wooden toy who believes he can really breathe and doesn't understand that when he moves his arms, it's only because the puppet master is pulling his strings."

This time, the reflection bursts out laughing.

"You're unbelievable! So is there nothing I can say that would convince you I'm just a normal kid? Okay, I'll try one more thing . . ."

He puts his shampoo bottle on the floor, then kicks it under the glass divider.

"Grab that bottle. You'll see it's perfectly real."

Tom looks down at the foamy bottle and reads aloud, "Mild shampoo. Honey and oats."

He staggers and has to grip the glass divider to stop himself falling.

"You . . . you wash your hair with that?"

"Yeah . . . Why? Are oats bad for ghosts or something, like garlic for vampires?"

Tom ignores this joke. He looks like he's struggling to breathe as he continues to stare at the bottle as if it were full of poison.

"So you don't remember anything?" he mutters at last. "You must have a hole in your head. You've totally forgotten certain . . . accidents."

"Whoa, Tommy! Don't get me wrong; I love ghost stories, but you're starting to give me the heebie-jeebies." He picks up his bottle and says, "I really do need to go now. But just in case we never see each other again . . . why don't you tell me how I died?"

Tom's face lights up; is his ghost finally ready to believe him? He turns toward the swimming pool.

"You drowned."

"Ah . . ." The reflection tries not to let his emotion show. "Okay, and what was my name? Maybe if I know that, it'll help me get some of my memories back . . ."

Tom is silent for a moment. Then he says, "Why are you using the past tense? You didn't change your name just because you died. Your name was, and always will be . . . Esteban!"

Esteban? the reflection appears to repeat silently. He bites down hard on his lip, as if he were trying to stop himself screaming, as if—all of a sudden—his memories have returned, and he's realized that he truly is dead.

He doesn't say another word, and—without glancing at Tom—he runs away through the locker room, paying no mind to the slippery floor under his bare feet.

He takes his clothes out of the locker, retrieves his coin from it, then dresses and leaves. As fast as he can.

In his balled fist, Esteban is holding a one-euro coin.

The one he used to lock his locker.

Third Age

The Young Soul

"Young souls are impatient, Maddi. They're ambitious, courageous. Selfish too. They are eager to make a mark, no matter the cost, unaware that they have plenty of time. So much time and so many other lives. If the world were filled only with young souls, it would soon be consumed in blood and fire. But without young souls, the world would be a cold, dark, lifeless place."

IV

Intuition

Apiphobia

14

"Have you seen my USB key, Gaby?"

"Your what?"

Through the half-open bathroom door, I see Gabriel poke his head out of the shower. Just his head. I'm in the bedroom, squatting by the bed, busy opening the drawers of the nightstand, emptying my jewelry box for the third time, shaking the sheets. I've already gone through the pockets of the clothes hanging in the closet.

"My USB key! The one with all the recordings of my sessions with Dr. Kuning."

"Where was it?"

Gabriel disappears back inside the frosted glass cubicle without waiting for my answer. His indifference irritates me. Before, he would have rushed out of the shower naked to help me, even if he was still dripping wet. Before, Gabriel was not self-conscious about his body.

Before . . .

Before what?

Before we moved to Auvergne?

Before our vacation in Saint-Jean-de-Luz?

Before I went crazy?

I start to yell, trying to make him understand how important this USB key is to me. "Shit . . . Don't you get it? Gaby, my whole damn life is on that key!"

His voice, muffled by the sound of running water, repeats patiently, "Where was it?"

"In my purse! Where else would it be? I always keep it on me."

I realize how ridiculous I sound, getting worked up like this. Obviously, it's not Gaby's fault. I'm just using him as a punching bag.

"Oh dear," the wet voice responds, with infuriating calmness. "You take your purse everywhere with you. Have you looked in the car? And at your office?"

Thanks a lot, Gaby! Why don't you just get out of that shower and help me search for it?

"Of course I have! I've looked everywhere."

"Well, I guess that just leaves the fifteen bedrooms and three floors of this place. I mean, a three-centimeter key in a building this size . . . it should be easy to find!"

So now he thinks the whole thing is a joke? For the fifth time, I empty my purse onto the bed. I turn it inside out, making sure there are no holes or burst seams.

I glimpse a hand groping around for a towel.

"Maybe if you were a little tidier . . ."

I force myself not to scream. Talk about the pot calling the kettle black! I look at Gaby's socks, boxer shorts, and pants rolled up in a ball at the end of the bed, and I want to smash my head against the wall. How long will it be before I'm being fitted for a straitjacket?

Where the hell is that damn key?

I try taking deep breaths to calm myself down. I look at the bed, at the rumpled sheets on the right-hand side. Gabriel always sleeps on that side now. Before, he didn't care which side of the bed he slept on. I breathe in his scent. It used to be so important to me, *before* . . . At one point, it was the only sensory input that kept me clinging to life during the night.

If I followed my thoughts to their logical conclusion, if I were to give in to my subconscious instincts, I think I'd be forced to admit the truth: that scent almost disgusts me now. That scent mingled with mine.

It's possible to avoid the affection of the person who lies beside you in bed; you can push away his hands when he tries to hug you, but you can't ever stop breathing his scent.

Giving up on the bedroom, I go out onto the landing. How can I possibly find my USB key in such a mess? The landing is covered with cardboard boxes that Gabriel brought with him from Etretat and still hasn't bothered to open. Old books, old DVDs, old video games. A huge pile of outdated electronic devices. Even his Gibson guitar has been abandoned there, stuck between boxes, undoubtedly out of tune.

He hasn't touched it for days.

Despite myself, I think of Esteban. My son would always play his guitar, for at least an hour every day, sometimes more than that.

Esteban was passionate, gifted, hardworking, determined.

Gabriel is superficial, mediocre, lazy, indecisive.

It didn't stop me loving him, though, all those years. What would have become of me if I hadn't had him? I should never forget the way he always said yes to me, without arguing or complaining. And why? Because I gave him a roof? Fed him, kept him warm . . . ? Cats generally don't stray far from home.

I'm being cruel, I know. Is Gabriel really nothing more to me now than some kitten too old to be abandoned? Do I truly feel nothing more for him than pity?

Knowing nothing of the storm inside my head, Gabriel calls from the bathroom, and his voice echoes through the empty rooms, the long corridors. Why did I choose to live in such a vast old house?

"Does it really matter if you don't find the key? Surely you can just ask your *good friend* Dr. Kuning to send you another one?"

Gabriel has recently added jealousy to his list of winning personality traits. Admittedly, I do spend more than an hour every evening on the phone with Wayan. I hang about in the parking lot, at the foot of the old ski slopes, talking into my cell phone while he listens and then trying to dissuade him from driving down to see me. He offered to do it again last night.

"It's only a six-hour drive, Maddi! That's nothing. I mean it. If I leave tomorrow morning, I could be in Murol by noon."

He doesn't seem to have accepted what I told him just before leaving Normandy: *You are not the kind of man who can abandon everything to follow the woman you love.* Wayan is the kind of man who will ask his secretary to cancel all his meetings for the next day, take the day off, and sweep a woman off her feet . . . for an evening, a night, at most a long weekend. But not to the point of giving up everything. Esteban was the same way . . . He was such a kind boy, but nobody could ever make him do something he didn't want to do.

Gabriel never even bothers asking me where we're going.

He's happy just to be with me.

Thank you, Gaby. Thank you for giving me that, at least.

And you have no reason to be jealous of Wayan Balik Kuning. I only spend so much time with him because I need him. In fact, I think it's because he's so far away that I'm comfortable talking to him so much. Last night, I even told him the next part of my plan. Or more accurately, since I am totally winging it, the most recent of my decisions.

"Wayan, I'm going to be honest. I've decided to go and see Amandine again. And Tom too. It's the only solution, since she won't come to my office anymore."

"Why, Maddi? What are you going to tell her?"

"I have a good excuse for the visit. She's ill; that's obvious. Everyone at the funeral could see it. So I'm really just being a good doctor."

"You didn't answer my question, Maddi. What are you going to tell her?"

"I'm . . . I'm going to warn her."

"Warn her about what?"

"The danger."

"Danger? What danger?"

"Tom was born on February 28. I read it on his file. He'll be ten in a few days."

"So?"

"You know perfectly well what I mean, Wayan. Esteban disappeared on his tenth birthday. I don't want the same thing to happen to this kid."

"Why, Maddi? Why should the same thing happen to Tom? He's not Esteban! And even if I accepted for a moment your belief that Tom is the reincarnation of Esteban, why would he be in danger? Maddi, what are you hiding from me?"

I hang up.

So that, Gaby, is why you have no reason to be jealous of Wayan Balik Kuning. Because I just want him to leave me in peace.

"Are you upset?"

Gabriel has finally emerged from the bathroom. He comes toward me, bare chested, a towel wrapped around his hips. He's handsome, no doubt about it. He looks at me like a cat begging to be forgiven.

"Yep."

"Because of that USB key?"

"Yep."

"You think someone might have stolen it?"

This is a subtle way of pointing out that I am irresponsible, that if the key was so important to me, surely I would have kept it safe, not carried it around in the chaos of my purse. Come to think of it, why didn't I do that? Because I wanted it on hand all the time? Because nobody could possibly know what it meant to me?

"No. Why would anyone do that?"

Gabriel puts his arms around me. He's still wet. He smells like his soap—like wood and freshly cut ferns. I decide I do like that smell after all. He looks deeply into my eyes, as if he can read me like a book.

"There's something else. Something else is worrying you. Tell me."

He annoys me, this selfish cat, with his animal instinct.

"Yeah . . . I . . . The police want to talk to me."

"Oh God!"

He looks at me as if I'd just committed armed robbery.

"About Martin Sainfoin. I examined him, you see, a couple weeks ago. Just the usual heart exam—he was fine. There were no warning signs. I even signed a certificate so he could keep cycling."

"Well, if there was nothing wrong with him—not a heart murmur or anything—then you have nothing to worry about. Right?"

"I hope so. The cop I talked to on the phone sounded kind of strange."

Gabriel hugs me.

"Forget it. It's not your fault."

He's always been good at this, my big cat, purring around my feet, making me feel better. Especially when he's hungry.

He kisses my cheek and steps back. "What's for dinner?"

I don't answer. I'm caught up in my thoughts.

Forget it. It's not your fault.

I am trying so hard to believe that.

Esteban was not my fault . . .

Martin is not my fault . . .

Will Tom not be my fault either?

Gaby moves closer, as if he wants me to hold him in my arms, but I shiver and tenderly push him away.

"Sorry, you'll just have to wait. Right now, I need to find that key!"

15

He stares at the key, enthralled

Is it possible that such a tiny object, less than three centimeters long and flat as a matchstick, could really contain the secrets of someone's whole life? People think a life can be held inside a coffin or an urn. But in reality, it can fit inside a thimble, including all the photographs, all the videos, all the conversations, all the words.

He carefully inserts the key into the laptop. Nobody saw him take it from her purse. Nobody could suspect him. Anyone in the village could have grabbed it, because almost all of them have been in the doctor's surgery at least once.

He clicks on the main icon and gasps as two subfolders appear.

Maddi Libéri: 2010–2020

Esteban Libéri: 2003–2010

The USB key contains not only the contents of Maddi's therapy sessions, but Esteban's too. Why are they on the same key? Who was Esteban's shrink? It couldn't be Dr. Kuning, because he works in Normandy, and Esteban lived in the Pays Basque.

He thinks for a while, then decides to click on the second folder.

Esteban Libéri: 2003–2010

Dozens of audio files fill the page, lined up in three columns. Esteban saw a shrink every week for seven years.

He makes a quick mental calculation: there must be more than three hundred files here. Where to start?

He moves the cursor, hesitates, then settles on the file marked 03/15/2004. So Esteban would have been . . . four years old. Two more clicks: the folder opens instantly, and he just has time to press pause before the sound bursts his eardrums. The laptop was set at maximum volume. Esteban's voice would have echoed all through the house.

A silent sigh of relief escapes his lips. He glances around, listens carefully to make sure nobody is about to walk in on him, then plugs in the headphones.

He checks again and confirms the door is closed and the room empty. Once the headphones are covering his ears, he'll be drawn into the story and will pay no attention to anything around him. He'll be as vulnerable as a lizard when it sheds its skin. Or a snake.

He presses play.

The psychiatrist's deep, calm voice fills his head.

"Hello, Esteban."

"Kaixo, doktore!"

Esteban, he realizes, is speaking Basque. Presumably he just said the equivalent of "Hello, Doctor."

The doctor answers in French. "Esteban, do you remember? Last week, you were supposed to tell me about a memory, a memory you often think about, that sometimes makes it hard for you to fall asleep. I know it's a scary memory, something you would like to forget, but in order for that to happen, you have to tell me about it first. Do you understand? You have to face it down, so the memory is scared of you instead of the other way around. Do you think you can manage that?"

"Yes, Doktore!"

There's a hint of defiance in Esteban's voice.

"Go on, then. I'm listening. I'll try not to interrupt too much."

Esteban switches to speaking French. "It . . . it was summer. I was still very young, younger than I am now. We went on the train to the top of Larrun. There was a line to get on the train going back down the mountain, so Mommy said we should walk instead. And we did. But after a while, I got tired of walking. So, to stop me whining, Mommy said we were going to play a game . . ."

Esteban's voice is sounding smaller and shakier.

He can hear the boy's fear coming through the headphones.

He closes his eyes. He is somewhere between the summit of Larrun and the Basque coast, on a hiking path used by tourists and wild horses.

And he's with Esteban.

"One, two, three . . ."

"Mommy, you're counting too fast!"

Esteban tiptoes away as quietly as he can.

"No peeking—don't cheat!"

Esteban watches her, just in case. Mommy has put her hands over her eyes, but she could easily open her fingers to see. He keeps walking slowly until he reaches the big rocks. Then he starts to run.

"Eleven, twelve, thirteen."

Mommy told him she would count to fifty and then she would shout, "Coming, ready or not!" She told him he shouldn't go too far. He looks around for a hiding spot. In the grass? No, it's not tall enough. The wild horses must have eaten it all.

Behind the rocks?

No, too easy.

He looks up at the big tree in front of him. If he's brave, he could shinny up the trunk and reach the lowest branches, then climb to the higher ones. He hesitates . . .

No, too dangerous!

"Thirty, thirty-one, thirty-two."

Mommy's voice sounds far away, but he needs to hurry. He looks around, in search of an idea. He could go to the other side of the little river. That's how the heroes escape from dogs or wolves in the cartoons he watches; the water puts their pursuers off the scent. Mommy could sniff him out if he's not careful. She always says he smells good, that he smells like a baby after his bath, although he doesn't like it when she says that.

Once across the river, he enters a field. And he can't believe his eyes: there's nowhere to hide. The grass still isn't tall enough. The grass here must have been eaten by the cows. There are at least ten of them standing in front of him. He knows a cow isn't dangerous, but still . . . their horns, their hooves. He'll have to find a hiding spot farther on.

"FIFTY! COMING, READY OR NOT!"

He hears Mommy in the distance. He has to make up his mind. She's on her way, and he still hasn't found a hiding spot.

Quick! He starts running. From time to time, he turns to look back. This really sucks. If Mommy comes this way, if she crosses the river, she'll see him right away, as easily as if he were standing in the middle of a football field. He looks around in all directions, trying not to cry. He wants to shout, *Mommy, STOP; it's not fair; let's start again. And count to a hundred this time* . . . And then he sees them.

Five little huts, lined up at the end of the field. They look like doghouses, but they're too small for that. Or maybe big mailboxes . . . Anyway, they're the perfect hiding place. The closer he gets, the more certain he feels. There's just enough room for him to fit beneath the floor of one. If he crawls all the way under, Mommy won't be able to see him.

Esteban takes one last look back. Nobody on the horizon, except the cows. But they're not going to tell on him. He sprints.

As he gets close to the little houses, he notices a few bees. But that's okay. Mommy has told him that bees—and other buzzing, flying things—only sting you if you bother them. Besides, he doesn't have time to check if it's a bee, a hornet, or a wasp, because Mommy will be here any second. He dives, like a rugby player, straight under the huts. A forward roll, like he does on the couch, and then he's lying with his back on the ground, his head under the floorboards, out of sight, eyes fixed on the entrance to the field.

"Estebaaaan!"

Mommy is calling him. He can hear her, but he can't see her yet. His heart is pounding, the way it does when he plays war games with his friends. He tries to stop breathing so he can hear better. At first, he thinks he can still hear himself breathing, even though his mouth is shut and he's pinching his nose. As if his lungs were wheezing. Desperate for air, he breathes out.

Still no sign of Mommy. She was probably too scared to cross the river. A smell fills his nostrils then, one he loves, a sweet smell that brings with it memories of waffles and breakfasts. It's the smell of honey. Where can it be coming from? Not from those two or three bees. For the first time, he looks up at the planks a few centimeters above his head.

Esteban's heart stops beating.

He can see them, close enough to touch, through the wire mesh nailed between the planks. Hundreds, maybe even thousands, of bees. Locked in the five tiny wooden, honey-scented prisons.

"Estebaaaaaan!"

Mommy has reached the entrance to the field. He can see her now.

Esteban knows he can't stay there, that he must ease himself out as quietly as possible and move away without scaring the insects that are buzzing above his head, knows that he should not start running until he's far away. He knows all this, but he can't move. He's like a statue. He feels sure that the bees will spot him if he wiggles a single finger. Nothing can survive a cloud of angry bees, not even a bear or a wolf. All he can hear now is their buzzing; all he can smell is that horrible scent of honey.

He is going to die here; he knows it. Mommy won't recognize him; his head will be swollen by a thousand bee stings . . .

"Estebaaaan?"

Mommy isn't far away now, but she will never find him if he doesn't answer. And if he does answer . . .

Oh well.

Esteban will never be sure who made the decision. His legs? His mouth? His heart? His brain? Or all of them at the same time?

He yells, at the top of his voice.

"Moooommy!"

And he drags himself out from under the hive, too fast, too hurried, banging his head, scratching his arms. He keeps crawling, but the panicked insects are already out. The Basque sky suddenly darkens. Esteban is on his feet, and they pour down on him: a dense rain of wings and stingers, a storm of blades through which he runs screaming. The last stings are the most deadly.

"Moooommy!"

"Estebaaan . . ."

He keeps running. Mommy's arms are there, a few meters away. Nothing else can happen to him now. Even if he feels like his head is about to explode. Even if he itches all over, so badly that he wants someone to cut his arms off to stop him scratching. Even if his last thought, before losing consciousness, is one last tiny black dot in the sky and the terrifying smell of honey.

◆　◆　◆

"You were very brave," says the psychiatrist when Esteban has finished his story. "Your mommy told me what happened afterward, because of course you don't remember that. The ambulance came very quickly, and you were taken to the hospital in Bayonne. Your mommy was very frightened, at least as frightened as you were. But don't worry; all their stings will fade. You will be left with nothing but a bad memory of honey and of bees."

"In Basque, they're called *erleak*!" Esteban says proudly, vibrating his lips to imitate a bee's hum.

The buzzing sound fades inside the headphones, like a detuned radio. The session is practically over; only another thirty seconds to go, according to the cursor moving along the timeline.

He lowers the volume on his laptop, while wishing the recording weren't only an audio file. He would like to be able to see what that psychiatrist looked like. Presumably it was someone in Saint-Jean-de-Luz. He's looked at the folders, but can't find any names.

How does one go about identifying the person behind a voice?

"I can speak Basque as well as you can," the shrink replies to Esteban calmly. "But you're going to have to be brave now. For the past five months, it's been too cold for bees. The warm weather will return soon, though, and that means there will be flowers that need pollinating. As soon as you go outside, they'll be there, all over town, even by the seaside."

"That's okay," Esteban blusters. "I'll just hide in the sea. Bees can't swim!"

"Yes, I've heard you love swimming. So you're not scared of the sea? The wind? The big waves?"

"No! Never! Because the waves, even the biggest ones, always bring you back to the beach."

16

Nectaire Paturin hears Savine Laroche coming long before she pushes open the door of the mayor's office. She is the only one who drives that fast up Rue de l'Hôtel-de-Ville, parking her car in a single maneuver and then running up the steps to the terrace and erupting through the doors like a volcano.

"Hi, Nicky. So how's the investigation going?"

In her hand she grips a blue-cheese panini purchased at the village bakery. She hasn't yet found time to eat lunch. Nectaire, on the other hand, has cleared his desk, covered it with a small red-and-white-check tablecloth, laid out silverware, a glass, a bottle of red wine, and warmed up a meal in the office microwave: *tripoux*, a local specialty—calf's stomach, carrots, and potato *truffade*—which he left simmering on the stove all night long.

"Give me an update," the social worker says, grabbing a chair and sitting in front of him. "What did you find out about Martin Sainfoin's death and Maddi Libéri's past?"

The secretary slowly tugs at his tablecloth, smoothing out the last few wrinkles.

"Would you like a glass of Côtes-d'Auvergne? It's a Saint-Verny from behind the craters that Souche found for me."

"Later! We'll have a drink if you've done a good job. So come on, Sherlock . . . I mean, Poirot . . . No, what was your nickname again? Clouseau, that's it! Now tell me what you found out . . ."

Nectaire, with all the ceremony of a professional sommelier, uncorks the bottle and pours half a glass. Then he slides the cork back in again, observes the color of the wine, and sniffs the bouquet, before finally allowing himself the tiniest sip.

"Mmm . . . So, you were saying?"

"Your investigation. Have you made any progress?"

"Not really, no."

Savine takes a huge bite out of her panini while frantically unscrewing the cap from a bottle of Volvic.

"What are you waiting for?"

"You."

"Me?"

Nectaire drapes a napkin over his lap and picks up a fork.

"I called Hervé Lespinasse, the lieutenant at the gendarmerie in Besse," he informs her, "but he wouldn't tell me anything. He simply confirmed that an autopsy was conducted before the funeral. He didn't know any more than that. Apparently, the entire matter is in the hands of the regional police in Clermont."

The social worker sighs. She takes a big gulp of mineral water to wash down the charred panini.

"You were right to retire. Clouseau, you're off the case!" She gazes bitterly at the rest of her panini, melted blue cheese dripping toward her fingers. "No hard feelings. Bon appétit!"

Nectaire takes the time to cut his calf's stomach into thin slices, and to taste a parsley-flecked piece of potato, before looking up at her.

"Wait just a minute before you give up on me. The hunt for the truth is like fishing; it's about patience. And Inspector Clouseau has baited the hook. All that's left to do is dangle it in the water . . ."

He takes another bite of the truffade, followed by a sip of the Saint-Verny, and pats his lips dry with the napkin. Then, at last, he picks up his cell phone. As he dials the number with one hand, he puts the index finger of his other to his lips. He clears his throat, then puts the phone on loudspeaker.

Someone picks up, but it is Nectaire Paturin who speaks first.

"Clermont Regional Police? This is Lieutenant Lespinasse, from the station in Besse, inquiring about the latest news on Martin Sainfoin."

At the other end of the line, the policeman goes off to check. Not for a second does he question the caller's identity. Nectaire has the precise, hurried tone of one cop speaking to another down to a tee. Nectaire's call is passed from department to department until finally—a phone receiver having been left on a desk—they hear the sound of footsteps approaching.

A deep voice says, "Lespinasse? It's Moreno from the crime squad. Your timing's perfect. We've just got news."

"Ah," says Nectaire, careful to speak as little as possible, even if it is unlikely that Moreno would recognize his small-town colleague's voice.

"We were about to call you, in fact," he goes on. "It'll all be in the papers tomorrow, and Judge Charmont is going to make an announcement. But I don't know if you follow the news out there in the back of beyond."

"Okay," Nectaire says mirthlessly. "So?"

"We got the detailed results of the autopsy this morning. To make a long story short, Lespinasse, we found C01AA03 in Sainfoin's blood. I'm sure you have no idea what that is, but to put it in layman's terms, this C01 stuff is what's known as a cardiotonic, an active ingredient that speeds up the heartbeat. You might know it by another name—digitalis."

"Shit!"

Nectaire is so surprised that he makes no attempt to disguise his voice. Moreno, though, doesn't seem to notice. As far as he's concerned, those rural cops are all interchangeable.

"Yeah. Shit, as you say. But the coroner is certain: Martin Sainfoin ingested, drank, or ate the equivalent of half a dozen foxglove leaves. That's about forty grams—enough, when added to his efforts to reach the top of the Col de la Croix-Saint-Robert, to make his heart explode."

"Shit!" Nectaire repeats.

"Yeah, but I think we're the ones who are gonna have to deal with this shit," Moreno concludes. "Sorry, Lespinasse, but this is a criminal case. You'll just have to keep handing out speeding tickets to farmers. Don't be too disappointed—at some point, the pros simply have to be called in to do their job . . . Now I'd better get going, unless you have anything else to add?"

"Just this, Moreno. And I'll put it in layman's terms so you can understand . . . Go fuck yourself."

◆ ◆ ◆

Nectaire carefully puts his tripoux into the bamboo box—he will share it tonight with Aster—then slides the cork back into the bottle of Saint-Verny, wraps the baguette in a cloth napkin, and folds up his tablecloth. Perhaps he'll have more of an appetite that evening.

Next, he puts the paperclip magnet, the ink pad, and the pot of ballpoint pens back in their precise places.

"My God," he moans. "Martin was murdered."

"With digitalis," adds Savine.

Digitalis is a flower that grows all over Auvergne, on every path, on every mountainside; all the local children are taught by their parents, as soon as they're old enough to go on walks, that these pretty flowers, in the shape of pink and purple bells, contain a dangerous poison, and that they must never, ever touch them. Martin Sainfoin knew that fact better than anyone. His having digitalis in his blood could not be an accident. He must have been poisoned.

When Nectaire has finished tidying his desk, he reaches out to the whistling kettle behind him.

"Would you like some tea?"

"Not really, no."

The secretary observes the social worker's anxious grimace and takes a few seconds to react.

"You don't think I—"

"Poisoned Martin? Of course not! Just like you didn't poison Alain or Géraldine or Oudard or any of the others who drank that infusion—or ate the rum flougnarde—that afternoon before he went up the mountain on his bike. We've all known each other for years. Martin was almost part of the family. He must have consumed the digitalis before that. Or after. On the other hand, if Martin was murdered, maybe it's because he . . ."

Savine's throat is so dry, she cannot finish her sentence. Nectaire manages not to offer her a cup of tea again. He even hesitates to take out his sachets of dried leaves.

"Because he . . . ?"

"Because he discovered something," Savine says breathlessly. "About Amandine and Tom Fontaine. Remember? He wanted to talk to me about them. He said that in front of everyone. But first, he wanted to check on something . . . What did he need to check, Clouseau?"

At last, Nectaire opens a drawer and tosses a few black leaves into his cup of boiling water.

"I have an idea," he says. "Look at this . . ."

From another drawer, he takes out a folder, opens it, and spreads a dozen photographs across his desk. Savine leans down, intrigued. Each image shows a thin, blond boy with pale blue eyes. In some pictures, the boy is riding a bike; in others, he's playing a guitar. One picture shows him on a beach, wearing a pair of swim trunks.

"So what do you think?" Nectaire asks.

"What do you expect me to think? They're photos of Tom."

Nectaire takes a sip of his beverage.

"Actually, they're not."

"What do you mean? I think I'm capable of recognizing Tom when I see him. I've been looking after him and Amandine since he was born."

Nectaire Paturin is inhabiting the character of Inspector Clouseau again, speaking with a little more rapidity and precision than usual.

"You won't believe this, Savine, but the kid in these pictures is called Esteban. And he's Dr. Libéri's son!"

Savine collapses onto the nearest chair.

"My God . . . Are you sure? Where did you find these photos?"

Clouseau gives a triumphant little smile. He takes another sip of his tea.

"It wasn't difficult. I just looked at Maddi Libéri's Facebook page. Her whole life is on there!"

Savine frowns.

"So you're saying this kid and Tom are twins? Or doppelgangers at least . . . Well, that would explain a few things. Not least the way she looks at Tommy."

"You're right about one thing," says Nectaire. "Tom and this Esteban certainly look alike. Disturbingly so, I would say, based on these photographs. But they aren't twins. And I know that, Savine, because these photos posted on Facebook were taken ten years ago! Do the math—Esteban Libéri must be twenty years old now."

Savine's brow is now so puckered, it resembles the local mountain range.

"These are from ten years ago? Hmm, so maybe the doctor is suffering from empty nest syndrome? Her little Esteban is all grown up. And now he's left home, she feels nostalgic, so when she sees this kid who looks just like him . . . she falls in love."

Empty nest syndrome? Nectaire raises an eyebrow.

"Listen, Savine. Inspector Clouseau has only one motto when it comes to hunting the truth: there's no such thing as chance—everything is connected. In the end, all the pieces will fit together. For example, why do you think Dr. Libéri moved to the very village where her son's doppelganger happens to live?"

Savine whistled admiringly.

"She . . . she knew he lived here. You think she came to this village purely because of the boy's resemblance to her son. But that's crazy, isn't it?"

"Completely crazy, yes. But it's far saner than believing in chance, don't you think? There's a rational explanation for every mystery.

Perhaps the two boys' resemblance could be explained by them having different mothers but the same father? That's what my instinct tells me."

"And Inspector Clouseau's instinct is . . ."

"Always wrong, yes! So the answer is simple, Savine. If you want to find out the truth, listen to me and then begin searching in the exact opposite direction."

He drinks the rest of his tea, feigning disappointment.

"Hold your horses, Clouseau," says the social worker coolly. "Let's just stick to the facts for now. Have you uncovered any other strange coincidences?"

"Yes! For example, I discovered on the internet that Maddi Libéri used to be a member of the Stork's Cradle, the Belgian charity; the list of all its members is published online. That charity is banned in France due to controversies concerning antiabortion groups. I did some reading . . . How can I explain this? Let's say there's an ultrasound that suggests a child will be born with dwarfism. There are some people who believe this should lead to a therapeutic termination, and others who think that if you start aborting children because they are too short, we will one day all end up exactly the same height. The former are—"

Savine raises her hand to interrupt Nectaire before he can fully develop yet another theory on how there are two kinds of people in the world.

"Okay, I get it. I'm lucky to be alive, given that I'm less than five feet tall. But which camp does this Stork's Cradle group belong to?"

"It's on the side that is against women getting abortions, obviously."

They're both silent for a moment. Nectaire stands up and walks over to the sink, holding his empty mug.

"I'll keep searching, Savine. Shall we meet up at the end of the day to go over what we've found out? At the terrace of La Poterne in Besse, say?"

This is a perfectly logical choice: Nectaire lives in the center of Besse, above his sister's store, La Galipote, which is only fifty meters from the bar's terrace in Place de la Poterne. But this is also the precise spot where Martin Sainfoin was supposed to meet Savine . . .

"Will you . . . ," Savine stammers. "Please promise me you'll be careful."

"I promise. No cycling. No sports. I'll save my energy to stick a few stamps into my book . . . and to go fishing for the truth, of course." He gives Savine one last smile. "You're going to be amazed when you see what a magnificent fish Inspector Clouseau catches for you . . ."

17

It's not easy maneuvering out of the parking lot at the Besse gendarmerie. Thankfully, a young female cop, who can't be more than twenty, guides me out with smiling efficiency.

"Carry on straight and you're there, madame!"

The gendarmes were adorable.

I wave to the young policewoman and rejoin the road to Murol. I feel so much lighter than I did before. The gendarmes told me three times at least that I have nothing to worry about.

It's not your fault, Doctor. You were right: Martin Sainfoin didn't have any heart problems. That's all we can tell you for now, but we wanted to reassure you.

Thank you!

It's a relief, even if it doesn't really make any sense to me. If Martin Sainfoin had no heart problems, then what happened to him? The gendarmes were all smiles, very reassuring, but there was something odd about the whole thing. They were all excitable and mysterious, almost as if . . . as if Martin Sainfoin had been murdered.

I force myself to stop thinking about it. This story no longer concerns me now that I've been exonerated. I stare at the Puy de Dôme in the distance—its strange summit, shaped like an elephant's back, the radio mast sticking out of the volcano's head. I try to find a music station on the radio so I can clear my head and concentrate. I still haven't found that damn USB key. I can't believe that anyone could have stolen it from me. Could I have put it away somewhere, and then forgotten?

I'm already entering Murol when the static clears from RFM Auvergne. Jean-Jacques Goldman is singing "Pas Toi." My first consultation isn't for another hour: I postponed them all, since I didn't know how long the gendarmes would want to keep me there. I have a whole hour to kill. Should I stop at my office or drive back to the Moulin? I'd have time to drink a coffee, to have a hug with Gaby, who's probably still in bed . . . Before I know it, my decision has been made for me: I've passed Murol and am driving along the winding road that runs beside the Couze Chambon. Another five kilometers and I'll be home. I wonder if Gaby has made coffee . . .

Goldman's guitar is still gently bleeding when I catch sight of the sign for Froidefond. The bridge over the stream is ahead of me, the red-watered fountain to my right. Amandine's farm, La Souille, lies below.

Nothing can erase you, I think, as Goldman keeps singing his sad old song about loss.

The front door of the farmhouse is open.

Without thinking, without trying to work out what's going through my head, I slam on the brakes.

Amandine Fontaine is waiting for me on the doorstep. She could hardly miss my MiTo parked in her yard. I deliberately chose not to be discreet; the tires sent gravel flying as I parked the car, a doctor responding to an emergency.

"Is there a problem, Doctor?" Amandine asks.

Is she playing a role, or is she genuinely concerned?

"No, don't worry. I just thought I'd drop in on you. A routine check, you know. We're neighbors, after all. I drive past your house every day. I just came to find out how you're doing."

Amandine is suspicious. If I ask her for permission, she'll say no; I can tell. So I don't ask. My doctor's bag lends me a certain authority. Without giving her a choice in the matter, I step forward, determined. Against all expectations, she moves out of my way.

In a detached tone, I ask, "Isn't Tom home?"

"No, he rode his bike to the pool."

Gazing toward the living room, I say, "Actually, that's good timing."

My eyes linger on the piles of unironed laundry, on the table that hasn't been cleared. Lidless jam jars are baking in the rays of sunlight pouring through the open window. Dish towels are covered with cat hair. In the cold, dusty fireplace, which looks as though it hasn't been lit for an eternity, there are piles of books, newspapers, and toys.

"It's you I wanted to see, Amandine," I add.

"Me? Why?"

"Because I'm a doctor. I saw you at the cemetery the other day. You couldn't even stand straight."

Abruptly, Amandine stops leaning against the wall and stands at attention, like a palace guard caught dozing by an officer.

"It was the heat . . . the emotion. I'm fine now."

"If you say so."

My gaze moves from Tom's schoolbag, tossed in a corner of the room, to the half-torn wallpaper, which looks as though Amandine decided to change it one day, then gave up. I stare at the boxes lined up on the floor, filled with earth and plants that are difficult to identify.

"I look after myself, Doctor. I thought I was pretty clear about that."

And to make it even clearer, she stares at the herbs in those boxes. It appears she uses a mixture of plant-based medicines and homeopathy. I continue my inspection: on a chair, there's a wobbly stack of books about mountain flowers and mushrooms. There are posters on the walls: a beach with the words *Save the Planet* carved into the sand; a heart-shaped tree; the earth designed to look like a ticking time bomb. There are quotes and poems that have been copied out on blank sheets of paper and pinned all over the place: "Elevation" by Baudelaire, "So Many Forests" by Prévert, "The Shepherd's Hour" by Verlaine, "Txoria Txori" by . . .

"Txoria Txori"?

I flinch with surprise.

"Txoria Txori" is the most famous Basque poem of all. Esteban knew it by heart, as did every child in his school. There is a Basque folk song based on the poem, and he liked to come up with new arrangements for it on his guitar. What is that poem doing here, hung on the wall of a farm in Auvergne? Did Amandine and Tom bring it back from their vacation in Saint-Jean-de-Luz? But why that one? And why a copy written in Basque? Surely neither of them can speak a word of that language . . .

Amandine's voice is sharp behind me.

"What are you looking for, Doctor? I have to be honest: there's something about you that creeps me out. I don't know what it is. The way you look at my kid, maybe. Or the way you keep hanging around my house. What's your problem, exactly? Is this some sort of social investigation? You think it's not clean enough here? That I'm a bad mom? Are you planning to report me to the authorities or what?"

Stammering, I retreat. "No, no, not at all . . . Do you . . . Could I use your bathroom?"

Amandine glares at me. She doesn't believe I have any urgent need to pee. She knows my request is just a way of buying time, of continuing to spy on her . . . And yet, how can she refuse?

"There's a hole. At the end of the garden."

I stare at her.

"Just kidding. It's down that corridor. First on the left."

The bathroom smells of sandalwood incense. Tom's drawings have been taped to the walls. Some are recent, some much older. I examine them all, but I can't find anything suspicious, nothing but the usual childhood fodder of suns, skies, fields of flowers, green volcanoes. Although, on a few of the pictures, I do spot two tall figures and one small one: so Tom has a dad! Of course, the thought had already occurred to me that Tom and Esteban might have the same father. But even that isn't sufficient explanation for their astonishing resemblance.

I move closer to the picture, but I'm not going to learn anything about the identity of Tom's father from this stick figure. The drawing is dated: *05/19/2013*. Tom would have been three then. The rest of the wall is devoted to paintings celebrating Mother's Day . . . one for every year since Tom was a toddler: 2013, 2014, 2015.

I dwell on the 2016 picture. It shows two cats sitting by a bouquet of flowers. Under that, three words have been scrawled. Three words that contract my heart.

maite zaitut ama

Three words in Basque that Esteban spoke to me so often.

I love you, Mommy.

I stare, hypnotized, at the next three years: 2017, 2018, 2019. The same Basque words are written on each of them.

maite zaitut ama

So Tom didn't learn them six months ago while vacationing in Saint-Jean-de-Luz, on the Basque coast; those words of love were painted as soon as Tom knew how to write, at six years old. And yet Tom has always lived in Auvergne—here, at the farm. He was born at the Sorbiers Clinic in Issoire; I read that in his medical file.

How could Tom have learned Basque? The Basque language, also called Euskara, is one of the most complex in the world. It's also one of the most geographically restricted languages: it is taught only in Euskadi—the Pays Basque—and hardly anyone beyond that land speaks a word of it.

◆ ◆ ◆

I come out of the bathroom. This time, I'm the one who can barely stand straight.

"Are you okay, Doctor?"

Amandine's voice is icy with irony. She is leaning against the stovepipe.

No, I am not okay . . . I know I'll never have another opportunity to return to La Souille. If I'm going to find out the truth, it has to be now.

"Yes, thanks . . . I'm just . . . I was just surprised that your son can write in Basque."

Amandine doesn't blink.

"So?"

"I lived there for ten years. Does Tom speak Basque?"

"I don't see how that's any of your business, Doctor."

I won't give up. What do I have to lose now?

"Are you Basque?"

Amandine smiles, her hand pressed against the stovepipe.

"We went to Saint-Jean-de-Luz for a week last summer."

"And your son learned to speak the language in a week?"

Amandine glares at me. War has been declared now.

"He's a bright boy. What's your point?"

"I just want to protect him. That's all; I promise. It'll be his birthday in two days. The twenty-eighth of February."

"Yes, I'm aware of that, thanks. And don't worry; he'll have presents and a cake. You can put that in your report to social services."

I ignore her hostility and take a deep breath.

"I had a son, called Esteban. He looked a lot like Tom. He would have been twenty now."

Amandine points a soot-covered finger at me.

"Why are you using the past tense?"

"He disappeared. On his tenth birthday. I . . . I don't want the same thing to happen to Tom."

Suddenly Amandine's face is warped by cold fury.

"*You don't want the same thing to happen to Tom?* Is that a threat, Doctor? Get out! Get out of my house; get out of my life; and get the hell out of my son's life."

She gestures with her chin at the front door.

"Goodbye, Doctor. I don't ever want to see you again."

18

5:30 p.m.

Nectaire is late. That's not like him.

Worried, Savine checks her watch. She's sitting on the terrace of La Poterne, as far away from the other customers as she can get, sheltered from them by the leaves of some potted strawberry trees. Besse is still busy at that hour. Under the streetlamps, around the fountain on Place de la Poterne, there are stalls that sell charcuterie and honey. At some stalls, wool hats and scarves are offered at reduced prices, while at others the cost of walking sticks and straw hats has ballooned. There's a joyous end-of-winter atmosphere in the town's small medieval center, almost as if a war has just ended. As if the people were proud of having triumphed—degree by degree, thanks to their unshakable determination—at making summer last forever.

Savine does not share this festive feeling. She looks up at the bell tower of the Saint-André church to check that her watch isn't running fast.

5:37 p.m.

Where on earth could Nectaire be? He's always on time. Always so careful. He's never in a rush because he never has to be. What could he have found out?

"You haven't ordered?"

Nectaire!

Savine exhales with relief. The secretary has just appeared from behind the strawberry trees. Bizarrely, he is wearing sunglasses, a Vulcania sun hat, shorts, and a tartan shirt that matches his socks.

"I was waiting for you."

"Okay, two beers, then. Because I have a *lot* to tell you!"

◆　◆　◆

By the time Nectaire has finished blowing on the foam of his Doriane Blonde, Savine's glass is half-empty.

"So tell me, Clouseau; did you find out anything about that Belgian charity, the Stork's Cradle?"

He blows delicately, and a few clouds of foam fly into the air. Her excitement quickly fades.

"No. Nothing. I didn't have time. I've been busy all day."

"You didn't have time?" Savine almost spits out her beer at this. "Come on, then; give me your report! Preferably before nightfall . . ."

Nectaire cautiously touches his lips to the foam, like a nervous swimmer dipping a toe in the cold ocean, then finally begins to speak.

"Don't worry; it's worth the wait. So . . . according to her Facebook page, Maddi Libéri lived in Saint-Jean-de-Luz for ten years, then Etretat for the next ten. I decided to start with the Basque part of her life, so I called the police station there. The telephone rings; someone picks up, and I say, just like this, 'Hello? This is Lieutenant Lespinasse, from the station in Besse. We have a homicide on our hands here, and I need some information.'"

Nectaire stops and looks to her as if for applause.

Savine sighs. "Okay, I get it; you're a genius. Please go on."

"To be perfectly honest, I didn't really know what I was hoping to find out, but as soon as I mentioned the name Maddi Libéri, all hell broke loose. I was passed to a certain Lieutenant Iban Lazarbal, who remembered her well. Very well, in fact. Now listen to this . . . Esteban,

Maddi Libéri's son, disappeared one morning in June ten years ago, on the beach at Saint-Jean-de-Luz."

"Esteban? Tom Fontaine's doppelganger? He disappeared? And he was never found?"

"Ah . . . Yes, he was, actually. One month later."

19

Xenoglossy.
The ability to speak a foreign language without having learned it.
I parked my car just after crossing the Froidefond bridge. I drove just far enough to get away from the farm, but not far enough to get too close to the Moulin. I need to take in these new developments and gather my thoughts before I go home. My eyes are trained to my phone's screen.

> There have been numerous cases of xenoglossy, and often they make the news. Yet in most cases, there is no scientific explanation for them. They generally involve children.

I scroll through the Wikipedia page.

> In the absence of any rational hypothesis, such cases are frequently regarded as miracles. The most famous case of xenoglossy appears in Acts of the Apostles chapter 2 at Pentecost, when the first disciples of Jesus Christ gathered and the tongues of fire landed on each of them, signaling the coming of the Spirit in an episode of inspired communication that allowed the disciples to express themselves in languages other than Galilean and to be understood by strangers. Yet another theory, an alternative to the

*explanation of miracles, suggests that because knowl-
edge of an unlearned language is stored in part of the
brain, if it hasn't been learned, then it must be innate. In
other words, it belongs to our cerebral memory, and is
therefore a recollection of a previous life.*

I let my head fall backward. Outside my window, the volcanoes tilt; the sky turns and is pierced by thousands of pine trees. Esteban spoke Basque; not fluently, but enough to get by. Less than fifty thousand people in France speak that language . . .

My ability to reason flies back to the Pays Basque, making a leap of ten years in a single instant.

I hadn't wanted to believe the cops in Saint-Jean-de-Luz that morning in July 2010, when they showed me the body of that drowned kid.

I refused to accept the theory of an accident. I refused to believe all the evidence.

So how, today, can I believe this is only a coincidence?

How can I not believe that Esteban is alive?

That he lives still, somewhere, inside Tom's head.

20

Nectaire takes a swig of beer to give himself courage.

"Yes," he repeats. "Yes, Savine, they found Esteban. One month later. Out at sea near the Corniche d'Urrugne, a cliff located a few kilometers from the beach at Saint-Jean-de-Luz. He'd drowned. Lazarbal's voice still trembled when he talked about it, ten years later. They spent a month searching for him, all over southwest France, even into Spain: asking for witnesses, scouring the local forests. They considered every possible theory: an accident, a runaway, a kidnapping. And it all ended, a month later, with the reality that everyone had imagined, without wanting to: the boy had simply drowned. The ocean was dangerous that morning, with strong currents. That's how the experts explained the fact that Esteban's body was found three kilometers away from where he had vanished four weeks before."

Savine looks deeply moved. Nectaire knows that she has devoted her life to saving children. The beer glass shakes in her hand. She does, however, manage to ask a question.

"But a body . . . in the ocean . . . for a month. How did they identify it?"

"It was the body of a ten-year-old boy. He was wearing a pair of indigo trunks. Really, that was all they needed to identify him. But, of course, they did all the DNA tests and so on too. Lazarbal confirmed to me that the body really was that of Esteban Libéri. Even if . . ."

Clouseau sips his beer.

"Even if . . . ?"

Another three sips.

"Even if his mother, Maddi Libéri, never accepted it. She continued talking about him as if he'd simply disappeared. She ordered several second opinions of the DNA analysis, which all confirmed the initial conclusion. But she refused to believe her son had simply drowned. She remained convinced that he must have been kidnapped."

"And . . . since he was never found alive, murdered?"

"QED."

The two of them are pensive for a while. So Dr. Libéri *had* been carrying that dark secret around with her . . .

The death of her child.

Of course, it all makes sense now. Nectaire mentally constructs a theory, and he guesses Savine is coming to the same conclusions: that Maddi Libéri must have seen Tom Fontaine somewhere, perhaps simply a photograph on the internet, and been struck by how strongly he resembled her son. So struck that she had quit her job and moved here, to be near him. So struck that she felt compelled to talk to him, touch him . . .

"Do you think," Savine murmurs, "that Maddi Libéri could be so desperate for her son to be alive that . . . that she could have sought out another boy to replace him? Even ten years later?"

Nectaire doesn't reply. He watches a bee fly between their empty glasses and the red fruit on the tree. He patiently waits until the bee returns to their table and starts to drink from a spilled drop of beer, and then—with an astonishingly rapid movement—he grabs his glass, flips it over, and traps the insect inside.

Savine can't believe her eyes. Is this really slow, old Nectaire? She is trying to think of some ironic remark she could make, when her phone rings. As soon as she picks up, a panicked voice yells into her ear, "Savine? It's Amandine!"

21

Evening slowly darkens above the volcanoes. Beneath the blood-orange sky, the craters turn aquamarine, like necklaces of pearl islands in some unreal archipelago. The black stones in the hamlet of Froidefond, having baked all day in the relentless sun, now seem able to breathe at last. Tom, too, catches his breath; he has ridden all the way uphill from Murol to Froidefond without stopping. He swam five hundred meters in the pool before that; all he needs now is to start running, and he'll be ready for the Lac Chambon triathlon.

He leans his bike against the damp granite basin of the fountain and resists the temptation to drink the red water that pours from the copper faucet. Mommy has told him never to do that. And yet, from the farmyard, he often sees walkers, especially older ones, going there to fill their flasks. He knows the legend, of course. Everyone around here does.

The little black dot hurtles downhill, several bends above Froidefond. At first, it's no bigger than a fly, but it grows as it comes closer until it is exactly the same size as him.

A boy. And he's riding the same bike as Tom. Well, perhaps a slightly newer model—the handlebars aren't rusted, and the steel wheel rims are still shiny.

Tom is happy when the boy stops to speak with him. He is the only child in the hamlet, so a visit from a friend, even one that's a figment of his imagination, is good news. Tom waves to the boy, who waves back.

As before, he feels as though he's looking into a mirror—a mirror that can talk and ride a bicycle.

"Hi, Tom," says the mirror.

Without hesitation, Tom replies, "Hi, Esteban."

The mirror leans his bike against the fountain, too, and frowns.

"That's not my name! I told you before, at the pool. Do I look like a drowned kid?"

"What's your name, then?"

The mirror hesitates, as if his identity were some closely guarded secret, then finally gives up.

"All right, if it makes you happy, call me Esteban."

Tom grins, then stares enviously at the brand-new bicycle.

"What are you up to?"

Esteban opens his hand to reveal a one-euro coin gleaming in his palm.

"Going to Murol to buy bread."

He closes his hand again.

"Can I come with you?" Tom asks.

"I thought I was a ghost?"

"Well, even if you are a ghost, apparently you need a bike to get down there, and you'll have to pedal it to get back up again."

"You really are totally nuts. If I drowned, why would I be here now, talking to you?"

Tom sighs. "Didn't I already explain this? You died at the same moment I was born, so your soul came to live in my head. And since it's my birthday soon, you've come to mess with my mind. You know, like a dream. Or maybe a nightmare."

Esteban takes the backpack off his back and rests it on the edge of the fountain.

"Nice! Do I look like a nightmare?"

He opens his bag and takes out a box of chocolate-chip cookies and a bottle of Coke.

"Want some? I don't mind sharing . . . Maybe I'm not your worst nightmare after all, huh?"

Tom nods. He bites into the cookies—they seem real. Esteban eats some, too, he notices, and he feels a little perturbed that a ghost can have such a big appetite. Suddenly, they don't know what to say to each other. As they take turns drinking Coke, Tom looks around: above them, the houses of Froidefond with their closed shutters; his home, La Souille, just below; and all around, meadows bright with daisies and dandelions. There are a few bees buzzing in the distance. Instinctively, he flinches. When his hand shakes suddenly, half the Coke pours over his neck.

"Shit!"

Esteban is watching him curiously.

"You're afraid of bees?"

"Yeah," Tom admits. "The doctors call it apiphobia. And it's a pain in the ass. Because normally you don't see bees until May, right? But thanks to climate change, they're already here in February! You can't imagine what a nightmare that is . . ."

He uses the sleeve of his sweater to wipe the Coke from his neck. He can feel the sticky liquid trickling under his clothes.

"Actually, though, you can, can't you?" Tom continues, annoyed. "Because it's your fault I'm so scared of bees."

"Gee, thanks! Blame me for everything, why don't you?"

Tom remembers the honey-and-oats shampoo Esteban used to wash his hair at the pool. "You're lucky you're a ghost, so you don't have to worry about being stung anymore. Maybe that's why you don't remember."

"Remember what?"

"Your fear of bees."

Esteban puts the cookies and the Coke bottle back in his bag, then says, "I've been thinking about it, you know. Since I met you at the pool. When I really concentrate, I think I can bring back some memories . . . I see . . . I see a game of hide-and-seek . . . There are mountains all around, and the sea in the distance. A river, some cows . . . I see five hives, too, although I don't know what hives are. I think they're doghouses or something. So I decide to hide there, and I—"

Tom interrupts this speech by clapping his hands. "Bravo! Well, obviously you *can* remember when you put your mind to it. No need to finish the story—it's not a fun memory, for either of us."

As he straps the backpack on again, Esteban stares at Tom.

Esteban puts his hands on the handlebars of his bike and glances at his watch. "I really should go, anyway, before it gets so dark that I crash my bike." He winks at Tom. "I'm just a beginner ghost. I can't even walk through a closed door. Oh, by the way, you should probably get washed before you go home."

Tom looks down at his beige sweater, which is covered with spreading Coke stains.

"You could just clean up in the fountain . . ."

"No way! That water isn't drinkable . . . I'm not even supposed to touch it."

Esteban straddles his bike. "Yep, you really are a loon."

"Don't be stupid," Tom replies angrily. "Everyone knows the water in that fountain—"

"Watch out!" Esteban shouts. "Behind you!"

Looking startled, Tom turns around. Three bees are hovering close to his sweater, lured there by the sugar. He waves his arms around frantically like a puppet with tangled strings, but all that does is enrage the insects. Esteban is about to call out: "Calm down! Don't move!" But Tom is already running.

Esteban watches as Tom crosses the road, climbs the embankment, and enters the field that slopes down gently toward the mountain stream, leaving a trail of crushed grass in his wake.

Only one or two bees are brave enough to pursue the beige flower that is trying to escape them.

Never before has Tom run this fast. He doesn't think, just charges downhill. With every step, he goes farther, faster, like a snowball gathering speed. Stopping is impossible; his legs are moving too quickly, and ignoring the orders his brain is sending. And the bees are still there—Tom can sense it.

What a mistake he made, running away from the fountain! He went the wrong direction. Chose the closest field, with the steepest slope. He'd thought that would help him escape the insects, but everywhere he looks the sunlit field is full of buttercups, poppies, and daffodils. The flower stems are knee-high, and with every step he takes, he has the feeling that he's disturbing hundreds of bees that are busy gathering nectar, and that they will unite in their fury against the giant idiot who tried to run them over.

How many are hunting him now? He doesn't have time to look. Besides, the one thing he's sure of is that he mustn't turn around. He has to keep running.

The river isn't far now. There, at the end of the field. If he can just make it out of this flowery trap, he'll be saved. Tom runs and runs. Is that his own breath he can hear buzzing in his ears, or is it still the bees?

His sneakers enter the river with a splash. The water is his last hope. Mommy will be furious, because this is his only pair of shoes, but who cares. But the water comes up to his ankles, no higher, and walking through it disturbs nothing but the stones rolling under his feet. Several times, he almost slips.

He hopes he's outdistanced them—the bees must have stayed on the other bank—but the stream is no more than a meter wide; as soon as he steps onto the other shore, where bogbeans and irises are growing, the trouble will all start again. Unless he keeps going into the undergrowth straight ahead? In the shade of the pines and chestnuts, there are no spring flowers yet. He'll be safe there.

Another few meters. Tom's old Converse sneakers squelch like he's splashing through a wading pool. The water grows ever colder as he hurries across; he's under the cover of the trees at last. Now, he thinks, he really is safe. It's dark in this forest with a river running through it; there's no colorful confetti to lure those monsters in . . . And yet he can hear a humming sound again, very close, as if there's a nest in a tree trunk, as if those three bees were only beaters sent to force him into a trap where the rest of the swarm waited.

He'll have to keep going: farther into the forest, down along the stream. He allows the current to pull him farther downriver. Surely they'll give up in the end.

But that hum is getting louder . . .

The water comes up to his knees now. Suddenly, he remembers the stream's name. He read it on a map once. Hell's Creek. Oh, so what, it's only a name! He can't give up. He mustn't stop. He moves his foot from stone to stone under the water, taking care to choose the biggest, the most stable; careful not to fall . . .

Tom doesn't have time to catch his balance before he sees the void gaping ahead. He only has time to understand that the humming noise he heard was the roar of a waterfall. He only has time to guess at its height—about fifteen meters—and to remember its name, Wolf's Leap, and to stare in terror at the jagged rocks below, like fangs upon which his body will be impaled. He only has time enough to realize all of this . . .

Before he falls.

V

Adoption

Wolf's Leap

22

"Tom!"

"Tooom!"

Night has almost fallen. Savine follows the white beam that shines from her phone. She should have brought a flashlight, but she didn't think of it. Amandine called her fifteen minutes ago, in a panic.

Tom hasn't come home!

Savine didn't hesitate; she left Nectaire on the terrace of La Poterne. Amandine isn't the kind of woman who worries over nothing; she's more the type of mother who lets her child roam free, who always says everything is fine, so if she's calling for help . . .

Amandine's lamp sweeps through the gloom a few steps away. They walk down through the meadow, trying to illuminate every inch of it.

Tom hasn't come home, Amandine told her between sobs. *He went to the pool this afternoon. I found his bike leaning against the Froidefond fountain, and Monsieur Chauvet saw him running through his field toward Hell's Creek.*

They arrive at the river.

"Toooom!"

"Tooooom!"

Still no sign of him.

Did he cross the stream? Maybe he got lost in the forest beyond? In less than half an hour, it will be totally dark. How will they find him then?

"Toooooom!"

Amandine is almost screaming now. She's cracking up, thinks Savine. Amandine, who is normally so detached, so confident. Savine goes over to her and gives her a hug. *It'll be okay. We'll find him.* The social worker puts on a brave face, like a captain in a storm, but she, too, is a hive of anxiety. *Oh God, if something's happened to Tom . . .*

She tries to think rationally, to reassure Amandine.

"Tom must have crossed the stream. That means he's in the forest somewhere between Froidefond and Murol. We'll get a search party out looking for him. The whole village. We'll search the forest from—"

Savine's cell phone rings just then. She answers without turning off the phone's flashlight.

It's Nectaire. "Have you found him?"

"No . . . ," she says. "Not yet."

"Where are you?"

"By Hell's Creek. At the end of Monsieur Chauvet's field."

Silence. Nectaire must be thinking. *Hurry up, Clouseau, for once in your life . . .*

"Have you been as far as Wolf's Leap?"

"Wolf's Leap? Surely Tom wouldn't—"

As soon as the words are out of her mouth, Savine realizes that Nectaire is right, that of course a boy might go that far, that this is the very thing they have to fear. The mountains around them are full of waterfalls, but Wolf's Leap is the most dangerous of all, particularly if one reaches it from upstream. There's a fifteen-meter drop, and the water splits into a double fall that crashes into a huge natural pool.

"I'll call you back."

In the glow of the phone's light, Amandine blinks like a tawny owl. "What?"

"Come on; follow me."

Savine goes first, running hard across the stream.

Down the hill ahead of them, Tom's little body is floating on the small lake at the foot of the waterfall.

"Tommy!" Amandine screams. "No, no, no, Toooommy!"

In fact, it's just his legs that are in the water. The boy's head and torso are washed up on the shore, like a piece of driftwood.

Amandine shoves past Savine. She rushes down the slope with its dark, sharp stones. Savine, still in shock, doesn't even have the presence of mind to tell her to be careful. The frightened mother skids most of the way, her butt bumping over rocks, her hands grazed by them. By some miracle, she lands on her feet, and in one piece, at the bottom of the waterfall.

"Tommy!"

She jumps into the river. The freezing water comes up to her waist. Using slippery rocks to hold herself up, she crosses to the other side and hurries over to her son's body. She calls his name again.

Tom reacts. He shivers, coughs, spits.

"Mommy . . ."

He's alive.

Savine is there, too, now. She helps Amandine to drag Tom out of the water, to pull off his soaked sweater, his pants, his sneakers, to check that he's not injured. Tom's whole body is shaking with cold. Savine covers him with her jacket before grabbing her phone.

"What are you doing?"

Amandine is leaning over her son, whispering words of comfort.

"Calling the doctor."

"No . . . no," says Amandine through chattering teeth, pressing her wet body against Tom's. "There's no need. We can—"

"You don't have a choice. He's hypothermic. He needs medical treatment now."

"Not . . . not Libéri," Amandine stammers, clinging ever tighter to Tom.

"Don't be ridiculous," Savine tells her. "She's the only doctor in the area."

23

Tom is in bed, lying next to Monstro, his stuffed whale, the sheets pulled up to his chin, three blankets covering him. I lean over him.

"It's okay, Tom. You're going to be fine. You were very lucky, you know, that you didn't land on a rock. And that your mommy found you so quickly. Now get some rest. I've given you some medicine to help you sleep. When you wake up, you'll have a few aches and pains—and a big bruise on your ankle. It won't stop you walking, though. But remember: no cycling tomorrow!"

I asked Amandine to leave me alone with him, but she refused. I take my time tucking him in, ruffling his hair, while I examine every detail of his room: a wooden Pinocchio doll hanging from the ceiling; the homemade lyre leaning against the opposite wall; posters of surfers pinned to the walls—photographs taken in Hendaye, Bidart, Hossegor—cut out of Basque magazines. Euskadi again . . . Esteban worshipped the great surfing champions, too, but that made more sense: he lived close to some of the biggest waves in Europe. Tom couldn't exactly have learned to love surfing from watching his idols ride waves on nearby Lac Chambon.

I try to buy a little extra time by smoothing out the folds of the bed. I would like to be able to look at all the rest of it—a small pile of books inside a box, a few scattered CDs, not many toys—but I know I won't be given the chance.

"Leave him in peace now, Doctor."

Amandine speaks softly, but it's an order all the same.

What choice do I have? I leave his bedroom.

Savine Laroche is still standing in the living room. She tries to clear a space amid the chaos to hang Tom's drenched clothes. Amandine hadn't bothered; evidently, her first thought had been to change out of her own wet clothes and put on a long, embroidered sari.

I give myself time to breathe. I rushed here the moment Savine called me, leaving Gabriel at the kitchen table with the two plates of lasagna—a dinner that he had made, for once.

When I got here, Tom was lying on his bed, half-asleep and muttering about how sorry he was, saying that it hadn't, however, been his fault—he'd been scared because he was all alone; he'd run away because the bees were trying to sting him.

Bees? I wondered: Was I hearing things? Was it possible that Tom, just like Esteban, suffered from apiphobia?

Savine Laroche looked startled, too, but not for the same reason. "You were all alone?"

She said that Monsieur Chauvet, before watching Tom sprint through his field, had thought he saw him chatting with another boy his age near the fountain.

Why would Tom lie about that?

"Never mind," Amandine had said. "We'll never know the truth either way. Tom has far too much imagination."

She seemed to have already put the incident behind her. I couldn't believe it. Her son had narrowly escaped death, falling from the top of a waterfall, and Amandine Fontaine was acting as if he'd only slipped in the shower. Now that her hysteria was over, it was as though the accident had been erased from her memory. It took all my self-control not to shake her, slap her, tell her a few hard truths. I have encountered so many of these irresponsible mothers during my career, women who react emotionally but do not . . .

"How much do I owe you, Doctor?"

Amandine has closed Tom's bedroom door. She speaks softly this time, but it's still an order.

I'm too surprised to say anything. I've just treated her son after an emergency—leaving Gabriel alone with his candlelit meal, arriving here five minutes after the call—and she wants to throw me out already?

Amandine repeats her question as if nothing of significance has happened, as if she wants to just get on with her life, as if tomorrow Tom will once again cycle to the pool, go swimming, run away from more bees.

"Doctor . . . how much do I owe you?"

"Nothing," I reply with equal coldness.

But I can't leave it at that.

"Tom was very lucky, you know," I tell her. "He could have drowned. He could be dead. You . . . you need to take better care of him."

Amandine has opened the door. She looks pale in her gold-embroidered sari.

"Goodbye, Doctor."

As I'm leaving, Savine Laroche grabs her wool jacket and smiles at me. I'll take that as a thank-you. She hugs Amandine. She has the soft eyes of a perfect nanny, the type who takes better care of the baby than the mother does.

"I'll walk out with you, Dr. Libéri."

24

The starless night swallows us up in darkness. My car is parked a few meters away, at the other end of the farmyard; Savine's 4x4 is a little farther off, at the entrance to the hamlet. I'm about to grab my keys, to make my MiTo's eyes flash, when Savine puts a hand on my shoulder.

I flinch, as if some invisible branch had clawed me.

"We need to talk, Maddi. Do you mind if I call you Maddi?"

I don't object. Maybe I feel the need to unburden myself. "That's fine."

We walk past our cars. There isn't a single streetlight shining in Froidefond, so we navigate the darkness by the sounds of the night—the Couze Chambon flowing under the bridge, the croak of a toad, the rustling of trees.

"What did you want to talk about?"

"I don't like beating about the bush, Maddi, so I'm just going to come out and say it. I've been doing some research. On you."

Savine gives me a brief rundown of everything she's learned: Saint-Jean-de-Luz, Etretat, my photos on Facebook, Esteban, Lieutenant Lazarbal's investigation, the physical resemblance with Tom . . .

I am stunned.

How could she have found out so much about my past? My Facebook page contains nothing but a few photographs and some simple biographical details; it's a facade, a veneer behind which I can hide.

"You moved here to be close to Tom, didn't you, Maddi? Because he looks like your son. Your son who drowned."

How could she have gleaned all this information? Did Lazarbal tell her? Don't policemen believe in professional confidentiality? I try to think as fast as possible. I guessed someone would uncover my secret eventually, of course. Esteban's disappearance was in the news ten years ago. My name appeared in the newspapers. These days, no one can escape their past. What choice do I have now, but to be as honest as I can?

We walk between two stone walls. A shutter bangs in the wind; the house in front of us is probably abandoned. Three slender threads of light filter from the house next door—two ghosts watching television?

"Listen, Savine. I assume you don't mind if I call you Savine? Tom isn't just Esteban's double. It's way, way more complicated than that."

I don't know how many times we walked through the three little streets in that hamlet, how many times we passed the same ten houses, the fountain, the bridge . . . Three times? Six? Ten? Enough, in any case, for me to tell her everything, methodically, clinically, sticking to the facts, following chronological order, from the indigo trunks to xeno-glossy, listing—without fear of ridicule—all the mind-boggling similarities between the two boys. I am protected by the darkness, unable to read the pity on Savine's face as she listens patiently to the ravings of a woman with an overactive imagination.

I'd been unable to read it on her face, but as soon as I finish speaking, I hear that awful pity in the intonation of her voice.

"Maddi . . . wouldn't the most logical explanation be . . . that you made all this stuff up?"

"You don't believe me, do you? You were polite enough not to interrupt, but you don't believe a word I just said."

"Who could possibly believe all that?"

"You! You saw the results of Tom's fear of bees. You saw the Basque words pinned to the walls of his room, that homemade guitar, that brown birthmark on his abdomen, when we took off his wet clothes . . . You know Tom!"

"But I don't know Esteban."

"I can provide proof. Photos, videos, police reports."

Silence envelops us. Have I convinced her? For an instant, I cling to that hope, before Savine's voice trails sadly through the night.

"And after that, Doctor? Even if everything you told me was true . . . what would it change?"

She stops in her tracks, and lightning bursts from her mouth.

"Esteban died ten years ago."

The lightning strikes me, and I flounder in the shadows. My words are scattered. I try to gather them, assemble them in order, but they keep collapsing.

"I . . . I could never bring myself to believe that."

Another streak of lightning hits me out of nowhere. No roll of thunder, no warning.

"But, Maddi . . . even if all the cops in the world, all the experts, were wrong . . . even if it wasn't your son they found drowned near the Corniche d'Urrugne . . . Esteban would be twenty now! Tom cannot possibly be him."

The words escape me, before my reason can silence them.

"Unless . . ."

"Unless what, Maddi?"

"Unless Tom is my son . . . reincarnated."

We continue walking, in silence, toward the two cars. Where have the stars all gone? Is one of the volcanoes belching smoke like a factory chimney, under cover of the night? All I can make out in the distance is the rounded peak of Sancy. I imagine that during snowy winters, the lights of snow groomers are sometimes mistaken for shooting stars.

It is Savine who breaks the silence.

"You don't believe that, Maddi. You're a doctor. You're a rational woman. You believe in science, not that kind of . . . superstition."

I smile.

"A few months ago, Savine, you would have been right. I would have laughed in the face of anyone who talked about reincarnation. But give me another explanation! The facts speak for themselves. And . . . there's something else I can't ignore."

I hold my breath for a moment, then blurt it out.

"Tom is in danger!"

"In danger?"

I've been brooding about this for several days. Isn't it Savine's job to protect children? She has to listen to me!

"Open your eyes! The kid almost died today, falling off a waterfall. Isn't that enough for you? He rides his bike fifteen kilometers to the pool at Super-Besse every day. And what about their house? Do you really need me to give you a list of all the basic health hazards there? His mother refuses to take him to a doctor. And refuses to see a doctor herself, I might add. Tom is a dreamy, affectionate, brave, gifted little boy. His living there, at La Souille, it's like . . . like the Little Prince being kept in a dungeon!"

Savine says nothing. I take that for acquiescence. She's a social worker; she's bound to agree with me. Besides, we're back in front of the farm now. The house looms above us, its windows all dark. Savine stops next to her Renault Koleos and opens the door.

"You're wrong, Doctor," she says angrily, surprising me. "I've known Amandine for years. I'll be the first to admit that she's not a perfect mother, nor the world's best housekeeper. And it's true; she does have some idiosyncratic theories about how people should only eat what they grow themselves, how doctors are bad for the health . . . She's not a big fan of scientific progress, I agree. But I'm absolutely certain that she loves her son, and that Tom is not in danger."

She turns on her headlights. To chase away the monsters lurking in the darkness? She's speaking a little more loudly now.

"You know, Maddi, Amandine survives on welfare payments. It's hard to find a job around here without a college education or a driver's license. So renovating La Souille, changing the wallpaper in the living room, replacing the rusty tractors in the yard . . . those things aren't her main priorities. It's easy to talk about self-improvement when you don't have to worry about where your next meal is coming from."

I am about to protest these baseless accusations. I've treated hundreds of patients since I graduated med school, and I've seen just as many neglectful parents among the middle and upper classes as I have among the poor.

Savine seems to read my thoughts.

"You know perfectly well, Doctor, that you have no objective basis for accusing Amandine Fontaine. Your opinion of her, and the way she's raising Tom, is—how can I put this?—somewhat biased."

Of course. How could I deny that? Savine Laroche is a smarter, subtler person than I imagined. I try to meet her eyes, but her car's headlights blind me. So I speak, with as much determination as she just did.

"I think you misunderstand me. I never said that Amandine Fontaine was putting Tom in danger. I never blamed her for anything. I am simply convinced . . . that she is incapable of protecting him."

"And you are capable? Is that what you're driving at?" All compassion, all pity, has drained from Savine's voice now. "Maddi, I don't have to be a shrink to read you like a book. So let me just point out the obvious: you suffered a terrible, traumatizing loss ten years ago. Like many mothers, you refuse to accept the death of your child, and perhaps even—at the risk of offending you—you refuse to accept responsibility for not having looked after him well enough, and so your brain is trying desperately to escape the weight of that guilt. I'm afraid it has invented another opportunity to save a child, as a way of protecting you from the terrible truth about your own past. But what are you expecting to happen, Maddi? Do you think you can find redemption?"

I want to slap her. Instead, I just spit out my words.

"I don't bear any responsibility. Esteban was kidnapped."

"Oh, come on! Be honest with yourself. How can you believe your theory of some mysterious kidnapper? Isn't it much more likely that your son simply disobeyed you? Or . . . you told me he was afraid of bees, right? Maybe he just saw one and panicked, ran into the ocean . . ."

Savine turns off her headlights, and darkness falls around me again. Our conversation is lasting longer than she expected, I suppose, so she wants to save her battery. A bee, or a wasp . . . Should I admit to her that I've thought of that idea myself, so many times? It would explain why no one ever found that one-euro coin. Esteban hadn't gone into the water to swim, but merely to take refuge, still wearing his espadrilles . . . and then a wave swept him away. So the culprit, then, would be an insect? It would be so simple to think that. But no, Savine, I'm sorry . . . I will never, ever silence the voice in my head that screams, *No, it wasn't an accident!* Esteban was kidnapped. He was stolen from me.

I take a step forward. I hear Savine breathing; I smell the odor of stale tobacco.

"Now listen to me. Listen carefully, Savine. I am not crazy, even if someone is trying to make me believe I am. And to make others believe it too. If you want to help Tom, instead of investigating me, you should try to answer all these questions: Why did Amandine spend her vacation in Saint-Jean-de-Luz, when there are thousands of other beaches in France? Why was Tom wearing the same swim shorts as Esteban? I can show you the photographs if you like. Why does Amandine refuse to let a doctor examine her, even though she's so sick she can barely stand? What is she hiding? I could go on . . . They mentioned Martin Sainfoin's death on the radio tonight. The judge said he was leaning toward the theory that Martin had been poisoned. I'm not crazy, Savine. It's all connected! It's all connected!"

Savine Laroche looks taken aback. I hear her breathing quicken. I push home my advantage. I click on the key fob and, thirty meters away, my MiTo flashes its headlights.

Now I am the one chasing away the night's monsters.

"I should go," I say. "I have someone waiting for me."

Internally I laugh. If Gabriel is waiting for me before he eats his dinner, it will be the first time. I bet he left my lasagna on the table to go cold.

"Yes, me too. Good night, Maddi. But, please, leave Tom alone."

"Who's going to make me? You? Esteban was abducted on his tenth birthday. Tom will turn ten in two days. I won't let whoever stole my son from me . . . steal him from me again."

25

Savine studies her reflection in the window of La Galipote. She parked under the streetlamp on Place de la Poterne. The social worker's tired face, her graying hair, the taupe wool jacket she wears . . . all of this mingles in the display window with the witch masks, plastic spiders, and magic wands that Aster Paturin sells in her store.

She rings the bell.

"It's Savine. Sorry I'm late."

"That's okay; come on up."

Aster and Nectaire are sitting at the table in the large attic room above the store.

"Have a seat."

Her plate, her glass, her silverware are all in place. Savine is used to their hospitality, their fascinating company. Aster and Nectaire are just like a married couple. They invite people, cook meals, pour drinks, converse passionately, argue tenderly, their disparate personalities forming a solid whole—providing everyone who lives in the surrounding area plenty of fodder for jokes. All they lack is a family—children and grandchildren to fill up their old age. They have plenty of love. It's not the same as having a romantic relationship spiced by desire, of course, but their partnership is no less loving for that.

"We saved you some tripoux."

Savine tries not to let her disgust show. She's gotten used to everything since moving to Auvergne . . . everything except the local habit of eating a baby cow's bowels drowned in carrot sauce.

"How's Tom?" Aster asks anxiously.

Savine is grateful for this question since it gives her an excuse not to start eating her tripoux. She describes in detail how the boy ran through Monsieur Chauvet's field, then fell over the Wolf's Leap waterfall, before reassuring them: Tom is going to be fine.

"Phew," says Aster.

Savine knows how fond she is of Tom. Before opening her store, Aster did a bit of everything: school assistant, youth center leader, nanny, even babysitter—all jobs that put her in contact with children and gave her the opportunity to exercise her true passion. Aster is a storyteller. Aster the Witch: this is how all the local children, from Orcival to La Bourboule, know her. Aster and her puppet theater. Aster, recounting the incredible adventures of the Galipote in the land of volcanoes. She's given up all that now. Like all witches, goblins, and elves, she has been rendered obsolete by the rise of electronic screens.

"You should eat," Nectaire urges her. "It'll go cold."

Savine suppresses a grimace, but Aster is as skilled at reading facial expressions as she is at reading palms.

"Lay off her. Can't you see she's not hungry? Pour her some more wine instead! What's the matter, Savine?"

Savine hesitates, then repeats almost every word of her nocturnal conversation with Maddi Libéri, before concluding, "Maddi Libéri is a good doctor; I have no doubt about that. She is a strong, sensible, independent woman. But there's something about her I don't understand. Of course, there's no mystery as to why she hasn't gotten over her son's death ten years ago. But obsessing about someone else's kid? I'm afraid she really believes Tom is her son. More than that, I'm afraid she might do something terrible."

Aster fiddles with her bead bracelets.

"You know, Savine, it's possible to be perfectly reasonable, rational, educated, and cultivated . . . and not to accept the death of the soul. Not to accept that everything dies, everything rots, everything ends up eaten by worms. One can, quite seriously and even scientifically, believe that something—whether you call it soul or consciousness or spirit—survives."

She rubs the back of her neck, as if her copper necklace were too heavy, and barks at her brother.

"Nicky, please get rid of that bowl of tripe! Can't you see it's making her want to throw up? And bring back some cheese and charcuterie."

Savine studies Aster's pendant: a simple copper wire twisted in spirals, ending in a thicker golden stem.

"Go ahead, Aster," she says. "I need to understand. Explain it."

"What?"

"All of it. Reincarnation, karma, the migration of souls."

Behind them, Nectaire carefully covers the serving dish of tripoux with plastic wrap, then writes the date and time in permanent marker on the transparent plastic film before putting the plate in the fridge. Aster stares at the social worker with her hypnotic witch's eyes.

"I'm going to skip over the subject of Hinduism and other religions because I suspect it's not really your cup of tea, as Nectaire would say. But you can search online the name of Professor Ian Stevenson. He studied thousands of cases, all over the world, of children who claimed to remember past lives."

Aster goes on to describe the "Stevenson model," which includes the children's physical, somatic, and mental anomalies such as unexplained birthmarks, phobias, and abilities, as well as the trauma from previous lives, which often ended in early, violent deaths.

"And is he serious, this Professor Stevenson? I mean, is he a scientist? Does he have a laboratory? Is it just a bunch of hot air, or can we believe it?"

"What exactly are you referring to when you say, 'Can we believe it?'"

"The stuff he's talking about. Those testimonies—are they true or not?"

"In your opinion, what enables someone to determine whether something is true or not?"

"I . . . I don't know . . . I guess if most people think something, it must be more true than false."

"So if we include Hindus, Buddhists, one-fourth of Europeans, and almost a third of Americans, then a majority of people on this earth believe in reincarnation. They are convinced that our body is merely a form of clothing . . . and that our soul survives it."

"And so you change clothes when the old ones wear out; is that right? Is that what reincarnation is? The soul is like a flea, jumping from person to person, or from a person to a dog, from a dog to a cat, from a cat to a rat . . . Is it as simple as that?"

"No, it's not that simple. On the contrary, it is a long journey. A journey of which we remember nothing, under normal circumstances. Except when it goes wrong . . ."

"What do you mean, 'when it goes wrong'?"

Nectaire offers them a large plate of charcuterie and an assortment of local cheeses: blue, Fourme, Cantal, and—of course—Saint-Nectaire.

"Ah, that, my dear," Aster replies, twirling her pendant, "is something nobody understands. That is the mystery. Why do certain souls return while others do not? Why do some knock on the door of the brain so that they won't be forgotten, while others are more discreet, subtly influencing us without our awareness? You know what I mean: instinct, intuition, the sixth sense . . ."

Savine nibbles a slice of cured ham.

"Doesn't your Professor Stevenson have a theory about that?"

"He does. According to him, if you set aside children's individual testimonies, which are always vulnerable to fabulation, there remain three irrefutable proofs of a reincarnation: birthmarks, phobias, and xenoglossy."

Behind her, Nectaire whistles.

"Whoa . . . If what Dr. Libéri says is true, Tom's three for three!"

"The more powerful those proofs are," Aster continues, blithely unaware of her brother's sarcasm, "the more violent the death in the previous life. These are the souls that return."

Savine has eaten almost nothing. Nectaire carefully wraps her plate, too, in plastic wrap, and Savine is surprised that he does not embellish his slow ritual with a theory about the world being divided between those who wrap their food and those who don't; those who keep their leftovers in Tupperware boxes and those who just leave them on the plate.

"Would you like an infusion?"

"Sure, Nicky."

He heads discreetly toward the kitchen. Even before he reaches the door, Aster is on her feet by the dresser. She picks up two small glasses and a bottle of the gentian-infused Fourche du Diable.

"Well, if we wait for Nicky to finish up, we'll probably die of thirst . . ."

They take small sips, savoring the citric bitterness of the liquor.

At last, Savine says, "Okay, let's imagine that Esteban really has been reincarnated in Tom's body. What proof do we have that Esteban himself isn't the reincarnation of someone else before? Or that Tom won't be reincarnated in another body if something happens to him?"

"What you are describing is samsara," Aster replies. "The cycle of reincarnation. Do you really want me to teach you about Buddhism?"

"If you keep it simple."

"Okay. In layman's terms, samsara is a cycle of life in which one is imprisoned, a cell constructed from suffering and illusion. Only our karma—the sum of our actions—will enable us to escape it and reach nirvana. Look, that's what this necklace symbolizes." She holds the pendant up for Savine's inspection. "It's a unalome: the spirals recall our previous lives, and the torturous path to awakening, which is represented by this straight golden line. But believe me, my dear, before we can reach that wonderful place, there are many steps we must take first. To start with, the passage from the infant soul to the mature soul."

Savine finishes her glass, still staring at the pendant.

"What do you mean?"

"The infant soul is the beginning of the cycle of lives. The mature soul, on the other hand, comes after many previous existences. For example, look at Nectaire and me. I am clearly an infant soul, and Nicky is a very fine specimen of the mature soul."

"That is the secret of all good pairings!" adds Nectaire from the kitchen. "Don't you remember, Savine? I was telling you about this on the way back from the funeral. The world is split between the two: infant souls who cross the road wherever they feel like it, and mature souls who always use pedestrian crossings; infant souls who eat a meal in five minutes, and mature souls who can sit at the table for hours; infant souls who travel all over the world, and mature souls who are content to admire the landscape through their window; infant souls who have thousands of CDs at home, and mature souls for whom the sound of birdsong is enough . . ."

"Okay, Nicky," Aster interrupts him. "I think we get the point."

For all their quirks, Savine enjoys watching this endless playful exchange between brother and sister. She adores Aster's whimsical nature, but also Nectaire's quirky philosophizing. Thinking over his descriptions of people who are always running, she realizes that she herself must also be an infant soul . . . which would make Nectaire her perfect partner.

Except he already has a woman in his life. What might Aster the Witch do to Savine if she were ever to steal her brother away?

Aster refills their glasses.

"But if you're simply interested in mysteries and the supernatural," she goes on, "there's no need to bring Buddha, Shiva, or the Dalai Lama into it. We have lots of fascinating folktales here in Auvergne. It's because of the volcanoes, I think. The eruptions, the fire, the sulfur, the bowels of the earth, the descent into hell . . . you get the picture. Go downstairs to my store and you'll find whole books about the exploits of the Galipote, the witch of the mills; about the village under Lac Pavin;

about miraculous waterfalls and poisoners; even that old legend about the Froidefond fountain. Did you know, Savine, that it has long been known as the Fountain of Souls?"

Nectaire bangs the mugs down on the table.

"Ooh, Aster the Witch is going to tell us all the old tales! Please spare us that nonsense, Sister. And also your snakeskin talismans and your so-called tonics containing extract of digitalis. My instinct tells me that this Esteban case has a perfectly rational explanation."

"Really, Clouseau?" Savine smiles. "In that case, it won't be long before little green men start pouring out of all the craters around here."

"Ha ha, very funny."

With surgical precision, Nectaire positions an infusion ball in each cup before looking up to finish responding to Savine.

"Nevertheless, at dawn tomorrow, I plan to go fishing again. I am going to call Lazarbal, the Basque policeman who led the search for Esteban Libéri, then dig up information on the Stork's Cradle, and after that, I will turn my attention to the bakery."

Aster mockingly plants a tender kiss on her brother's cheek.

"Will you bring me back some croissants, dear?"

"Ahem, no, Aster. I'm sorry . . ." Nectaire blushes. "What I meant is that I'm going to call Le Fournil de Lamia bakery in Saint-Jean-de-Luz. The morning Esteban disappeared, he was supposed to go there to buy bread. His mother had given him a one-euro coin that, according to Lazarbal, was never found."

Aster pours a generous measure of gentian liquor into her tea, ignoring Nectaire's grimace at this sacrilege.

"Why would it be found?" Aster shrugs. "He used it to pay for his boat ride across the river to hell."

Nectaire and Savine are frozen with their teacups in midair.

"Surely you've heard that story before?" Aster demands. "For centuries, people would place a coin in the mouth of the deceased so he could pay for his trip to the other side of the River Styx. Only those who could pay the boatman had a chance of being chosen by the guardian of hell to go in the boat, and therefore to return among the living."

Nectaire sips his herbal tea, but Savine's mug is still suspended in front of her face.

"And those who got in the boat," she says. "How were they chosen?"

Aster twirls her unalome pendant one last time. The copper circles flash and shimmer.

"The guardian of hell is a judge, and his is the last judgment. So there are only two ways that someone can be allowed, after death, to return to the land of the living. Either the dead person is innocent, and he will be permitted to return to earth to avenge himself. Or he is guilty, and he will return . . . to be judged and punished."

26

As usual I ignore the hundred empty spaces beside the Moulin and park as close to home as I can, with my MiTo straddling the sidewalk. Before opening the front door, I briefly check my reflection in the glass. My tired face blends in with the old posters for the Chambon-des-Neiges ski resort that are still pinned to the wall of the entrance hall.

Does nothing make sense anymore? Am I coming undone? Am I the one who needs a doctor? Should I listen to that voice screaming in my head? The one that says, *Follow your instincts. Don't make the same mistakes as in the past. Esteban is back. Hasn't he sent you enough signs? How many more do you need before you understand? You have a chance to redeem yourself. Tom is in danger . . .*

I open the door. I climb the stairs. I feel as if my brain were about to explode.

◆ ◆ ◆

As I expected, my lasagna has gone cold on the table, the ground meat steeping in an unappetizing pool of tomato sauce.

I throw it straight in the trash.

"So?" Gabriel asks from the sofa, sounding surprisingly worried.

I assume the clanging of the trash can's lid must have woken him. But when I walk over, I see that Gaby is sitting in front of his laptop, wearing nothing but a pair of shorts that reveals the top of his butt crack. The aluminum spotlight above him shines prettily on his bronzed back.

"He's okay," I say. "He fell from the top of a waterfall, but he's more scared than hurt. I stuffed him full of Tramadol. He'll sleep like a baby, and tomorrow he'll be fine again."

"Phew."

Gaby seems relieved. Is he pretending to be interested in my work, for a change? Why would he care so much about a kid he's never seen?

"Sorry I abandoned you at dinner."

"No big deal, it's your job." Having apparently lost interest in the subject, he's already turning back to his computer screen. "I'm used to it."

I go over to Gaby. I need to touch him, to feel him. I put my hands on his bare shoulders and begin to massage them. He appears to like it, although he doesn't turn away from his laptop.

"So what are you up to?" I ask.

"Exploring a new world. Still *MTW-1*. Don't you think we'd all be happier if we lived in a world of our own creation?"

"I don't know."

"We totally would! Look, in *My Tidy World One*, you can take as many risks as you like. If you screw up, who cares. You just erase it all and start over. You can even die, because you have as many lives as you want."

I smile, although Gaby can't see me. Or perhaps he can, in the reflection on his computer screen? *Maybe*, I think, *this is what's happened to me: I'm living inside a video game.*

Gabriel is sweet tonight: affectionate, attentive. Why can't I love him anymore? Because it's "Game over"? Because Esteban is the only one I want to play with now?

"Oh, by the way," Gaby says, still without tearing his eyes away from the screen. "Did you ever find that USB key?"

I shake my head as I continue to rub his back.

"Nope."

Thank you for asking, at least. For pretending to care. I know I should talk to you, confide in you, if I don't want to go completely crazy. I should lean on your shoulder, be content with your kisses.

I dig my thumbs into your clavicles. I want to hurt you. You don't complain.

I'm sorry for that too—that I just can't seem to talk to you anymore. I guess I can't stand the idea that you will tell me you believe me, when in reality you don't. I don't want your pity. I have to deal with this myself, without being judged. Don't be jealous, Gaby, and don't be angry; there is no other man in my life but you.

I haven't called Wayan back, even though he is harassing me by text.

Are you okay, Maddi?

I'm worried.

I'm there, if you need me.

You can ask me anything. ANYTHING. You know that.

I care about you more than you realize . . .

I should call him back.

I should reassure him.

I should . . .

"Um . . . you're kind of hurting me."

I relax my fingers. Gabriel's neck and shoulders are red, as if I'd tried to strangle him.

"Sorry, Gaby. I'm sorry."

I should go to bed.

I need to be ready tomorrow.

Because the day after tomorrow is Tom's birthday.

I am going to listen to the voice screaming inside my head. I know what I must do.

Tom needs me.

27

This time, before clicking on the file, he checks to make sure the volume on the computer is turned down. Then, before plugging in the headphones and placing them over his ears, he listens for any noises in the house. He hears nothing, not a single sound, not even someone breathing in the distance. It must be almost two o'clock in the morning. Who could possibly imagine that he's awake?

Before listening to the interview, he takes the time to read the highlighted title.

Session no. 78—09/29/2009.

So Esteban was nine years old.

◆　◆　◆

"Hello, Esteban."

"Hello, Doctor."

He hears footsteps, the scrape of a chair on the floor, the rustle of fabric. Presumably Esteban is taking off his jacket. Then there is no more interference, only the conversation itself, punctuated by occasional brief silences.

"If it's okay with you, Esteban, I'd like to pick up where we left off last time. Do you remember? You told me that there was something bothering you, but you found it hard to talk about. And that you didn't want your mommy to know about it. Do you think you're ready to discuss it now? I promise, it will be our secret."

" . . . "

"You know, the longer you leave it, the more difficult it will get. Secrets are like spiders, Esteban: if you lock them away, they don't die; they just grow bigger."

"My secret . . . is already a very, very big spider."

"I'm not scared of spiders," says the doctor.

" . . . "

For the first time, the psychiatrist's voice betrays a hint of irritation. "Come on, Esteban. This isn't a game. You have to tell me."

"I have to . . . I have to die."

The next silence seems to go on forever. Finally, trying hard to sound casual, the shrink says, "You have to die? Oh, is that all? And why would you want to do that?"

Suddenly the words pour in a rush from Esteban's mouth. "So I can be reborn somewhere else, Doctor, in another body."

The boy's assurance is a strange contrast to the psychiatrist's careful language.

"Who . . . who put that idea in your head?"

"I can't tell you."

"Okay. Let's come back to that later. Just explain it to me, then. Why don't you want your own body anymore? Why would you prefer a different one?"

"You won't tell?"

"No, I told you. I promise that everything you say to me will be our secret."

"Okay. Well, Mommy can't love me in this body. It's . . . it's like the clothes I'm wearing are too dirty or worn out or something. So I have to change them."

Another, longer silence.

"Esteban, this is serious, what you're telling me. Do you know that? So I am going to have to ask you to promise me something too. You mustn't do anything that might . . . that might put you in danger . . . without telling me first. Do you swear it?"

". . ."

"Promise me, Esteban."

"I . . . I can't, Doctor. It's not up to me."

"Then who is it up to?"

"I can't tell you."

Another silence. The longest yet.

"Okay, Esteban, okay. If you can't tell me who, maybe you can tell me where and how this is going to happen?"

"How? I don't know, Doctor. But *where* . . . I think it'll happen underwater. Deep in the sea. It's like an upside-down world there. Half of Saint-Jean-de-Luz was swallowed up, years ago, and if you go down far enough, you can still see houses down there."

"Who told you that, my boy?"

"Mommy."

"But . . . was it Mommy who told you to . . . change your body?"

Esteban laughs, happily, mockingly. Clearly the shrink doesn't understand anything.

"Of course not! She doesn't know about that."

A final, interminable silence. Has the therapist run out of arguments?

It is Esteban who breaks the silence.

"Don't worry, Doctor. It's not the place where you leave your body that matters. What matters is choosing the right moment. You see? You just have to aim right. So that your next life is better than the one before."

"Don't you like your life before? I mean, your life now . . . You know what I mean."

"I do! Of course I do. But like I told you, Doctor, I'm doing all this so Mommy will love me more."

"Your mommy loves you, Esteban. Believe me. She could never love anyone more than she loves you. But listen to me. I think I'm going to have to talk to someone. One of my colleagues. Another psychiatrist. A specialist. To . . . to help you."

Those are the last words spoken before the file ends.

He keeps listening until the end, though, alert for the faintest breath or murmur. He thinks about the shrink's last words, *Your mommy loves you, Esteban. She could never love anyone more than she loves you.*

He feels a desperate urge to weep.

If only Esteban had aimed right . . .

28

I spot Tom at the foot of the Serrette hillside, in the first bend above Lac Chambon. He is on foot, pushing his bicycle beside him. He wasn't able to pedal more than fifty meters uphill.

In truth, I suspected this would happen.

I suspected that Tom, every bit as stubborn as Esteban, would get back on his bike as if nothing had happened and ride to the pool again. I suspected that his neglectful mother Amandine would let him do it, despite my advice. I suspected that his ankle would be fine on the descent to Murol, as long as he didn't put his weight on it, but as soon as he had to start climbing . . .

I slow down as I pass Tom and park my MiTo beside the embankment, a few meters above him. I open the passenger door so he realizes I am offering him a ride. Tom stops alongside the car and gives me the embarrassed look of a runaway schoolboy who's just bumped into his teacher.

"What are you doing, Tom? Didn't I tell you not to ride your bike today?"

"I know, Doctor, but—"

"Come on; get in. I'll take you home. I'm sure you'll survive if you don't pedal or swim for one day."

Tom hesitates. However irresponsible his mother is, she at least must have warned him not to get in a stranger's car.

Does Tom consider me a stranger? I'm his doctor, and a doctor is like a police officer, a mail carrier, a teacher—an adult in whom all children can put their trust. Anyway, I don't give him a choice: I'm already out of the car, opening the trunk and lowering the back seat.

"See? We won't even have to take the wheel off your bike. Come on; that's an order. If you keep putting weight on your ankle like that, you'll be spending the whole holiday in bed."

Tom examines the contents of the MiTo's trunk as if searching for ropes, bags, saws: the kind of stuff you'd expect to find in a psychopathic kidnapper's car. Finally, he makes up his mind and smiles at me.

I swallow and cling to the car door.

That smile . . . it's Esteban's.

I force myself not to show what I'm feeling, and the two of us work together to lift the bike into the trunk. I do everything I can not to meet those sea-blue eyes of his, of Esteban's, because I fear if I did, I would drown in them. The eyes are the mirror of the soul; everyone knows that. My son's soul lives behind that gaze. How could I doubt it even for a second? Behind those irises, he is smiling, laughing, thinking, looking at me. Perhaps he will recognize me soon?

"Shall I get in the front seat, Doctor?"

His voice startles me from my thoughts. Are the last defenses of my reason falling one by one?

We both look at the bicycle, which fills all the space at the back of the car.

"I don't think you have much choice."

We get in, buckle up, set off. Not a single car has passed us through all of this. If I did want to kidnap Tom, it would be the perfect crime. How careless his mother is, letting him ride these deserted roads every day.

I signal, make a U-turn.

"Shall I take you back to Froidefond?"

Tom nods. He seems relieved to see me driving back toward Murol. We pass through the tiny village of Saint-Victor-la-Rivière. A smiley-face sign by the road lights up after checking my speed. Thirty-eight kilometers per hour. I slow down even more, turn off the radio, and—as casually as I can manage—say, "*Goazen! Etxera buruz.*" ("Here we go. Homeward bound.")

Tom does not look surprised. He replies as though he doesn't even realize we are no longer speaking French.

"*Bai . . . eskerrik asko.*" ("Yeah . . . thanks.")

"*Euskaraz hitz egiten duzu?*" ("You speak Basque?")

"*Pixka bat.*" ("A little.")

"*Non ikasi duzu?*" ("Where did you learn it?")

Abruptly, Tom stiffens. The surreal nature of our conversation suddenly seems to hit him.

"*Inon!*" ("Nowhere.")

Nowhere?

Tom's expression has changed. I bite my lip. It was stupid of me, trying to move things forward too fast. He'll be suspicious of me now. Without signaling, I turn off onto a dirt path. Tom watches as the Saint-Ferréol church shrinks into the distance.

As if reading his thoughts, I explain, "It's quicker than going through the center of town."

The truth is I would rather skirt around Murol than go through the center, so that nobody can see this boy in my passenger seat. Tom, looking worried, hangs on to the door handle as my MiTo snakes between fields on the narrow, bumpy road. One kilometer farther on, we see the main road straight ahead.

"I told you; it's a shortcut to Froidefond."

Tom looks up at the dozen or so houses in the hamlet that cling to the hill in a ragged line, almost on top of each other, as if carved directly into the volcanic rock of the valley.

"Doctor, why did you speak to me in Basque?"

My fingers tense around the steering wheel.

I stop at a yield sign, even though there's no one coming. There's no rush. La Bourboule, twenty-five kilometers. Clermont-Ferrand, thirty-seven. Froidefond, just three. At last I set off, slowly. The road leads straight up to the village from here.

Trying to sound as natural as possible, I say, "Wouldn't you prefer to call me Maddi? Now that we're friends, I mean . . ."

Tom stays silent. Like Esteban, he's too smart to fall into an adult's trap: when he asks a question, he wants an answer, not another question.

Doctor, why did you speak to me in Basque?

He will only confide in me if I confide in him. I take a deep breath and begin.

"*Hala izan* [all right], Tom. The truth is, I lived in the Pays Basque for a long time. In Saint-Jean-de-Luz to be exact. Very close to the beach. I lived there with a boy—a boy your age. He looked a lot like you. And, like you, he loved to swim . . ."

Another three bends; a sign to the right reads "Froidefond, 1.5 km." The car sways slightly from side to side; Tom stares straight ahead. I need to keep trying to tame him, this little frightened fox.

"He really liked music too . . . Do you like music?"

The car is filled with morning light. We drive through a forest, and the sun flashes its rays at us between the tree trunks. I convince myself that I've seen a glimmer in Tom's eyes.

"Yeah, although I don't have a proper instrument. I like listening to songs, though, and then working out the notes—well, the sounds anyway—with flutes I make from reeds or this guitar I built from string and wood."

"Froidefond, 0.5 km," says another sign. To my left, a dead end leads to a B&B. I slow down. Never before have I done such a good job of respecting the speed limit on these empty roads. Tom's last revelation circles my head.

I like listening to songs and then working out the notes. The ability to reconstruct a melody from memory after listening to it is the precise definition of perfect pitch. Esteban had that gift too. A gift possessed by less than 1 percent of the population.

I drive past the sign for Froidefond at less than thirty kilometers per hour. In the end, though, I run out of time: I arrive and park next to the fountain, close enough to Tom's home that he doesn't wonder what I'm doing, but far enough away that Amandine won't be able to spot my MiTo from the farmhouse.

He's in a hurry to get out.

"Thanks . . . Maddi."

His hand is already on the door handle. I try not to make any sudden movements. I smile as I gently pull him back by his sleeve. *Don't scare him,* I remind myself.

"Just a second, Tom. I have one last question. Yesterday, Monsieur Chauvet told us that there was another boy here, near the fountain, before you ran into his field to get away from the bees. He even said the two of you were talking. But you . . . you said you were alone."

Tom's frightened look makes me feel sick. I used to hate it when, on the rare occasions Esteban lied to me, I had to raise my voice to make him confess the truth. I felt as though all our closeness would be destroyed forever. All mommies must feel the same way when doors are slammed and ugly words are uttered. And yet surely no child has ever abandoned his mother over an argument? I force myself to sound stern.

"Monsieur Chauvet has no reason to lie. This is important, Tom. Was there another boy with you?"

I think Tom is afraid. I think I'm scaring him. He practically hiccups the word out. "Yes."

I smile at him. I touch his cheek with my hand. I know I shouldn't, but my fingertips know every pore in his skin, every dimple, every tear balanced between the corner of his eyelids and the wings of his nose.

Tom is petrified. I whisper into his ear, because secrets have to be whispered.

"Do you know his name?"

"I . . . I can't tell you."

"Why not?"

"Some . . . some things are beyond our control."

Tom pronounces these words like a prayer learned by heart. His voice, almost inaudible, sounds like it's scratching against his throat, like a trickle of water caught in a dried-up stream. I can't let him suffer like this; I have to take him in my arms to comfort him. I lean toward him . . .

Instantly, Tom recoils and grips the door handle.

He tries to open the door, but the handle is jammed. He tries again, shaking it harder and harder, unaware that I have locked it. That he can only escape once I have decided to let him go.

I put my hand on his shoulder, to calm him down, to pull him back toward me.

"Don't be afraid, Tom. I just want to know. That boy . . . what's he called?"

My hand is resting on his shoulder, and I can feel his whole body shaking. I know I can soothe him. I know he will recognize my warmth, my tenderness. I have to protect Tom. I know he's in danger. I have to know who this friend is, this child his own age who failed to warn anyone that Tom was in trouble, who would have borne responsibility for Tom's death if we hadn't found him when we did.

"Just tell me his first name."

A grimace distorts his beautiful face. Deep lines appear in his forehead. The words he speaks next sound as if they have been torn from his mouth.

"His name is . . . Esteban."

"Esteban?"

Esteban?

Did Tom really say that?

So Tom knows Esteban?

Has he seen him? Spoken to him? Monsieur Chauvet must have been mistaken. Tom was on his own, talking with Esteban inside his head. Or Esteban was talking with Tom. It's the same thing, essentially. The ultimate proof that . . .

I have lost focus. Tom starts hammering against the passenger-side window. Calling for help. But who can rescue him in this deserted hamlet, other than me?

"Please, just a second, Tom. This won't take long, Esteban. I have so many questions for you. Nobody will hear you; the door won't open. But I don't want to hurt you; I just—"

The driver's-side door bursts open. Light pours in.

Before I can react, a huge hand reaches over me, grabs Tom by the waist, and hauls him out of the car. I don't have time to make the slightest movement before the hand reaches back inside, grips my collar, and chokes me, pulling at me like I'm a sack of potatoes. My jacket gets caught on the gearstick, then rips. My face grazes the full-grain leather seat, and I find myself catapulted onto the dark stones of the sidewalk. My knees and elbows are bleeding.

The man standing before me is tall, bearded, tattooed from neck to wrists. He motions as if to kick me, then changes his mind.

"You bitch!" he spits. "What the fuck are you doing to my kid?"

VI

Interrogation

The Surfer's Return

29

Savine Laroche hawks up a mouthful of phlegm that she hopes contains all the nicotine that's been stuck to the walls of her lungs. The Château de Murol is still another good hundred meters up ahead. This is her favorite walk. She likes it best in the mornings, when the tourists aren't yet out and about, when she is alone to enjoy the climb through hazel trees and, after she reaches the top of the eagle tower, to savor the panoramic view of scattered hamlets, wooded volcanoes, and fairy-tale lakes.

Her phone rings just as she's starting up the steepest section, a gravel path that leads to the first battlements. As she answers, she notices that Nectaire has already tried calling several times. Her phone never rang, though; presumably there was no signal up here.

"Savine? It's Nectaire. Where are you?"

"I'm halfway up the north face of Kilimanjaro, so I'm going to have to catch my breath while you talk."

"Okay. Well, listen to this . . . I just spoke to Iban Lazarbal— you know, the cop in Saint-Jean-de-Luz. He and I are becoming good friends, even if he still thinks I'm called Lespinasse and I'm head of the Besse gendarmerie. Anyway, I started by asking him about the Stork's Cradle. So get this: the charity's big thing is baby hatches."

Savine stops dead, halfway up the hill.

"Baby what?"

"Baby hatches! Or foundling wheels, if you prefer; that's what they were called back in the Middle Ages. They're also known as baby windows in Germany, life cradles in Italy . . . You get the idea. In most countries they're perfectly legal, but not in France."

"What on earth are you talking about, Clouseau?"

"This stuff goes back centuries. Baby hatches are these little drawers built into the wall of a hospital or a church or some other public building. They're heated, comfortable, sheltered from the wind and rain. Like little nests for—"

"Abandoned babies? Is that what you're telling me?"

"Exactly! Anyone would think you were a social worker or something . . . Anyway, in France, a woman isn't required to register her name when she gives birth, but she's also not allowed to abandon her baby. It became illegal in 1940. Back then, in all the old poorhouses of France, you could still find those towers for abandoned children that had accepted thousands of orphans over the years through those drawers, going all the way back to the Middle Ages. Recently the system has been reintroduced in several countries—Germany and Switzerland, for example—and certain charities, the Stork's Cradle among them, are campaigning for its reintroduction in France."

"What a horrible idea!"

"I don't know. From the baby's point of view, I think that's debatable . . . Do these hatches encourage parents to abandon infants if they simply cry too much, or do they save the lives of children who might otherwise end up in a dumpster? It's a tough question, one that might split the world in two. In the first camp—"

"Yes, I get the idea!" Savine says, panting.

During Nectaire's long tirade, she started walking again and has now reached the black stones of the first battlements. She is crossing a large square courtyard, buffeted by the wind blowing through the arrow slits.

"Didn't you have some news to tell me?" she begs, hoping he will get to the point.

"I'm coming to that. As I said, Dr. Libéri is on the members' list for that charity. So I called Lazarbal and asked him if . . ."

"If?"

Nectaire has stopped talking. Savine has had time to climb up to the ruined castle. The mountains are still illuminated by full sunlight, but the temperature is notably colder now than it has been in recent days, especially here on this esplanade, where there is no shelter from the wind.

"Nectaire?"

What the hell is he doing? Is this just a way of drawing out the suspense, or has he gone off to make a cup of tea?

"I asked Lazarbal," Nectaire finally says, "if Esteban was really her son. And . . . bingo! You see, Clouseau does have an instinct for these things . . . Get this: Esteban Libéri was adopted. Before that, he was left, at three months old, at a clandestine baby hatch operation run by a Stork's Cradle activist outside the hospital in Bayonne."

"Shit."

"Lazarbal says there's no doubt about it. They investigated the matter thoroughly. Maddi Libéri adopted the baby. As a single parent. That's pretty rare—adoptable babies are usually reserved for couples, but single women are allowed to apply too. It took a long time, but Maddi Libéri got what she wanted in the end. Lazarbal gave me the rundown on the whole adoption procedure managed by the child welfare services. There's a whole bunch of red tape to get through. Dozens of visits from social services during the first two years, psychiatric reports . . . But Maddi Libéri passed with flying colors. Apparently, she was the perfect single mother."

Savine, shivering, listens to Nectaire while she looks around from her observation point: at the cars streaming past on the main road; at the tourists walking along mountain paths; at the children in the meadow above the Couze Chambon, playing cops and robbers, or vampires and hunters, or customs officers and smugglers. She recognizes

Eliot and Adam, armed with sticks; Enzo and Nathan, perched in a tree; and Yanis, off to one side, hatless and alone.

"A perfect mother," Savine murmurs. "Well, at least for the first two years . . ."

"I phoned the baker in Saint-Jean-de-Luz too," Nectaire tells her.

"Oh, from Le Fournil de Lamia? The place where Esteban was supposed to go buy bread?"

"That's the one. The baker was probably busy kneading when I called, but I left a message saying he *needs* to call me back."

Savine groans at this heavy-handed pun. She is freezing now, her fingers turning to ice where they grip her cell phone.

"What are you expecting him to tell you?"

"No idea. But this is the Clouseau method: no stone left unturned."

Savine feels she has to get out of this icy wind before she turns into a statue. She is reluctant to go back down the hill, though, for fear her phone will lose the signal in the middle of their conversation. The children have left the meadow below, she notices, and found a better place to hide.

Nectaire is midway through a theory about how there are two kinds of people in the world when it comes to choosing the type of baguette they buy from the baker, when the phone rings behind him in the mayor's office. Savine sighs with relief. As usual, Nectaire puts the phone on loudspeaker, so the social worker hears the subsequent conversation just as if she were in the room.

"Hello, this is Le Fournil de Lamia. You called us?"

Thankfully, Nectaire summarizes the situation with relative rapidity. Savine hops from foot to foot to try to get warm again. No way is she going to move and risk missing this call. The girl on the other end of the line is clueless, though; she only started working there nine months before, she explains, so she's going to fetch the boss.

The sound of footsteps on the loudspeaker is drowned out by Savine's own shoes stomping up and down.

Finally, the bakery owner arrives, and Nectaire has to repeat the whole story.

Oh please, Clouseau, hurry up! Savine can practically hear the baker scratching his head as he whistles and says, "Whew, that was a long time ago. Let me think . . ." Savine's legs lose all feeling as the man racks his brain before concluding, "No, I don't remember, sorry. Maybe it was my wife who served him?"

Savine is about to scream, but by some miracle Nectaire is spared the need to recite his story a third time because the man's wife has been standing beside him throughout this conversation, listening to every word.

"Yes, Lieutenant, of course I remember little Esteban Libéri. What a sweet boy he was. And handsome too! That whole story was just so sad. He used to come here with his one-euro coin every morning. One baguette, not too well-done . . . and he would use the thirty centimes of change to buy a canelé."

"A canelé?" Nectaire repeats.

"Yes, it's a Basque specialty. A little cake made from rum, vanilla, custard, and caramel," says the baker's wife. "We normally don't sell them individually, but I always made an exception for that boy. He loved them . . . Our canelés are pretty famous, though. People come from Hendaye and even from Spain to taste them. They're very special. We make them with honey."

30

"Home, Tom! I don't want to hear another word; just go home."

The boy limps off toward the farmyard. I don't know what scared him more: the man's violence or my behavior.

I am still lying on the sidewalk. The tattooed man brings his motorcycle boots a few centimeters from my face.

"You, follow me. We're going to have a conversation. Somewhere quiet."

No offer to help me to my feet. No look of concern at my bloodied knees, my grazed hands encrusted with black dust. He just stands beside me, as wary as a security guard who's just caught a customer stealing, ready to grab hold of me—by the hair, if necessary—if I show the slightest sign of trying to flee.

I take my time standing up. This gives me time to observe him. He's muscular, with a lumberjack's arms and a weightlifter's thighs. His hair has been shaven to within a few millimeters of his scalp.

He shoves me toward La Souille. Tom is already inside the house, and I can see Amandine at the window, a motionless blur between the straw-colored curtains.

Another few shoves in the back, forcing me away from the road. A gray cat, sleeping in a pool of sunlight, runs off in alarm. I am obliged to jog forward, sending hens flying. The birds take refuge inside a broken barrel, presumably once used to capture rainwater. We pass a heap of stinking, oozing compost.

"That's far enough," the man says.

We come to a halt inside the barn with the ruined roof, in front of a vehicle the size of a tractor-mower, covered by a big beige tarp. The tattooed man stands there, legs slightly apart, like a wrestler waiting for me to enter the ring.

Okay, no need to wait for the bell. Round one.

I rub my face with my dusty, bleeding hands, hoping the blood and dust will look like war paint, and demand, "Who are you?"

The muscleman gives a small satisfied smile.

"Who are *you*?"

I have nothing to hide.

"Maddi Libéri. I'm the doctor in Murol. Tom is my patient. I was—"

"You were harassing him!" the man interrupts. "You were molesting him. You've been prowling around him like a kidnapper. You want to know what I'm doing here? Amandine called me. Because she's scared. Because you're a fucking psychopath. That's exactly what she told me: *Jo, come quick, there's this crazy woman stalking Tom. She hides behind the fountain to spy on us. She's sick. She's capable of anything.*" He stares at me with his steel-blue eyes. "And obviously she was right."

I hold his gaze.

"And you are . . . ?"

"Jo. Tom's father! You didn't get that?"

Shit. I remember now the words he shouted: *What the fuck are you doing to my kid?* I was so stunned in that moment of being dragged from the car, everything else was immediately pushed from my mind. *Of course* Tom has a father . . . I try to cover my shock by going on the attack.

"I'm glad to know he has one. Apparently, he doesn't see you very often."

"I'm there when he needs me. And I don't have to justify myself to you. I'm a snowboard instructor, so obviously there's nothing to do here this winter. I went to the Pyrenees to find work."

I examine him again. He must be about thirty. His body may be in perfect shape, but his face is already showing signs of aging—too much wind and sunlight, perhaps, or too much alcohol and too many drugs. He looks sure of himself, determined, independent; intelligent in a certain way, and stupid in every other.

"Okay," says Jo, "so we've got the introductions over with . . . What now? Should I call the cops? I saw you in the car—he was trying to get away, and you were holding him back."

He takes a cell phone from the back of his jeans.

"I got it all on video, so don't try to deny it."

Reeling from this new revelation, I try to think clearly. Well, at least I know where I stand now. I raise my hand calmingly, as if to say, *Let me explain.* He looks suspicious, but he lets me speak; he needs to understand what's going on. He doesn't interrupt me as I give him a brief résumé of my life: Esteban's disappearance, then all the similarities between him and Tom. I say only the minimum about the physical details—their resemblance, the birthmark, all of it too bizarre to be explained fully in a few words—and emphasize the other coincidences: the indigo trunks with the little whale logo, the vacation in Saint-Jean-de-Luz, their love of music and swimming, their fear of honey and bees, the Basque words . . .

Jo leans against the tarp-covered vehicle. He looks crushed by this accumulation of facts. Inside the farmhouse, behind the curtains, Amandine continues to watch us. There is no sign of Tom.

Jo waits for a while, making sure I've finished my account.

Have I convinced him? Or at least sowed a seed of doubt in his mind?

His gaze is like a scalpel in my forehead.

"You're completely nuts!"

I can't believe it. Was he even listening? I explode.

"Everything I told you is true! And you know it. If you want me to stop acting irrationally, then give me a rational explanation."

Jo sighs irritably, as if I were wasting his time, then speaks to me in a voice stiff with sarcasm.

"A rational explanation? What planet are you from? Do I really need to spell it out? Ten-year-old kids who like music and swimming aren't exactly rare, you know. Oh, and kids who are scared of bees? Wow, what an amazing coincidence! Tom's scared of spiders, too, and snakes. When he was little, he was afraid of monsters hiding under his bed. I bet your Esteban was too. And I bet he liked Big Macs and pizzas, and loved watching *The Avengers*, and dreamed of having a toy *Millennium Falcon* . . . Well, guess what? Tom is exactly the same!"

Bastard. Esteban never set foot in a McDonald's. And he disappeared ten years ago, before his *Avengers* comics were ever made into a movie.

"Your son speaks Basque, despite never having learned it. Scientists call that xenoglossy."

"Oh, really? Fascinating. So maybe he's going to wake up tomorrow speaking Mandarin? Or compose cantatas inspired by Mozart's ghost? Are you really that dumb? I'm a surfing instructor. Didn't you notice the posters of Kelly Slater and Jérémy Florès on the walls when you searched his room?"

I was here to look after your son, asshole.

"I spend the winters here, when it snows," he continues, "and the summer in Guéthary, Hossegor, Biarritz . . . all those beach resorts on the Atlantic coast. I taught him how to say *maite zaitut ama*. He learned his Basque from me."

I stare at Jo and say, "Go on, then; say something in Basque."

"I really am going to call the cops."

"Why won't you do it? Just speak Basque to me, to prove you know it."

"And then what? Are you going to check if I wear Basque espadrilles and like the taste of Espelette peppers?"

He chuckles at his own joke. I realize I'm going to get nothing from this man. And yet I can't just give up.

"What about the indigo trunks Tom was wearing? Indigo with a whale logo. Did you choose those? Don't tell me you harpoon whales in the Arctic too?"

Jo's smile doesn't falter.

"No . . . It was Didine who bought the trunks."

I look at him blankly. "Who?"

He rolls his eyes. "Amandine," he explains, as though talking to an idiot. "Tom's mom. Maybe she was thinking of me when she got them because I'm not there often enough." He tells me that although everyone calls him Jo, the name on his birth certificate is Jonas. "Remember Jonas from the Bible, or Jonah as some people call him?" he says. "The prophet swallowed by a whale? Maybe that's why she bought trunks with that logo. And if that isn't enough to convince you, Tom loves *Pinocchio* too. Did you see the wooden puppet in his bedroom? He named his stuffed whale Monstro. Do I need to go on, or do you remember the Disney movie?"

This bastard has an answer for everything, as if he knew what questions I would ask in advance, as if he prepared his defense. But why would anyone go to such lengths unless they had something to hide? I have to admit that his arguments have unnerved me. Or would have done, were it not for the boys' physical resemblance, their identical birthmarks . . .

"Are you trying to see if my nose is growing?" Jonas jokes.

He bursts out laughing.

No, his nose is not growing. He is perfectly composed. Too perfectly. He has left no room for doubt. Yet surely any father would be shocked by what I've told him. He's bluffing, or stalling. Or he simply doesn't want to let his guard down in front of me. But once I've left . . .

He waves his cell phone in front of my face.

"You know what we're going to do, Doctor? We're going to leave it here for now. I'm going to forget this incident, and you're going to vanish from our lives. Deal?"

Without waiting for my response, he pulls hard at the beige tarp behind us. It's not a tractor-mower that's beneath it, but a brand-new four-wheeler. Suddenly, Jonas looks far more interested in this vehicle than in his son's health. He ogles it for several seconds before turning to face me.

"But before we go our separate ways and forget everything that's been said, I have a favor to ask you, Doctor."

Strange. That's the second time he's called me doctor in less than a minute. He didn't do it at all before.

"I want you to examine Didine."

I understand. He's just come back to La Souille after being away for several months, so he must be shocked by Amandine's condition. Presumably she told him the same thing she always tells me: that she refuses to see a doctor.

"Of course, Jonas. Don't worry; I'll treat your wife."

This time, the tattooed giant looks genuinely concerned.

"It's not exactly *treatment* that I mean, Doctor. I think it's . . . a little more complicated than that."

31

Savine leans against the radiator.

The heat radiates through the fibers of her Gore-Tex pants, cooking her butt. She moans with relief. After almost freezing to death on the battlements of the Château de Murol, she could barbecue herself like this for hours. Long live Auvergne, with its volcanoes and geothermal energy!

"Could you maybe close the window?" Nectaire asks from behind his desk, his hands over his collection of Guatemalan stamps. Savine has turned the heating on full blast, but she's smoking a cigarette and blowing the smoke out through the open window.

"Let me just finish this first."

Nectaire shrugs, then watches for a few seconds as Savine blows hot and cold.

"Would you like some tea?"

"Oh, give me a break from your damn tea!"

Yes, there's the confirmation he was looking for. Savine is definitely in a bad mood. All because of the canelés at Le Fournil de Lamia? He carefully slides his stamps into a drawer.

"So you feel the same way I do? You don't understand?"

"There's nothing to understand," Savine spits. "On the way back from the Château de Murol, I saw his motorcycle parked on the Froidefond road, just in front of the fountain. Jonas is back! He's returned to bother poor Amandine. I thought he might leave her alone this winter, given the lack of snow, but no, he must have decided he wants to ride a four-wheeler or go mountain climbing."

Nectaire is surprised. He doesn't understand why Savine is so upset by Jonas's return.

"Okay. So Jonas Lemoine, the most handsome tattooed surfer in Auvergne, is back. But we have bigger fish to fry right now; don't you think? Didn't you hear what the woman from the bakery said? Esteban Libéri used to eat a honey canelé every morning!"

Savine takes a drag of her cigarette. She doesn't show any signs of having heard Nectaire.

"You should watch out," he warns her. "If Souche, Géraldine, or Oudard smell tobacco in here—"

"It's really bad timing, that's all!" the social worker cuts in. "Why did Jonas have to come back now, especially given the state Amandine's in?"

The secretary frowns. He has no idea what Savine is talking about. Anyway, Amandine and her surfer can wait; he's still preoccupied by his own idea.

"Don't you understand the significance of that daily canelé? It means that, contrary to what Maddi Libéri claims, her son did not hate honey. Hence, he presumably had no phobia of bees either. Which means she's been telling us fibs right from the beginning. If you follow that line of reasoning to its logical conclusion, it means that—"

"Amandine should just kick him out for good! I can guess what he's telling her now. *I'm back to stay this time, babe.* And Amandine will fall for it all over again. Until he goes away. He's a wherever-I-lay-my-hat, girl-in-every-port kind of guy, and he's not about to change. But right now, it's the last thing she needs, with Tom messing about and Dr. Libéri prowling around him."

"Speaking of whom . . . ," Nectaire says eagerly. "If Maddi Libéri lied about the apiphobia, she might well have lied about all the rest. The more I think about it, the more certain I feel there's something off here."

Savine takes a final drag, then stubs out her cigarette on the windowsill.

"He's going to break her heart again, that bastard, and I'm going to be stuck trying to put the pieces back together."

Nectaire continues to think out loud, unsure whether Savine is listening.

"I need to call Lazarbal again. There's something I don't understand. He must have questioned the bakers, too, so he must know about the canelés. But did he know about the phobia of honey? This is some case, I tell you . . . Just when you think all the clues are pointing in the same direction, you find there's something missing, like the last puzzle piece . . . or a spot you can't fill, like the last space in a sudoku . . . and you have to go back to square one."

Savine slams the window shut.

"What were you saying, Nicky? About going back to square one? I'm afraid you'll need to do exactly that now, because I haven't heard a word you've said."

She gazes around the office with a look of disappointment.

"Didn't you make me any tea?"

32

I put my stethoscope back in my bag while Amandine buttons up her shirt.

"Don't worry; you're fine. You just need plenty of rest."

She stands up, then sits down on the couch. Without Jonas here, she would never have agreed to lie down and let me examine her. She glares at me now, as if I just did something unforgiveable. As if I stole her secret.

An instant later, she gazes adoringly at her tattooed hero. Jonas is still standing, one hand imprisoned inside Amandine's; his other holds a bottle of beer.

Amandine is the submissive type, one of those women so blinded by love that they go through their whole lives never knowing whether they were fated to be like Penelope or whether they chose that destiny. Living the sacrificial existence led by the wives of sailors, truck drivers, explorers . . . and surfers. The kind of woman who despises anyone incapable of such passion and patience, anyone who settles for their second choice, all those other women who will never know the intoxicating joy of a reunion after months of separation. She is the kind of woman who one day, when Odysseus finally comes home, will be able to yell at the whole world, *I was right!*

The kind of woman I will never be . . . Amandine must truly despise me.

How long will Jonas stay this time? I have the feeling he's only here for a short stay, that his odyssey is far from over. But why should I care? At least he had sufficient sway over his Didine to make her see a doctor.

I try to defuse the situation. I move my hand slowly toward Amandine's belly, but she pulls back as far as she can while still holding Jonas's hand.

So I tell her simply, "It's okay; your baby is perfectly healthy."

Amandine is five months pregnant. Not that you would guess it to look at her. She always wears baggy clothes, and her abdomen is still relatively flat. I give her two prescriptions, one for an appointment with a gynecologist in Aubière—because she hasn't seen a specialist at all yet—and the other for Spasfon and metopimazine, in case she needs them for pain or nausea. I tried to convince her, using the simplest words I could think of, that nobody gives birth alone on a farm nowadays, that nobody should rely on plants to get them through childbirth, that there are such things as ultrasounds and amniocenteses, and—at the very least—pregnancy Pap smears, and that all of this is for the good of the baby.

I don't know if Amandine listened to me. I leave the referral and prescriptions in plain sight, on the coffee table.

I don't know where Tom has gone. Probably he's in his bedroom upstairs. I really wish he would come down. Or at least that I could catch a glimpse of him at the top of the stairs.

And ask him to forgive me . . .

Ask him . . . Oh, I still have so many questions for him.

A shadow falls across me. Jonas's bulky figure has approached. He holds out his hand, smiling carnivorously.

"No hard feelings, Doctor? Just leave my son alone, okay? I'm back now, so there's nothing to worry about. I'll keep an eye on him."

I have no choice but to leave.

My gaze tries to cling to something as I head toward the door. That Basque poem, maybe? Tom's damp jacket, on the floor in the entrance hall. His pair of sneakers, still wet because Amandine hasn't put them somewhere to dry. Though where could she dry them? The fireplace is such a mess that it would be impossible to light a fire.

I step outside, still trying to memorize everything I see. Leaning against the wall of the house: Tom's bike, which Jonas pulled out of my car one-handed, as though it were no heavier than a toy. The four-wheeler in the barn. The frightened hens. Jonas watches me, standing in the doorway. I stare back defiantly for an instant, then turn away, feeling troubled. His pale eyes are just like Tom's.

I have to get in my car. I have to leave.

But where should I go?

Where is Tom?

I don't want to go to my surgery.

I don't want to go home and see Gaby.

I don't want to leave Tom alone.

33

"Hi, Esteban! I didn't think you'd ever come back."

Tom is leaning against the fountain. Esteban is riding his bike along the asphalt road. He brakes when he comes alongside Tom.

"Where's your bike?"

"I'm not allowed to ride it at the moment. I'm not allowed to go swimming either."

Tom rolls up his pants leg and pulls down his sock to reveal his bruised ankle.

"Ouch . . . And it happened because of the bees?"

"Yeah. I hate those things. Although you weren't much help either . . ."

Esteban leans his bike against the fountain. He looks genuinely sorry.

"What could I have done?"

"Well, you could have called the police when I didn't come back."

"Have you forgotten I'm a ghost?"

Tom can't help grimacing at this.

"Only when it suits you. Anyway, never mind. We're quits, because I had to tell them about you."

This time, Esteban bursts out laughing.

"Given that I live inside your head, I don't see how anyone could catch me."

They stand there in silence for a moment. Tom glances back at the farmhouse. Nobody can see them; all the curtains are drawn.

"My father came back," he says finally. "I'm going to need you even more now, Esteban. I'll need to talk to you . . . Because I'm going to be alone now. My father doesn't come home very often, but when he does, he just stays in the bedroom with my mom so they can . . . well, you know. When he's here, I don't exist anymore. I become a ghost, just like you."

"So, what do you do?"

"Ride my bike, go swimming. When I can. And when I can't, I stay inside and try to play guitar."

"You've got a guitar?"

"Nah, not really, just this thing I made. And I've never had lessons or anything."

"I have. I'll find you a guitar. And I could teach you too!"

Esteban is leaning down to open his backpack. Tom smiles at him sadly.

"Thanks. But it's not a big deal. My father will leave soon; he always does. And for a month afterward, my mom will cry her eyes out."

Tom is silent again for quite a long time. He sniffs back a sob.

"You know what I wish, sometimes, when I think about my father?"

"No, what?" Esteban tears open a packet of cookies with his teeth, listening.

"I wish he would die."

"Seriously?" Esteban takes a bite of a cookie, then offers one to Tom. "You want one? Chocolate chip and honey."

Tom makes the sign of a cross with two of his fingers. "No way! *Vade retro*, nectar of the devil!"

They both laugh. Esteban chokes on cookie dust, and Tom steps back so the crumbs don't touch him.

"Are you really so scared of honey that you'd let me choke to death? Move out of the way; I need some water." Esteban continues to cough.

Tom doesn't budge. "Don't. I told you last time; it's forbidden. This fountain is . . . for the dead."

Abruptly, Esteban's coughing stops. Whatever was stuck in his throat has gone. He observes the reddish-colored water pouring from the rusted copper faucet, overflowing the granite bowl, and leaving behind a fiery smear on the oxidized stone.

"For the dead? I don't think so. I've seen plenty of living people stop here to fill their flasks and—"

"Have you seen the color of the water?" Tom cuts in. "It comes from the center of the earth. Straight from hell. The old people around here call it the Fountain of Souls."

Tom stares, fascinated, at their dual reflection in the scarlet water. They both look as if they've been flayed, the skin of their faces removed to reveal the bloody flesh beneath.

"Go on, then," Esteban says impatiently. "Tell me the story."

"The old people here say that when someone is about to die, you have to fill a cup with water from the Fountain of Souls and make them drink it. Then right away, you have to give a pregnant woman a drink of the same water from the same cup. That way . . ."

"That way, what?"

"That way, the soul can pass from the dying person's body to the unborn baby's."

"Whoa!" Impressed, Esteban whistles. "But you'd need to have a pregnancy and a death at the same time. That can't be easy to organize . . ."

"It's happened before, I think. There are stories about that stuff going back centuries."

Tom has turned toward the farmhouse. His gaze follows the cracks in the walls up to one of the upstairs windows.

"I should go, Esteban, before my father flips out. I'm not allowed out of the yard." He stares at the drawn curtains, which are the same color as the house's cob facade. "I'm just making the most of it while they're in the bedroom. But you should go have fun—ride your bike, go to the pool. If you're in my head, that means I'll be able to ride and swim, too, kind of, without hurting my ankle."

Esteban puts the cookies away in his backpack, then straddles his bike.

"Still as crazy as ever, I see."

"I don't know . . . You seem less and less like a ghost to me."

Esteban is already riding away. Tom watches as he speeds down the hill before vanishing from sight at the first bend. He just has time to shout, "Actually, I'm starting to believe you might really be alive!"

34

Amandine stays in Jonas's lap, even though she can already feel him shrinking inside her. She puts her hands flat on his torso—she's so light, he will hardly even feel the pressure—and keeps undulating her hips, to make the pleasure last as long as she can.

She has never loved any man the way she loves Jonas. There's nothing she can do about it—it's physical, chemical. No matter how many times he cheats on her with all his little girlfriends, going away for six months and coming back suntanned, telling her to wash and iron his clothes, which still smell of those floozies he's fucked, she'll never turn him away.

Jonas is lying underneath her; her thighs grip him like a vise. She's not going to let him go anywhere. She'll give him five minutes' rest before starting over.

Actually, make that one minute.

Jonas kneads her breasts with his hands, then moves his hands over her belly. His warm palm covers her navel.

"Looks like a crater," Jonas murmurs. "The super-cute crater of a brand-new volcano."

His fingers follow the rounded curve of her belly. Amandine grabs his wrist and pulls it away.

"Don't; I feel like a monster!" she moans. "I hate having this big fat belly."

Jonas looks up. His pale eyes examine her.

"It suits you. Some curves . . ."

He sits up enough to brush her nipples with his lips.

"Your tits look great."

"I hate them! I feel like a cow."

"Idiot. You're beautiful and you know it."

They're both sitting on the bed now, chest against chest, she on top of him, he inside of her.

"I'd prefer it if you thought I was ugly . . ."

"Huh?"

"And loved me anyway. Because there are so many women who are prettier than me."

"Idiot!"

Jonas kisses her. Amandine surrenders to the pleasure. They are both on the verge of climax, but she has to hold hers back a little longer.

With a long moan, Jonas comes first.

"I love you, Amandine. I love you to death."

Jonas strolls naked through the living room. Amandine also loves men who don't bother getting dressed after sex. Men who don't fall asleep or take a shower; men who wear her scent like a badge of pride, who need something strong so the fire doesn't die out too quickly.

Jonas pours himself a glass of whiskey.

He stops in front of a sheet of paper containing a few lines from the poem "Txoria Txori," which is pinned to the wall in a gap between torn wallpaper.

"You put it on the wall?"

"Of course."

Amandine, who is also naked, moves closer to him. She puts her arms around his waist, kisses the back of his neck. She hugs him tight. Time has stopped. Every instant with him is an eternity.

She reads the poem over his shoulder, even though she knows it by heart, in French and in Basque.

> *If I had cut his wings*
> *He would be mine*
> *And he would not have left.*
> *Yes, but then . . .*
> *He would no longer be a bird.*
> *And for me,*
> *It was the bird that I loved.*

Amandine repeats the last line softly, her lips close to Jonas's ear. "'It was the bird that I loved.'"

She kisses him again, the two of them fitting perfectly together. She will fit herself to him for as long as he needs her. For as long as he wants her.

"You see," she whispers, "I do understand. When you love a bird . . ."

Jonas turns his head, and only his head. Their lips almost touch.

"There's nothing to understand anymore, babe. This time, I swear, I'm going to stay."

Amandine just smiles, almost indifferent to the words.

I'm going to stay. How many times has she heard that promise? She believes it even less than she does Dr. Libéri's ravings. She forces herself to make her voice sound as detached as possible.

"No, Jonas, you're not going to stay . . . but that's okay. I'm used to it."

Jonas slowly frees himself from Amandine's arms. He pulls away a little, turns his body around, and draws his forefinger lightly over her belly. Amandine shivers.

"I'm going to stay for him . . . and for Tom. Tom needs me."

"Tom has always needed you."

"No, I don't mean that. He needs me now . . . because of all that stuff Dr. Libéri was talking about."

"Wait. Don't tell me you believe it?"

"I didn't say I believed it. But you have to admit it's pretty weird. Don't worry; I didn't let it show in front of her. But if even ten percent of what she said is true . . ."

Amandine stares into his silver eyes.

"That woman is crazy. She lost her kid, and since ours looks like him, she's obsessed with him."

Jonas's eyes move constantly around the room now, no longer looking at her.

"You're right. But I get the feeling it's not that simple. I might seem like some moron who only cares about skiing and bikes, but there are still things I want to understand . . . And I don't understand this. I'm going to talk to Tom about it. It's about time I acted like a dad."

Amandine runs her fingernails down his skin, as if she hasn't heard a word he's said.

"I still want you."

"Sorry, Didine, I think you've really worn me out this time."

He walks to the nearest window and draws the curtain.

Even in her disappointment, Amandine is struck by his beauty. Every muscle in his body is illuminated by the slender beam of daylight. Will it always be like this with him? The more she desires him, the more he runs away. And he comes back to her as soon as she starts to forget him. She wonders for a moment . . . What if he's telling the truth? What if this time Jonas really is going to stay? She's never asked him for anything, not even when she became pregnant the second time; she has never blackmailed him or tried to hold him back. And she never will.

It's the bird that she loves.

But what if the bird wanted to build his nest here?

She knows she shouldn't let that thought take root in her head.

Besides, Jonas has already moved on. He is now staring through the window at some invisible point behind the curtain.

"What are you looking at?"

"Where did Tom go?"

"He's probably just hanging out near the fountain."

"No, he's not there."

Amandine moves closer. She knows the yard by heart; she knows Jonas by heart; and she knows he isn't looking toward the hamlet, but the other way, toward the barn.

"Go for a ride. I know you're dying to."

"No," says Jonas, without taking his eyes off the ATV. "I told you; I'm staying with you."

"Go, idiot. And come back quick. I'll never believe in a tomorrow with you. Just promise me tonight."

"I'm promising you the rest of my life!"

Amandine kisses him so hard, he can hardly breathe.

The rest of his life?

She shivers. Her skin is all goose bumps.

No, she's not dumb enough to believe him again, is she?

Jonas hurriedly puts on his boxers and jeans.

"I don't want to leave you or Tom alone ever again."

He pulls a sweater on over his bare torso.

"Anyway, that doctor can't just have made it all up! The physical resemblance. The birthmark . . . I mean, her kid—this Esteban—would be twenty now." He laughs as he tries to untangle a pair of socks. "I'm only twenty-nine, so I can't be *his* dad."

Suddenly overcome with modesty, Amandine picks up the blanket from the couch and wraps it around her body. She watches her surfer struggling with the socks. Would she still love him this much if he did build his nest here? For the rest of his life? It's the bird that she loves, yes . . . but an eagle, not a canary!

Jonas reaches for his boot and, in the same offhand tone, says, "In fact, if the only logical solution to explain the physical resemblance between those two kids is that they have the same father . . . then maybe I'm not Tom's dad either."

Amandine glares into his steel-blue eyes.

"Listen to me, Jo. I've never had any other man since you. Tom is your son!" She touches her belly. "And so is this one; I swear it on their lives. Now, go have fun . . ."

She leans slowly over the coffee table and picks up the two prescription sheets Dr. Libéri left behind. She lines them up neatly, then rips them in half. She does this again and again, until they're nothing but confetti, which she lets rain from her hands into the trash can.

"No, Didine," Jonas protests. "That's not a good idea."

She puts her finger to her lips, telling him to shut up and finish getting dressed while she grabs a blank sheet and a pen, and starts to write.

Jonas is ready to go out. Amandine, wrapped up in her blanket, watches him.

Yes, oh God yes: she would love him even more with every passing day if he did build his nest here.

She gives him one last kiss.

"Go enjoy your ride, Jo. You'll have the whole mountain to yourself." She hands him the sheet of paper. "While you're out, could you pick up a few things for me? I made you a list . . ."

But no: the previous kiss can't be the last one . . . *This* will be the last one: she kisses him feverishly, breathlessly, then opens the door with a heavy heart and lets it fall shut, after whispering, "Come back quick."

35

Wayan Balik Kuning listens to the phone ring once, twice . . . twelve times before she finally picks up. The psychiatrist gives a long sigh of relief.

"Hello, Maddi? I thought you'd never answer. I had a really hard time finding your address and your landline number. Don't you ever answer your texts? I had to go to the mayor's office and—"

"Is that . . . Dr. Kuning?"

Wayan pauses. That is not Maddi's voice.

"Gabriel?"

Silence.

"May I speak to Maddi, please?"

"She's not here."

Gabriel's voice is curt and cold. Wayan knows that Gabriel has always considered him a rival. Masculine instinct? Well, he isn't wrong . . .

"Where is she?"

"No idea."

Wayan feels helpless in the face of Gabriel's aggressively blunt replies.

"So . . . is she well, at least?"

"Great! She works constantly. She loves her new job, and everyone here loves her!"

Wayan curses inwardly. He doesn't believe a word of this nonsense.

"She's stopped replying to me, and I don't understand why."

"Maybe she doesn't need you anymore. You should be glad she's better, right?"

"Well, I'd like to make sure of that."

"There's no problem here. She's doing fine."

"Gabriel, this isn't a joke. Maddi . . . needs me."

"Apparently not, if she's not replying to your texts."

Wayan can't just give up, having found out precisely nothing, but how can he get past Gabriel's defenses?

"I . . . I really need to speak to her. It's important."

"Sorry, Doctor, but I honestly don't know where she is."

He's lying; Wayan feels sure of it. But Gabriel isn't going to give him anything. Will he even tell Maddi that he called? What should he do? Call the landline again later, hoping Maddi picks up first? Continue to send her texts? Change his number and call her cell phone? But would she answer a call from an unknown number? Maddi is much more than a patient. He guessed—and accepted—her biggest secret. He knows her entire life, her doubts, her flaws. How many times has he saved her from falling apart?

Etretat to Murol. A six-hour drive, according to Mappy. What the hell is he waiting for? Auvergne is hardly Bali.

"Gabriel, this is important. Please tell her I called. Ask her to call me back. I'm . . . I'm worried."

Gabriel makes no promises. He ends the call on an almost cruelly happy note.

"No need to worry, Doctor. I'm looking after her."

And hangs up.

◆ ◆ ◆

At the Moulin de Chaudefour, Gabriel unplugs the landline, in case that leech of a shrink tries to call again. His gaze drifts through the window toward the grass-covered summit of Mont-Dore, now turning red in the setting sun. Throughout his brief conversation with the doctor, Gabriel told the truth at least once.

He has no idea where Maddi has gone.

36

I parked my MiTo in front of the jetty at Lac Pavin. Nobody could miss it there. There's only one way in, and only one parking lot, practically deserted in this snowless winter. I'm alone apart from a few walkers who have almost finished their tour of the lake.

It's a beautiful spot. Lac Pavin is a circle of water about one kilometer in diameter. When the sun shines, it's a turquoise gem set amid gleaming pine trees. In bad weather, it's a dark blue trap. Pavin's moods are ever-changing, like the eyes of a tormented beauty.

I approach the calm-looking water. Swimming is forbidden here. You can take a boat out on the lake in summer, but that's all. The lake is the deepest in the whole of Auvergne, almost a hundred meters. It is also the most recently formed, and the most dangerous in the region, thanks to the concentration of gas in its depths. It has been at the heart of all the local legends ever since the violent volcanic explosion that formed this perfect crater almost seven thousand years ago.

As I walk toward it, the lake turns from sapphire blue to topaz, from topaz to magenta, from magenta to indigo. The luminosity changes with every step, as if inhabitants of the lake's deep waters are lighting fires, opening windows, moving about, making love, disturbing the water with strange shadows and brief flashes of light.

I know the old stories—Pavin is bottomless; a whole village drowned inside it; it is a place of diabolical dread; one day it will awaken in a deadly eruption that will transform the inhabitants of the region into pillars of salt, and the landscape into clouds of ash.

And yet it looks so serene. I walk slowly along the edge of the glassy surface. Not a breath of wind troubles it since it's sheltered on all sides by an army of pine trees.

I walk along the edge of my madness.

The surface of the lake is as smooth as an iron plate.

What happens if a person sinks down into its depths?

What lies at the bottom? What is there to see?

Where are you, Esteban?

Please, I'm begging you; give me a sign.

I'm alone now. The last walkers have disappeared. It takes just over an hour to make the tour of the lake. In some places, the path drifts between pines; in some, it goes all the way down to the water. As I walk, I pick up stones and throw them as far as I can, without even giving them the hope offered by the brief immortality of a ricochet.

I prefer a simple dive, an ephemeral crater, thousands of ripples.

And thousands of questions inside my head.

When Jonas appeared back on the scene, my hopes had been briefly raised. I had almost forgotten that Esteban had parents before me. I know nothing about them. What if it was Jonas, or Amandine, who'd abandoned Esteban in a baby hatch that morning in September 2000? No, it's impossible—both Jonas and Amandine are far too young. They're barely thirty. They couldn't have been more than ten when Esteban was born. And anyway, I never believed that genetics could explain that astonishing resemblance between Esteban and Tom, let alone their birthmarks. All the scientific articles I read were clear on that point.

Which would leave only one explanation . . . Reincarnation?

I throw another stone in the water, which is now such an intense oil blue that I half expect the rock to get stuck in it, like a seabird near a leaking tanker. But no, it sinks straight down. Is that what happens to everything, in the end?

As for the other similarities between the boys . . . Jonas gave an explanation, but it didn't convince me.

Does the surfer really speak Basque, or does he just know a few one-liners that he uses to seduce the local waitresses? *Edateko bat nahi zenuke?* (Would you like a drink?) *Oso polita zara.* (You're very pretty.) *Maite zaitut.* (I love you.)

And the indigo trunks? He told me that Amandine bought them, and theorized about why she chose a whale, but why did she choose that particular design? All kids love music, he said, and maybe that's true, but not all kids make their own lyre. And sure, all children grow up fearful of something, but not specifically of bees.

I throw another pebble in the water. I am almost three-fourths of the way around the lake now. It's an easy walk: the path follows the shoreline, skirting around a few tree roots, widening before you have to cross a stream, narrowing when you need to climb some rocks, before returning to its circumscribed route. I have no desire to go back to the Moulin de Chaudefour. In fact, what I want to do is just keep walking around and around the lake. There are too many questions circling my head, in a wild procession. I need to sort through them, separate them; it's the only way I will be able to find my way. I have to be strategic, precise, organized.

I have almost reached the jetty. A simple wooden pontoon on stilts, advancing over the water.

On the dock, my MiTo is waiting for me like a docile animal. Lost in my thoughts, I haven't picked up any more stones.

There are three main points on which I need to focus.

The first one is to find categorical proof that even if it is a scientific impossibility, Esteban is living inside Tom, or Tom inside Esteban. I have to put myself in the state of mind of a scientist who's willing to explore beyond appearances, beyond previously held knowledge.

The second point, consequently, is to protect Tom, or Esteban—the name doesn't really matter; if I save one, I save the other—because I know they are in danger. Esteban was, Tom is: that is what they're trying to tell me. That is the meaning of all these signs, which only I have read.

I press the button on my key fob, and the car's headlights flash. I hadn't noticed two fishermen walking by; they startle at the sight of the MiTo suddenly coming to life.

I keep thinking. The first two points make sense only if I find the key to the third. And that is: Who is hiding in the shadows? Who kidnapped Esteban ten years ago? Who is preparing to kidnap Tom, tomorrow perhaps, on his tenth birthday? Who killed Martin Sainfoin? All of this has to be connected. Who is capable of distorting the way things appear, so that nobody will believe me?

I finish my walk, thinking that life and death are nothing more than a single loop that can be repeated as many times as I can walk around this lake.

Who will kill again, eliminating anyone who gets close to the truth . . . ?

37

Jonas parks his four-wheeler near the Cascade de la Biche, the waterfall near the old ski resort. He takes his time observing the Chaudefour Valley: the Dent de la Rancune mountain facing him, the sharpened points of Sancy in the distance (the only peaks among Auvergne's small mountains worth climbing), the pylons that once held up the ski lifts at Chambon-des-Neiges. His eyes scan the landscape for any sign of a forest ranger. Ever since the valley was classified as a preservation site, it has been strictly prohibited to ride a motorized vehicle here. Not that a mere rule will stop Jonas from doing what he wants. He knows every slope and every path of this valley.

Those pylons planted among the pine trees have made him feel sad ever since the closure of the ski resort. Once useful, they are now nothing more than blots on the landscape, steel ghosts; they ought to be pulled down and scrapped, but the materials aren't worth the price of renting a bulldozer. It was here that Jonas learned to ski, on the beginner slopes of Puy Jumel, when he was Tom's age. Back then, Auvergne was covered in two meters of snow from November to February.

This fucking planet . . .

He turns off the four-wheeler's engine. Time to get to work. He takes Amandine's list from the pocket of his jeans.

Honeysuckle.

Raspberry bush.

Whitebeam.

Nettles.

Blessed thistle.

Blue gentian . . .

She must have found these recipes in an old witchcraft handbook. A tisane made from flowering oats to soothe the future baby, a decoction of dandelion roots to guard against indigestion, motherwort to enrich her milk, a homeopathic dose of false hellebore just to piss him off. Any normal girl would simply go to the pharmacy! And yet he will pick all these damn weeds for her. Why? Because Didine isn't any normal girl. He's had plenty of eccentrics and hysterics in his life, dozens of girls who think they're unique. He always realized in the end that it was just a tactic, a trap to lure wild males; once they'd got the leash around his neck, they always became just like other women: boring, annoying, possessive.

Amandine is different. With Didine, it truly is the bird that she loves.

A bird that is now bringing her these stupid stalks and twigs in his beak!

Jonas leans down.

Fuck, how is he supposed to tell the difference between honeysuckle and false hellebore? When he was Tom's age, he knew all the plants in the valley. With a little effort, that knowledge will come back. He will take the time to teach Tom, too, just like his father taught him. His father traveled all over the world in the merchant navy before returning here to settle down.

Jonas has spent ten years surfing the waves of his life, collecting women and hangovers . . . He's had enough.

Amandine needs him. The baby she is carrying needs him.

Above all, Tom needs him.

Tom isn't doing well, and that's probably his father's fault.

Jonas had a long, long talk with his son before going off on this four-wheeler ride.

◆ ◆ ◆

Shit, let's just get this over with. Now what the hell does blue gentian look like?

Jonas walks a little farther along the path. He orients himself using the dikes, those huge blocks of granite that rise above the forest, in shapes as strange as their names—the Tooth of Bitterness, yes, and the Cockerel's Crest, the Monk's Needle. According to his memory, which dates back to the previous millennium, gentian usually grows at the base of trees. The plant needs shade, but sun too. A bit like Didine, it's hard to please, never satisfied with . . .

"Hello, Jonas."

The tattooed giant looks up, unsurprised. All he sees is a backlit silhouette, but he has no problem recognizing the other person.

"You got my message, then?" he says. "Perfect. I think this place is about as discreet as it gets."

"True."

He continues searching among the ferns, more concerned for now with crossing another item off his list than engaging in conversation.

"Do you know what blue gentian looks like?"

"No idea."

"Ah well . . ."

Jonas pushes tufts of grass out of the way with his foot.

"Let me know if you spot something blue, or maybe even yellow, with a long straight stem and pointed leaves . . ."

The surfer is amused by the idea of making his visitor stew for a while. And stews are always better with some herbs.

"In your message, you said the matter was urgent. I got here as quickly as I could. What's so important that—"

"Tom told me everything," Jonas says.

He pulls three grass stems out of the ground and stuffs them into the bag on his back, without even turning around. He takes another three steps into the forest, forcing the visitor to follow him through ferns and brambles.

"It wasn't easy, getting him to talk," Jonas continues. "I had to shake him up a bit, but he spilled it all in the end. All the stuff you put in his head. You groomed him with your bullshit, like a fucking cult leader preying on the vulnerable."

Jonas bends forward. He thinks he's spotted some motherwort, the most precious of all the ingredients on the list. Maybe this is his lucky day . . . He's found this flower. And he's about to cut out the tumor that's been making Tom sick.

"You can tell the cops all about it," Jonas says. "But first, I'm going to let you defend yourself. Tell me why. Why did you do it?"

He crouches down, thumb and forefinger pinched together in such a way that they won't damage the petals of the motherwort when he cuts its stalk. Behind him, a foot crushes a piece of fallen bark. The approaching figure blocks out what little light remains in the under-growth. Jonas glimpses a dark shadow on the tree trunks, an arm raised, a branch held like a sword.

He spins around, faster than a cat.

He'd expected this, anticipated it. With a powerful backhand, Jonas knocks away the heavy branch. With the other hand, he grabs the shad-owy figure by the throat and shoves it against the nearest pine.

"I suspected . . . but I wanted to be sure. You're sick! Sick enough to kill. Was it you who murdered Sainfoin? And you were ready to eliminate me, too, right?"

Jonas tightens his grip around the shadow's throat while his left hand gropes around inside his pocket, in search of his cell phone. The shadow is choking; its feet are kicking, arms waving. But Jonas, sure of his own strength, doesn't falter.

"What would you have done to Tom if I hadn't come back? If Didine hadn't called me?"

The shadow's eyes are bulging; it is slowly losing consciousness. Its arms fall to its sides, its circulation apparently cut off. Jonas moves closer to that face, now even paler than the whitebeam flowers in his bag.

"All your little schemes, they're over now. I'm back. And I promised Didine I'd stay with her for the rest of my life."

"And . . ."

The shadow is trying to speak. Saliva dribbles from its lips, flows into its throat, preventing it from swallowing.

"And you are going to keep . . ."

The shadow gasps for air.

"Your promise."

Jonas suddenly releases his grip.

There's a searing pain in his stomach, bad enough to make him bend over double. He remains upright, though, blood pouring from the wound, covering his hands. He was overconfident, he realizes; the shadow was concealing a knife in its pocket, waiting for him to come close enough that it could stab him. But no mere knife wound is going to stop him from strangling this monster . . . His hands seek the murderer's throat again. This time he will show no mercy.

The blade sinks into his flesh a second time. He can't do anything to evade it. Jonas realizes his reflexes have been dulled. His vision is blurring. His legs can barely hold him up now.

He feels a strange heat under his motorcycle jacket, in his stomach— hot liquid escaping and only his second skin of leather preventing his guts from pouring out.

The blade sinks in a third time, and Jonas collapses to the ground. This time, the knife touched his heart.

His mouth spits more blood than words.

"Why?" he manages to ask. "Why?"

Jonas can feel his life leaving him. Never would he have imagined that anyone could die so quickly. Is that really all death is? A simple wave, taking you away? Too sudden, too unexpected for you to be able to surf it . . . Just a moment's inattention and it's all over. *I'm sorry, Amandine, I'm so sorry.*

"Why?" he asks one last time.

His open bag rolls to the side. Around him, the motherwort, the whitebeam, the blessed thistles, are scattered across the ground. The shadow's cold voice reaches him just before he dies.

"Because Tom needs me."

VII

Premonition

Dinner at La Potagerie

38

Savine sits at her desk and sips her tea.

"Thank you, Nicky."

As far as she can gather, it's a mix of wild thyme, marjoram, and meadowsweet. It took Nectaire almost an hour to make it. Honestly, she can hardly even taste the pinch of licorice and the dash of star anise . . . In fact, she's not even sure she could tell Nectaire's tisane apart from the stuff you get in tea bags at supermarkets. She doubts Nectaire would be happy if she told him that, though. She imagines she would sense in his voice a hint of bitterness, a pinch of annoyance, a dash of vexation. Savine's long tirade on Jonas and Amandine's complicated relationship did not seem to interest him very much.

Nectaire has just gone over the story again from the beginning: his phone call to Saint-Jean-de-Luz, the baker's wife, the honey canelés that Esteban Libéri would eat every day.

"The more I think about this," Nectaire says, "the more certain I am that there's something off. Esteban couldn't really have been apiphobic if he loved the taste of honey."

"Maybe eating honey was his way of getting revenge on the bees?"

Nectaire rolls his eyes and, without bothering to respond, punches in a number on his phone. Just before he presses the final digit and puts the phone on speaker, he says, "You want to hear Clouseau in action? Listen and learn . . ."

Three rings.

"Hello, Iban?"

Nectaire winks at Savine, to make her understand that calling Lieutenant Lazarbal by his first name is a subtle strategy to put him at his ease with a fellow colleague.

"It's Hervé. Remember me? Lieutenant Hervé Lespinasse, from Besse."

Nectaire lays the niceties on thick. He's not far from asking how Iban's kids are doing, the temperature of the sea at the Grande Plage, the wind speed, the size of the waves . . .

"Hurry up, Clouseau!" Savine hisses. "Get to the point or he'll hang up on you."

"Anyway, the reason I was calling, the reason for this Basque-Auvergnat partnership if you will, is that we have a murder on our hands. Poisoning. With digitalis. Maddi Libéri is on the list of possible prescribing doctors, so we have to do some digging, as they say, into her past."

Savine cringes at Nectaire's terrible imitation of a folksy local policeman.

Ignoring her, Nectaire launches into an interminable summary of everything he has learned about Dr. Libéri: her son's adoption, his tastes and phobias, his movements on the morning of his disappearance, the beach, the towel, the rugby shirt and the espadrilles, the one-euro coin, his phone call to Le Fournil de Lamia . . .

"Just so you know, Iban," Nectaire adds in a sincere tone, "I would like to make it clear that I'm not following up on your investigation to make sure you didn't miss anything—I'm sure you didn't—but, well, better safe than sorry, as they say . . . So, where was I? Oh yes, the phone call to the baker's assistant, then the baker himself, and finally his wife, who told me about . . . canelés!"

If Lieutenant Iban Lazarbal finds this speech a little long-winded, he nevertheless sounds impressed.

"Very good, Lespinasse. Covering all that ground, ten years later. And I'm glad to see that you've joined my camp."

"Your camp? What do you mean?"

"Those who have always doubted the 'simple accident' theory."

"Ah . . . How many of you are there?"

"There are two of us, now you're on board."

For the next fifteen minutes, Lazarbal talks and talks, with Nectaire restricting his contributions to a few onomatopoeic interjections.

"To start with, Hervé, when Maddi Libéri informed us of her son's disappearance, we had three theories. Only three. That he'd drowned. That he'd run away. That he'd been kidnapped."

"Uh-huh."

"Naturally, we all thought drowning the most likely scenario, since all it would have taken was for the boy to disobey his mother. But when we didn't find his body, the other two possibilities came into play. They were rapidly narrowed down to one, because when a ten-year-old kid runs away and isn't found pretty quickly, it generally means either they've had an accident—which would effectively be theory number one again—or they've run into bad company."

"Yup."

"For three weeks, we threw everything at the search: posters; radio broadcasts in French, Basque, and Spanish; photos in the newspapers . . . Kidnapped children were not quite the big media story then that they are now, but even so, I doubt anyone in the region was unaware that Esteban Libéri was missing, or didn't know what he looked like. When, twenty-nine days later, we found his body floating in the sea near the Corniche d'Urrugne, it came as a relief for many members of our team. And I must admit I felt it, too, even if *relief* is perhaps the wrong word."

"Mmm-hmm."

"No more mysteries. No more mysterious kidnapper scaring all the families from Bordeaux to Bilbao. The kid drowned, simple as that, and the body must have been carried there by the current . . . Of course, the mother didn't want to accept this: if it was an accident, that meant she bore some responsibility for his death. So, after collaborating with us harmoniously during those first four weeks, since we were her only hope, she suddenly became—how to put this—a pain in our ass."

"Ah-ha."

"Exactly, Hervé. She was a doctor; she had money; she could pay lawyers to go over everything, and they in turn paid experts to tell them whatever they wanted to be told: for example, that the body couldn't have drifted from the beach at Saint-Jean-de-Luz to the cliff because the currents that month would have taken it in a different direction."

"Hmm . . ."

"Yes, indeed. Except that Esteban's body had indeed been found in the sea close to the cliff by Urrugne. They analyzed the water in his stomach, the traces of algae and plankton in his lungs. All of it proved nothing. They examined his body for signs of a struggle, but given how long his body had been floating in the ocean, any conclusions drawn would inevitably be . . . let us say, speculative. Nevertheless, the private medical examiners—yes, that is a thing, apparently—claimed they had detected some subcutaneous bruising that, in their opinion, must have been caused by strong pressure exerted by two adult hands upon the child's forearms. Now, Maddi Libéri said she was absolutely certain that Esteban did not have those bruises on the morning he disappeared . . ."

"Ah?"

"Most of my colleagues had already moved on. In any case, it was up to the judge to decide, and as far as he was concerned, the case was closed. But Basques are stubborn, Hervé. Yes, almost as stubborn as Auvergnats! And there were several little details in this case that had always bothered me. The pair of espadrilles we never found, for example. We searched everywhere, on land and in the sea. If Esteban had left them on the beach, or even if he'd worn them to go swimming, I feel sure we would have found them. On the other hand, if he'd met up with someone—someone who'd kept them . . . And then, like you, I found out about the canelés."

"Hmph."

"Can you imagine? Publicly questioning the conclusions of such a big-news case over two espadrilles and a thirty-centime patisserie? Nobody cared about that detail, particularly since, on the morning he disappeared, Esteban didn't even set foot inside the bakery. Nobody wanted to hear that we found ourselves presented with two contradictory pieces of information. On the one hand, little Esteban was terrified of bees and the smell of honey; everyone I interviewed agreed on that— his teachers, his music professor, his psychiatrist. On the other hand, unless the baker's wife was lying, Esteban would buy a honey-flavored cake every morning."

"Uh-huh."

"So, the only logical conclusion to be drawn was this: Esteban was not buying those patisseries for himself, but for someone else."

"His mother?"

Lazarbal is silent for a moment, presumably surprised that his colleague has finally expressed himself using actual words.

"No," replies the Basque cop. "Maddi Libéri always said she didn't know about the canelés. As far as she was concerned, Esteban just kept the change. That was his reward for running to the bakery every morning, and she assumed he put the coins in his piggy bank."

"So, if I'm not mistaken, Iban," Nectaire says, suddenly voluble again, "your theory is that, between visiting the bakery and going home every morning, Esteban would meet up with someone. Someone . . . hungry?"

"Precisely! You've hit upon the very idea that struck me at the time, Hervé. I interviewed all the homeless people in town, without discovering anything. I interviewed the early-morning street cleaners, the dawn dog walkers. I never found a single witness. In the end, it seemed most likely that the kid was just too shy and polite to refuse the gift of the canelé from the baker's wife, which probably cost more money than he had in change, and that he tossed the honey cake in the first trash can he passed, or fed it to the birds."

"Hmm."

"I know, Hervé, I know . . . but do you have a better suggestion? This enigma slowly drove Maddi Libéri insane. She was obsessed by the idea that someone was behind the abduction of her child, and she couldn't believe that we had no leads. Not only that, we'd plastered posters of her son all over the coast, and we couldn't take them all down. So she saw Esteban's face every time she went outside . . . There might still be posters of him around here even now. In the end, she moved to Normandy after a few months and started a new life there. I hope she's happier now. All I know is that she began seeing a psychiatrist. Esteban had seen the psychiatrist too . . . It was through chatting with the doctor that I started having doubts again. And that's what led to my fourth theory, the most horrible of them all."

Nectaire is shocked into silence, unable to think of an appropriate noise.

"Suicide, Hervé!"

"Shit!"

It is Savine who shouted this.

"Is there someone with you?" Lazarbal asks, sounding unpleasantly surprised.

"No, no."

"Because what I'm telling you is confidential."

"Yeah, yeah, absolutely. It was just our intern, young Laroche . . . She was bringing me some, uh, tea . . . And I poured it out. Because what the hell do I want with tea, eh?"

"You're weird, Hervé."

"Weird? Why do you say that?"

"It just doesn't sound like you're calling me from a police station."

At that precise moment, as if to reassure Lieutenant Lazarbal, a police van speeds along Rue de l'Hôtel-de-Ville, sirens wailing, before shrieking to a halt outside the mayor's office. The vehicle's doors burst open, adding to the din. Nectaire has other questions he wants to ask the Basque lieutenant, among them the names of Esteban and Maddi's psychiatrists, but the gendarmes are already opening the door.

"I'll call you back, Iban. Something's come up."

Well, at least Lazarbal ought to believe he's a cop now . . .

At that moment, all the other employees in the building rush downstairs from their various offices to see what is going on. Souche, Géraldine, Oudard . . .

Three policemen enter. Lieutenant Lespinasse stands in front of Nectaire, who instantly fears the worst.

Have they come here for him? Has he been unmasked? But surely they wouldn't make this much fuss over a simple case of identity theft . . . Besides, Lespinasse doesn't look angry, just a little stressed.

"The forest rangers in the Chaudefour Valley spotted a four-wheeler near the Dent de la Rancune. And when they went to investigate, they heard a scream."

Nectaire bites his lip. Savine comes to stand close to him.

"A scream?"

"Yes. It was your sister."

"Aster?"

Nectaire is so surprised, he knocks over his mug. The tepid tisane splashes all over the floor, making a puddle of soggy herbs. It looks as if hundreds of ants are drowning at their feet.

"She's fine; don't worry," Lespinasse adds quickly. "We're not here about her, but what she discovered."

Savine, Nectaire, and all the other employees—about ten of them now—stand waiting, mouths gaping.

"A corpse. About thirty meters from the four-wheeler. The body is Jonas Lemoine's. And by all indications . . . he was murdered."

39

I carefully squeeze the contents of the syringe—a Valium solution—into Amandine's arm, then look up at Lieutenant Lespinasse.

"She should sleep for several hours, with that in her."

It was Sergeant Louchadière, the only female cop in the brigade, who helped me put Amandine on the bed in her room. Amandine had become hysterical when the gendarmes came to tell her about Jonas's death. It took four of them to subdue her, and they'd called me to come urgently.

Tom, apparently, showed no reaction to the news. He's in his room. Nobody really knows how much he's understood, although surely he heard the bare fact that his father is dead. The cops decided to let Amandine explain things to him when she wakes up. Until then, Sergeant Louchadière will stay at the farmhouse with them. I've been told that she has some training in psychology. She assured me that Tom will be fine, that he doesn't seem upset, and that she is keeping an eye on him.

I grit my teeth. Sergeant Louchadière is in her twenties. I bet she just attended a few psychology lectures at university before dropping out and joining the police.

"I'd like to see Tom," I tell her. "I know how to speak to children. Tom needs me."

Lieutenant Lespinasse cuts my attempt short.

"Thank you for your help, Doctor. We'll call you if we need you again. The medical examiner will take over for now."

A polite way of informing me that I need to leave. With his lumberjack beard and his dwarflike build, Lespinasse looks more like a welfare worker from Middle Earth than a hard-bitten cop. For him, I'm guessing, a policeman's work is 10 percent authority and 90 percent compassion. He holds out his large hairy hand.

"Anyway, given that we've had two murders in a week, this will all be taken out of our hands in a few hours by the Clermont police."

Not that this fact is preventing the local cops from avidly searching the room. What do they hope to find amid all Amandine's mess? I head regretfully toward the front door. It would look suspicious if I stuck my nose in any further. And besides, I have a feeling I'll be seeing all these people again pretty soon, when they come to interrogate me. I'm sure my row with Jonas a few hours before didn't go unnoticed. Someone in the hamlet must have heard us, Monsieur Chauvet, or one of the other neighbors, listening from behind their shutters . . . and even if there were no other witnesses, Amandine will undoubtedly tell them when she wakes up. I consider telling them my side of the story now. But what exactly can I say?

That Jonas attacked me because I was giving Tom a ride in my MiTo? That I'd picked Tom up because he looks like my son, but also because of more than a simple physical resemblance between the boys. *Lieutenant, I'm talking about . . . reincarnation! No doubt Tom's father was killed over what he knew about the connection, just like Martin Sainfoin. No, I don't have an alibi for the time when Jonas was stabbed to death. I was alone, at Lac Pavin.*

Would the gendarmes really buy any of that?

For now, they're paying me no attention because they're too busy picking up anything in the room that might have been used as a weapon—kitchen knives, scissors, screwdriver, fireplace poker—and sealing them inside plastic evidence bags.

Finally, Lieutenant Lespinasse turns around and is surprised to find me still standing there.

"Is there anything else, Doctor?"

I smile, shake my head to reassure him that everything is fine, and leave. How long do I have before the cops come knocking at my door? An hour? A night? A whole day?

I walk across the farmyard and start my car.

I know what I have to do next.

◆ ◆ ◆

I enter the mayor's office. I had a feeling I'd find these two here. The most mismatched pair of investigators in the region. The mistrustful, energetic social worker and the cunning, anal-retentive secretary, sitting side by side. An improbable and yet extremely effective partnership.

I politely refuse the hot drink that Nectaire Paturin offers me—no time, I say—and the chair that Savine Laroche pushes toward me—no need, I tell them—before asking them simply to listen to me, without interrupting.

I give them a brief summary of the latest events, starting when Aster Paturin discovered Jonas Lemoine's corpse in the Chaudefour Valley: Lieutenant Lespinasse calling to ask me to sedate Amandine; his gendarmes searching La Souille before the arrival of the Clermont police; Tom Fontaine being left in the supervision of Sergeant Louchadière.

"What, little Jennifer from Saint-Victor-la-Rivière? Well, well . . ."

Clearly, Savine Laroche knows the young sergeant—in fact, I get the impression she knows everybody around here—and she doesn't seem to consider Jennifer Louchadière exactly the next Kay Scarpetta.

I have to come clean. I have no choice. I need Savine and Nectaire, and I've already gathered that they have a head start on the cops' investigation. I describe my day in a few words: Tom and his bike picked up in my MiTo, Jonas's muscular intervention, our conversation at La Souille, my long walk around Lac Pavin . . .

"So basically," I say, "I have a motive and no alibi. I'm the ideal suspect."

"What do you want from us?" Savine asks.

The social worker is a smart woman. She knows I've come begging for help. I see Nectaire Paturin write something, then slip the sheet of paper in front of his colleague, as if I wouldn't notice, or be able to read the words upside down.

Don't trust her.

I look into Savine's eyes, careful not to lower my gaze to the scrawled words on the paper. She's the brains in this duo. Nectaire is just her sidekick.

"After everything you've found out about me, you must think I'm crazy. So listen: I'm not asking you to believe me, only to help me."

It's a trap.

Savine barely glances down at the secretary's scribble.

"Help you to do what?"

"To save Tom!"

Nectaire raises his pen.

"Because you think your son has been reincarnated in this kid? And that it'll all happen again: the disappearance, the drowning . . . Sorry, but where the river of hell and the samsara and the infinite cycle of cursed souls and all that other nonsense are concerned, you've come to the wrong place. You should try my sister instead. La Galipote, number seven, Place de la Poterne, in Besse. You can't miss it."

He gives a small self-satisfied smile.

"Go on," says Savine, as if Nectaire had not spoken a word. "Why would Tom be in danger?"

Thank you!

I try to reveal everything as quickly as I can, because I know this is my only chance to convince her.

"We're dealing with a monster here! A monster who lurks in the shadows. One who has planned the whole thing from the beginning. Tom will be his next victim. And we only have one day to save him. I know it's hard to believe, but Esteban fell victim to this predator ten years ago. Esteban knew him! So he's trying to warn us. That's why he's entered Tom's head—it's a call for help. To . . . to break the curse."

I don't believe a word of this.

Savine Laroche ignores the piece of paper her friend has slipped in front of her. She takes out a cigarette. I can see her thinking about lighting it, wondering whether she should trust me. She looks me straight in the eye.

"Well, I agree with you about one thing, Maddi: there is a murderer at large in the area. As for the rest, all your Buddhist and Hindu theories . . . well, as an old agnostic, I find it pretty hard to swallow. I'll need some more . . . scientific proof."

"Scientific proof? Sorry, Savine; you'll just have to take my word for it. I, too, am navigating between reality and . . ."

"A DNA test!" the social worker says suddenly.

Nectaire is so surprised, his pen slips across the paper. I can hardly speak.

"A . . . a what?"

"A DNA test! You claim Tom and your son are practically twins, and that they have the same birthmark, right? So let's start with the simplest method and see if they share the same genes. You're a doctor, Maddi; surely I don't have to explain this to you?"

Nectaire writes, upside down and with unusual alacrity:

This is crazy!

My thoughts are in turmoil. Savine Laroche has caught me off guard.

"You must still have some of Esteban's belongings, right?" Savine says. "As the social worker here, I can easily get hold of some of Tom's stuff . . . And you, Nectaire . . . as a former cop, I'm sure you can make sure we get the results quickly. This way, we'll know!"

We'll know what? If there's a family connection between Tom and Esteban? How can I refuse?

Besides, what if Savine's pragmatism is the solution? What if there really is a rational way to deal with this?

Savine deftly evades the little kick that Nectaire tries to give her under the table, crumples up the sheets of paper covering her desk, and even flashes me a complicit smile.

"Frankly, Maddi, what do we have to lose? As long as you have nothing to hide . . ."

40

"I've come to see Tom."

Sergeant Jennifer Louchadière has been left alone at La Souille by her colleagues. Her task is to stay there until evening, and to make sure before she leaves that both Amandine and her son appear stable. The other gendarmes from Besse have all gone to the Chaudefour Valley to investigate the crime scene. They have been able to reconstruct with some degree of precision the path taken by Jonas's four-wheeler along the walking paths where all motorized vehicles are strictly forbidden, then by Jonas himself, on foot, after he parked the quad bike at the base of the Dent de la Rancune.

There are, however, no signs of his murderer. Did he follow Jonas into the valley, or did they arrange to meet? Lespinasse leans toward the second hypothesis since it's an isolated spot, and Jonas's cell phone has disappeared. If they did meet up, the murderer, too, must have parked nearby. It seems unlikely that he walked all that way on foot. Consequently, the gendarmes are searching the countryside, hoping to discover a clue before the Clermont police seal off the entire valley, leaving the local cops nothing to do but show them around and play babysitter.

Jennifer Louchadière shifts from foot to foot in the entrance hall.

"Sorry, Savine, I'm afraid that won't be possible."

Savine knows Jennifer. She took her under her wing for a few months when she was a teenager. Her parents had asked the local social services for help: Jennifer had been caught dealing drugs at her high school, the Lycée Apollinaire, and she was failing all her classes, too busy attending rave parties in the craters to bother studying. Who could have imagined back then that ten years later she would be on the other side of the law?

"Just five minutes, Jennifer, so I can make sure he's okay. I know that boy."

"I can't let you in. Lieutenant Lespinasse told me that—"

Sure of her authority, Savine interrupts.

"Just call Hervé. What are you worried about? This poor kid just lost his father. We're all in the same boat. Your job is to find the murderer; mine is to make sure this little boy isn't going crazy. Did you leave him alone in his room?"

Jennifer Louchadière shyly nods.

"And what's he doing, sleeping?"

Jennifer Louchadière shyly shakes her head.

"What the hell! And you're just staying here at the house without even speaking to him?"

Savine Laroche brusquely pushes past the sergeant. She knows she's won the argument, that Jennifer won't dare to stop her, but even so, she doesn't want to let the matter go.

"I'm going to check that Tom is okay and that he doesn't need anything. But after that, you need to stop playing *Call of Duty* on your phone and stay close to the poor boy!"

"Tom? Tom?"

Savine gently closes the door behind her. Tom is kneeling on the floor, playing with a dozen action figures spread out before him. Savine has a feeling she caught him by surprise, that he hid something as soon as she came in, but when she looks around, all she sees is a plastic sailboat on the worn blue carpet with some little plastic men scattered around it.

"How are you doing, Tom?"

The boy gives her a long, sad smile. Savine wishes she had time to talk properly with him, but she can't hang around—there's a good chance that Jennifer might actually call Hervé Lespinasse. In any case, she has a meeting in fifteen minutes at the parking lot of the Old Tower, behind the mayor's office, with Nectaire and Maddi Libéri. And she needs to provide the promised object.

She glances at the bed and spots it, leaning against the pillow.

"Tom . . . Tom, listen. I have a little favor to ask you. Can you lend me Monstro for a few hours?"

41

The tiny parking lot is already deep in dusk shadow. The perfect ambience for a conspiracy. Murol is vanishing behind a fine mist that haloes the stones of the Old Tower with a certain mysteriousness: a ghostly atmosphere of bats and flying witches. In the moonlight, Savine's orange Koleos looks almost brown. Beside the social worker's 4x4 are my MiTo and Nectaire's old Renault 5.

"Here you go," says Savine, handing the secretary the stuffed whale wrapped inside a plastic bag. "Mission accomplished."

I agreed with her that Monstro was probably Tom's most beloved belonging, likely to harbor traces of his spit, his hair, his skin. And she assured me that she would have no difficulty wrapping up the whale and hiding it under her jacket. Jennifer Louchadière was hardly going to body-search her. I open the trunk of the MiTo and hand my bag to Nectaire.

"And this is mine."

I try to smile, to look natural, but my throat is tight. The bag contains about ten different pieces of clothing belonging to Esteban, the ones he wore the week before his disappearance, which I've never had the courage to either wash or throw away. For a long time, I could smell him on them. But, like my hope, the scent gradually evaporated. Still, Esteban remains present in every fold of those garments. I know that DNA traces can stick around for decades, even centuries. All it takes is the smallest drop of saliva, sweat, urine . . .

Nectaire weighs the bag in his hand before glaring at me.

"You kept all this?"

He sighs, then very carefully puts the two bags into the back of his Renault 5.

"There really are two kinds of people," he groans as he stands up. "Those who throw out everything as they move through life, and those who carry the weight of their pasts on their backs."

The mist continues to rise, leaving the village behind and accumulating at the base of the battlements. The Château de Murol, surrounded by this bloom of vapor, looks like a rocket about to blast off.

"Okay, Nicky, we get it," Savine quickly interjects. "There are slugs and snails, shrimp and winkles, those who sleep under the stars and those who drag a caravan behind them . . ."

I observe this strange duo with a kind of fascination. They are like an old married couple who don't want anyone to know they're married. They share the same codes, the same squabbles, the same games. And yet they are both single. For now.

"But," Savine goes on, "let's save the philosophizing until we meet up later at Le Fourche du Diable. Now, are you sure your old colleague will run the DNA tests for us?"

"Boursoux? Oh yes! We've kept in regular contact since I left the police. He lives in Royat, near La Grotte des Laveuses. We belong to the same philately club, except that, while I collect volcanoes, he specializes in stamps of caverns from around the world."

We are silent for a few seconds. I cannot think of anything to say to that.

"Ah, the unbreakable bond between you crazy stamp collectors . . . ," Savine says finally.

Nectaire Paturin is supposed to take these samples to his colleague in Royat tonight. It's only a thirty-kilometer trip, but he examines his

Renault 5 as if he were preparing for the Dakar Rally. Tire pressure, headlights in full working order . . .

"Oh, so I'm the crazy one, am I?" mutters Nectaire as he checks the rubber on his windshield wipers. "You're asking me to compare the DNA of two twins—twins born ten years apart!—and *I'm* the crazy one . . ."

42

The road turns abruptly to the left before Serre Haut, more than fifty meters above its twin hamlet, Serre Bas. This is one of the most beautiful views between Besse and Royat, and one of the most dangerous too. As Nectaire takes it in, his old Renault 5 continues straight on.

Shit.

The secretary steers one-handed into the skid. The car zigzags for a few meters before stabilizing.

Shit, shit, shit.

He almost had a fatal crash, and Lazarbal still isn't answering.

He leaves the cell phone pressed to his ear, listening to the empty ringing, then leaves another message. "Iban? It's Hervé . . . Hervé Lespinasse . . . from Besse. Listen; I need to speak to you; it's urgent. Call me back." He has called at least ten times already, and this must be the fourth or fifth message he's left. He tried calling the Basque policeman as soon as the gendarmes left the mayor's office, after announcing the news of Jonas Lemoine's death. Before Nectaire was forced to hang up, Lieutenant Lazarbal had begun telling him that Esteban and Maddi were both seeing a psychiatrist, and he had mentioned a fourth theory: that the kid had committed suicide.

At the mayor's office, Nectaire and Savine spent a few minutes researching the matter online. Suicides among children under ten are rare, but they do happen. More than ten cases every year. Suicidal threats—*I'm sick of this; I'm going to kill myself*—are far more common, affecting one in seven children, but they almost never translate into actual suicide attempts. For a child, the concept of death is quite complex: before six, they cannot distinguish between death and sleep; until ten, they tend not to regard death as a definitive end. It's only later that a new idea becomes a reality: death as an unknown realm. The way the child imagines this realm can vary widely, depending on the factors of family environment, experience of grief, education, and religion.

In conclusion, the theory that Esteban killed himself is perfectly plausible. Of course, Nectaire could have asked Dr. Libéri about this theory himself, but that isn't the Clouseau method. He prefers to gather evidence first, to search, to dig, to figure out the lay of the land. And only then, when he feels fully prepared, to go into battle. Maddi Libéri hasn't told them everything; he feels sure of that, and all his instincts are telling him to be wary of her.

Now the question is, Should he trust his instincts?

The road to Royat continues to wind back and forth, all tight curves and hairpin bends. He needs to make another phone call. It's impossible, with one hand, to turn the steering wheel and shift gears, so Nectaire simply keeps going in second gear, the engine screaming in protest whenever he gets up above forty kilometers per hour. He hates modern gadgets—hands-free phones and all that stuff. In his mind, GPS systems are guilty of a genocide: the extinction of paper maps, just as emails and texts have killed off paper letters—and, even more crucially, envelopes bearing stamps.

To make the next call, he slows down to below thirty kilometers per hour. The car's engine coughs and judders.

Shit and double shit.

Aster isn't answering either.

According to the Besse gendarmes, his sister was the person who discovered Jonas's corpse. Are the cops still questioning her? And, if so, why? She found the body more than four hours ago.

Royat, at last.

Never before has Nectaire taken such a long time to cover the thirty kilometers between Murol and this small spa town. He parks at the spot he and Boursoux agreed upon—beside the wash house, close to the grotto and the Tiretaine River. As soon as he gets out of the car, he shivers with cold. The temperature has fallen more than ten degrees since noon. The north wind is blowing harder, its icy gusts seeming almost to whisper, *It's all right; I'm here; winter can begin now . . .*

Boursoux, wrapped up in a winter jacket that makes him look like an obese raccoon, rushes over to meet him. Nectaire has known Boursoux for almost thirty years. They were already friends when he worked for the police in Clermont-Ferrand; while the other cops were saber-rattling, gung-ho types, Nectaire and Boursoux preferred to form the rear guard, the backup team, the grupetto. The unbreakable bond between beta males . . . They have remained friends ever since, exchanging stamps at the philately club every Saturday. Nectaire has promised his cavern-obsessed friend some extremely rare stamps of the Hang Son Doong grotto in Vietnam in return for a simple, discreet favor.

"Hurry up, Nectaire," Boursoux pleads, blowing into his hands. "It's freezing out here. And all hell's broken loose at the station."

Nectaire speeds up as much as he can. He grabs the two bags from the back of his R5. He's already explained to his former colleague what he wants him to do—a DNA test of two samples.

Boursoux stares in frank astonishment at the stuffed whale, visible through the transparent freezer bag, then at the children's clothes supplied by Maddi Libéri.

"Jesus, Nicky, what's this all about? Are you trying to find out if you're the kid's father?"

Nectaire doesn't correct Boursoux. If the thought that Nectaire might have a small legion of illegitimate children all over the French countryside provides his friend with added motivation, so much the better. He can tell him the truth later, when this case has been solved.

"I can't tell you anything. Sorry. How quickly can you get me the results?"

Boursoux gives him a curious look, as if searching for the charming Casanova who has been hiding all these years behind the mask of the mild-mannered stamp collector.

"Is tomorrow morning soon enough? I can prepare the samples tonight, and the information will be sent to Beijing before midnight. We have an agreement with them. We investigate during the day; they analyze the data at night. Scientific expertise is like little plastic toys: you get twice as much for the same price if you outsource it to China."

Nectaire acts amazed at how much progress has been made in policing since he left his job. "Whoa! So, um, any . . . any news on that murder this afternoon? Have your colleagues unearthed any leads?"

"The crime squad from Clermont has arrived. They're up there now, in the Chaudefour Valley." Boursoux is still blowing into his hands and rubbing them together, as if hoping to produce sparks. "I'd rather keep warm in the lab, personally. They'll just end up searching with flashlights and catching a heavy cold."

"So you can't tell me anything?"

"Sorry, Nicky, you know how it is. I'm already taking a risk analyzing your kids' stuff. Anyway, for now, I don't think anyone really has a clue. All I know is that they're checking out the alibi of the person who found the body."

Nectaire's heart feels as though it's been hit by an atom bomb. Boursoux doesn't seem to realize that the person in question is his sister.

"From what I've heard, they found an anomaly in her story," his friend continues. "There's a twenty-minute gap between her finding the corpse and calling the cops."

43

I stay behind in the parking lot with Savine, my neck wrapped in a scarf and my hands dug deep inside my coat. I watch Nectaire's car turn onto Rue de Jassaguet and drive away. Savine watches the Renault 5, too, and the rows of intertwined fir trees that are illuminated by its headlights, like surprised lovers, before being swallowed up by darkness once again.

I have to think of a way to thank her.

"Nectaire must really love you, to do something like this for you."

Savine turns to me, frowning.

"What's that supposed to mean?"

Oops, apparently I've hit a nerve. Anyway, it's horribly cold, so I beat a quick retreat.

"I'm freezing; aren't you? So I guess it's not just a legend after all— you really do have winter in Auvergne."

The social worker smiles at me. She's acting like the cold doesn't bother her, but my guess is that, under her taupe jacket and orange scarf, she's shivering just like me. Suddenly I have an idea, and I share it without thinking.

"Why don't we go somewhere to warm up? You know, a cup of tea or a bowl of soup or something. Anything to get out of the cold . . ."

She hesitates. But not for long.

"I'll take you to La Potagerie. You'll love it! It's not far."

Savine lights a cigarette, and I take a few steps back to text Gaby.

I'll be home a little late. Don't wait for me to eat dinner. There are burritos in the fridge you can warm up. Gabriel doesn't offer a word of protest. How many women would envy me my freedom? I try to remember the last time he and I went out to a restaurant together. It must have been weeks, maybe even months ago.

◆　◆　◆

Behind its austere facade, La Potagerie has a generous heart. It's a sort of microcosm of Auvergne.

A black basalt wall, a menu barely visible in the dim light, a door that's practically hidden and whose frame is so low that anyone taller than five foot five has to duck as they go inside . . . But when they do, they find themselves inside a warm cavern with a vaulted ceiling.

A few tourists are already here. The owner, a woman with pink cheeks, leads us to a table near the fireplace. A cooking pot straight from a fairy tale is suspended above the flames.

"You should try the soup," Savine tells me. "Brittany has its crêpes; Cuba has its rum; and we have our soup."

She hands me one of the menus from the tabletop.

"All the 'cocktails' are good."

I open the menu and, to my amusement, discover the list of improbably named soups. The Bloody Puy-Mary (tomato, Cantal cheese, celery), the Morille-tôt (mushrooms, sour cream, chestnuts), the Bleu Lagoon (asparagus, blue cheese, wild nettles), the Dike-qui-rit, the Aubergine Fizz, the Margueritat, the Bougnat Colada . . .

I order a Bloody Puy-Mary, while Savine goes for a Bleu Lagoon. Feeling suddenly warm, I remove my scarf, gloves, and coat.

"Thank you," I say with complete sincerity, "for the test."

Savine just shrugs and waves my thanks away.

"You can thank me afterward. Or not. Depending on the results."

But I'm still curious.

"Why did you agree to . . ."

"Help you?"

In our spot near the fire, Savine is already as red as a copper pot. Anyone who's met her once, spent a few hours with her, or had only a superficial working relationship with her would surely see only a dynamic, hardworking woman with her rural common sense, welcoming arms and tireless legs, and lava-warm heart. Of course, Savine is all of that . . . but there is so much more to her. I sense in her a subtlety, an acuity, even a femininity. There is something inexpressible in her that makes her unique.

Savine flashes me a conspiratorial smile and says, "At our first meeting, I remember you kept telling me that Tom was in danger. Since then, Tom's father has died after talking to his son. Martin Sainfoin was murdered after telling me he'd learned things about Tom and Amandine Fontaine. I no longer have any doubt: those crimes are connected to some secret hidden at La Souille. And yes, Tommy is in danger. A better question, Maddi, would be: Why have I agreed to trust you?"

In the curves of the copper cooking pot, the reflection of her smile widens.

"First of all," she goes on, "I trust in my instinct, and you don't have the profile of a killer. I must also admit, at the risk of being considered as crazy as you, that the resemblances between Tom and Esteban are rather striking."

The restaurant owner brings us our steaming "cocktails." The soups come with hollow wooden spoons instead of straws, and two baskets filled with thick slices of bread take the place of the traditional bowl of peanuts.

"But that doesn't make us accomplices," Savine points out. *Slurp.* "I haven't forgotten that you've been prowling around that child as if he were yours, and I still believe that Amandine is a good mother who loves her son and is entitled to raise him the way she wants." *Slurp.* "And you somehow forgot to mention to me that Esteban wasn't your biological son but was in fact adopted. Neither did you tell me that after his disappearance, his body was found a few weeks later, drowned."

Slurp.

44

Nectaire sets the dining-room table with two glasses, two plates, and two sets of silverware. Aster, though, is not yet home. He's tried calling her at least ten times, alternating the calls with attempts to get in touch with Lazarbal. Neither of them has picked up once.

Nectaire is worried. He can't get that phantom twenty minutes out of his head. What could his sister have been up to? He knows what a divisive character she is. Some people in the village love her eccentricity, but others, with their somewhat medieval attitudes, regard her as an actual witch and would probably burn her at the stake given half a chance.

6:56 p.m.

The sun has set. The streetlamps are shining in Place de la Poterne, illuminating the old stones in timeless colors and creating the impression that every night, once the tourists disappear, the town is teleported back to its own past. In the halo of copper light, Nectaire sees a few snowflakes whirling.

Where could Aster be? What kind of trouble has she gotten herself into? Is it worse than the trouble he himself is in?

Perhaps the smell of cabbage will bring her running? Nectaire lights the gas under the pan. When Aster is in charge of getting dinner ready, she just puts the leftovers in the microwave for three minutes. But Nectaire prefers to warm them on the stove, as gently as possible, for half an hour.

There are two kinds of people . . . , Nectaire starts to muse, while watching the iron shutters come down one after another over the store windows of Place de la Poterne. A man in a shirt and tie waits outside the hairdressing salon; he just has time to raise his collar against the cold before he is assailed by two young children and a blond woman, who puts her arm around his neck.

There are two kinds of people in the world, Nectaire thinks. *Lonely, single idiots like me, and people who have made a success of their life.*

To shake off this melancholic turn of thought, he returns to the question of Aster. Where the hell is she? And why isn't Lazarbal taking his calls anymore? All Nectaire wants to ask him is the names of Maddi and Esteban Libéri's psychiatrists. How many shrinks can there be in Saint-Jean-de-Luz? Maybe he should just search for the person himself . . .

Nectaire is on edge. While continuing to stir the hot pot in the pan, he types a few words into his cell phone's search engine.

Psychiatrist Saint-Jean-de-Luz

Only three names appear, each one located with a red dot on a map the size of a postage stamp. But he only needs to zoom in.

Sofia Côme

Gaspard Montiroir

Jean-Patrick Chaumont

7:03 p.m.

Are their offices closed by now? Nectaire has nothing to lose, and nothing else to do while his hot pot is simmering. Time to get to work, Clouseau! One little click and a number on the screen dials itself.

Three rings, then a robotic voice asks him to leave a message. Apparently even psychiatrists use machines to answer their phones . . .

"Dr. Sofia Côme? This is Lieutenant Hervé Lespinasse, from the Besse police station in Puy de Dôme. We're currently investigating a double homicide, and we have reason to believe that these crimes could be linked to two of your former patients, Esteban and Maddi Libéri. Please call me back at this number. It's urgent."

Nectaire lets go of his spoon and clenches his fist.

One down!

He clicks on the second number.

Are you working late, Gaspard?

45

Slurp.

I sip my Bloody Puy-Mary. It's delicious. Its rustic appearance, just like Savine's, conceals an infinity of subtle nuances. I brood on the words she has just spoken.

And you somehow forgot to mention to me that Esteban wasn't your biological son but was in fact adopted. Neither did you tell me that after his disappearance, his body was found a few weeks later, drowned.

I wasn't wrong. These two—Miss Marple and Hercule Poirot—make a surprisingly effective team. So they know about it all? The baby hatch, the adoption, the disappearance, the body found near the Corniche d'Urrugne. Almost as if Lazarbal has told them everything . . .

I watch Savine as she dips a whole slice of bread into her Bleu Lagoon.

In a quiet voice, I say, "It's true I didn't tell you the whole truth, but I didn't lie to you."

Savine uses her spoon to rescue the icebergs of bread soaking in her bowl.

"Because you never truly believed that Esteban was dead?"

I fish a few celery sticks from my own soup before giving her a sad smile.

"Dead? Living? Let's just say it's . . . more complicated than that. Or more muddled, anyway. For four weeks after Esteban's disappearance, I clung to the hope that he was alive, somewhere. Imagine, Savine, when the cops come to tell you, one morning, that they've found the body of a ten-year-old boy; you try to convince yourself that it's not the body of *your* boy. By the time all the identifications have been made, it's already too late; you've spent too long hoping; you can't give up now, so you clutch at straws—maybe the police made a mistake, or it's a conspiracy . . . You go through every possible rational explanation, and once you've exhausted those, all that remain are the irrational explanations—the afterlife, the survival of the soul, caught in limbo, before . . . being reincarnated."

Savine wipes the corner of her mouth with a thick beige napkin. She looks down at the bluish reflections on the surface of her bowl, then gazes into my eyes. Perhaps in Auvergne they read soup the way other people read tea leaves?

"Once again, you're not lying to me, but you're still not telling me everything."

I try to look surprised, hoping this will convince her of my sincerity.

Savine isn't fooled. "Something has bothered me about this whole story from the beginning. How could a woman like you— independent and educated—how could you, even when confronted with such an accumulation of coincidences, believe in a blatantly supernatural explanation?"

I give up on my attempt to look like a rabbit in the headlights, and instead stare into her sky-blue eyes. I decide to tell her everything. Is it the warmth in this restaurant that pushes me to do it? Is it the fact that Tom will turn ten in less than four hours? Is it because I've hardly spoken to anyone in the past three weeks, apart from Gabriel? Or because I need an ally?

"Okay, Savine, you win. I'll tell you a few little secrets. Painful secrets, which I would rather not have to dredge up again."

The social worker puts down her napkin.

"Esteban used to see a psychiatrist, from an early age. Because of his adoption, obviously. And because of his apiphobia. But six months before he disappeared, he started saying some strange things to his psychiatrist. He implied that . . . that he wanted to change his body to a different one . . . because I wasn't his real mother. That I couldn't love

259

him enough the way he was. He'd also discovered that a whole section of Saint-Jean-de-Luz, its coastal neighborhood, had been swallowed by rising waters three hundred years ago. That fascinated him. He used to talk about an underwater world in which he would abandon his bodily shell. Well, he didn't use those exact words, but that's what he meant."

Savine says nothing. I continue, feeling increasingly nervous.

"Esteban's psychiatrist was called Gaspard Montiroir. I authorized him to waive the code of confidentiality so that the cops could have access to the recordings of all his sessions with Esteban. The police had to know everything if their search was to be successful. Only in the end, everyone, even Gaspard Montiroir, ended up concluding that . . ."

Tears well in my eyes. I can't finish my sentence. Savine hands me her thick cloth napkin.

"That he'd committed suicide?" she murmurs. "Lazarbal's fourth theory. You think he deliberately drowned himself?"

I twist the napkin in my hands. Thick as it is, I feel strong enough to tear it in half.

"NO!" I shout.

The few other customers in the restaurant turn to stare. Even the copper cooking pot seems to tremble. I repeat, more quietly, even while the flames of rage are still burning in my eyes: "No! I know he didn't. Nobody understood. Esteban would never have invented that story of underwater worlds and body changing on his own. Someone put those ideas in his head. Someone he met that day, with his espadrilles on his feet and his one-euro coin in his hand. Someone who kidnapped him. Someone who is going to do the same thing to Tom, tomorrow . . . on his tenth birthday. You must believe me, Savine. You are . . . my only hope."

As I utter that final word, an icy wind runs down my back, from the nape of my neck to the base of my spine. The breath of death. It takes me a few moments to realize that the door of the restaurant has just been opened. I turn around. A couple walks in, ducking under the low door and dusting white flakes from their winter coats.

Outside, it has started to snow.

46

He watches the snow swirling in the halo of the streetlamps. It isn't really settling on the road as yet. The black asphalt swallows up each snowflake, melting them all into slush, but it's a losing battle. There are just too many. Tonight, whiteness will win out—here, at least. Perhaps in Murol, or in Besse, the cold will be slightly less intense, a degree or two lower, and that will be enough to turn the night's precipitation into a cold rain rather than a snowfall. The roads will be icy tomorrow morning.

He turns on his computer, feeling reassured. Nobody will disturb him tonight. No need to bother with headphones; he can just use the speakers.

He scrolls down the long list of files and stops at the last one.

Esteban Libéri, 02/12/2010.

Two clicks, and a deep, warm voice fills the room. A voice he recognizes, obviously.

"So you're Esteban?"

"Yes."

Never has Esteban's voice sounded so shy to him.

"Dr. Montiroir has told me a lot about you."

". . ."

"He let me listen to your sessions, too, so I could get to know you. Almost as well as he does."

" . . . "

"I understand why you might feel nervous. You've known Dr. Montiroir for years. But . . . but you see, sometimes, it's best to see a specialist. It's the same with all doctors. If your teeth hurt, you see a dentist; if you're worried about your heart, you see a cardiologist. One doctor can't cure everything."

"I . . . I'm not ill."

"Of course not, Esteban. I was just comparing it to those things to help you understand. Some psychiatrists are better at explaining dreams, others at explaining fears, and others at . . . well, anything that has to do with death."

Esteban's voice suddenly rises.

"I don't want to die, Doctor! I never said that to Dr. Montiroir! I just want to change my—"

"Okay, Esteban, okay. Let's take it slowly and calmly. We have a lot of work ahead of us. First, we need to learn to trust each other."

◆　◆　◆

Aster opens the door to the apartment above La Galipote. Nectaire immediately leaves his hot pot and his phone; he's been dividing his attention between the two. Nobody has called him back: not Lazarbal, nor any of the three shrinks.

"Where have you been?"

Aster makes some strange movements with her fingers, which presumably signify, in the sign language of witches, *Just a second, Nicky; at least let me take off my hat and coat first.*

Drops of melted snow fall thickly from the coatrack where she has hung her items. Nectaire pretends not to notice. He will mop the floor later.

"Are you hungry?"

He turns off the gas under the hot pot.

"Those bastards kept me at the station all afternoon," Aster complains. "They kept going on about my 'movements' today, as if I have to justify myself to them. Lespinasse even threatened me, 'Madame Paturin, it's for your own good. If you don't have an alibi . . .' Unbelievable! I find the corpse for them, and that's how they thank me? What do they think? That witches think it's good fun to kill anyone who ventures into their forest alone?"

Nectaire doesn't say anything for now. He serves the hot pot as if nothing has happened, but he can't stop thinking about Boursoux's words: *There's a twenty-minute gap between her finding the corpse and calling the cops.*

"Was . . . was Jonas already dead when you found him?"

Her fingers make a gesture again, but this one is a little cruder. Any policeman, even a poor one, would be able to interpret it easily enough.

"Oh, I forgot—you're a cop, too, aren't you, Nicky?"

"Have a seat instead of talking nonsense."

Aster sits down, warms up, and calms down. Nectaire pours her a glass of Saint-Pourçain, then waits until his sister has her mouth full before asking, "So, what's all this about an alibi?"

"Nothing, don't worry. All witches have their secrets. Do those gendarmes really think I'm going to tell them where I pick my herbs? Anyway, it's not really the alibi they're worried about."

Nectaire almost chokes. "So . . . what are they worried about?"

"The knife that was used to stab Jonas: a Thiers Gentleman. I'm the only one in Besse who sells that model. Lespinasse isn't the sharpest knife in the drawer himself, but even he made that connection."

Nectaire takes a big gulp of wine to prevent cabbage leaves from spurting out of his nostrils.

"Did . . . did someone steal a Thiers Gentleman from your store?"

"No, Nicky. Someone stole two of them."

"As I was saying, Esteban, Dr. Montiroir told me a lot about you. What did you call him, by the way? Dr. Montiroir . . . or Gaspard?"

"Doc . . . Doctor."

"Yes, I'm not surprised. But some doctors prefer to let children call them by their first name. A little like your teachers in elementary school. We can decide about that later if you like. I also had a long chat with your mom. I hope you'll understand that I wasn't betraying you. Everything you told Dr. Montiroir, and everything you tell me, will stay in this room; it will remain between the three of us. There's only one exception: sometimes, if . . . only if it's something very important . . . we will have to talk to your mom about it. Does that make sense?"

He hears only the faint rustling of clothes, a pen being tapped against a table, the ticking of a clock.

"We can get started now, Esteban, if you're ready? Dr. Montiroir said you'd told him about an underwater world—far, far beneath the surface of the sea—a world where you can see life upside down, and where you can change your body. Could you tell me about that place, too, in your own words?"

◆　◆　◆

"Two Thiers Gentleman knives? Stolen? From La Galipote?"

Nectaire sits there with his silverware suspended in midair.

"Calm down, Nicky. Anyone could have done it. I'm not the type to put surveillance cameras in my store, or metal detectors near the door. By the way, your phone is buzzing . . ."

Shit, Nectaire thinks. *It must be Lazarbal, or one of the shrinks.* He'd forgotten all about them. He hates it when events snowball like this, speeding up and growing bigger instead of waiting quietly in a neat line for his attention.

He picks up after hesitating over whether to let go of his fork or his napkin.

"Dr. Gaspard Montiroir," announces a dynamic voice. "You called me?"

"Yes . . . this is Nick . . . um, sorry, I mean Clouseau . . . No, no, not Clouseau, that's just my nickname—some of my colleagues can be a little cruel, you understand . . . But anyway, this is, as I'm sure you know, Lieutenant Hervé Lespinasse."

Aster is trying so hard not to laugh that she almost spits out her hot pot. Gaspard doesn't sound so amused.

"I was under the impression that this was urgent, Lieutenant."

Having gotten over his initial surprise, Clouseau composes himself and speaks with his usual calm meticulousness, summarizing the events behind the double homicide in Besse and concluding with Maddi Libéri's connection to the case, and the disturbing resemblance between her son Esteban and Tom Fontaine, son of the second victim.

Apparently, Nectaire passes this test: the psychiatrist no longer seems to harbor any doubts over his identity.

"To be honest, Lieutenant, there's not much I can tell you. You should contact Lieutenant Lazarbal; I'm sure he has all the case files. I was questioned at the time, naturally. Maddi Libéri agreed to let me waive the code of confidentiality. I told the lieutenant everything I knew, but curiously, even though I was Esteban's psychiatrist for most of his childhood, I wasn't there for his most important revelations."

"What do you mean?"

"Well, I'm not sure how much I can tell you. But, oh, it was ten years ago, after all, and it's all in the police files anyway, I'm sure . . . All right, I will say this: six months before his disappearance, Esteban began telling me some rather strange things—suicidal ideation, morbid fantasies. I have to admit I was frightened. This went well beyond my realm of expertise. Most of my patients are depressed elderly women who tell me about the complicated relationship they have with their husband, or with their poodle once their husband is dead. So I suggested to Maddi Libéri that a more specialized colleague should probably take over."

"Do you know his name?"

"Yes, of course, although he left Saint-Jean-de-Luz a long time ago."

He can clearly make out the ticking of a watch now on the recording. Maybe the drip-drip-drip of a fountain in the distance. A creaking chair. Perhaps Esteban is rocking from side to side.

"It's okay; you can tell me. The first words are always the hardest. After that, the others will follow more easily. I know it's not easy, but you can trust me. I . . . I have helped many other children. I have a lot of experience in this domain. Do you think you can trust me?"

"Y-yes, Doctor . . ."

"No need to call me doctor. I'm not like Dr. Montiroir—I would prefer you to call me by my first name. My full name is Wayan Balik Kuning, but you can just call me Wayan. Okay?"

47

I watch the snow fall, hypnotized. My bedroom window is steamed up. A thin layer of powder snow covers the parking lot of the Moulin de Chaudefour. I can no longer tell where the road ends and the embankment begins, or where the valley starts to grow steeper. Pine trees and pylons all look the same. The mountain in front of me is already nothing more than a long white slope ending at the foot of the former hotel. Winter is coming, retaking possession of the place, like a merciless army whose cold determination cannot be stopped, only admired.

I got back to the Moulin before the snow started falling more heavily. As soon as Savine saw the weather, she urged me to drive home. "Be careful," she told me. "The winter has three months of snow to catch up on." I paid for our meal and walked her back home, to a pretty little town house with orange shutters on Rue de Groire, close to the mayor's office.

"See you tomorrow morning, Maddi!" she called. "Nectaire will call me as soon as he gets the results. I'm not going to lie to you—I don't believe all this stuff for a second . . . but if the DNA results for Tom and Esteban are identical, or at least show a family connection, I'll pay for you to eat at La Potagerie every night until we're both retired!"

The snowflakes are growing bigger, thicker, as if feeding on the few lights in the neighborhood—a distant streetlamp, some passing headlights—making the night look darker than ever. Poor Savine, will you really be able to afford to buy me dinner every night? I am certain the results will be positive. I know that Tom is Esteban, and that Esteban is Tom. I have given up trying to understand how it's possible. I have mentally burned all my class papers on genetics; I have ceased struggling to rationalize everything. With other people, I can still maintain the illusion, but deep within, I know. I know that my son has come back to me.

The parking lot, the sidewalk, the road signs all vanish as if they had never existed. Snow is an invitation to erase everything.

A thought, which I've managed to keep at a distance until now, returns to haunt me. What if something were to happen to Amandine? What if, after losing his father, Tom—as I have to force myself to call him, even if I know his real name—what if Tom lost his mother too?

Could . . . could I look after him?

How long would it take before he forgot that borrowed name, Tom, and remembered his own? Esteban.

How long before he once again became the boy he has never truly ceased to be? A few months? Less than a year? What would he need? A new home, comfortable, welcoming, loving. A real guitar too. A music teacher. Intensive lessons. There's no time to lose. Talent can so quickly drain away in a child once they're over ten. What else? A big swimming pool? A lake? Or, why not, the sea? A calm sea, obviously, without any big waves . . . the Mediterranean?

I am soothed by these insane thoughts, enveloped in a snowy night that makes everything appear unreal, a magical interlude of a single night: like Christmas without tinsel or lights or illusions.

Gabriel sleeps beside me. The sheets are twisted around his body, as though he refuses to share them with anyone else. He's selfish and individualistic even when he's asleep. Although . . . when I got home this evening, I found a small gift waiting for me on the table. Gaby's handwriting was on the attached card. *For you. Bon courage! I love you.*

11:50 p.m.

The radio alarm clock shows me the time in its fluorescent-green digits.

Ten minutes from now, Esteban will be ten years old. I should never call him Tom again. Except in front of other people, for whom I must put on an act.

Outside, the snow unfolds its white shroud over the countryside. In preparation for the most macabre of ceremonies?

It will all come down to what happens tomorrow . . . I must save him. Who could judge me for doing that?

When life offers a second chance, who would refuse it?

11:51 p.m.

Inside my head, a voice keeps repeating, *Esteban is in danger; I have to save him.*

I already know I won't sleep a wink tonight.

Who could keep me company? Who could help keep me from sinking into hell forever?

I could wake Gabriel . . .

Or call Wayan . . .

Or just curl up with my memories. Unwrap them one by one, like opening cardboard boxes that have been kept in the attic, like taking out old knickknacks, like rehanging old paintings, so that everything will be ready when my son returns.

Tomorrow.

Fourth Age

The Mature Soul

"When souls reach maturity, they approach their final voyage. They save time rather than spending it. They are no longer searching; they are at peace. To other, younger, hungrier, thirstier souls, they can appear as if they no longer have any desires. They are simply replete. No longer having anything to prove or discover in this world, they are the guardians of its peace."

VIII

Destination

A Boat on the Lake

48

First, Tom hears the pattering of mice. He listens to the sound of their little paws, but he can't work out where they are.

Are they hiding behind the walls? Under his bed? He pulls the sheets over his head, takes shelter behind his pillow, and tries harder to concentrate. This is all he can do tonight: listen to sounds, try to guess where the shadows are moving in the darkness, on the alert for the faintest of drafts. He isn't sleeping. He won't sleep. Without Monstro, he finds it impossible to close his eyes or trust the night; without his stuffed whale, there is nothing to scare away the nightmares, the dark monsters, the pattering of mice.

That's it; he's worked out where they are.

The mice are on just the other side of his window. They are scratching at the shutters to be let in. And not only with their paws, by the sounds of it. *Tac tac tac.* Unless there are thousands of them . . . Maybe they're too cold outside? Maybe they simply want to get warm? Or maybe they only want to talk to him?

Tom gets out of bed. He is very careful not to make the floorboards creak, even if he knows his mom won't wake up. She told him that evening that she was going to take some pills to make her sleep, that she wouldn't wake until late tomorrow, that he'd have to make his own breakfast and so on.

As soon as he opens the window, the cold hits him. He is wearing only pajamas. The wind blows under the shutters, pushing at the snow that has piled up on the edge of the wall. A layer thick enough that he could draw a heart in it, or write a word, or make a snowball.

Tac tac tac.

The mice are growing restless. Although Tom realizes now that it's not actually mice that are causing the sounds. No mice could ever have climbed this high. Maybe they're bats? He concentrates so he can listen to the night.

"Tom . . ."

He hears a cry, carried on the wind. Muffled by the snowflakes, it sounds like a whisper.

Someone is calling his name.

"Tooom . . ."

He has no choice. He's not afraid. He must know. He pushes the shutters wide open. Suddenly the curtains flap like wings, and snowflakes pour into his room like butterflies, only to quickly melt in the warm air. Tom's pajamas are flecked with frost. Another burst of small stones rattles the open shutters.

Tac tac tac.

"Tooom," whispers the voice in the night.

Tom stares through the darkness. The voice and the handfuls of gravel are coming from the right, from someplace close to the barn with the collapsed roof. The barn doesn't offer much shelter, but he guesses that is where his nocturnal visitor is hiding. He scans the darkness, his eyes gradually growing used to the dazzling white of the farmyard below. Every abandoned object—old tractor, pile of manure, broken barrel, smashed flowerpot—has been transformed into a ghost, covered in a freshly laundered sheet. He spots some footprints in the snow and follows them until he discovers a small figure leaning against one of the barn's pillars.

He recognizes him instantly.

Esteban.

Ignoring the cold, and the snowflakes that are making his pajamas cling to his frozen skin, he waves happily at his friend.

The wind carries another muffled whisper to his ears.

"Happy birthday, Tom! Come on; come down here. I've got a surprise for you."

◆ ◆ ◆

Tom pulls on a sweater and the first pair of jeans he finds in the laundry basket, then tiptoes downstairs in socks, putting his sneakers on only once he's at the front door.

He's quieter than a mouse. Mommy's asleep. The policewoman went home a long time ago. He grabs his fleece hoodie—a pumpkin-colored Fumerol, slightly too big for him. Its pockets bulge with the gloves and hat that are stuffed into them. He doesn't bother checking that everything's there; he just opens the door and walks out into the snow-filled night, with his hands and head bare to the elements.

Before Tom has taken half a dozen steps, his sneakers are already drenched. Normally, he doesn't care about the hole in his sole, because he's good at avoiding puddles and sharp stones. But nobody can glide over five centimeters of snow.

Esteban is waiting for him, still leaning against the pillar of the barn. He's better equipped than Tom. Moon Boots, woolly gloves, ski jacket.

He looks with surprise at Tom's snow-covered hair.

"You should cover up, Tom. You'll catch your death out here."

Tom obediently removes the hat from his pocket and pulls it onto his head.

"So? You said you had a surprise for me?"

"Yep, follow me."

Esteban heads out of the farmyard.

"You don't mind a long walk, do you?"

"No problem," says Tom proudly, although his socks feel as cold and wet as if he were soaking them in a bucket of ice.

Out on the road, they're sheltered from the wind by the houses, and the snow falls less heavily than in Froidefond.

"I couldn't bring your birthday present here," Esteban explains. "It's too big. I've got it at home. You're into music, right? So you'll love this."

Tom shivers, hopping from foot to foot so his sneakers don't freeze to the ice around the fountain.

"This instrument is to die for, seriously," Esteban goes on. "But first, there's something I have to ask you."

"Okay, but let's keep moving. Or I'll turn into a block of ice."

"All right, we can walk in the middle of the road. The snow's not as thick there."

Esteban is right about the amount of snow, but the middle of the road becomes slippery as soon as they start moving faster.

"Aren't you cold?" Tom asks, trembling.

"I'm a ghost, remember!"

"Yeah, a ghost in a ski jacket . . . So, what did you want to ask me?"

"It's important, Tom. You know how I told you that some memories have been coming back to me, like with the bees? Some of the memories are really weird. I hope you don't have the same ones."

Along the roadside, the skinniest trees sag under the weight of the accumulating snow.

"Are you talking about nightmares?"

"Worse than that," says Esteban. "I know you love swimming, right, at the pool or in lakes during summer? But have you ever wondered if there's anything at the bottom? Another world, I mean. Invisible. Hidden below the surface of the water. If you go down there, and then come back up, you become someone else."

Abruptly, Tom stops walking. He doesn't feel cold anymore.

"You . . . you remember that too? I've never talked to anyone about that. It's MY secret. How can you know about it if you're not a ghost? If you haven't come out of my head? And just when I was starting to think you must be real because you're wearing Moon Boots . . ."

Three bends below them, there's a flash of light, but neither boy sees it.

"Did you really think I'd go out wearing just a sheet in weather like this?"

Tom smiles. Is he really talking to himself? Has he gone out alone into the night? If he closes his eyes, will Esteban vanish? Should he go back to his bedroom now instead of continuing to walk forward, his feet freezing, to who knows where? Is he dreaming? Maybe if he pinches himself, he'll wake up warm in bed?

Esteban looks so alive. And he's Tom's only friend. Tom doesn't want him to disappear. So when Esteban starts walking again, Tom follows him, limping slightly so he doesn't put too much weight on his right foot.

The car enters the hamlet just as they're leaving Froidefond, a few meters before the bridge. It moves slowly, silently, its headlights dimmed, like two yellow eyes belonging to a wild animal trapped in the sudden snowfall, searching for some foolhardy prey it can devour.

The bridge is completely frozen. They slide more than they walk now, each clinging to a side of the parapet.

"Okay, I'll trust you," Tom says loudly, sounding more confident than he feels. "You're kind of a weird ghost, but you're a cool one too. I bet not many ghosts remember birthdays and give out presents."

Esteban, still gripping tightly to the frozen bridge railing, turns to his friend.

"Seriously, Tom, don't you think it's time we gave up on that game?"

"Wh-what game?"

"I'm not a ghost. You know that. And my name isn't really Esteban."

Tom seems to lose his balance. He clings to the railing so he doesn't fall. Is the Couze Chambon, down below him, frozen?

"So, what's your name?"

As Esteban is about to answer him, the beast's yellow eyes appear suddenly behind them.

The halo of light scans the bridge—illuminating the two isolated creatures—before exploding into the night, beams on bright, blinding them.

"Watch out, Esteb—"

Tom's yell gets caught in his throat. There is no longer anyone on the other side of the bridge. The boy has vanished, and he is alone in the night as the beast charges toward him.

49

The snow stopped falling early that morning—just before sunrise, as if its intention had been to create the perfect backdrop for people to wake up to. The subtle shades of pink on the volcanoes' gentle slopes. The dancing shadows of fir trees on the white carpet, immaculate except for a few jackdaws' claw marks. All of it a delicate harmony, disturbed only by the ballet of snowplows scraping the asphalt with their steel blades. The roads are drivable, as long as I take it slowly, stay in the middle of the road, and don't meet anyone coming the other way.

Never has it taken me so long to cover the three kilometers between the Moulin de Chaudefour and Froidefond. Almost thirty minutes. As I left the former resort, I had the feeling that the ski lifts were about to crank into action again, the parking lot to fill with cars, the slopes to come alive with zigzagging skiers.

But no. I encountered nothing but silence and a few crows. Nothing but a quiet morning, and a fearmongering journalist on the car radio forecasting another snowstorm that would hit midmorning, even more violently than the one the previous night.

"Everybody, please stay home!"

I spot the orange Koleos parked at the entrance to La Souille. No Renault 5, though. Nectaire is supposed to bring the results. He's the last to arrive, uncharacteristically. A bad sign? I shake that thought from my head. We arranged to meet at eight o'clock, and the Murol church bells haven't yet rung. He isn't even late.

As soon as she sees me arriving, Savine gets out of her car, wrapped up in the same kind of thick khaki parka Alpine hunters must have worn in the last century. Her military look clashes with my bright purple ski jacket, which must be visible from kilometers away.

I was the one who chose the meeting place. Here, at La Souille. Once we have the DNA results, whatever they are, we will have to act quickly and in concert.

I remain convinced that Tom is in danger.

Savine steps toward me, wearing a Siberian ushanka that looks like it predates the Russian Revolution. Her orange scarf flutters in the wind. We parted as good friends last night, but this morning she looks like a bear woken in January.

What happened since we went our separate ways?

"Do you know a Wayan Balik Kuning?"

No *hello*, no *how are you*, no *Nectaire's on his way with the results.* Just a gut punch.

I catch my breath, then reply, "Yes, he's my psychiatrist."

"Not only yours, apparently. He was Esteban's too. How come you didn't mention that yesterday?"

I feel as if someone threw a snowball at my neck, the ice is melting down my back.

"How did you find out his name?"

"You'll have to ask Clouseau that. Or Nectaire, if you prefer. He called me last night. He can be surprisingly shrewd sometimes. He tugged gently at the thread—he's good at that—and the whole story came out . . . Your son changed his psychiatrist a few months before he disappeared. Why didn't you mention *that*?"

The mention of Wayan's name came as a shock, but I've calmed down now. Does it really matter whether there was one shrink or two? I mumble an explanation.

"I was trying to keep the story brief, that's all. When Esteban started saying weird things—about wanting to change his body, to find a submerged world at the bottom of the sea, to be reborn in a different body—Gaspard Montiroir panicked. He was afraid of having a suicide on his hands, so he passed the buck to a colleague in Saint-Jean-de-Luz who had more experience dealing with childhood trauma. You see, Savine—nothing very mysterious."

"Except that, after your son disappeared, this Dr. Kuning moved to Normandy, where he opened a practice in Le Havre. And then, a few months after that, you moved to Etretat . . . less than thirty kilometers from his new office."

The icy water on my back warms up. I understand now why she's so suspicious: Savine doesn't believe in coincidence. Should I admit the simple truth? Yes, I followed Wayan. I needed therapy after Esteban disappeared, and Dr. Kuning seemed like the obvious choice. When he moved to Le Havre—an opportunity for him to work with one of the largest laboratories of clinical psychiatry in France—I felt lost. Everything happened so quickly after that: the police showed me a body and told me it was my son's; the search was over, they said, and the case closed. There was nothing to keep me in the Pays Basque. I tried to find somewhere to go. It didn't really matter to me where it was, as long as it was far away from Saint-Jean-de-Luz but still close to the sea. Royan, Lorient, Dunkirk, wherever . . . I had stayed in touch with Dr. Kuning, though, so Etretat seemed like a natural option. I needed him. I may even have been in love with him, without admitting it to myself . . . Then Gabriel showed up.

I meet the social worker's gaze. She is a tough little woman; I have the impression that nothing could knock her down, not even a snowstorm or a volcanic eruption.

"I'm sorry, Savine, but that part of my life is none of your business. It has nothing to do with . . ."

I hesitate. I almost said Esteban. I bite my lip. *Tom* . . . I have to say Tom in front of her.

"With Tom."

"If you say so."

She drops the subject, but I can't. My curiosity is overwhelming.

"What did Dr. Kuning tell you?"

"Nothing. Nectaire spent the whole evening trying to call him, but there was no answer."

I know exactly how he feels. I did the same thing last night, and Wayan didn't answer my calls either. Strange that he should be so silent, after sending me so many texts . . .

I rub the mist off my watch face.

8:07 a.m.

Where could Nectaire Paturin be?

Savine looks worried too. She twists her body to extricate her phone from under her parka. Nectaire is never late.

"Nectaire?" she shouts, holding the phone hard against her ear as if that might help her to hear better.

And he always answers when someone calls him. Doesn't he?

"Nectaire?"

I stare at Savine; then we both look at the road. The snowplows have made it sparkle like a cut diamond.

What if Nectaire, in his old Renault 5, has had an accident?

50

Nectaire doesn't dare brake. He doesn't dare shift down a gear either, because for that he would have to grow a third hand; he needs two to cling tightly to the steering wheel. And he certainly doesn't dare accelerate, even if he knows this is the recommendation: drive a little faster and maintain that speed. No fits and starts, just the faintest movement of the steering wheel.

Easy to say . . . Nectaire has managed reasonably well so far. He's been driving slowly but surely from Besse toward Murol, concentrating hard, dreaming up an imaginary codriver for a rally race in which it is the most precise driver, rather than the fastest, who would be declared the winner. *Hairpin bend in three kilometers,* his navigator would tell him. *Slow down and move three millimeters to the left.*

He had been feeling pretty pleased with himself, until his phone started buzzing in his pocket. Obviously, he couldn't do anything—couldn't move a muscle to pick it up; could only listen to it ringing over the car's speaker system.

"Hello? Hello? At least have the balls to answer me! I don't like being made to look an idiot."

Incapable of responding, Nectaire lets his Renault 5 slide toward the roadside.

"I just called Lespinasse. The real Lespinasse. At the police station in Besse. Naturally, I told him that there was another guy doing his work for him."

The R5 drifts softly into a pile of dirty powder snow, leaves, and branches that were spat out by a snowplow.

"I don't know who you are, but believe me, I am going to find out. And when I do, you'll have some explaining to do."

Beep beep beep.

Nectaire presses on the gas, but the Renault's wheels spin uselessly, unable to pull out of the rut.

In his jacket pocket, he can feel the weight of the envelope containing the DNA test results, which Boursoux sent him electronically at six o'clock that morning and which he printed at home. All he had left to do then was deliver them.

But he has failed at his mission.

51

8:32 a.m.

"There's something wrong. Nectaire should be here by now," Savine says, visibly panicking. "Why isn't he answering his phone? It's not normal . . ."

I am touched by her anxiety. Would she be capable of kissing him, if Nectaire suddenly turned up now? Of admitting that she was terribly scared, that she doesn't want to lose him, that . . . she loves him?

"I'm going to look for him," she says. "My car has four-wheel drive and snow tires. And there's supposed to be another storm in less than an hour . . ."

The end of this sentence is drowned out by the roar of an engine, and we both cover our faces to block the stench of burned rubber. Then, stunned, we watch as the Renault 5 pulls up outside the farmyard, hood and wheels smoking, as if Nectaire has driven all the way from Besse in first gear.

The white paint is covered in mud, melted snow, wet leaves, and dozens of handprints, as if an entire regiment had pushed it out of a ditch. Nectaire Paturin climbs stiffly out of his R5, an envelope in his hands.

"I made it. The firefighters from La Bourboule had to get me back on the road, but I made it."

I step forward. I want to tear the envelope from his hand.

"Savine told me about your bet." Nectaire smiles strangely. "Dinner at a restaurant every night until retirement if the two DNA tests are identical."

I reach out to take the envelope, but he raises his hand as if asking for patience.

"I was sure you were lying, Dr. Libéri. That your twisted mind was inventing all these similarities. All my instincts told me not to trust a word you said . . . Once again, Clouseau was wrong."

At last, he passes me the envelope and forces himself to make a joke.

"You're going to have to work overtime, Savine, to pay for all those meals."

I tear open the envelope and let it fall onto the snow. I barely look at the logos and official stamps, the tricolor icon at the top of the page, and the Chinese ideogram at the bottom. I just read the result . . .

DNA TEST No. 17854—Comparison of batches 2021-973 (Esteban Libéri) and 2021-974 (Tom Fontaine)

The genotypes of the two batches are identical.

Reliability rate of 99.94513 percent.

Consequently, the two samples provided must come from either the same individual or from monozygotic twins.

I consider the implications of this revelation. Only twins can possess the same DNA. Tom and Esteban cannot possibly be twins . . . Therefore, as impossible as it seems, they must share the exact same bodily shell. They are one and the same person.

I hear Nectaire yelling to Savine behind me:

"This is more than we can handle. I'm calling the police . . . and I'm going to tell them to bring an exorcist."

I turn toward the farmhouse. I know Amandine never locks the door.

"Wait!" Savine calls, coming after me.

I pay no attention. I turn the door handle and go inside. I repeat the same words over and over again:

"I have to protect Tom."

"The police are doing that," Savine reassures me. "There's a policewoman on duty here, Jennifer Louchadière."

Nectaire runs up to her and says, "No, Savine. Louchadière went home last night. The gendarmes said everything was under control here, and she needn't stay."

For half a second, I wonder how Nectaire can be so slow in every aspect of everyday life, yet always so well informed.

"Anyway," I call back, rushing toward the stairs, "the police will never believe this reincarnation explanation. Any investigation they carry out will be limited to their own narrow version of reality. It'll be like searching for a murderer in the night and hoping he happens to pass the only lit streetlamp. Amandiiine!"

I am yelling now. Even if she's still in a Valium stupor, I'm determined to wake her. I hear Savine rushing after me.

"No, Maddi . . . wait. Wait for the police."

I reach her bedroom door. Amandine is sleeping on her side. There's a cup containing some sticky liquid on her nightstand.

"Amandine, answer me; this is important. Has Tom said anything about changing his bodily shell? Or going to an underwater world? Or being reborn in another child's body?"

Amandine doesn't react. She's totally out of it. I run across the landing like a fury.

"Tom, Tooom."

Savine stands, barring my way in her Siberian KGB uniform.

"Take it easy, Maddi. We've taken a step forward with that DNA test. We now know there's something strange going on. We're with you; we can testify, but you have to let the police do their job."

I push her out of the way. I need to get past her. I need to see Tom. I open his bedroom door.

And freeze in the doorway.

Tom isn't there.

I stare incredulously at the unmade bed, the sheets pushed back as if Tom had just got up to visit the bathroom. I see his pajamas abandoned on a nearby chair. Evidence that Tom got dressed in a rush and went out in the middle of the night?

It's all happening again.

I turn around to face Amandine's bedroom and yell even louder.

"Where is Tom?"

She doesn't move a muscle. As if everything going on around her is just a nightmare that she refuses to face.

Savine grabs my arm.

"Maddi, please, calm down."

"Don't you understand? Esteban disappeared on the morning of his tenth birthday! It's all happening again."

Nectaire is standing at the bottom of the stairs.

"No!" he shouts. "Don't touch anything in that room. If Tom has been kidnapped, it's a crime scene. Every detail could be important."

Before he has climbed three steps, I am already yanking out drawers and rummaging through their contents. Books, notebooks, sheets of paper go flying. I search his room, panic-stricken. I have to find something, anything, even if it's only the smallest of clues. I failed ten years ago. I didn't see it coming then. I wasn't prepared. I can't fail a second time. I have to find out where he's gone. Who led him there . . .

I yank all the hangers out of the wardrobe. Shirts, pants, sweaters fall to the floor. I kick hard at the bottom of the closet. My foot goes through the plywood. There's no false bottom.

"Maddi, you have to stop this," Savine pleads.

No, what I have to do is find him.

Through the open door I catch sight of Nectaire, phone to his ear, presumably calling for backup. Doesn't he understand anything?

I drag the sheets off the bed. I toss the pillows over my shoulder. Nothing.

There has to be something here. Tom needs me. Tom is in danger. The police won't believe me, just as they didn't ten years ago. They'll waste too much time.

Savine stands behind me, looking helpless for once. She's given up trying to stop me.

I bend over and try to move the mattress, but I can't manage it. I feel as if I'm losing energy, as quickly as if my blood were pouring out through a wound. I stare imploringly at Savine.

Help me.

She sighs. She, too, I sense, has left the rational world behind. It's too late to pull back now. We must descend into hell. We can resurface later, to explain what can be explained. She helps me drag the mattress off the bed. It falls flat on the floor, raising a thick cloud of dust. I cough, and my eyes sting, and at first all I see are a few broken slats.

The cloud disperses, like the sea retreating.

Beside me, Savine freezes. She grabs my hand. When you are sinking into the irrational, when you have nothing left to cling to, you must cling to another person.

Under his bed, Tom has built a model. I doubt anyone has ever seen it, certainly not his mother. Tom knew that no broom would ever come here and destroy his secret creation.

I am stunned by the precision of the details: the church bell tower, the clock on the train station wall, the school playground, the sign of the golden croissant outside the bakery. It's all there: every streetlamp, every roof, every chimney. An entire village. No people, no animals. Just the village itself, painted blue. The paint that covers the floor and the baseboards under the bed makes it perfectly clear what Tom intended: he has painted an underwater village. Not having a psychiatrist to talk to about the visions in his head, he built them in the real world instead.

Savine's hand is holding mine so tight, she's crushing my fingers.

In the distance, I hear Nectaire shouting.

"Wake up, Amandine! For God's sake, wake up!"

291

I hear voices, even farther away, recounting those persistent legends. A village was swallowed up by Lac Pavin. A whole village. The same legend, the same story as the one in Saint-Jean-de-Luz.

I understand.

Savine tries to hold me back, but nobody—nothing—could do that.

I hear Nectaire yelling again in the bedroom across the hallway.

"Amandine, please wake up."

I hear Savine behind me, pleading.

"No, Maddi, stay here."

I am no longer listening. I can still win. I can still save him.

I rush out of the room and hurtle downstairs. Without a backward glance, I run outside. The wind is howling, and snow is pouring from the sky once again.

52

"Amandine, wake up!"

Savine is kneeling by the bed. She pinches Amandine's arm, but there's no reaction. She looks at the pills scattered over the nightstand.

"Oh God, what have you taken? Wake up, love, wake up."

She puts her hand on the woman's belly.

"If you won't do it for yourself," she says, "do it for your child."

Nectaire is standing in the bedroom, staring anxiously through the window at the farmyard below. Maddi's MiTo has disappeared, and the tire tracks have already been covered by fresh snow.

"Where did she go?" he says.

"No idea. Help me, Nicky! Fetch me a wet towel or something."

Nectaire struggles to react. He has already called the police station in Besse, but with the snowstorm returning, it will take them a while to get here. There is too much information fighting for attention in his head: the surreal DNA results, Tom's disappearance, Maddi Libéri driving into the storm . . . it's all whirling like the snow. His instincts are telling him . . .

"Get a fucking towel! She's burning up, and her breathing is too slow."

Nectaire stammers an apology, then—too scared to ask where the bathroom is—starts to panic, opening the door of the wardrobe before realizing he's not going to find a towel in there.

"What has Maddi done?" he wonders aloud.

"Nothing. Just hurry up. The bathroom's the first door on the right."

Nectaire takes one step forward, then another.

Crack.

Broken glass underfoot. He leans down and carefully picks up—between his thumb and forefinger—a syringe.

"What the . . ."

Savine reacts instantly. With a quick glance, she takes in the same thing Nectaire sees: viscous brown residue stuck to the shards of glass. She pushes the sheets away, grabs hold of Amandine's limp arm, turns it over, and examines the veins in her wrist. She finds a tiny hole, ringed with a crust of dried blood. There are bruises, too, on her arm and wrist.

"She didn't do this on her own," says Savine, her voice shaking. "Someone drugged her. Last night. The man who kidnapped Tom, it has to be . . ."

"Or the woman . . ."

"What woman?"

Savine is searching for other needle marks on Amandine's skin, but she doesn't appear to find any.

"The woman who kidnapped Tom!" Nectaire holds the broken syringe in the palm of his hand. "Look at this. You can't find this sort of medical equipment at a high-street pharmacy. And the injections are clean and neat—professional quality. It was a doctor, or a nurse, who did this."

"You don't mean . . ."

"How many doctors do you know around here? Who have we suspected from the start of wanting to kidnap Tom? Who vanished as soon as we called the cops? Who's been stringing us along from the start? Who could have provided us with those clothes—and just *claimed* they used to belong to her son—for that damn DNA test? She's been to La Souille several times before; she could easily have picked up some of Tom's clothes—they're lying around all over the place! All she'd have to do is bend down and grab some. God, how stupid we've been! It's the only explanation."

Savine picks up Amandine's wrist and presses her thumb against the purple vein. She tells Nectaire that Amandine's pulse is weak but steady. Nectaire carefully drops the remains of the syringe onto the nightstand, while continuing his monologue.

"I knew I should have followed my instincts . . . I was right all along. She wants to escape with the kid. What did she say, Savine? Where did she go?"

"She . . . she seemed obsessed by that story of the underwater village."

"Same as her kid!" Nectaire exclaims. "That's exactly what the shrink told me. And that boy drowned. Except in his case, the place where half the town vanished under the ocean was Saint-Jean-de-Luz."

Savine's and Nectaire's eyes meet and widen at the same moment.

Lac Pavin: the legend, told to them so many times by Aster, of the drowned village at the bottom of the lake. A town punished by the devil for all its sins.

"She must be there now!" Savine cries. "She must have taken Tom there."

Nectaire's face lights up briefly with a glimmer of admiration, perhaps even love.

"I'll go," she says.

The heroes are never the ones you expect them to be.

"No, stay here," Nectaire tells her. "Amandine needs you. Call the station in Besse and tell them to meet me at Lac Pavin."

53

Lac Pavin, spread out before me, looks like a vast mirror surrounded by frosted pines, their shivering doubles reflected in the icy water. Snowflakes are cascading down by the thousands; the luckiest ones cling to branches, pile up on the lakeshore, while all the others die in the lake, disintegrating as soon as they touch the surface, like so many kamikaze pilots.

I slow down but drive as close to the lake as I can, onto the wooden jetty. I feel the planks creaking under the car's tires. At last I stop, but—even with the handbrake on—my MiTo continues to move forward for more than a meter, sliding helplessly on the packed snow. It comes to a halt only at the very end of the jetty, a few meters from the water.

I exhale. I've made it. The first part of the trip was pretty straightforward, on roads that had mostly been cleared, but the second part—after Besse—was a disaster. It was then the storm had suddenly worsened. The wind had swept up the snow piled up at the roadside and on the branches of pines, mingling it with the blizzard that was falling from the sky. My headlights had illuminated only a thick curtain of whiteness. I could practically see the level of the accumulated snow rising before my eyes.

The farther I drove, the more I felt as if I were traveling through a tunnel, one that was closing in on itself behind me. A long and silent tunnel. The snow fell soundlessly onto the car roof; the tires seemed to float over the ground. The radio gave the only indication of other life, even if the signal was muffled and staticky. The local journalist kept repeating the same advice: do not go outside; the storm will be over in four or five hours, but it will be extremely violent; the meteorologists are predicting more than a meter of snow this morning. The whole region will be cut off. Whatever you do, stay home. Only travel if it is absolutely essential.

I open the door of the MiTo and step out onto the jetty.

Rescuing my kid is absolutely essential, right?

My feet skid from under me, and I grab hold of the door. Shit . . . Beneath the layer of powder snow, the ground is pure ice. It's like a skating rink that could transform, at any moment, into a slide. The lake stretches out in front of me. I put on my mauve hat and my white wool scarf, and I button my purple ski jacket all the way to the top. I squint to keep the snow out of my eyes.

I cannot see anything at all through the curtain of falling snow. No parked cars, no tire tracks, footprints, or sled marks. Nothing but the frozen lake and the white pines that surround it like an army of twisted skeletons.

But I have to find him.

Esteban is bound to be here. I can't be wrong.

Did he come here of his own will last night, during the lull in the storm? Or was he abducted?

Has he already . . .

I observe the smooth surface of the lake, upon which millions of snowflakes have already sacrificed themselves.

Has he already drowned?

No, impossible.

I creep forward along the jetty, shouting loud enough to wake the whole galaxy.

"Estebaaaan."

There's not a single ripple on the surface of the lake. To my left, the path that runs around the lake is hard to make out, and the signposts appear blank.

All I can see is whiteness.

"Estebaaaan."

I start walking along the path. I have to cling to the branches. The path slopes down toward the shore: one misstep and I'll be taking an ice bath. The surface of the lake is covered with a thin fog of condensation. The water cannot be much warmer than the air, but the mist offers the illusion that it is boiling hot, a gigantic cooking pot heated by the flames of hell.

It's unimaginable that Esteban could have dived into this, genuinely believing that he would find a drowned village below the surface. If he did, someone must have influenced him.

"Estebaaaan."

I hold the note so long that snowflakes enter my mouth. I spit them out, continue walking, and reluctantly call out the other name.

"Toooom."

Still no answer, not even an echo to mock me, to make me believe that someone else is here.

"Toooom. Estebaaaan. Toooooom."

I keep going along the circular path. A hundred times I almost slip. Every new meter is another trap: a pit of soft snow where I sink thigh high, followed by a clearer part where the driven snow has left behind only a patch of ice.

Yet I keep moving forward. My MiTo is now nothing more than a small igloo at the edge of the ice floe. I've almost reached the opposite bank, which means I am already halfway around the lake.

Already?

How long have I been here? Fifteen minutes? Thirty? An hour? I use my teeth to tear off my right glove and shove my hand into my pocket, in search of my phone.

Seven calls, three messages. That's all I have time to read before the screen is covered by snowflakes. I wipe them away furiously, then try to shield the phone with my hand.

Savine, of course. Savine has been calling and calling. They must surely have called the police. And she and Nectaire are not stupid: they're bound to have thought of Lac Pavin.

My fingers skate uselessly over the screen, but I keep trying to wake it, and finally it obeys me.

Wayan tried to call too. But there's no voice message, no text.

My hand is freezing, my face raw. I put the cell phone in my pocket and put my glove back on before my fingers turn to icicles.

"Estebaaan. Toooom. Estebaaan . . ."

I resume my chaotic walk. I brush past pine branches, and the slightest touch sends tons of snow pouring over me. Sometimes, when the path is too narrow, the branches scratch at my face.

I am no longer paying attention to the pain or the cold. My eyes are drawn to the surface of the lake, the only element in the landscape not devoured by snow; a black hole indifferent to the surrounding cataclysm; a calm body of water with a perfect, almost transparent reflection.

My vision is blurred, but I think I can just make out the shapes of roofs, hear the sound of a bell ringing, children laughing.

"Estebaaaan?"

Is it all going to happen again?

Is the water going to close over him once more, and over the secret he keeps?

The identity of a silent killer who will never confess.

Will I never see Esteban again?

Will the pain overwhelm me again?

Will they fish a drowned child from the water, four weeks from now? Will I . . .

I have almost finished the tour of the lake. My MiTo is only a few meters ahead of me. The jetty. A few benches. A few mooring posts where rowboats and paddleboats are tied in summer.

The snowstorm grows even denser, the flakes attacking my face. I keep my eyes wide open all the same. Let them sting me, blind me. I don't care.

A small boat is moored to one of the posts. A boat I don't remember seeing when I first arrived. How could I have missed it?

Is it an illusion?

"Esteban?"

My throat, half-strangled by the boa scarf, lets only the smallest thread of sound emerge from my mouth.

I can hardly believe my eyes.

He's there. In the boat.

Right in front of me.

I recognize his jacket, his hat, his blond hair frosted with snow.

"Estebaaaan!"

This time I yell loudly enough to set off an avalanche.

Esteban does not turn around.

"Tooom!"

Tom doesn't hear me.

It doesn't matter. I run toward him, every footfall an invitation to slip.

I don't care about the snow; I don't care about the ice.

No, it is *not* all going to happen again. This time I have found him. This time I can save him.

54

Nectaire spots the MiTo right ahead. It's blanketed with snow, but the shape of the bodywork is unmistakable. Nobody but Maddi Libéri possesses a car like that around here. He keeps driving, his tires sliding on the ice. How long has Maddi been here? How much of a head start on him does she have?

He doesn't brake as he gets closer to the lake—he's already driving slowly enough—and instead simply lets his Renault 5 drift gently in neutral into the MiTo's rear bumper.

It's a soft collision. The car sputters to a stop.

He exhales. He made it, at last. He should feel a sense of release, but his fingers are tensed so tightly around the steering wheel that he can't let go. His vision is distorted by thousands of black-and-white dots, as if he's spent hours watching a blank screen.

He almost crashed a dozen times on his way here, almost got lost; he in fact did stall the car, struggled to climb the few ascents, lost control during the interminable descents . . . He nearly gave up many times, but he made it in the end.

He takes a deep breath. His hands are as stiff as a Playmobil figure's.

What has gotten into him, deciding to act the hero? Has he done it to make Savine's beautiful, tired eyes shine with admiration? Because there are still a few drops of cop blood flowing in his veins? Or simply because he didn't think things through, because he only followed his instincts, because he hates having the wool pulled over his eyes, because he had to find out . . . the truth?

He has paid dearly for this truth.

The drive to Lac Pavin took two hours, the Renault never going more than ten kilometers per hour. A bicycle would have beaten him in a race. He'd trembled at every crossroads, cursing his own bravery, wondering if it was really him driving that car, if it was true that Nectaire Paturin was the only motorist who had been reckless enough to venture out in the middle of that tempest, the R5 moving so slowly that his mind kept wavering between absolute concentration and rambling thoughts—imagining himself safe and warm at home, making a cup of tea, watching the snow through the window, examining yesterday's stamps because no mailman was going to come today—talking to himself inside that metal cage, behind the nervous swish of the windshield wipers.

What in the world had he been thinking?

He hadn't seen a single 4x4 between La Souille and here, not a single rescue vehicle. There had been nothing on the roads but his old Renault 5.

Aster could tell this story to generations of children—how her brother the hero had gone out alone to conquer the worst storm in a decade. There are two kinds of people in the world, he thinks—normal people and crazy people. But perhaps everyone crosses the red line into madness at some point in their life . . .

He has finally freed his fingers from the steering wheel.

He assumes the MiTo must be empty, but the layer of snow that covers it makes it impossible to see inside. He wipes the condensation from his window with the back of his hand. For an instant, he hopes that Lespinasse and his brigade are already here, but no, he sees no sign of any other vehicle.

He's alone. On the shore of the lake.

And somewhere close by, Maddi Libéri is hiding.

◆ ◆ ◆

Before going out to confront the snowstorm, Nectaire leans over to the glove box and takes out the Sig Pro in its leather holster. In fifteen years of working for the crime squad, he never once used it. It is one of his only souvenirs from that period of his life, this pistol that he kept without a permit, along with a fingerprint kit and his official police badge. A premonition? Had he guessed, somehow, that he would have to wait to be a secretary at the mayor's office before he'd have cause to remove the weapon from its holster?

He opens the car door. The snow accumulated on the Renault 5 falls in a sudden heap, as if the roof has come off. He waits for the white cloud to disperse before placing his two solid hiking shoes onto the powder. The cleats dig into the snow. The shoes are Rossignols, a birthday present from Aster four years ago . . . Until today, he hadn't even taken them out of the box.

With his hood up, he advances along the frozen jetty, like a bird of prey with sharpened claws. After that odyssey in the car, his eyes can distinguish even the tiniest detail between snowflakes, as if his brain has cobbled together a sort of decoder to pick up an encrypted channel. He turns his head 180 degrees, looking from one shore to the other, but sees nothing, no sign of life, not even a crow or any other bird. Nothing but the blank surface of the lake surrounded by thousands of ghost trees.

She's here, though. He knows she is.

His senses are tingling, like he's a trapper at the North Pole tracking the last polar bear. What's happening to you, Nectaire? He touches the butt of his Sig Pro for reassurance, while staring harder at the surface of the lake.

Is there a drowned village somewhere beneath it? He thinks about the legend that Aster likes to tell, thinks about the model of it that Tom built in secret . . . Then he notices something. A tiny ripple, a barely visible wave on the surface of the lake, moving with an evenness that leaves no doubt: it is not caused by the wind. It is a perfect arc, one that gradually widens before breaking on the shore and being replaced by another, just as perfect as the first.

Rings in the water.

But not like those rings created by a stone thrown from the shore or skimmed across the surface. No, these rings are slow and regular, the kind that are born out in the middle of the water, made by a simple, precise, repeated impact on the surface. The kind that are born from the swaying of a boat, the movement of an oar.

Impossible, Nectaire tells himself. Who could possibly be out in a boat in weather like this?

He utters a curse word that is lost in this milky landscape, then carefully turns and walks back to the Renault 5. He opens the glove box again and takes out a pair of binoculars. They are National Geographics, the model Aster sells to tourists. He congratulates himself for being so organized; the Renault might be rusty and dented on the outside, but everything inside it is exactly where it should be.

Back to the lake, his hawk's claws digging into the snow. The binocular's copper circles press against his swollen eyelids. He curses as he adjusts the focus, as he meticulously wipes the lenses clean every ten seconds, incapable of telling whether it's his vision that's blurred or just the melted snow he's seeing, trickling down the glass. Meter by meter, he scans the flat, dark surface. He almost expects to see the neck of the Loch Ness monster surging out of the water, but no, there's nothing. He's close to despair when he spots another circular ripple. He raises the binoculars little by little, following the circles back to their source.

Oh my God.

He makes out the shape of a boat floating on the lake. A few oar strokes betray the silent presence within.

He zooms in closer, adjusts the focus again, widening his eyes to prevent his lashes from disturbing the view.

Hell's teeth!

There's no doubt about it. He recognizes Tom's pumpkin-colored Fumerol hoodie. And, beside him, the purple ski jacket, mauve hat, and white scarf of Maddi Libéri.

The steel cleats of his hiking shoes seem to be stuck in the planks of the jetty.

What the hell is that madwoman doing with Tom out on the lake? And where the hell are Lespinasse and the other cops? What the hell should he do now? He thinks about firing his pistol into the air. But then what could he do after that?

He continues to monitor the boat through his binoculars. It is moving away. It will soon become nothing but a colored dot, before fading from sight altogether.

He has no choice. He has to follow it.

Along the path around the lake.

◆ ◆ ◆

Nectaire stops, out of breath. He has never walked this fast before in his entire life, and every step exhausts him. He has to plant his cleats as deeply as they will go, get a solid grip on a branch, then lift his foot up, which is as hard as pulling a nail out of a plank. And then do it all over again. And again.

He is making progress, though, faster than he could have believed possible. The binoculars bang against his chest; the Sig Pro bounces along inside his pocket.

What is Maddi Libéri planning to do with that kid? Why would she want to row all the way to the other side of the lake? Why not just walk around it?

He grabs onto the trunk of a pine tree for a moment, adding his weight to that of the snow and making its low branches sag. His heart is beating too fast. He must have overestimated his own strength in his desperation to rush through the section of the path that deviates from the lakeshore for about a hundred meters, winding between pines before descending toward the water again. But he doesn't have time to wait for his heartbeat to slow down. He puts the binoculars to his eyes and searches for the boat. Or, failing that, then at least the ripples in the water.

He can't find any ripples at all. There's nothing but the smooth, empty surface. As if the lake were covered with a thin layer of ice that healed up after swallowing the boat and its passengers.

He curses. This makes no sense. Lac Pavin isn't frozen. He has to have gotten closer to them with all this walking, and they can't have turned back.

Where the hell are they?

Have they had time to moor the boat?

Well, yes, they must have done, if it's not on the lake anymore.

Nectaire walks a little closer to the shore, unsure where the path ends and the water begins. His cleats give a sharp screech as they scratch a rock.

Don't go any farther. Don't panic. Just observe and analyze.

He keeps his eyes wide open as the twin circles of the binoculars scan the lakeshore, right along the edge between the white carpet of the path and the puddles of snowmelt that cover the shore. He can see every detail; if the boat was moored there, he . . .

He spots it.

Washed up on what looks like a small cove.

The boat is empty.

His first reflex is to imagine the worst. They sank. They jumped into the water. They swam down to that ghost village under the surface of the lake, and the abandoned boat simply drifted to its present position.

He continues to examine the boat through the binoculars: he sees the oars balanced on the rail, the rope knotted through the iron ring at the bow. He follows the rope by slowly moving the binoculars. The other end of the rope is tied to the branch of the closest tree.

If his cleats were not so securely planted in the ground, Nectaire would dance with relief.

They haven't drowned! They've simply moored the boat. They must have continued on foot.

He sets off again. He has to catch them. Surely even a clumsy old bear like him can walk faster than a ten-year-old child. Even if his shoes weigh a ton, even if his thighs are getting stiffer and his knees are creaking.

He claps his hands together, then slaps his legs. Come on; let's do this. Even as he starts walking again, Nectaire tries to organize his thoughts.

What is Maddi planning to do? The lake is a dead end, sunk into a deep crater. To reach the jetty—and the MiTo—they are going to have to either pass him on the lake or walk all the way around . . . To what end? What is the point of this crazy hike?

Nectaire speeds up, or at least he feels like he does. He never notices himself moving slowly, except when he's measured against other people. Maybe he's actually losing ground on Maddi and Tom. Does he have the energy to walk any faster?

◆ ◆ ◆

He has almost reached the cove. He stands, exhausted, looking at the moored boat. Lactic acid is burning in his thighs. Can he go farther without taking a break? Without catching his breath? He hasn't brought anything to eat or drink. Snow is pouring into his face, a few flakes sneaking in to chill his neck, despite the buttoned-up hood. Nectaire is about to yell with rage when he glimpses a light on the road leading to the lake: it is behind the jetty, behind the MiTo, behind the Renault. A car! A car with a light flashing blue through the fog. It's a police car.

No, make that two police cars. Savine must have done it—convinced Lespinasse to go out in this storm. Now the only exit is blocked.

Whatever Maddi Libéri had in mind, the trap is about to close on her.

His fingers grip the butt of his Sig Pro.

Good work, Clouseau, good work.

◆ ◆ ◆

Finally, Nectaire arrives at the cove. He is feeling increasingly confident on the snowy path. Knowing that reinforcements have arrived has given him access to a reservoir of energy he didn't know he possessed. He has enough breath in his lungs to emit long sighs of relief.

Thank goodness, the boat is still bobbing in front of him, one end resting on a white bed of snow that descends in a long white bridal sheet toward the lake. Thank goodness, the rope that moors it to the shore is still tied to the nearest tree. Thank goodness, he can see two rows of different-sized footprints in the snow ahead—an adult's and a child's. Nectaire starts to breathe more easily. Somewhere in his mind, without daring to fully imagine it, he had considered the possibility that Maddi Libéri might have thrown Tom into the lake before rowing to the shore and attempting to escape on foot.

But no, two passengers obviously got out of the boat and left their fresh footprints on the small white beach before joining the path and walking along it for a few meters.

Wait, why only a few meters?

Nectaire looks closer and sees that it's true: the tracks before him stop dead.

It's impossible . . .

There's nothing here but the lake to his right, a steep cliff rising to his left, and the path continuing straight ahead, covered in an immaculate white carpet that, to judge by the thickness of the snow, nobody has trodden upon for at least an hour.

This is ridiculous, he thinks. They can't just have flown away.

And yet, the reality is undeniable. They can't have turned back, or he would have passed them; they can't have gone any farther, because their footprints would betray them. There is only one other way out . . . The lake? But why would they have gone into the lake then? Because the police arrived? He cannot imagine the astonishing determination it would take to dive into that icy water.

Nectaire is at a loss. Once again, it's all happening too fast. Everything is swaying, whirling, like those millions of tiny snow-white butterflies that surround him; even his steel cleats are not enough to help him keep his balance. To stop himself from falling, he puts his hand on the closest rock: a basalt column that descends vertically until it almost reaches the lake, leaving barely a meter of path between the cliff face and the shore.

Ow!

Nectaire's palm is gripping not the smooth wall of volcanic rock, but rather something rough and bumpy, a strange excrescence that is at once hard and granular. He scrapes away the accumulated snow and stifles a cry of surprise.

The rock is red. Bright red. And less than a meter higher up, there's another like it, this one sunshine yellow. He discovers a third, turquoise blue, just below the red one, above his right foot.

It takes him a few seconds to understand: these are footholds.

Looking up, he spots another dozen. While he stupidly counts them, his brain is working feverishly. Of course—he's at the bottom of a climbing wall. Lac Pavin is famous for its boat rides, the unique color of its water, its depth, its drowned village . . . and its rock climbing. A good spot for beginners, from what he can remember hearing. The local schools bring students here on field trips.

In the summer, it's packed with people . . .

But in the winter? In this freezing white apocalypse? With a ten-year-old kid?

Is Maddi Libéri hoping to escape Nectaire and the police . . . by *climbing*?

Instinctively, Nectaire looks up. The driving snow lashes his face, but he squints through it, searching for any hint of shadow or movement above him. But it's impossible to see. He can't pull back far enough from the cliff, and the others are too far ahead. How could Maddi Libéri have convinced Tom to follow her on such a mad escapade? Tom must be climbing the wall of his own will; she could hardly drag him up there if he was resistant.

What should Nectaire do? Follow them? Put his own hands and feet on those holds? No, it's impossible. He gets vertigo just from standing on a step stool. No amount of determination is going to get him up that wall . . . The only solution is to tell Lespinasse as quickly as possible, so that he can catch them at the top. But where at the top, exactly, should Lespinasse go? Nectaire can't see anything beyond the climbing wall.

Then the idea pops into his head of its own accord. To see them, he needs more perspective. And to do that, he has to move back from the wall . . .

His cleats grip the ice. This time he runs, sending the powder snow flying. He yanks on the rope, and the branch snaps off. He throws everything into the boat, wood and rope together, and moves closer to push it, one foot in the snow, the other in the icy water. The cold bites into his flesh, up to his knees. But he ignores the feeling and jumps into the boat. Grabbing the oars, he plunges them into the water, his legs frozen, his arms on fire, eyes riveted to the cliff face.

The farther away he rows, the more he can see. He starts to make out what's at the top of the cliff: a platform, located in a clearing in the thick woods.

Have they already made it there? Snow-blinded, he tries to distinguish their bodies flattened against the rock wall. The wall seems less intimidating now, viewed from the lake—less steep, less vertical, with numerous crevices where a climber can gain a hold—but he cannot find any trace of the two fugitives.

Where have those ghosts gone?

He drops the oars and lets the boat drift.

He has to warn Lespinasse quickly. The electric blue lights are still flashing above the jetty, but Nectaire is too far away to make out the gendarmes.

He takes out his phone, checks that he has a signal, and glances back at the wall. This time he spots them.

They are right at the top. He can see Maddi's ski jacket and Tom's fleece.

What now? He has to choose, quickly, between his phone and the binoculars. Between Tom's safety and his own curiosity . . .

There's no time to hesitate.

In that split second before he can choose, staring bare-eyed through the thick curtain of snow, he thinks he sees Maddi Libéri leaning down to help Tom reach the last hold and hoist him onto the platform. He thinks he hears Maddi Libéri cry out. And then silence.

He can't believe it. He sees Tom's body tip back, fall, fall, like a rock that's come loose from the wall, before smashing into the lake's surface a hundred meters away.

Nectaire drops everything—binoculars and phone—and he picks up the oars and rows, as hard as he can, until his lungs wheeze and his shoulders feel as though they are about to dislocate. He thrashes the water with the fierceness of a machine, as if he were striking Maddi with the oars, as if to warn her, *Don't you take that child any farther* . . . but when he gets to the epicenter of the ripples, only a few moments after Tom's body crashed into the lake, the surface there has already healed over. The water is smooth and pure again, like a mirror. And beneath its surface, Tom must still be sinking: thirty meters, sixty meters, a hundred . . . arrowing down to that other world, far from the land of the living.

IX

Arrest

Jonas Caves

55

I open my eyes.

The first things I see are words. Basque words, which I translate in my mind.

> If I had cut his wings
> He would be mine
> And he would not have left

The poem is pinned to the wall facing me.

> It was the bird that I loved

The words dance inside my head, like a nursery rhyme.

> It was the bird that I loved
> It was the bird that I loved

I think I hear children laughing, and shouting, too, the sound of waves, the buzzing of a bee.

"Dr. Libéri, are you awake?"

The voice seems to come from beyond my dream. I try to turn my head, but everything flips over: a dirty ceiling followed by a rickety wall, the doors lying flat; then everything freezes in a close-up of my feet. I feel as if I were inside a video shot on a cell phone whose owner has forgotten to press stop.

"Dr. Libéri?"

The voice is coming from above me. I raise my head, and this time I see them.

Three cops.

The camera grafted to my eye has finally stabilized. I recognize Lieutenant Lespinasse, the bearded man with kind, monk-like eyes; young Louchadière, who doesn't dare meet my eye; and the third one . . . Salomon, I think. He's a giant who looks like a mountain guide from the Himalayas.

"Where . . . where am I?"

It's a stupid question, I realize, recognizing the mess in the fireplace, the ragged curtains, the collapsed piles of laundry, the flies hovering around the dining-room table . . . I'm at La Souille.

"You were asleep for a long time," Lespinasse explains. "We've been waiting more than two hours."

"Waiting for what?" I try to sort my scattered thoughts. My brain feels like it's buried under snow.

"For you to explain, Dr. Libéri. To tell us what happened."

"What happened?" I curse the slowness of my mind. Am I really incapable of doing anything more than repeating the policeman's questions? I have to snap out of it.

I move my hands, my feet. I realize I'm lying on the sofa, wrapped in a blanket. The three gendarmes are sitting in chairs, in a semicircle, facing me. One couch, three cops. It's like some weird mix of a police interrogation and a psychoanalysis session.

"I . . . I don't remember anything."

Lespinasse sighs.

"I was hoping you would be more cooperative."

He looks desolate. He stands up and walks over to one of the windows. I glance around the room. I spot Savine's khaki parka and Nectaire's gray winter coat hanging beside mine on the coatrack in the entrance hall. So they're here, too, somewhere. Waiting upstairs, perhaps, or in the kitchen, for the interrogation to end.

Lespinasse pulls the ragged curtain aside. Daylight barely enters the room. It's as dark outside as it is in here and . . . I don't recognize a thing. The farmyard is now merely a chaos of white dunes. The snow hasn't just covered everything up; it has concealed even the shapes of the objects beneath it. Impossible to tell the difference now between the four-wheeler and the old tractor, or the manure pile and the woodpile. Even the other houses in Froidefond, visible in the background behind the falling snow, look as if they've been completely buried under white powder.

"The storm's going to last another couple hours," explains Lespinasse. "And nobody is permitted to set foot outside during that time. So, your lawyer coming here, or us letting you go before we've finished questioning you . . . those things are not going to happen."

What am I doing here?

Images return to me, growing more precise and unambiguous as they lose their coating of semi-reality. I see my MiTo parked on the jetty at Lac Pavin. I remember walking along the path that circles the lake, in the snow. And the last image flashes in my head. Esteban in the boat, just ahead of me. I see myself running toward him . . . then it's all a blank . . . until I wake up here.

Lespinasse comes back to his chair. I don't give him time to sit down.

"Where is Esteban?"

He was in the boat. What happened after that?

Sergeant Louchadière's eyelids flutter faster than a wasp's wings. Lespinasse gives Salomon a searching look, as if seeking help with answering my question.

I repeat it, forcing myself not to yell.

"Where is Esteban? What am I doing here?"

Lieutenant Lespinasse calmly sits down on his chair. Again, he looks to his colleagues' eyes for support; finding none, he takes a deep breath and starts to speak.

"We found you on the platform at the top of the climbing wall near Lac Pavin, in the middle of the woods up there. You weren't moving. Our assumption is that, after the accident, you must have fainted, and when you fell, you banged your head on a rock. The blow knocked you unconscious for two hours and left a nasty wound above your left eye."

I touch my forehead, my temple, and feel the elasticated fabric of a large Band-Aid stuck over a makeshift compress. Accident? What accident?

"You can thank Salomon for the bandage," says Lespinasse. "He's the one who nursed you. Given the weather, we knew we were on our own. So I decided the simplest thing was to bring everyone together here. All the witnesses, all the clues. We don't have a choice. We're going to try to get everything done in this farmhouse—interrogations, hearings, identifications."

Am I even listening anymore?

An accident? Above Lac Pavin? That's all I retain of his speech. In my last memory, I was running along the lakeshore toward the jetty. Toward a boat. And inside the boat was . . .

Trying desperately not to think what this all might mean, I repeat, "Where is Esteban?"

The wound on my head, which I hadn't even noticed before, is now aching horribly. Lespinasse gives me the same kind of pitying look I imagine nurses give patients when they lose their marbles.

"Your son died ten years ago, Madame Libéri. In Saint-Jean-de-Luz. He drowned."

Bastard. I knew the cops wouldn't understand. I knew talking with them would leave me banging my head against a wall. That they would refuse to listen, refuse to consider the possibility of anything that did not fit their vision of reality. I take a deep breath and try, like Lespinasse, not to raise my voice.

"Okay, if you say so. So let me rephrase my question . . . Where is Tom?"

Lespinasse looks me straight in the eyes. His gaze is unblinking, unwavering.

"Tom drowned, Madame Libéri. Two hours ago. His body is a hundred meters underwater. At peace . . . at least, I hope so."

Is it my horrified expression, my paralyzed hands, my body's convulsions, that force him to clarify further?

"Tom is dead, Dr. Libéri," he says. "You kidnapped him. You ran away with him. And, with your recklessness . . . you killed him."

56

"Omelets for everyone?"

Nobody answers Nectaire's question. Nobody has any appetite. In fact, nobody has even thought about eating, even though it's one o'clock in the afternoon and they are going to be stuck at La Souille for many hours yet.

"Well, I'm going to start cooking," Nectaire says, "and you're all welcome to eat some."

He moves between the gas stovetop and the hot oven, presumably hoping that the heat will dry his soaked clothes. He left his hiking shoes in the entrance hall because the metal cleats made a screeching noise when he walked.

"Okay," says Lespinasse, "let's have a five-minute break and take stock. Jennifer, don't let Maddi Libéri out of your sight. Even if she'd be unlikely to get far in this weather."

The lieutenant invites Savine Laroche and Fabrice Salomon to sit with him at the kitchen table. Watching them pace around like pigeons in front of a bakery has been making his head spin.

"Fab, you checked on Amandine Fontaine?"

"Yep," replies the giant. "Her condition's stable. She's resting. I think someone gave her an injection of oxycodone. Hard to tell how much . . . If she'd been given an entire syringe, she would already be dead. If it was only a few milligrams, she'll be fine, and the baby will be too. I don't think there's any point calling for an ambulance in this weather. She's better off here, in the warmth. Besides"—Salomon hesitates for a moment, then gives a small smile—"we have a doctor in the house now."

"Excellent, Fab," remarks Lespinasse. "Though you might also have mentioned that the doctor in question probably knows the exact dosage of opioids in Amandine Fontaine's bloodstream, since she is almost certainly the one who gave her the injection."

There's a brief silence, broken only by the sound of cracking eggshells. Lespinasse turns a weary eye to Nectaire.

"My suggestion is that we stop all these private investigations and pool all our knowledge on this matter. That way, we should be able to get a clearer picture of what's occurred. Agreed, Nectaire?"

Eyes lowered and frying pan raised, Nectaire nods.

"Perfect," says Lespinasse. "We'll deal with your decision to conduct a parallel investigation a little later. I'll persuade Lieutenant Lazarbal to hold off strangling you while you explain to me how you came to be on a boat in the middle of Lac Pavin. For now, let's just try to gain a clearer understanding of what actually happened."

"I'll start and you can stop me," Lespinasse goes on. "It all began ten years ago, when Maddi Libéri lost her son. He drowned. In the Atlantic. Maybe it was suicide; more likely he just disobeyed his mother and went swimming; perhaps because he was afraid of a bee. Maddi Libéri felt guilty and never got over it. She started to believe that her son, Esteban, had been reincarnated in another boy who looked like him—Tom Fontaine. She even moved to Murol just to be closer to him. All the rest is hypothetical, but we can speculate that her obsession shaded into madness, and that she began manipulating everyone, including little Tom, filling his head with her nonsense about reincarnation."

Savine raises her hand.

"Objection!"

Lespinasse nods at her, like a judge inviting a lawyer to speak.

"Manipulating everyone? Sure, in theory: Why not? But how could she have gotten in contact with Tom Fontaine? She only saw him two or three times, almost always in front of other people. She spied on him; that's true. She was obsessed with him. In fact, I think I was the first one to realize that. But I don't see how she could have, as you put it, 'filled his head' with anything."

Behind them, the frying pan sizzles. From the smell, they all guess that Nectaire is using up Amandine's mushrooms and chives.

"It wouldn't have been that difficult, Savine. Do you have any idea how many crazy people there are on the internet, and the garbage they inflict on children? And Maddi Libéri is apparently addicted to the internet: her whole life is posted on social media, or—more pertinently—the part of her life that she wants people to know about. Anyway, back to my account. We can safely assume that Maddi Libéri, along with Tom Fontaine, had been planning this for several months, maybe even years. How else do you explain the model of the drowned village that Tom built under his bed? She invented a list of coincidences that made it look like Tom resembled her son. Same tastes, same phobias. She even killed people to achieve her aims. Martin Sainfoin, Jonas Lemoine. Anyone who might thwart her plan. We can also note, in passing, that she has no alibi for either of those murders. Besides, who better than a doctor to prescribe digitalis and add it to some harmless medication? And one hour before Jonas Lemoine's murder, witnesses saw Maddi Libéri's MiTo parked in front of the jetty at Lac Pavin. Was she already casing the place then?"

Nectaire, frying pan in hand, whistles in admiration.

"We've been over her timeline," Lespinasse continues. "She had a lively altercation with Jonas Lemoine not long before he was murdered."

"Everything came together on Tom's tenth birthday," the lieutenant goes on. "This date was the nerve center of her obsession. She neutralized Amandine by injecting her with an opioid; we'll leave it to the doctors to tell us whether or not she intended to go so far as to kill her and her unborn baby. After that, Maddi Libéri kidnapped Tom, whom she now called Esteban, because by this point, she had lost all sense of reality."

This time, it is Fabrice Salomon who raises his hand.

"Question."

"Yes, Fab?"

"Where did she intend to take the boy? What was her plan, once she'd abducted him? And what was the point of this whole charade afterward, and before?"

Lespinasse leans back in his chair. He sniffs the enticing scent of mushrooms. That cretin Nectaire certainly seems to be a better cook than he is a policeman. The lieutenant is perturbed. He has three homicides on his hands, one of them a child, and this bastard is managing to make him feel hungry!

"How should I know?" Lespinasse replies, for the first time showing a hint of irritation. "No doubt a shrink would explain that Maddi Libéri was seeking to exorcise her past; or to go back in time to before her son drowned, in order to save him before his tenth birthday. To be able to accomplish that, she needed events to happen again, in an almost identical way . . ."

"Objection!" Savine says, this time without bothering to raise her hand. "So according to your theory, Maddi Libéri's plan was premeditated long before. You're saying she methodically planned the kidnapping. But she kept warning me and Nectaire about it! It was her darkest fear, in fact, that Tom would be kidnapped today."

Lespinasse catches another whiff of omelet and tries to stay focused.

"Well, either she's truly demonic and took advantage of your naivete"—Savine's face twitches at this—"or she is completely crazy and doesn't remember what she's done. I'm sure I don't need to get into those details. Watch any cop show on TV, and it's always the same story: personality issues, schizophrenia . . . Basically, part of her brain is unaware of what the other part is doing."

Nectaire looks up from his frying pan for an instant.

"But what about all that nonsense this morning? The boat trip on the lake. Climbing the rock wall . . ."

Lespinasse looks suddenly more assured. Clearly, he's already done some thinking on this particular point.

"We could imagine various scenarios, but in my opinion, Maddi Libéri wanted to make us believe that Tom drowned in Lac Pavin. She rowed out to the middle of the lake to leave a clue there—a hat, a scarf, or a glove belonging to Tom, for example. She knew that, because of the lake's geology, it would be very difficult to fish out a body, leaving room for doubt. Everyone would believe Tom was dead, then, but she would drive off with him and raise him under another identity."

"That makes sense," says Nectaire admiringly, adding a pinch of salt. "She believes that her own child was kidnapped ten years ago. So, in her mind, she's just taking back what was stolen from her."

"But," Lespinasse continues, less vulnerable to Nectaire's compliments than to his culinary talents, "her plan went awry. Because you turned up at the lake and you saw her. Then we arrived, cutting off her chance of escape. We were too far away to see her, of course, but she couldn't miss our flashing lights. She no longer had time to carry out her staged drowning. She had no choice but to flee with Tom—Esteban in her mind—and there was only one possible escape route: the climbing wall. An act of madness in weather like this . . . You know the rest. Tom slipped and ended up drowning for real. Just like her own son, ten years before. She wanted to save him, and she killed him."

Lespinasse pauses, as if waiting for a round of applause. He thinks that maybe that idiot was right about the omelet. They could be here for a while, and he'll need a clear head for the interrogation—him alone against the two Maddi Libéris, the respectable doctor and the reckless psychopath. Not to mention that he came back soaked and exhausted from his adventure at Lac Pavin.

He feels even wearier when he sees Savine Laroche raise her hand.

"It's a bit much, though, isn't it?" she says, without waiting to be given permission to speak. "The idea that she could have convinced Tom to go out in the middle of the night; then to get into the boat with her, during the worst snowstorm in years; and finally, to climb, using his bare hands, up a twenty-meter wall . . ."

Nectaire lowers the gas flame under the frying pan and briefly contemplates his work of art.

"Come on, Savine," he says. "You saw the model of the drowned village that Tom built under his bed. The same garbage that Maddi's son told his psychiatrist. That model alone is proof that she brainwashed him."

"We will check everything," Lespinasse says. "Computers, cell phones, mail. We'll question Tom's teacher, the leaders at the youth center, the lifeguard at the swimming pool. I swear to you, Savine, we will uncover the truth."

"Sorry," the social worker says, "but I still don't believe it. I talked with her; I ate dinner with her. And I know Tom. He's a daydreamer, that's true, but he's a smart kid. Not the kind who would be easily manipulated. How you can imagine even for a second that he—"

Lespinasse, finally losing his temper, cuts her off.

"And you think the parents of kids who've been radicalized could have imagined such a thing? What world are you living in? There are guys in Syria and Afghanistan who manage to persuade ten-year-old children to blow themselves up with explosive belts, or to kill their brothers and their parents. Surely I don't need to tell *you*, Savine, that a child's brain is like modeling clay."

"And Maddi Libéri's brain," Nectaire adds, "is a mess. If Clouseau were to give you any advice—other than recommending a glass of Saint-Pourçain to accompany this omelet—it would be to call her psychiatrist."

"You have her psychiatrist's number?" Lespinasse explodes.

Nectaire Paturin does not bother replying. He just takes his phone out of his pocket and calls the number that he has already tried calling a dozen times before.

"Teamwork," he says as the phone rings and rings. "Dr. Wayan Balik Kuning, from the psychopathology center at the university hospital in Le Havre."

The phone rings one last time, then falls silent. Not even a voice mail or an answering machine. Why does this psychiatrist never answer, despite all the messages Nectaire has left him?

Sergeant Louchadière approaches the kitchen, lured by the delicious smells.

"It's your turn on guard duty, Fab . . ."

Salomon looks regretfully at the plates on the table and is about to unfold his giant body, when Nectaire's phone starts ringing. Could it be the psychiatrist calling him back? They all hold their breath, and Nectaire puts the phone on loudspeaker.

"Hello, Nicky? Nicky? It's Aster, your beloved sister."

They all stare at the phone in silence.

"Are you still stuck with the witch burners of the Inquisition?"

"Ahem . . . yes . . . and . . . they can hear you."

"Perfect! So you're all there, are you? The three musketeers— Salomon, Lespinasse, and Louchadière? Can you hear me? I've been thinking about that stolen knife, the one you found in poor Jonas's belly. I've been going over the whole day in my head. I don't have hundreds of customers, you know . . . and I did notice one who could have swiped something from my store. Thinking back, he did act a little strangely. He asked me to fetch all these rare stones from the back room—gypsum and amethyst—but in the end, he just bought some cheap knickknack."

"Do you know the guy's name?"

"Just his first name. I've only seen him once before—at the cemetery. He was with Maddi Libéri. And you mentioned him to me briefly once, I think. It was Gabriel."

Lespinasse slams his fist on the table, which makes the plates shake and clatter.

"Who is this Gabriel?"

Savine and Nectaire look shocked. Is it possible that Lespinasse and his team believed Maddi lived alone? Then again, who would have bothered to say anything? Prior to that morning, there had been no need for the police to pry into Dr. Libéri's private life.

When no one answers, Lespinasse addresses Nectaire directly.

"So where is he, this Gabriel?"

"At home, I imagine," says Savine. "The Moulin de Chaudefour, where he lives with Maddi."

"Yeah, he probably hasn't gone out picking mushrooms in this weather," Nectaire adds.

As if to punctuate his sentence, the smell of burning mushrooms, chives, and eggs suddenly fills the kitchen, quickly followed by a cloud of smoke. Nectaire rushes over to the frying pan that he has—just for a minute, but a minute too long—forgotten to watch. Louchadière coughs and Salomon grimaces, but Lespinasse just waves the smoke away and stares at the thick white mist behind the window. The snow-storm is at the peak of its ferocity.

"Salomon," he says, turning toward his deputy. "You've climbed the Annapurna, the Dent Blanche, and the Aconcagua, right?"

The uniformed colossus nods.

"It's barely three kilometers from here to the Moulin de Chaudefour. Even less if you cut through the forest. So get out there and walk to the Moulin de Chaudefour. I want you to pay a visit to this Gabriel."

57

Gabriel hears a noise. Holding the knife tight in his fist, he moves from deep inside the cave he's in toward its entrance.

From where he stands, he can survey the entire Couze Chambon valley, though the endless curtain of snow makes it hard to see much. Maybe the blizzard is a blessing in disguise, Gabriel thinks. He can see that there are no hikers, no cars, no signs of life at all. If there were, he would spot them in an instant. In this moment, the only living creatures in view are two crows gliding through the sky above.

Two spies? Sent by whom?

While he stares at the white horizon, Gabriel is also listening. It was a cracking sound that made him leave the shelter of his cave. Too loud to have been produced by anything other than a living being. Motionless, Gabriel listens to the silence. Maybe it was just some rodent, lured from hibernation by the unseasonably warm weather and then caught in this snowstorm. A fox? A squirrel? A vole? Or a curious human?

Gabriel remains on the alert, but he hears no more sounds, spots no movement. Oh well. He ducks down and goes back inside, to the rear of the cave, which is warm and dry and sheltered from the wind.

Of course, like everyone around Murol, Gabriel has heard about the Jonas Caves. Jonas . . . another coincidence? It has to be, unless Tom's father was named after these strange volcanic caverns sculpted in the red tuff cliff that overlooks the valley. Gabriel once did some research on these caves: dug more than two thousand years ago by historic cave dwellers, or troglodytes, they form an actual complex of living spaces. Five hundred meters long by five hundred meters high; five floors; seventy apartments. A labyrinth large enough to shelter close to a thousand people.

He has had time to lose himself in this maze and to start to find his way, helped by a few signposts. The site is closed in winter, so there's little chance of being surprised here by a stray tourist.

Bent double, he makes his way forward through the narrow passageway until he reaches one of the most remote cavities: the oven. This space is where he put his belongings.

The room's gentle warmth welcomes him as he enters, as does the delicious smell. He'd left a few chestnuts roasting in the fire. The chimney dug out of tuff works as well now as it did two thousand years ago. All he'd had to do when he got here was set fire to a few branches that were abandoned there and then close the room's heavy wooden door. After that, he'd been able to dry his clothes, warm his bones, and . . . wait.

There's no risk of the smoke betraying his presence here, he thinks. The sky is too overcast for that. Even so, he tenses his fingers around the knife handle. He needs to stay vigilant. Until now, he has done well: nobody has seen him; nobody could possibly suspect that he's here. He must continue this way, calmly, with a clear head. He will use his knife to shell a few hot chestnuts, drink some water, and then start looking through the rooms, one by one.

He has already investigated the biggest spaces: the chapel, the master's house, the attic, the bakery. He has inspected about ten rooms, moving silently, searching for the only room that truly matters . . .

That cracking sound again.

This time, Gabriel hears it clearly. Should he go toward the cave entrance again? It's probably just a bird that landed on a frozen branch, maybe a rodent that has sniffed his odor or—more likely—been drawn here by the warmth. The most reasonable thing to do would be to extinguish the fire, then continue exploring.

How much time does he have? Have the gendarmes already noticed his disappearance? Whom have they interrogated? What has Maddi told them? What has Dr. Kuning told them? What has Aster the Witch told them? Has she snitched on him?

He knows he must be careful, now more than ever.

If anyone approaches—be it hare, dog, or human—he must be ready to strike.

He decides to forget about the chestnuts and lets the fire die. It's too much of a risk.

Still bent double, waving his knife blindly in front of him, he shuffles toward one of the corridors.

He must be ready to kill.

To kill when he finds the most important room of all.

A room with four walls, white with lime.

The dying room.

58

"Think, Madame Libéri! Try to remember."

Lespinasse is asking me the same questions for the umpteenth time. I am still lying on the couch. He has returned to sit facing me. What does he think will happen if he continues on this way? That he will make me crack? That I will fill all the holes in my memories with the story he wants to hear?

"I'm just trying to help you, Madame Libéri. There are several possible truths."

Does he really think he can lure me into his clumsy traps?

There are several possible truths . . .

Because I have several personalities, is that what you mean, Lieutenant? Because I'm a schizophrenic in denial? Dr. Libéri and Miss Hysteria.

No, no, no! I refuse to believe their theory. I am not crazy. Someone is trying to drive me crazy. I must not waver from that conviction.

I am not crazy. Someone is trying to drive me crazy.

"Okay, we're going to start over from the beginning," Lespinasse announces, clearly struggling to stay patient.

The lieutenant is interrupted by a stampede of footsteps above us. A second later, someone hurtles downstairs.

"Hervé! Hervé!"

I recognize Sergeant Louchadière's voice.

"Hervé, it's Amandine. There's something wrong."

I do not wait for the lieutenant's permission. I jump off the couch and rush out of the room. Lespinasse makes no attempt to hold me back. We all run upstairs, Lespinasse first, then me, Louchadière bringing up the rear. Nectaire and Savine, alerted by the yelling, come running too.

Amandine has been in stable condition since this morning. From what I've gathered, the police believe I injected her with a powerful painkiller, oxycodone, an opioid responsible for more overdose deaths than any illegal drug. As soon as I see Amandine, I can tell that her condition has suddenly worsened. She is curled up on her bed. Her breathing, which was already irregular, seems to be inexorably slowing down. She appears to no longer be responsive to sounds or to physical pain. All the symptoms of an overdose. Her skin is extremely pale, almost blue. If we don't act quickly . . .

Lespinasse takes out his phone. By the time he reaches the top of the stairs, I hear him cursing the emergency operator.

"For God's sake, I don't give a shit about the weather! This woman is pregnant. In Froidefond, just above Murol."

Amandine's pulse is growing thin and unsteady. Her brief convulsions are followed by long seconds when she doesn't breathe at all. Louchadière holds me back, while Nectaire and Savine rush to the patient's bedside.

"I don't expect you to send a helicopter," Lespinasse shouts. "I'm just asking you to get here as fast as you can."

In the corner of the room, I spot my doctor's bag, which Salomon borrowed from me to look after Amandine.

"Okay, they're on their way," the lieutenant announces at last, after hanging up. "They'll be here in about thirty minutes. Well, that's the optimistic estimate. They have no idea what road conditions will be like."

Nectaire freezes. Savine is holding Amandine's hand, trying to stop her from moving, which won't help at all. Amandine needs chest compressions, and she needs them now, but that alone will not be enough.

"I'm such a fucking idiot," Lespinasse hisses. "I can't believe I sent our only qualified first-aid worker to check on a suspect . . ."

Louchadière is still blocking my route to the bed. Are they too afraid to ask me? Do they dare try and stop me? I shove the sergeant out of the way and grab my bag.

"In less than a minute," I say, "Amandine will be short of oxygen. After two minutes, the consequences for the baby will be irreversible. After three minutes, mother and child will both be dead."

Louchadière panics. Lespinasse hesitates. Nectaire closes his eyes, and Savine's lips move in prayer.

Amandine, for her part, just lies there suffocating. After each convulsion, her apnea lasts longer and longer. One gap goes on so long, everyone looks like they think her heart has stopped for good.

"Do it," the lieutenant shouts.

I rush over.

"Nectaire, Savine, hold her still."

They press down on her arms with their whole-body weight. Louchadière and Lespinasse come over to take her legs. Too late for the heart massage.

"An injection of naloxone will calm her down," I say in an authoritative voice. "Her breathing will go back to normal. If the ambulance isn't here an hour from now, she'll need a second dose."

I act quickly. Every movement counts. Each one must be precise, assured.

Amandine, who can't weigh more than fifty kilos, starts twitching on the bed despite the quarter ton weighing down on her.

"Hold her! Now!"

Eight hands grip her as firmly as a vise, two on each arm, two on each leg. She is immobilized for a few seconds, long enough for me to stab the needle in her shoulder.

I exhale.

"Okay, you can let go now."

They all stare at me, still mistrustful.

Don't they understand that, even if I have committed acts of which I have no memory, right here, right now, I am Dr. Libéri, not Miss Hysteria? I can't stand their suspicious eyes. I toss the empty naloxone box in Lespinasse's face.

"Do you want to read the label?"

Not that there's any need. Amandine's condition has already visibly improved.

I put my hand on her belly. Her breathing is normal once again. She'll be okay. The baby too.

"Thank you."

Savine is the first one—the only one—to say it.

Louchadière sits down on the bed, as if wanting me to give her an injection too. Maybe something for anxiety. Nectaire holds Savine's hand. Lespinasse is looking at his cell phone.

"What the hell is taking Salomon so long?"

None of them, apart from Savine, dares look me in the eye. Who am I, to them?

A murderer or a heroine?

Or both?

It feels like fate is playing a dirty trick on me.

I have just saved the life of a mother and her child, a child about whom I know nothing.

And yet I couldn't save my own child.

Esteban, Tom . . . whatever you want to call him.

I am a doctor. I spent years studying, passed all my exams. I have healed hundreds of patients, have diagnosed cancer, heart failure, rare allergies, enabling dozens of strangers to survive. I have devoted my life to prolonging the lives of others. I have worked ten hours per day for thirty years. I have listened to people's complaints without ever complaining myself, have dealt with depressives without getting depressed, have treated cases of chronic fatigue without flagging . . .

And yet I couldn't prevent the death of the only person I cared about.

So maybe you are right, Lespinasse, Louchadière, Nectaire, and maybe you, too, Savine . . . Maybe Miss Hysteria does exist, does lurk somewhere deep within me, because Dr. Libéri is clearly cursed.

Doomed to heal everyone except the sole being she truly loves.

◆ ◆ ◆

Footsteps echo in the stairwell. Someone's coming upstairs.

The steps are light and graceful, barely even audible.

Could it be Salomon, who has already turned back, defeated by the storm on the Sancy?

Impossible: his footsteps would be five times louder.

Then who?

Who would dare come to La Souille in the middle of such a blizzard?

Five pairs of curious eyes turn to the bedroom door. We are almost expecting to see some fantastical beast enter the room, some supernatural being with a gift that has enabled it to brave this tempest.

We are not wrong.

A dark figure appears before us, flecked with thousands of snowflakes. When she shakes them off, there stands before us, dressed entirely in black, a witch.

59

Gabriel weaves through the corridors dug long ago by the caves' inhabitants, out of the surrounding rock formed from volcanic debris. Those people must have been dwarves, he thinks as he ducks, bends, or crouches with every step. Some of the corridors have collapsed, and he has to clear them by hand. In some places, the snow has poured in, blocking the way, and he is forced to turn back.

He memorized the map of it all beforehand, though, while examining the signs posted at the caves' entrance. The maze isn't as complicated as it seems, in fact. There are five floors, each containing rooms in various shapes and sizes, all arranged in neat lines. The more elaborate rooms have colonnades, skylights, alcoves carved into the stone. Some of the others are no more than bare cells where the local youngsters like to hang out, to judge from the empty beer bottles, plastic bags, and upturned crates Gabriel finds in there.

Gabriel is not cold. Curiously, the wind hardly seems to penetrate the corridors of these cliffside caves. Maybe those ancient builders had some understanding of insulation, achieving it through the habitations' orientation, by avoiding exposure to dominant winds or rainfall.

He continues on, while keeping himself hidden.

◆　◆　◆

Gabriel has reached the top floor and visited all the rooms but one. This room is separated from all the others by only a few meters, but you have to go outside again in order to enter it. He concentrates on his progress, trying not to graze his hands or bang his head. It must be weeks since anyone has crawled through these tunnels. Each dark bend hides a new trap: the volcanic rocks are sharper than the blade of the knife in his belt; the fragile stalactites are like swords suspended above his head, ready to fall at the smallest misstep.

Gabriel tries not to think too much, not to let his rage overflow. He is angry with Kuning, that handsome, honey-tongued psychiatrist; with Aster, that nosy old witch; obviously with Maddi, too, who has never given him the love he deserves. He is mad at the snow, the wind, the volcanoes. He is furious with this entire region, where it either doesn't snow enough or snows too much. He seethes at the whole world.

But he has to stay calm and clearheaded.

Finally, he glimpses a light at the end of the rocky passageway.

The tunnel ends there, ahead of him. He steps closer to the void and discovers a stunning view, far more striking than the one from his previous observation post. White volcanoes stretching into infinity, and a snowfall so powerful that it looks as though it won't stop until the craters have all been filled. In the dazzling fog, he can just make out, to the north, the massive outline of the Château de Murol and the spire of the Saint-Ferréol church.

He takes the time to orient himself. If he trusts in his memory of the map he consulted outside, then about twenty meters to his right, the wall of red tuff ought to open onto . . . the dying room, the place where corpses were stored in days gone by. The cave dwellers dug it so it would be separate from the rest of the village. So, they must have had some knowledge not just of insulation, but of hygiene too . . .

Gabriel decides to stay where he is, at the border between the tunnel and the snow outside. From there, he can watch the dying room: impossible to miss that hole carved into the sheer cliff. His partial view includes the limewashed wall and the bars blocking the entrance to its cavity. He knows he must resist the urge to get a better view by stepping outside, but his curiosity is so strong. The dying room is very close: he'd only have to climb up a few steps crudely carved into the cliff's edge to reach the stone platform outside its iron bars. He is about to do this—he already has one foot outside the tunnel—when he hears another cracking sound, very close by.

Instinctively, Gabriel grabs the handle of his knife. He isn't afraid; he is prepared for this. He knows that someone is bound to return. He just needs to be ready, completely ready, to spring when the moment comes. He listens, alert as a hound sniffing its prey. There are no more sounds, but Gabriel senses that his prey is there somewhere, hiding in those tunnels.

He moves slightly, pressing more closely against the wall of red volcanic rock. From his position, he cannot possibly be seen from below, or from outside. He, however, can survey the entire hole-ridden cliff face and, most importantly—outside, just above him, to the right—the barred entrance to the dying room. Gabriel slowly looks up at it.

He thinks he sees a shape move behind the iron bars. He squints in concentration. Thanks to the rocky overhang that partly protects the cliff face from snowfall, Gabriel has a perfectly unobstructed view of the white-walled cave.

At last, he spots the prisoner inside it. The curved figure advances toward the padlocked railings.

Gabriel observes him, scrutinizing every detail of his face, every expression, every gesture. The prisoner appears terrified, his fists gripping the iron bars as if he might be able to rip them out with his bare hands. His hair is soaked, his cheeks black from having been rubbed too often, his eyes red from shedding too many tears. He seems to have trouble standing straight, his feet slipping as he clings to the bars.

But despite all this, Tom is alive.

X

Incarceration

The Fountain of Souls

60

Aster's elegant boots leave little puddles of melted snow behind them in the hollows of the worn wooden floorboards. I must look at least as stunned as Lespinasse, Savine, and Louchadière. Only Nectaire seems unfazed by her sudden appearance.

Aster throws back her wide black hood, then shakes the last snowflakes from her long white hair.

"For Hecate's sake," she says with a smile, "it's not witch-friendly weather out there! My broomstick is completely frozen."

I register each person's reaction. Savine, sitting on the bed, listens distractedly to Aster while concentrating on Amandine's pulse, which is growing steadier. Nectaire observes his sister with fascination, apparently marveling that she is still capable of surprising him after more than forty years of living together. Sergeant Louchadière, on the other hand, stares through the window at the sky, perhaps searching for the white vapor trails left by a Nimbus 2000? Lespinasse is the first to speak.

"You walked here all the way from Besse?"

Aster unfastens her long cape.

"Amandine needs me. And, at the risk of blowing my own trumpet, Lieutenant, I'm not the kind of person to be daunted by a few snowflakes. I was born here. I know every mountain path. Snow is like people—it always gathers in the same places. All you have to do is avoid the most popular spots."

Lespinasse appears unconvinced by this. He looks out at the layer of snow covering the rooftops of Froidefond—more than thirty centimeters thick—and seems to be calculating how many times that ought to be multiplied to estimate the thickness of the powder snow covering the paths beyond. Three times? Five times?

Aster takes advantage of his silence to unbutton the black fur coat she is wearing under her cape. Rabbit, weasel, or skunk?

"You weren't born back then, kid, but let me tell you, the winter of '85 was a lot harsher than this little flurry. I was thirteen at the time, and it didn't stop me climbing up to Mont-Dore every day to bring my mother what she needed for her cooking pot. That snow lasted three months, not three hours, and yet every morning when the teacher took the class register, not a single child was absent."

Aster seems sincere. I have no trouble believing that if Nectaire sent her a text, she would be crazy enough to climb up to Froidefond on foot. And yet, oddly, I don't trust her. I feel as if she's not telling us the whole truth. Amandine is fine, Lespinasse assures her. The ambulance is on its way. She's resting.

"And Tom," replies the witch. "Is he fine too?"

Under the shelter of her fur coat, Aster is wearing her copper unalome, along with a leather cartridge belt, strapped to her chest, that contains a whole series of small glass vials.

"Listen to me, Lieutenant Leper-ass," she says. "I've known Amandine and Tom since they were born. I rocked that little girl in my arms, just as I rocked her son in my arms twenty years later. Just as I've done for most of the kids around here. As a little girl, Amandine was slightly more receptive to my stories than most of the others, a little less spoiled by television, ready-made meals, and laboratory-manufactured medicines. She's a stable, well-adjusted girl, whatever else many people think."

That's aimed at me. Aster stares at me with her dark eyes, then at Amandine's bed.

"So if you don't mind, I would like to look after her too."

She unhooks her cartridge belt. Jennifer Louchadière watches her but does nothing. Lespinasse scratches his beard and sighs, no doubt wondering how he's going to cope with a doctor who believes in reincarnation and a witness who wants to heal the victim with bewitched herbal remedies.

As soon as Aster moves, the lieutenant claps his hands. Clearly, he has decided to put his foot down.

"All right, that's enough. I called for an ambulance twenty minutes ago, and they should be here soon. In the meantime, I want everyone out of this room, including you two lovebirds!"

Savine and Nectaire look surprised when they realize that the lieutenant is addressing them. The gendarme turns to Aster with a look of determination.

"You too, woman, out! And before you clear off, pick up your test tubes. Jennifer, stay here and keep an eye on Amandine. Check her temperature, check her pulse, and come give me an update every five minutes. Dr. Libéri, come down to the living room with me. Maybe your memory's magically returned? Sit in a chair or lie on the couch again, I don't care, but we're going to start over from the beginning."

This tirade seems to have its intended effect. Even Aster doesn't talk back. But Lespinasse has barely had time enough to emit a sigh of relief and flash a self-satisfied smile when Nectaire's phone starts to ring.

The mayor's office secretary carries out his trademark technique of answering while putting the phone on loudspeaker.

"Hello?" says a voice that I recognize instantly. "You tried to contact me?"

No one says anything.

"This is Dr. Wayan Balik Kuning, from the university hospital in Le Havre. How can I help you?"

Lespinasse grabs the phone from Nectaire's hand and walks into a corner, though he's still close enough for us to hear the conversation.

"This is Lieutenant Lespinasse from the police station in Besse. I'm in charge of the investigation into the double homicide of Martin Sainfoin and Jonas Lemoine. I'm glad to hear from you, Doctor, because I have quite a few questions for you. But first, I want you to listen to me."

In a loud voice, making no attempt to close the door or go into a different room, the lieutenant outlines the situation in clipped, quasi-military tones.

"All right . . . so what can I do for you?" Wayan asks.

Without answering him, the gendarme continues his account, listing my obsessions, my theories on reincarnation. I feel certain that he is deliberately talking this loudly so that I—and everyone else—can hear every word he says.

Wayan, meanwhile, listens, punctuating the end of each of Lespinasse's sentences with his usual *mmm-hmm*s.

I have heard that sound so many times before.

Where is Wayan? I have tried calling him several times since last night, and so has Nectaire apparently. Wayan, in turn, tried calling me this morning. Is he at his office in Le Havre? Why wouldn't he be? Or maybe he's by the sea somewhere, in Sainte-Adresse, Etretat, or Antifer . . . He always loved strolling along the beach. But no, what I hear in the background of their conversation is a song, as if Wayan is listening to the radio. Is he in his car? Or at the home of one of his mistresses?

"In summary, Doctor," Lespinasse says at last, "I think you know what I'm asking you. You have been Maddi Libéri's therapist for more than ten years. So my question is simple: Is she . . . sane?"

Thankfully, Wayan does not reply immediately. In the silence that follows, I hear the song end and a commercial begin. Wayan clears his throat. His voice is deep, composed, beautifully formal.

"Since you are asking me to be precise, I will make this as clear as possible, Lieutenant. Maddi Libéri is perfectly sane."

Thank you, Wayan.

"She went through a very painful grieving process," explains my favorite psychiatrist. "I treated her for many years. And I can affirm that my patient does not suffer from any form of schizophrenia, paranoia, or bipolar disorder."

Thank you, Wayan.

"While her behavior might strike you as strange, that is purely because of the events in her life. And with all due respect, Lieutenant, it is your job to make sense of those events, however incredible and inexplicable they might be. However, deciding that you can close your investigation by attributing all its ambiguities and inconsistencies to my patient's supposed insanity would not only be a grave professional error on your part. It would also, and above all, have the unforgivable consequence of leaving the real criminal at large."

Thank you, Wayan.

Lespinasse reacts as though he's been punched in the face. Wayan was sufficiently clear that his medical opinion cannot be doubted. I regret that he is so far away, in Normandy, and I wish now that I'd said yes to his generous offer before (*Just say the word, and I'll be there*), that I had not treated him with such contempt, as if he were an overly clingy admirer.

Wayan is a nice guy and a good psychiatrist, and for one night— just a single night of mutual debauchery—he'd also proved himself an excellent lover.

A long silence falls between the psychiatrist and the policeman. The only sound is the crackling radio playing in the background. A jingle blares at the end of the commercial. Then I hear a woman's voice:

"Be careful out there, everybody. Traffic conditions throughout the region are appalling. This is France Bleu Auvergne. Don't turn that dial!"

61

Tom has retreated to the back of the cave, to the corner most distant from the iron bars. It's darker there, and less cold too. He doesn't know how long he's been in this place. Several hours at least, although there's no way for him to check since he left his watch on the nightstand in his bedroom when he went out to join Esteban last night.

There's a nightstand here, too, in his white prison. And a bed, covered by three thick blankets. When he gets underneath them, he doesn't feel cold at all. When he tries to get up, which he does even though he still feels so tired, the warmth of the fireplace envelops him. It fills the entire corner of the room, and there's enough firewood to keep it blazing until summer. At the foot of the bed is a pile of books: *Twenty Thousand Leagues Under the Sea*, *Robinson Crusoe*, *Treasure Island*. He hasn't opened any of them. He's too exhausted. On the other hand, he has devoured the packets of cookies, the fruit, and the bar of chocolate that were arranged beside them.

Tom looks up. This time, he feels certain. He heard a noise. Last time, its source was a fox. To catch a glimpse of it, he'd had to stand still behind the bars for an eternity. A beautiful silver fox, as in a fairy tale. Is it the fox again?

Tom walks silently back to the barred window, even though it's a struggle to lift his feet. For a long time, he stares at the white landscape. He senses that the snowstorm is abating; a faint light is now illuminating the Château de Murol. Other wells of brightness pierce the sky above the isolated hamlets. Tom stares wide-eyed, on the lookout for the smallest detail, even if he can hardly stand now, even if his eyes sting and he still wants to cry . . .

"Hey, Tom. Pssst."

Tom stiffens, his hands tensed around the frozen metal bars. Was he dreaming? Did someone really call him? Well, it couldn't be the fox! A fox, even a silver one from a fairy tale, couldn't sp—

"Tom, I'm here. Give me your hand."

Tom turns to the right. His face lights up instantly with a big smile. "Esteban!"

"Grab my hand quick, before I fall!"

Tom slips his hand between the bars and grips the gloved hand that Esteban is holding out to him. The boy, balanced precariously on the narrow ledge of the cliff, steps forward carefully, then finally reaches the small platform outside Tom's prison.

The boys stand face to face, separated only by the bars.

"You came back, then? You didn't just forget about me this time?"

"No! Of course not. Why would you think that?"

"Are you . . . are you really alive?"

"Didn't you feel my hand when you held it?"

"Yes . . . but I could have invented that."

Esteban gives a heavy sigh, pretending to be annoyed.

"I walked three kilometers through the snow! I'm soaked, freezing, and shattered. The sick bastard who locked you up here is probably still prowling around nearby. And that's how you welcome me? Like I just popped out of your head?"

Tom hesitates. He feels lost. He puts his hand between the bars again and touches Esteban's frosted hair, his wet nose, his chapped lips.

"If I came straight out of your head, why would you bother putting me in a hat and gloves? You could just make me appear in swim shorts."

"Idiot!"

All the same, Tom now pictures Esteban in the indigo trunks he wore at their first meeting, in the swimming pool locker room. He concentrates, frowning. If he can undress this boy with his thoughts alone, that would mean he's just a figment of Tom's imagination.

"You've got to be kidding, right?" Esteban says with a smile. "You're really trying to strip me naked in weather like this?"

"You're getting on my nerves. I don't know if you're real or not anymore. If you're really real, prove it to me."

Esteban suddenly looks serious.

"How?"

"You know how. By getting me out of here."

With the little strength remaining to him, Tom starts to shake the rusted iron bars. Esteban, on the other side, does the same thing. But no matter how hard they grip the bars and shake, no matter how many times they do it, the bars don't budge a centimeter.

"I'm useless," sighs Tom. "I should have imagined a more muscular ghost, like Hulk or Iron Man."

Esteban snickers.

"My body is your body, remember. If you'd done boxing instead of swimming and cycling, maybe I'd be more muscular."

Tom puts his two arms out between the bars.

"Maybe I could start by fighting you?"

Esteban carefully steps back, to the edge of the platform, perilously close to the four-story drop. He takes off his backpack. As he starts to open it, he grins up at Tom.

"No more fighting. Look; I've got a surprise for you."

62

The voice from the radio continues to whirl inside my head, like a commercial jingle played on repeat.

This is France Bleu Auvergne. Don't turn that dial!

So Wayan is not in Normandy.

Wayan followed me here.

Is that why he wasn't answering my calls? Did he drive down here because I wasn't answering his? Where is he now? Stuck somewhere in the middle of the A71 highway with thousands of other motorists? But then why wouldn't he tell Lieutenant Lespinasse that? Why let a radio presenter betray his whereabouts?

I am not the only one wondering all this. Savine and Nectaire silently exchange a glance, like Miss Marple and Poirot, but Lespinasse reacts instantly. He walks away holding the phone, and I realize that the rest of the conversation between the two men will be private. He puts his hand over the phone's microphone and orders Jennifer Louchadière to "keep watch." I see him, cell phone glued to his ear again, walk along the upstairs landing, then close Tom's bedroom door behind him.

Sergeant Jennifer Louchadière proudly carries out her duty, watching us warily. She paces around Amandine's bedroom, looking suspicious, as if Nectaire and Savine, sitting calmly on the edge of the bed, might suddenly rise to their feet; as if I, stuck in the corner, may be about to make a run for it; or as if Aster, sorting through her vials on the small table, could very well turn around and—

Suddenly, Louchadière freezes, like a hunting dog scenting prey: Aster has just turned around.

Having chosen one of the vials, the witch moves toward Amandine's bed. The sergeant immediately stands in her way.

"Not another step!"

Aster opens her arms wide, the vial gripped tightly in her right hand.

"Jennifer, I've known you since you were knee-high to a grasshopper! Please get out of my way."

Jennifer trembles, but does not budge.

"Sorry, Aster, but you're a suspect. And you know why. You didn't call us until more than twenty minutes after you found Jonas Lemoine's corpse. We traced your phone. And you have refused to explain why. Not to mention that the knife used to kill Jonas came from your store . . ."

Aster takes another step, vial in hand. I watch from the corner of the room. Savine and Nectaire, sitting side by side on Amandine's bed like two shy young newlyweds, have not moved.

"Someone stole that knife, Jennifer; I told the police that. In fact, they stole two knives."

"That . . . that doesn't change the stuff about your alibi," the sergeant stammers. "Why didn't you call us as soon as you found Jonas's body?"

"Maybe I was hoping I could bring him back to life? You've always considered me a witch, haven't you, Jennifer? I remember how much you loved my stories when I told them at the school. Of all the kids there, you were the one who was most enchanted by them. Maybe that's even why you became a gendarme?"

I observe all this, silent and unmoving. Who will win? My money's on Nectaire's sister. What chance does young Jennifer have against a witch? I really have no idea what Aster wants to do, though.

The sergeant bends but doesn't break.

"Maybe, Aster, but that still doesn't change anything . . ."

"Yes, it does. It changes everything."

At last, Aster opens her hand. The vial in her palm contains a pale red liquid. A few drops of blood diluted in water? Louchadière's eyes mist over.

"Remember, Jennifer? Some say this water comes straight from the center of the earth. Others call it the tears of hell. I told you that story many times, didn't I? The Froidefond spring. The Fountain of Souls."

The sergeant looks out of her depth. Her eyes flicker with panic. She takes a step back, puts her hand on the holster of her Sig Pro, and appears to think about calling out to her superior officer for help.

"Don't . . . don't take another step."

"Listen, Jennifer. I'm going to tell you what I was doing during those twenty minutes, since you're so obsessed by them. I went to fill this bottle at the Fountain of Souls. I'm sure you haven't forgotten its powers . . ."

"N-no."

"When I got back to Jonas, he was very close to death. I made him drink a few drops of this water from the bottle. As a result, this water that I am holding now contains his soul."

Louchadière appears hypnotized by Aster's calm self-assurance. Her eyes are drawn inexorably to the copper unalome hanging between the witch's breasts. She steps back again, staring at Aster as if she were holding a grenade with the pin out, her fingers tensed around the butt of her pistol.

"You understand, don't you, Jennifer? Amandine has to drink a few drops of this water, from the same bottle. And the father's soul will migrate into the child inside her. You realize I don't have a choice, right? You realize how rare it is that all the conditions should come together like this, the father dying before the child is born? You do understand that we have to do this? For Amandine. For Jonas. For their future child. So that Jonas's soul doesn't migrate to the end of the world, and so that the soul of this child in Amandine's belly is not the soul of a stranger. So that they can be reunited in a single body. All of that was worth my making a brief detour, don't you think? A quick twenty-minute trip so that Jonas could, after dying, come back to life, here, at La Souille?"

Aster seems sure she's won. The story about the Fountain of Souls sounds like a fairy tale, and yet how can I of all people really question it? Neither Savine nor Nectaire makes the slightest movement.

"Move aside, Jennifer," Aster says. "Let me do it."

Aster pushes the sergeant out of the way and carries out a series of precise, resolute movements. She leans over Amandine, wedging her hand behind the patient's neck to lift her head without waking her, then uncorks the vial and raises it toward Amandine's open mouth.

In a flash, I see Jennifer Louchadière regain her balance, unholster her gun, and aim it at the witch's back.

"Stop, Aster! Stop this nonsense now or I'll shoot."

63

Tom's eyes grow wide.

"A surprise? For me?"

Esteban continues rummaging inside his backpack, balanced between the platform and the void, apparently without any feelings of vertigo. Tom, to the contrary, can see the landscape swaying before his eyes. His vision blurs as soon as he tries to focus on a point in the distance: the church spire, the castle keep, a snowy peak. If he weren't holding on to the iron bars, he would collapse. His legs can barely hold him up.

He wants to cry. He's so stupid! When will he admit that the boy in front of him is just a ghost? Would a living child really take so many risks for him? Climbing the cliff to get up here. Braving the cold and the snow. Only a true friend would do that. And Tom doesn't have any friends. Apart from the ones in his head.

And yet . . . He'd felt Esteban's gloved hand in his; he'd helped him climb up to that ledge. If Tom was really inventing it all, then he would know what Esteban is looking for inside his backpack, what he's about to take out. An imaginary friend can't surprise you. An imaginary friend doesn't wake you in the middle of the night to give you a birthday present. An imaginary friend is just a shoulder to cry on. He helps you to accept your nightmares, when they carry on after you've woken. He helps you to accept death, when that is all you have to hope for.

Tom feels tiredness overwhelming him, but he still finds enough strength to make a joke.

"Do you have a key, Steb?" The nickname falls naturally from his lips the first time he says it. "You are going to get me out of here, right?"

Esteban's hands are still deep inside his backpack, as if what he's seeking is both fragile and precious.

"No . . . sorry. Actually, do you know the name of the room you're locked up in?"

Tom looks at the limewashed walls around him.

"The white room?" he guesses.

"Nope! It's called the dying room. This is where they used to bring all the corpses, back in the caveman days."

Tom can't believe his ears. How could he have invented such a sadistic friend?

"I thought you came here to help me."

"I'm going to . . . Look what I found!"

Tom can't believe his eyes. Esteban is holding a small bottle of reddish water.

"You remember?" he says. "You told me about it, by the fountain. This water is from the Fountain of Souls. Just swallow a few drops, and if things don't go well, I promise I'll give the rest to your mother to drink."

If things don't go well? Is that really what his friend said? Does that mean he's going to be murdered too? Like his dad yesterday, and like Martin before?

"Go on," says Esteban. "It's not a big deal. When your mom gives birth, you'll be reincarnated in the baby. You won't have to do anything at all for four or five months. Sure, you'll have to wear diapers again, and learn to crawl and ride a bike, relearn everything from scratch basically, but there are loads of advantages too."

Tom can't tell if his friend is serious, or if he's making fun of him.

"Think about it, Tommy. You'll forget that Santa Claus doesn't exist, that you're scared of bees. Who knows, you might even become . . . a girl!"

Tom shakes the bars with one last surge of energy and hysteria. He already feels like a baby trapped inside the bars of a crib.

"This isn't funny, Esteban. Get me out of here!"

"Okay, I'll try; I promise."

He pauses, as if he heard another sound nearby . . . As if someone, in hiding, were spying on them.

"But first," says Esteban, lifting the bottle between two bars, "take a quick drink. Because you never know . . ."

64

"Stand back, Aster. Don't make me shoot."

Sergeant Jennifer Louchadière is still aiming her pistol at the witch, hands tightly gripping the butt of her Sig Pro, forefinger tensed around the trigger. Nectaire and Savine are on their feet now, close to Aster, but she stubbornly refuses to move away from Amandine.

"Please, Astie," Nicky begs her.

"Put the bottle away," Savine says.

"I'm not going to let you pour that filth in her mouth," the sergeant says threateningly.

Everyone has forgotten about me. I could leave and no one would notice. Aster is still holding the vial of red water in her hand, a few centimeters from Amandine's pale lips. She turns to stare at the policewoman, not daring to lift the bottle any higher but refusing to put it down.

"Jennifer," the witch pleads, "don't you understand? Some things are beyond our control."

Suddenly I feel as if a window has been opened.

Some things are beyond our control. Is that really what Aster just said? An icy blast hits my chest.

I've heard that phrase before. Yesterday morning. And it was Tom who said it.

The gust through the open window seems to sweep away years of dust to expose the naked truth: Tom and Esteban were bewitched.

Someone put these ideas into their heads, these tales about the migration of souls, the drowned world under the sea, water from hell, resurrection, reincarnation.

It was so obvious, now that I think about it.

A child's brain is like modeling clay. Who else other than Aster could have kneaded their minds into these insane shapes?

Jennifer Louchadière is still aiming her gun at Nectaire's sister. Has the policewoman understood too?

I am not the crazy one here. Aster is.

"What the hell's going on here?"

The voice thunders behind us. Lespinasse appears, cell phone pressed to his ear. Instantly, Jennifer lowers her pistol a few centimeters, and Aster takes two steps back.

The lieutenant stands directly in front of me. Is he still on the phone with Wayan? What could my former psychiatrist have told him? I have absolute trust in Wayan. Or at least, I had absolute trust . . . until I learned he was hiding somewhere in Auvergne.

"Your shrink just hung up on me!" he says irritably. "Either that or the line went dead. I called him back, but he's not answering."

His arm drops to his side, as if the phone weighed a ton.

"On the other hand," Lespinasse goes on, "Deputy Salomon just called me back. He's at your place, the Moulin de Chaudefour. I'm afraid he had to break a window to get inside."

This startles me. Why would he break a window? If he'd just rung the doorbell, Gabriel would have let him in.

"He's searched every room," the lieutenant continues. "It took a while, believe me. But he's absolutely certain. Gabriel is not there."

I feel as if the ceiling were spinning above my head. As if Aster were flying into the air, followed by Jennifer with her raised pistol, while Nectaire and Savine cling to the bars of the bed to stop themselves from being pulled upward too.

Of course Gabriel is at the Moulin! Where else would he be? Gabriel would not have gone out in this weather. He can spend hours, even days, in front of his computer. He would have told me if something serious had happened, something that had forced him to leave the house. I have absolute trust in Gabriel . . . don't I?

"Dr. Libéri," says Lespinasse, "where is Gabriel?"

The room is silent. I feel as if all the air has been sucked out of it. My thoughts become tangled in Lespinasse's thick beard, his bushy eyebrows, his dark gaze.

Should I speak? Reveal my secret? Do I have a choice?

"This is important, Madame Libéri. Do you have any idea where Gabriel could have gone?"

Will this madness ever end? Will the dead bodies keep piling up? How many crimes will I have on my conscience before they realize I need to be locked up?

"Madame Libéri, can you hear me? Can you give us any clue as to where he might be?"

I whisper. Maybe there is still one life I can save . . .

"Y-yes."

65

"Don't drink it all!"

Tom has swallowed half the water. He gives the bottle back to Esteban.

"Calm down. I'm not an idiot, you know."

Half the liquid still remains in the bottle—the same quantity for his mother as for himself. The red water doesn't taste bad. It's slightly metallic and slightly fizzy, like Coke if you don't screw the cap on properly.

"See, that wasn't so hard, was it?" says Esteban. "Now nothing bad can happen to you."

Tom wipes his mouth with his jacket sleeve. The red water has revived him a little. He looks up through the bars at the white sky. The mountain and the forests still resemble a fairy-tale landscape, full of ogres and hungry wolves.

"Thanks, Steb. Although I'd still rather not go through all that baby stuff again . . ."

Esteban laughs, and—for the first time since being locked up in the dying room—so does Tom.

"We'll still be friends if that happens, you know, although you'll be ten years younger than me. When I'm fifteen, you'll be a little five-year-old. So don't be jealous if I get all the girls, okay?"

"Ha ha . . ."

Suddenly they fall silent.

A new sound has just rung out, to their left, near the entrance to the cave complex. Is someone coming, slowly, furtively? Tom feels a cold gust of wind. When he talks with Esteban, he forgets all the rest—the cold, his fear—but as soon as something disturbs them, he starts to shiver again; he is terrified, freezing.

He quickly returns his attention to the entrance of his white prison, convinced that if he momentarily loses his concentration, his imaginary friend may vanish as quickly as he appeared.

But no, he was worrying about nothing. Esteban is still there, carefully putting the bottle of red water back in his pocket. It was probably just that silver fox, Tom thinks. Unless he invented that animal too . . .

"Steb! Steb!"

Tom shakes the bars again, but there's no belief behind the action. He has already tried unfastening the heavy padlock a hundred times.

"Steb, now I'm immortal, you need to get me out of here. You promised you would."

Esteban is fastening the straps of his backpack.

"I promised to try . . ."

"So, what are you waiting for? Try!"

Another cracking sound, even louder than before. Impossible to know where it came from, because it echoes through the caverns. Only one thing is certain: whoever made that noise is very close.

Esteban is up on his feet.

"I have to go, Tom. If I get caught, too, we'll be completely screwed."

Esteban has already begun walking back between the slippery stones and the footprints that he left in the snow on his way here.

"No, don't leave me."

Tom doesn't raise his voice. It's a prayer, spoken in a whisper.

Esteban takes one last look at him.

"Don't worry. I'm going to hide, but I won't be far away. It's the only way I can get you out of here. When whoever locked you up comes back, I'll attack him. Don't worry; I'm armed."

"No!" Tom begs.

Tears spring from the corners of his eyes. He wants Esteban to stay where he can see him. If he disappears, Tom knows that one second later, he'll feel sure the boy was nothing but a hallucination.

"Esteban, look at me. Swear to me you're not a ghost."

The boy raises his hand and flashes a confident smile.

"I swear it."

Tom has to remember that.

"Wait, wait . . . Last night, before you disappeared at the Froidefond bridge, you told me that your real name wasn't Esteban . . ."

The boy casts an anxious glance at the entrance to the cave, then at the other openings around him.

"Now isn't a good time, Tom."

Tom presses his face against the iron bars. His tears roll down the rusty metal.

"You have to tell me now! In case you don't come back. In case I die and become a baby again, and forget everything . . . Please, it'll only take a second. What's your name?"

66

Lieutenant Lespinasse hangs up on Salomon, drops his cell phone into his pocket, and grabs me by the collar.

"Quickly. Every second counts, Dr. Libéri. Where is he? Where's Gabriel?"

All eyes in the room—except for Amandine's, still closed in sleep—converge on me.

Savine looks perplexed, as if I've destroyed her fragile trust in me.

Aster, herded patiently but insistently by Nectaire, has moved away from the bed. Jennifer Louchadière's Sig Pro is now aimed only at the dusty floor.

Lespinasse grips me too tightly. He no longer resembles the friendly monk I imagined when this investigation began.

In a strangled voice, I reply, "I . . . I don't know exactly where he is, but . . . but I can find him."

"Sorry?"

He practically picks me up; his hands are nearly choking me. I can sense that he is suppressing the urge to hit me. *Let me speak, for God's sake! I'm as scared as you are about what might happen . . .* I try to breathe between each gasped word.

"There's a . . . GPS . . . tracking device . . . sewn into . . . his jacket."

The lieutenant immediately puts me down.

"You sewed a GPS tracer into the lining of Gabriel's jacket?"

I take a deep breath. I shoot another mistrustful look at Aster. Should I speak in front of her? My cell phone is tucked safely away at the bottom of my pocket; she can't take it from me. So what am I afraid of?

"Yes, Lieutenant. A tracking device. Three clicks online and you can control it. It's no bigger than a SIM card. Permanently connected to my phone. They sell millions of the things every year, for elderly people with dementia, hikers who don't have a compass, or even dogs without leashes."

For the first time in a long time, Savine speaks.

"But Gabriel doesn't have Alzheimer's. And he's certainly not a dog."

I roll my eyes. I'm sick of people judging me by their stupid moral standards. I try to explain.

"I . . . I work a lot. All day long. Gabriel is alone almost all the time. I trust him, but you never know. He might tell me that he stayed at the Moulin all day when in fact he went to—"

"Oh, who cares!" Lespinasse interrupts. "Give me your phone so we can find out where he's hiding."

67

"Please," Tom repeats. "Tell me your name."

He's pressed his face so hard against the iron bars, they've probably left stripes on his face. He is crying, pleading, stamping his feet. He doesn't want his ghost to forget him. Around him, everything is as white as death. Esteban continues to walk cautiously back toward the caverns.

"Don't abandon me!"

Esteban stops for a moment, balanced on the unstable staircase dug into the cliff face. He reaches under his anorak and proudly pulls out a knife.

"I told you, Tommy; I'm staying here. And I can fight for both of us."

The iron bars constrict Tom's chest. The steel padlock pushes against his belly. He feels as if he could become a ghost, too, as if he could pass through this cage, evaporating and then solidifying again on the other side. But only in movies can people do things just by imagining them.

Tom pulls ever harder at the bars. His face squeezes between them, the metal tightening around his cheeks, squashing his ears. He's like a half-deflated balloon, about to explode. His mouth twists. His temples buzz. The cold iron grips his brain like a vise.

"Please! I just want to know your name."

Esteban goes down another three steps. He's almost at the cave entrance. He flashes a big smile, then calls out four words before disappearing.

"My name is Gabriel!"

XI

Resolution

Safety Trace

68

"Give me your phone," Lespinasse repeats.

This time I don't argue. I hold out my phone to the lieutenant.

"Seriously, though?" Jennifer whistles. "Bugging her own boyfriend?"

I stare at her, stunned by her confusion. I realize that, unlike Savine, Nectaire, and Aster, she has never seen Gabriel. He's hardly been out of the Moulin de Chaudefour since we arrived, apart from turning up at the cemetery for Martin Sainfoin's funeral . . . and going swimming at the Hermines pool.

For all those who have not yet understood, I make things clear.

"Gabriel is not my boyfriend. He's my son. And he's only ten."

They all stare pityingly. I hate the guilt they make me feel. I hold on to my phone for a moment longer.

"Don't judge me, Lieutenant. Nor you, Savine. I love Gabriel. He's the flesh of my flesh. Without him, I'd have gone crazy ages ago. But you have no idea what it's like to raise a ten-year-old child on your own. A child I gave birth to barely four months after losing my first son. A child who is so different . . ."

I turn away from their eyes. I stare at the bare bulb dangling from the ceiling, the blistered paint on the walls, the straw curtains at the windows, before my eyes widen with shock.

Outside, the snow is blue.

I tense my fingers around the phone. In Amandine's room, all the others stop and look out at the azure gleam on the snow in the courtyard, as if the sky had trickled down onto the ground.

Savine is the first to react.

"The ambulance! Finally . . ."

She's right. The blue haloes, projected onto the white screen of the houses of Froidefond, whirl around as first an ambulance and then a fire truck drive into the farmyard. They've come in force, following the first rule of traveling through a storm: never go alone.

"Wait for me!" Lespinasse barks.

Louchadière presses her face to the window. Savine holds Amandine's hand and mutters a few soothing words. "It'll be okay; it'll be okay." Nectaire watches Aster.

Nobody's paying any attention to me.

I glance down at my phone for a moment. The SafetyTrace map appears on the screen. Gabriel is just a small red dot. I'm so used to checking the app during my brief pauses at work and never seeing that dot move away from the Moulin de Chaudefour that it takes me a few seconds to locate it.

The red dot has not gone far. It is flashing three kilometers from the Moulin, according to the map. Over toward a neighboring village. Saint-Pierre-Colamine.

What on earth is Gabriel doing there? I curse my imprudence. Before leaving the Moulin this morning, I made Gabriel's breakfast, squeezed an orange, took the butter out of the fridge, toasted some bread, and left a note on the table: *Have a nice day, goblin.* I didn't even open his bedroom door, for fear I might wake him.

If only I'd known . . .

Everything went so fast after that. Too fast.

I hear Lespinasse, at the foot of the stairs, welcoming the paramedics. I see Louchadière waving through the window. *Up here, up here!*

I look back at the red dot. My son is in Saint-Pierre-Colamine, less than three kilometers from Froidefond. Through the open door of Amandine's bedroom, I assess the length of the upstairs landing that leads to Tom's bedroom door, also open.

In a fraction of a second, my decision has been made.

I warned the cops, but they weren't able to protect Tom, any more than they'd been able to find Esteban.

I have to act. Alone, this time.

I drop my phone into my pocket. I hear Lespinasse and the paramedics starting to climb the stairs.

Now.

I breathe in and sprint through the narrow corridor. The last image I retain from Amandine's bedroom is of Savine's disappointed expression when she sees me running.

Doesn't matter. Don't look back.

I burst into Tom's room. Lespinasse is still only halfway up the stairs. I can't help glancing at the model of the drowned village under the bed. The cops haven't touched a thing. It is the bedroom, frozen in time, of a dead child who will never return. How many days and nights did I spend weeping in an identical mausoleum?

Not this time. I must not slow down. I must think only of Gabriel.

The mattress is still leaning against the wall. Perfect for sleeping on your feet, Nectaire would probably joke. I shoulder open the rotted wood of the window frames. No time to think about the way it hurts my shoulder blade: I grab the mattress in both hands, balance it on the window ledge, lie on it, gripping the sides, and let myself tip forward . . .

There's no danger.

I have another fraction of a second to persuade myself of that.

The barn is only a few meters beneath the window. The mattress and the snow will cushion my fall onto the roof.

A fraction of a second . . . before the mattress bounces off the barn, throwing me off, catching and tearing at two broken beams as I continue to slide. I flip over and land in a meter of fresh snow, at the foot of the old henhouse. My fall made no noise. Feathers rain down from the broken mattress, blending into the falling snowflakes. Nobody has seen me go. The flashing lights of the emergency vehicles paint the polar backdrop with a surreal fluorescent-blue glow, like an artificial aurora borealis.

Quick . . . I swim more than crawl through the snowdrift and hide behind one of the pillars. I take a second to check that the bandages on my head haven't been messed up; then I advance through the empty farmyard, doing my best to stay as concealed as possible.

I cross the road, or at least what I assume must be the road. The sky and the soft ground look so similar that I feel as if I were entering a giant chrysalis. I see the Fountain of Souls, also completely covered with snow. Only the red water is still flowing, digging a well in the snow that appears to descend all the way to the center of the earth.

I hear yelling behind me. I don't have time to listen, to work out whether it's coming from Louchadière, Lespinasse, or Nectaire, to imagine them aiming their guns at me, to wonder whether they will dare come after me. I rush through the alleys of Froidefond. Off to one side, I spot a lean-to beside what looks like an abandoned house. I take refuge in there, checking to see that nobody is following me. Enough time to take out my cell phone. To search for the red dot.

Gabriel.

The application locates me almost instantly, calculating the distance that separates me from my son. Two thousand eight hundred meters.

Barely a thirty-minute walk moving in a direct line.

I set off.

I enter the gently sloping field, eyes riveted to my 4G compass. Nobody else can possibly know where Gabriel is. Nobody can know where I'm going. Do I even know myself?

I make rapid progress. I understand how Aster managed to reach La Souille on foot, how Salomon was able to climb up to the Moulin: the roads are almost impossible to drive on, but the snow is soft enough to pack under my soles, forming a sort of magic staircase, new steps hardening beneath me with each stride.

Two thousand one hundred meters.

I'm already one-fourth of the way there. The gusts of snow have almost stopped; only a few snowflakes spiral lazily down from the sky now. I'm not cold, even though I'm only wearing a sweater. My coat is still hanging on the coatrack in the entrance hall of La Souille. I didn't even think about that as I dived out through the window.

Oh well . . . The bandages on my head at least protect me from the snowstorm's final blasts, even if Salomon tied them on too tightly. I can feel my blood beating against my temples, the bandages squeezing my brain, making me dizzy. I ignore the spinning sensation, and it stops anyway as soon as I look up from the phone screen.

I have to keep looking at it, though, have to continue going in the correct direction: straight ahead. Saint-Pierre-Colamine. I push away regret as I pull aside the frozen branch that blocks my path: I should have bought Gabriel a cell phone of his own; I shouldn't have told him he had to wait for his sixteenth birthday, or until college, or whatever excuse I used. I should have trusted my son, should have given him a phone instead of sewing a tracking device into his jacket. That's what any normal mother would have done . . .

I pull aside another branch. The field is sloping more steeply now.

One thousand nine hundred meters. Straight ahead.

But I'm not a normal mother. My son was kidnapped ten years ago. Nobody ever believed me, but I always knew. A cell phone is no use against a kidnapper; the only real way to find a kidnapped child is a hidden tracker.

One thousand eight hundred meters.

The snow suddenly feels more compact. I am still advancing cautiously when the red dot on the screen suddenly vanishes and is replaced by a blue rectangle.

A message.

Of course, Lespinasse, Nectaire, and the others must be searching for me. I've only made things worse in their eyes by running away. I read the message while I walk, paying attention to both activities. The slope is growing ever steeper, and a few rocks poke out through the snow.

Sorry, Maddi. I really wanted to help you. But all the roads are closed south of Clermont. You see, I am not perfect. I was so desperate to prove to you that I'm the kind of man capable of abandoning everything to follow the woman he loves. I came up fifty kilometers short.

Despite the cold, despite everything, I smile. It's very kind of you, Wayan, but now is not the best time. I tick off a mystery in my head—at least I understand why he was listening to France Bleu Auvergne now. Wayan simply wanted to pay me a visit, but did not anticipate the snowstorm. He drove all the way across France for nothing . . . How ironic.

I watch as Wayan's message disappears and is replaced by the map, the red dot. It's a shame he couldn't reach me. Wayan is one of the few people I might have been able to trust. Gabriel needs him, too, even if they have never met. I concentrate on the SafetyTrace app, my finger clicking on the menu, and for a moment I stop thinking about the steepness of the slope, the snow, the invisible rocks . . .

My foot slips, I fall, and I roll several meters downhill. Just before my face smashes into a rock below, I let go of my phone and wrap my arms around my head. Wind blowing, snow whipping, rock against flesh.

Thankfully, the snowdrift slowed me down, and I escape with nothing worse than a few bruises on my wrist. I have to keep going. But first, I need to find my phone . . . I have to stand up. I'm only two kilometers away from him.

I climb to my feet and, stunned at what I see, fall back onto my butt. *What an idiot . . .*

The path ahead is cut off. The field leads to a ravine, a sheer drop of thirty meters. It's impossible to descend, especially in weather like this and without any equipment. I stare down at the rock-strewn void, a few trees, the waterfall, which I can hear, muffled, distant, and buried under snow.

What a fucking idiot!

I measured the distance on my GPS—2,800 meters—and set off on the shortest route without searching for the fastest, without thinking about the fact that I live in the mountains, that between my blue dot and Gabriel's red dot, there might be summits, rivers, canyons, craters. There's no point hoping I can get any farther this way; I need to turn around and walk back to Froidefond, to the road . . . where the police will undoubtedly stop me.

But maybe that's the best solution? Maybe I should put my trust in the police this time. My sweater is soaked, as are my T-shirt and my underwear. I'll be frozen solid in less than fifteen minutes. And I'm wasting precious time. I'm messing everything up. If only I'd handed my cell phone to Lieutenant Lespinasse when he told me to, Gabriel would already be safe by now. I should call them. I should . . .

On all fours, I start digging frantically in the snow. I'm like some desperate animal now, digging its own hole, scratching and clawing with my frozen fingers.

I have dug away almost all the snow around my legs, without finding anything. I'm in despair, on the verge of cracking up. I realize suddenly that every handful of snow I move might just as easily be burying my cell phone even deeper.

I'm just some frantically burrowing animal that weeps, curses, prays.

On my knees.

Has any god heard me?

I lower my eyes. Through the whiteness, I think I can make out a dark, geometric shape.

Euphoric, I push aside the thin layer of snow.

Thank you, thank you, thank you.

Like a heart beating under the ice, a small red dot flashes before my eyes.

69

It took me less than five minutes to get back to Froidefond. I walked in my own footprints, certain this time that I would not get lost, certain that I wouldn't slip, galvanized by the cold spreading through my drenched clothes, driven by the fear that I would be transformed into an ice statue if I slowed down.

I promised myself I would call the police as soon as I reached the hamlet. That I would go back to La Souille. That I would give myself up . . .

Two thousand eight hundred meters.

The red dot hasn't moved. The tracking device is sewn into Gabriel's jacket, and in weather like this, he's bound to be wearing it. Only his mother would be reckless enough to go out in nothing but a sweater in the middle of a snowstorm.

◆ ◆ ◆

I am approaching the first houses in Froidefond when, just ahead of me, the Fountain of Souls lights up. As if I had triggered a movement sensor.

I don't understand. I look up. The stones of the fountain light up and then go dark, again and again, like an insistent miracle. I keep going, a few more meters, then notice the 4x4 parked just in front of the fountain.

Savine's Koleos.

She leans over and opens the passenger door as I reach the car.

"Get in!"

I hesitate. I look inside, thinking of the warmth, the comfort.

"Get in," Savine repeats. "I don't blame you for not trusting the cops. But wherever Gabriel is, you won't get there on your own. Not on foot. Not in that state."

Her gaze moves over me. With the bloodied bandage on my head, my frost-stiff sweater, and my wet jeans, I must look like a recently defrosted zombie. The halo of her headlights illuminates the black-and-white houses, captures a few last scattered snowflakes in the air. I stare at Savine.

"So you trust me? Why?"

The social worker replies immediately. "Instinct, as Clouseau would say. Everyone deserves a second chance, right? Even a third. Come on; get in; we're going to find your son."

This time, I obey. As soon as I'm sitting down and the Koleos sets off, my doubts evaporate. How long would I have been able to keep going out there, before collapsing? The car's filthiness assuages even my tiniest remaining qualms. How could Savine care about me messing up her Koleos when the door pockets are overflowing with cigarette stubs, half-eaten sandwiches, empty chip packets, and balled-up tissues?

"Where are we going?" she asks, her eyes on the road.

"According to SafetyTrace, Gabriel is somewhere near Saint-Pierre-Colamine."

My clothes are soaking the layer of dust and crumbs that cover the floor. Savine takes a second to think.

"Saint-Pierre-Colamine. Are you sure? There's nothing there."

"Gabriel is there. Is it a big town?"

Savine makes a quick U-turn. The little orange fir tree hanging from the rearview mirror spins frantically. The car's wheels grip the snow. She drives with furious determination, focused on the road ahead as well as our final destination.

"It's a shithole. Murol is a big city compared to that place. There's not a single store, not a bar. Honestly, apart from the . . ."

Savine's hands tense around the steering wheel. She grimaces.

"Apart from the what?"

"Apart from the Jonas Caves."

Jonas? Could that name really be a coincidence? I peer down the white road ahead of us. There's not a single tire track in the snow. No vehicle has been this way for quite a long time. I can't help crying out my next words.

"He's there, Savine! He must be. Let's go, as fast as possible."

The 4x4's wheels splash snow to either side. I balance the phone in my lap. The red dot flashes almost happily.

Two thousand seven hundred meters.

"We're on our way," Savine reassures me. "I'm going to trust you again. But I do need you to explain . . ."

"Explain what?"

"Why you're so cruel to Gabriel."

Savine is a good driver. She's used to these conditions, and her old 4x4 handles the icy patches better than a team of huskies. But even so, she can't go faster than fifteen kilometers per hour. In my head, I calculate that it will take us fifteen minutes to reach the caves. Maybe less. I look up hopefully at the sky—the clouds are parting, revealing unexpected pastel hues. I do everything I can to expel that word from my brain . . . Cruel?

"I'm going to be blunt," Savine warns me, confidently rounding a tight bend. "You act like you're some wonderful mother; you accuse Amandine of being irresponsible; you're obsessive in your desire to . . . to protect Tom. And yet with your own son, you're lax; you're absent; you're . . . irresponsible. I don't understand."

Tom . . . Esteban . . . Gabriel.

Tears trickle from my eyes. The red dot in my lap is a blur of light.

"Of course you understand, Savine. You know how the story started . . . I was thirty years old. I wanted a child, on my own. I was a liberated woman. I adopted Esteban, and for ten years he was the only man in my life. The only man in my life, but not the only man in my nights. The body has needs that the mind does not. You understand that, too, Savine; I'm sure. On rare occasions, very rare occasions, I would have a man over, like any single mother. They always left before Esteban woke up."

Another bend, a controlled skid. I feel like a helpless codriver in a rally car.

"And you got pregnant?" Savine prompts.

"Exactly. And I had to make that decision alone: to keep the child or not. Esteban was nine. He was starting to ask questions. He'd learned that he was adopted—I don't know how. I'd always planned to tell him about it when he turned ten. He was starting to say some strange things too. That was when he changed psychiatrists . . . When Dr. Wayan Kuning entered his life."

On a long straightaway, Savine shifts into third gear. The 4x4 manages almost thirty kilometers per hour.

"So you decided to keep the child? Because you were starting to feel that Esteban didn't need you as much anymore, that he was growing up, becoming independent. You needed a baby so you could feel like a mom again. Is that right?"

I look admiringly at Savine. She's as skilled in psychology as she is at driving.

"That's a pretty accurate summary, yes."

"It's a common phenomenon, Maddi," she says reassuringly.

I stare at the drop of blood in my lap.

"As soon as Esteban found out about the baby, he got it into his head that I would love the new child more than I loved him. Because he was adopted, and the new one would be truly mine."

"Again, Maddi, a perfectly normal reaction."

Savine's common sense is starting to get on my nerves. She sounds like an advice column.

"And is it also perfectly normal that the adopted child starts talking about changing his body so he can be loved more? About dying, so he can be reincarnated? You know the rest: the disappearance, the drowned boy, a dead body at the morgue that I refuse to recognize as my child's. I gave birth to Gabriel four months later, in Normandy. I loved him as best I could, I swear to you."

My screen says 1,600 meters. The snow on the road seems less thick now, but it might well be even more treacherous.

"Of course you love him," replies Savine, focused on the road. "What mother wouldn't love her child? But you can't help thinking that, were it not for Gabriel, Esteban might still be alive. And I suppose you couldn't help comparing the two boys too."

Once again, I stare at Savine. Everything she says is perfectly logical. Everything I experienced is perfectly logical. Yes, of course, in my mind, as Gabriel grew up, a little voice kept whispering: *At his age, Esteban could already walk, could already have a conversation, could ride a bike, swim, was interested in music, didn't spend hours on end lying on the couch.*

And yet I raise my voice and tell her, "Listen, Savine. I never blamed Gabriel for anything. I never belittled him. I was never cruel. If you knew how hard I tried to . . ."

I can't go on. I'm exhausted, tearful.

One thousand one hundred meters.

Savine smiles, her eyes still on the road.

"Maddi, a child can sense these things. The presence of another child who drank from the same cups as he did, slept in the same sheets, was held in the same arms . . . The presence of a dead child who did everything better than he did."

Nine hundred meters.

Gabriel is still just a motionless red dot.

"I know all that . . . I tried; I swear. I tried not to make Gabriel play music or go swimming. I really tried to focus on what he liked. On his personality. Maybe I tried too hard? Gabriel is so different. Esteban was extremely sensitive, intelligent, affectionate . . . Gabriel's the complete opposite: lazy, indifferent, passionless."

"So what?" Savine says, with a hint of anger. "It's the same in all families. One child might not be as beautiful or as gifted as another, but their parents still love them all the same, don't they?"

Of course! What does she think?

Savine turns off the road abruptly. The magic orange-colored tree, still hanging from the rearview mirror, starts to shake. It must have lost its peach scent ages ago. We bump along a narrow path, too narrow for two vehicles to pass side by side. It's impossible to tell whether the road is normally wider than this, or if it's paved. The wheels of the 4x4 grip the slope without any apparent difficulty. As we come out of the first bend, I catch sight of a strange monument—a hundred meters high, half a kilometer long—that blocks out the horizon. A ruined castle, I think at first, before realizing that it is in fact a natural cliff, with dozens of man-made caves dug into the volcanic stone.

The Jonas Caves? Is this where Gabriel is hiding?

Savine accelerates. I turn to her.

"I gave Gabriel all the same things I gave Esteban; I promise you. There was never any question of favoritism. But . . . I don't know; Gabriel just didn't seem to need me as much. He's a solitary boy. He can spend hours alone in the house, playing video games, eating whatever he can find in the fridge . . ."

"Most kids are like that these days."

Madame Know-It-All is really grating on me now. *Tom wasn't like that,* I want to scream.

Seven hundred meters.

The red cliffs appear and disappear with each twist in the road. Savine almost loses control of the car in one particularly tight bend, but I don't let the subject drop.

"I got home last night at nine o'clock. And that's the first time I've been out at night in three years. I'm doing my best, Savine. I work like crazy. Do you have any idea what it's like being a doctor? I'm bringing

Gabriel up on my own. I enrolled him in the closest private school, in Saint-Saturnin, so that he could stay there before and after classes while I worked, which he couldn't do in Murol. But he was sick when we got here, and he'd been doing some studies online. He still doesn't have any friends in Murol. And now the schools are on holiday. But even during vacation, the school says he has to study those stupid online educational resources provided by the Ministry of Education. I call him several times a day when I'm at work, to check on him. I leave him messages. I check SafetyTrace to make sure he's home . . ."

I am trembling with rage. I am not a bad mother! Why can't she stop lecturing me and just drive the damn car?

"And I'm going to tell you something else, Savine, since you've obviously hit a nerve. Everything was fine between me and Gabriel until eight months ago, until I went back with him to Saint-Jean-de-Luz, until we moved to Murol, until . . ."

Anger tightens my throat and stops me speaking.

Five hundred meters.

Savine takes advantage of my silence.

"Until you became obsessed with that ghost? With his big brother, who died before Gabriel was even born, and who came back from the dead to steal his place? To the point where you made him give up everything to come here with you? Do you have any idea what you have put that kid through?"

Why can't she shut up? I'm not going to let her keep throwing all these truths in my face. At least Wayan, when I talked with him about these things, didn't contradict me. But I can't stay silent.

"What do you expect, Savine? Do you really think I had a choice in the matter? All those coincidences . . . I didn't make them up! That astonishing resemblance, the birthmark . . . the identical DNA. You read those results. I was dragged into this madness, against my will. And Gabriel was dragged along with me."

Savine shifts down a gear, slowing as we pass through a tiny, snow-covered hamlet, and she lowers her voice, too, as if to defuse the tension. She's done her job as a social worker: she's delivered some home truths; she's lanced the boil. Now she needs to heal the wound.

Her voice is a little gentler now. "Since you arrived in Murol, how has Gabriel reacted to everything that's happened?"

Thank you, Savine.

"I . . . I tried to talk with him about it, at first. To be as open as possible. It was . . . difficult. I don't know if he was listening to me. He just . . . withdrew into silence, into his video games, into a sort of indifference."

Three hundred meters.

Savine smiles again. Without cynicism this time. In her voice, the only tone is empathy for Gabriel.

"Indifference? That was just the armor he wore when he was with you. Of course he was listening. Can you imagine all the questions he must have had? A big brother, who disappeared ten years ago . . . and now he's reappeared? A mother who hardly even looks at him anymore."

The boil is oozing. My face is striped with tears. Savine is right; she's right about everything. Thankfully, the red dot is close now. My blue dot is almost kissing it on the screen.

"I . . . I was so awful . . . cruel . . . He . . . he must hate me."

One hundred meters.

The red and blue dots have practically merged. Gabriel is here, very close, in one of the caverns in this cliff face, straight ahead.

Savine shifts into first, then reaches over and takes my hand.

"Don't be stupid, Maddi. Of course he doesn't hate you. A ten-year-old child is incapable of blaming his mother. He loves you. And the less love you show him, the more he will seek it out. Gabriel must have wanted to help you. He must have wanted to understand what was happening. He must have wanted to prove to you that he was up to the task. So that you'd love him . . . as much as you loved Esteban."

I don't say anything.

"Please reassure me, Maddi. You do love him as much as you loved Esteban, don't you?"

The Koleos has slowed almost to a halt. Savine is looking for a place to park, between the snowdrifts that line the road and the tuff cliff that towers above us, bloodred and perforated with gaping mouths ready to swallow up any lost tourists.

I wipe the tears from my face. My sweater is still wet. I take a moment to look intensely at Savine, before she parks, before we get out of the car, before we rush to find Gabriel. I want her to know that, this time, I am telling her the truth, the whole truth.

"Three days ago, even three hours ago, I would have said no. If the devil had made me an offer, I would have exchanged Gabriel for Esteban—or for Tom—without the slightest hesitation. I would have sacrificed my own child to have the one that was stolen from me handed back. I'm not going to lie: to me, Gabriel just seemed like an annoying preteen, a parasite, a mistake. Yes, that's what I thought: a mistake. But . . . but . . . Give me your hand, Savine."

I grab her free wrist and put her palm on my chest.

"Feel my heart. It's beating as fast as it was ten years ago. As fast as it was at Lac Pavin earlier. And it's not beating for a ghost this time; it's beating for my child, my living child."

Savine, with her other hand, swings the steering wheel brusquely to the side to park the car.

I am already opening the door, but I take the time to add, "So, yes, Savine. I am sure now. I love him just as much as I loved Esteban."

Before running toward the entrance to the caves—a few steps carved in the stone, lined by a snow-covered fence—I take one last look at the SafetyTrace app. Our two dots, red and blue, are perfectly superimposed. I'm so excited by this sight, I almost do not notice that in the distance—on the edge of the map that takes up the whole screen—a third dot, green, has just appeared, as if by magic.

70

We try to find our way through the narrow, low-ceilinged tunnels. We didn't think to check the snow-covered signboards because we were in too much of a rush. We ran straight into the Jonas Caves, climbing the first steps, while I yelled his name.

"Gabrieeel."

Most of the tunnels between rooms are not much more than a meter high, so, almost blindly, we move forward, bent double, before emerging into the natural light with each new room, most of them high and spacious. Savine has given me a quick briefing on these caves: seventy rooms, on five floors, used for millennia as either a refuge or a prison.

"Gabrieeeel!"

We enter the chapel without even glancing at the frescos. We cross through the master's room, paying no attention to the high, vaulted ceiling. We explore the bakery, the attic, the dovecote, without finding any signs of life. I know Gabriel is here, somewhere close by, but the SafetyTrace tracking device isn't precise enough to indicate which floor he's on; it can't tell me the name of the room, or how to find it without getting lost in this labyrinth.

"Gabrieeeel? Gabrieeeeel?"

What on earth is he doing in this maze? Why, and how, did he come here? Was he running away? Well, why not . . . After everything that Savine has made me realize I put him through . . .

I have to rid my mind of the image of Esteban, or Tom, drowned in Lac Pavin. I have to forget all those stories of reincarnation. I have to distance myself from that black lake that is swallowing my memories. I have to concentrate, keep going, and think only of my son.

Another room. A strange feeling of warmth. Savine hurries over and finds a few still-glowing embers in the wide fireplace. Someone lit a fire here, less than an hour ago. We look around at the pink walls carved from lava, at the smoke-blackened stones above the hearth.

"This must be the oven," Savine says. "Someone was hiding here."

The room is lit by a tiny skylight in a low ceiling. I walk over to it and stand on tiptoe.

"Gabrieeeel!"

My voice disperses in the icy air. All I can see through the skylight is the sky and the ridgeline of mountains. I am about to look for a better observation post—to lower my heels and take a step back—when I hear a voice.

A distant, high-pitched voice, but it reaches my ears and triggers a memory.

I would know that voice anywhere. Am I going crazy again?

It's not Gabriel's voice. It's Tom's . . .

No. Tom is dead. Esteban is dead. I mustn't think about them anymore. I must push the ghosts away. I must think only of Gabriel now.

Gabriel. Alive.

Savine comes over and joins me beneath the opening. Did she hear the voice too?

My hands grip the edge of the skylight, and I pull myself up as tall as I can. I yell at the top of my voice.

"Gabrieeeeel!"

The sound is loud and then fades, as if my voice were clinging to every crack in the cliff wall before giving up the struggle and collapsing.

"Here!"

The sharp edges of the skylight are cutting into my fingers, but I can't feel them. My heart leaps; my face lights up. This time, there's no doubt at all. It's Tom's voice.

And he's alive.

So Lespinasse, Nectaire, Louchadière, and all the other cops were lying to me? Why? What horrible game were they playing? I start to suspect some monstrous conspiracy . . .

Savine stands behind me, looking just as stunned as I feel. She heard the voice too.

I yell again, this time without thinking.

"Estebaaan!"

Savine glares at me. *Esteban?* Have I not remembered anything that she was trying to make me understand? That I have to forget that ghost, think of Gabriel. Or of Tom, in a pinch.

I look away. I'm sorry, Savine, but you're the one who hasn't understood. If Tom is alive, then so is Esteban.

"Estebaaaan?"

No answer. Of course, I'm being stupid. Tom doesn't know anything about his previous identity, his old name.

"Toooom?"

This time he answers right away.

"Here . . . I'm here!"

The distress in his voice is heartbreaking. Never before have I heard such a forlorn cry for help. *It's okay, Esteban; this time I'm not too late.*

The voice came from my right; I feel sure. Presumably he's stuck in one of those rooms, a little farther away. Without another thought, as if Savine didn't exist, I run into the first tunnel I see. It's even lower than the others: my bandages graze the ceiling, and I come close to banging my head with every stride. My sweater gets caught on the granite walls; I leave behind tufts of wool as I go.

"It's okay; I'm coming . . ."

Dead end.

I curse my misfortune. I chose the wrong tunnel. This one ends with an opening onto the void below. Oh well, I just have to go back the way I came, then choose another corridor. I'll keep shouting to orient myself, and listening; I'm bound to find him eventually. Before rushing back down the tunnel, I take a second to try to work out where I am by looking out the opening, at the holes in the cliff face. I can see about thirty of them, the highest ones ten meters above me, the lowest ones buried under snow, near the empty parking lot where we left the Koleos. That car is the only sign of life in the entire landscape, apart from the set of tire tracks that leads up to it, like the rails of a ghost train.

I follow the tracks for an instant, distractedly, before losing them, then picking them up again—but in a different spot, almost as if . . .

It's impossible; I know it is. There can only be two lines: one set of tire tracks, in the snow. I concentrate, staring at the immaculate parking lot, and then I see clearly what I hadn't noticed at first: the tire tracks of Savine's Koleos cross a different set of tracks.

I stop breathing.

A car came here: only a few hours ago, because its marks have not yet been completely erased. A car with tire tracks that are very easy to identify.

My head is spinning. I know who the monster is now. I know who kidnapped Esteban, who kidnapped Tom, who has been trying to drive me crazy all these years. I have to flee. I have to run. But first I have to yell, to warn him, to warn them. I don't know whom to call out to anymore. What name should I yell? Tom? Esteban? Gabriel? I have to choose, quickly, to decide, before . . .

I hear it. The voice bursts from the corridor behind me: a trail of powder, a blazing fire, a single word.

"Mommy!"

I turn around, my arms open to welcome him.

The stone, brought down with furious power, smashes into my temple and half of my right eye.

71

La Souille is a hive of activity. Four paramedics, five firefighters, and three gendarmes rush in and out, going up and down the stairs, trailing snow and mud, boots and doors banging, turning the house into an even bigger mess, an even louder cacophony.

"Where's your girlfriend?" Lieutenant Lespinasse demands, pacing around in front of the fireplace.

Nectaire stands motionless in front of the pinned sheet of paper containing the poem "Txoria Txori," as if he were capable of translating those few Basque words. *If I had cut her wings. She would not have left.*

"I need an answer, Paturin," Lespinasse says angrily. "Where has Savine gone?"

At last, the mayor's office secretary turns around, looking just as confused as the gendarme.

"I have no idea."

The lieutenant punches the mantelpiece. Snow and soot rain down on the books and magazines piled up in the hearth.

"Shit! So there are two women and a kid running wild. And we don't have a clue where they might have gone. I don't even know if they're together."

"Lieutenant?"

Four paramedics are standing in front of him. Three men and a woman, and it is the woman who speaks to him now.

"Amandine Fontaine woke up. We gave her a second injection of naloxone. She's going to be okay."

The four of them are standing in a line, like superheroes posing for a poster in the Paris metro. Military-style uniforms, with fluorescent belts, collars, and cuffs.

"Can I question her?" Lespinasse asks.

"If it's important, and it won't take too long, yes," the woman says.

The lieutenant is already on his way to the staircase.

"Lieutenant, I would like to question Amandine with you."

Nectaire, too, was surprisingly quick to react. He's standing in front of the stairs, blocking the lieutenant's path.

"Please," he adds. "I know how this works, and I've been investigating this case for the past week. I know more about it than you do, in fact."

Lespinasse does not have time to waste.

"Okay, we'll do it together."

He climbs the first step. This time, it's Aster who stops him.

"Lieutenant?"

"Sorry, no more places available!"

He looks up at Sergeant Louchadière, who is standing at attention at the top of the stairs.

"Jennifer, keep an eye on the witch for me. We don't want another runaway."

Nectaire's sister places her hand, noisy with bracelets, on the gendarme's wrist.

"Don't worry, Lieutenant; I'm not going anywhere. I just wanted to give you some advice. Please don't tell Amandine that Tom is dead."

Lespinasse was not expecting that.

"Why not?"

"Just give her some time. A few hours. She's still getting over the last shock. You can trust my intuition on this."

The policeman's bushy eyebrows frown as he stares, hypnotized, at the swaying copper unalome.

The Paturins and their intuition . . .

"The reason my brother has no intuition is that I got it all when we were born. Give Amandine a chance."

"A chance?"

"A chance to understand. Who? How? Why? Until you know the answers, there is no point drowning her in doubts."

The lieutenant makes no promises, but he nods as if to say he'll think about it, that he will bear her words in mind when formulating his questions. Aster smiles, opens her mouth, and whispers, "Thank you," then gives her brother a long hug.

Amandine looks like a porcelain princess forgotten on a doll's bed. A princess who fell asleep long ago and has just been woken in a very non-fairy-tale way, by noisy firefighters, with no kiss, and no sign of her Prince Charming anywhere.

Nectaire and Lespinasse carry in two chairs and place them at the end of the bed. Lespinasse speaks in a calm, empathic voice.

"Amandine, you . . . you were attacked last night. We think someone tried to kill you. By injecting you with an opioid. Did you . . . see anyone?"

Amandine is sitting up in bed, her back resting on three pillows whose embroidered designs match the white crocheted petals on her nightshirt.

"No . . . I was asleep."

Her long hair falls over her shoulders, like thin straps holding up the lacy fabric. She leans forward.

"Where is Tom?"

Amandine remains silent.

Should I tell her or not?

Nectaire's gaze weighs even more heavily on Lespinasse than Aster's words.

"We have other questions for you, Madame Fontaine."

"Where . . . where is Tom?"

This time, it is Lespinasse who does not say anything.

Amandine turns her porcelain face to Nectaire. She looks so fragile, as if a flutter of eyelashes could split her face in two. Yet she finds the strength to say, "I want to talk to Aster."

Lespinasse speaks as softly as possible. "That's impossible."

"Then I want to talk to Savine."

"She . . . she isn't here. Why do you only want to talk to those two?"

"Because I trust them. I trust your sister, Nectaire, and I trust Savine. And I don't trust either of you two."

Lespinasse doesn't flinch.

"Madame Fontaine, this morning we discovered a model village under Tom's bed. A model of a strange, drowned village. Did you know about it?"

"No."

"Do you remember the last time you looked under Tom's bed?"

"No. Probably years ago. It's his bedroom, his space—I respect that."

The gendarme forces himself to keep calm.

"I understand. Have you ever heard Tom mention that story of a drowned village, the migration of souls, reincarnation?"

"NO!"

Amandine's face has grown paler. It is almost translucent. Is she going to disappear, too, become invisible? Her voice, on the other hand, is growing more powerful.

"Why are you asking all these questions? Where is Tom?"

Lespinasse hesitates. The pendulum is swinging the other way now. It would be simpler just to tell her everything, but could she stand the shock?

Nectaire takes over before the lieutenant says something stupid.

"Amandine, listen to me. We're concerned about Maddi Libéri. I know you've had several arguments with her. You remember how she was talking about all those coincidences, those similarities between her son and Tom? We'd like to go over all that, if you don't mind. From the beginning."

Amandine trembles with rage. A few strands of her hair hang draped over her chest, like so many cracks in her heart.

"You're not still hung up on her bullshit, are you? Jonas explained all those so-called coincidences, one by one."

"Then let's go over his responses one by one," Nectaire replies patiently. "Jonas was probably killed because he understood something. Something that we need to understand too."

Amandine appears convinced by this argument.

"Go on," she murmurs.

Nectaire takes a deep breath.

"Let's start with the indigo trunks. This might seem strange to you, but to me that's the most intriguing coincidence. Probably because there's nothing supernatural about it. The others—the resemblances, the birthmarks, the shared phobias and passions, even the DNA test— can only be explained by magic, or by witchcraft . . . But those trunks? Esteban Libéri was wearing a pair with a whale motif—you can't deny that; it was in the police report written by Lieutenant Lazarbal. So, I'm sorry, Amandine, but I find it impossible to believe that it was pure random chance that Tom was wearing the same pair eight months ago, on the same beach, on the very day when Maddi Libéri was there."

Amandine sounds as if she's reciting a memorized answer.

"The whale was because of Jonas. It's a story in the Bible, apparently."

Nectaire glances at Lespinasse. Amandine's response doesn't explain anything. In fact, her reasoning only makes it more incredible that Esteban should have been wearing the same pair ten years earlier, when Jonas—whose name apparently inspired the purchase of Tom's trunks— was only twenty and Tom was not yet born.

"So was it Jonas who bought those trunks for Tom?" Nectaire asks softly.

Amandine takes a moment to think about this.

"No, I don't think so . . . Jonas never bought clothes for his son."

"Who, then? You?"

"No, I would remember that."

"Who, then?" Lespinasse and Nectaire ask in chorus.

Amandine racks her brain while leaning farther back on the feather pillows. If she slips, if she falls, her porcelain body will shatter.

"I . . . I think it was Savine."

XII

Execution

The Dying Room

72

There's a cut on my forehead, and blood is pouring into my right eye, but I am incapable of wiping it away.

My wrists and ankles are bound.

I am incapable even of crying out, of expelling the pain that burns my throat, of spitting out the venom of saliva and bile that is poisoning me.

My mouth is gagged.

I am on the ground in a cold, bare room, my back against a crudely carved lava wall. A dungeon of sharpened volcanic rocks, the very opposite of a padded cell.

"I'm going to tell you a story, Maddi. I'm going to tell you my story. I think you deserve that."

Savine Laroche is leaning against the only part of the wall that's covered with bricks. Facing me.

I don't want to hear her voice.

I want to listen out for the faintest sound beyond this room. I want to be attuned to the smallest cry.

I want to hear Gabriel's voice, if he calls me again.

Mommy!

Where is Gabriel?

I want to hear Tom's voice, if it guides me again.

Here. I'm here!

I scream inside my head, a deafening roar within my skull, loud enough to transform all my brain cells into the cells of a lunatic asylum.

Where are you?

"I'm going to tell you my story, Maddi. It's the unremarkable story of a lost girl. Don't worry; I'll spare you my childhood, my adolescence. Knowing about them would allow you to understand certain things— where I'm from, where I got to—but you're intelligent, Maddi; you'll read between the lines; you'll imagine the forest where I grew up, a lost soul. Les Aubiers, the poorest neighborhood in Bordeaux. I'll spare you all the times when I put my life in danger; I'll spare you the things I did with strangers in return for alcohol, drugs, love. I'll spare you my mistakes, my addictions, my false dawns and humiliations. I'll spare you my long descent into hell, and I'll start my story there, in the deepest pits of despair. I was just over twenty years old.

"I'd trailed after this boy. He was different from everyone else I knew—better looking, healthier. A surfer, a musician, a student at the Bastide campus. He was miserable at the university, happy whenever he escaped to the beach. Once or twice, between exams, he found consolation in my arms. He also found consolation in other arms, more suntanned and less bruised than mine, on the Miramar Beach, when he left the lecture halls behind. I don't think I can even remember his name now. Anyway, was it really his child? It's possible. And since there are no certainties, Maddi, let's just stick to that possibility. The other potential fathers on the list were not at the same level.

"I gave birth on my own, at the Belharra Clinic in Bayonne. I did my best, I swear. I tried, Maddi, to look after the child, to bring him up. I bought him a stuffed animal, some pacifiers and diapers, but day by day, I came to see that I wasn't prepared; I feared that I was putting my child in danger. There were a few articles in the newspapers back then, about that charity, the Stork's Cradle, and how they'd set up baby hatches all over France, including one on Rue Lasseguette in Bayonne. That baby hatch gave me a second chance. My son was three months old. He would be happier without me, and I would be happier without him.

"Or so I thought . . .

"I don't know if you can imagine what a mother feels, Maddi, when she leaves her baby in a drawer, closes it, and walks away. I don't know if you can imagine all the stories the brain can invent, to protect itself, to survive.

"My poor brain went for the simplest and most obvious option. To stop me turning back as I walked along Rue Lasseguette, away from the hospital in Bayonne, it promised me, *I will come back. I will come back and get you, my baby. Wherever you are, I will find you again.*

"It took me a long time—years—but I eventually kept that promise.

"As paradoxical as it might seem, abandoning my child is what saved me. Well, no, that's not quite true. The promise—obsessive, essential—of finding my child again, getting him back, raising him like any normal mother . . . that's what saved me. I left him in that drawer on September 29, 2000. I haven't touched drugs since that day. No lost souls have shared my bed since then. I became a student, and discovered that I had a gift: not that I was more intelligent than the others in my class, but I was much more motivated than any of them. And more experienced too. All the other trainee social workers were girls from good families who had never set foot in the neighborhoods and apartment buildings where they would have to work. My past mistakes became the fuel that fed my future. My goal to get my child back. After suffering so much, I was certain to be a better mother in the future. I had entrusted him to you, but I hadn't *given* him to you.

"Yes, it took me a while to find you.

"I had to be ready. Once I'd become a social worker, discovering where my child had been placed wasn't too difficult. My job gave me access to the files. It was easy enough to find dates, names, addresses. There aren't that many babies who are abandoned in hatches.

"It took me almost ten years to develop and perfect my plan.

"No matter what you might think, Maddi, you are far from a perfect mother. You work too much. Esteban was alone too often. It wasn't difficult to approach him without your knowledge, to chat with him, just for a few minutes at first, now and again, and then more regularly, and then every morning, like a ritual, whenever Esteban went to buy bread. He would give me a honey canelé; we would talk, and he would be home before you were out of the shower. I would also see him on the way to his music lesson, or near the swimming pool. No one notices a woman like me. People trust a woman like me. It didn't take long for me to get Esteban eating out of my hand.

"Especially since I told him the truth.

"You were not his real mommy; he was adopted. You were pregnant with a child who really was yours. Esteban loved stories, legends. He had lots of imagination, like all naive children. I planted the seed in his head and watered it day after day: he should go to the drowned world, change his life, or at least his body, so that you would love him more. But he had to keep the plan a secret.

"A few people came close to guessing the truth, like Gaspard Montiroir, his psychiatrist, but he chickened out. Or like that cop, Iban Lazarbal, but he couldn't prove anything. I was invisible.

"Esteban and I agreed that we should change his life on his tenth birthday. Of course, that story about changing his body was, for me, just a metaphor, and for Esteban it was just a game. No blood would be shed; nobody would be drowned. I just wanted my son back. And you had a child of your own on the way, so we were even.

"I have to confess my sole regret, Maddi. I went too fast. I wasn't patient enough. I thought I'd tamed Esteban, but he wasn't ready.

"That morning, he came to me of his own free will, at the edge of the beach, with that one-euro coin in his hand. Nobody noticed anything, naturally: there were no bees around, and Esteban didn't go swimming. He trusted me. But when, instead of his buying bread and a canelé like he had on the other mornings, I invited him into my car and drove away, he panicked. I had to park off the road, a few kilometers away, close to the Corniche d'Urrugne, to calm him down.

"I tried to tell him his favorite stories again—the upside-down world, the village under the sea—but he refused to listen. He was ten years old, and he knew the difference between stories and reality. The underwater world, reincarnation . . . all of that was just joking around; he had never wanted to die. Now he wanted to go home.

"I held his arms still. I had no choice now—I had to tell him everything. Not just that he was adopted, but that I was his real mother. We were finally together. We would be happy, the two of us. In the end, he hugged me. I thought I'd convinced him.

"I continued to console him. 'I'm not going to hurt you. You know me now. You can keep your first name if you like. You can write to Maddi occasionally.'

"He calmed down. I could feel his heart beating against my chest as I rocked him from side to side.

"'The two of us are going to go away, Esteban. I've organized everything. We'll go to a land where you can swim in the warm sea all year round.'

"Those were the most beautiful twenty seconds of my life. The only ones, really, that mattered. Twenty seconds together, at the cost of his life . . . was that the price I had to pay?

"He was mine at last. That was what I believed. I leaned down to kiss him, just one kiss. But he pulled himself free and kicked me in the chest. Then he opened the door and ran straight ahead, without turning back, barefoot, in the direction of the cliffs.

"Esteban was a good swimmer, but he had no understanding of distances or countercurrents. He jumped straight into the ocean.

"I've thought about it so many times since. And I understood. You had him for ten years, Maddi. Ten years: time enough to corrupt his mind, to make him believe that you were his real mother. And I only had a few moments. All I needed was a little more time, to convince him, to save him.

"Esteban's body was discovered twenty-nine days later.

"He wasn't there anymore, but what was that to you, really? You had your own child. You had another one.

"But what did I have?

"A pair of espadrilles and a one-euro coin that had fallen under the passenger seat of my car.

"Don't you understand, Maddi? I entrusted you with my child, and you lied to him, year after year. You confused him so much that he ran from me. You killed him. Yes, it was you!"

73

Through the dirty window, Nectaire watches the snow fall. The hamlet of Froidefond, the Fountain of Souls, the farmyard, all the vehicles that have left furrows in the snow: the fire truck, the ambulance, the police van, his old Renault 5 . . . and the empty spot where the Koleos was earlier.

I think it was Savine.

As soon as Amandine pronounced those words, Nectaire had jumped to his feet, thunderstruck.

Lieutenant Lespinasse realizes he will have to take over, so he now says gently, "Amandine, this is very, very important. Was it Savine Laroche who bought those indigo trunks?"

"Yes . . . I think so."

"You think so?"

"No . . . I . . . I'm not sure."

For a few seconds, Lespinasse digests this information or prepares his next question. Or perhaps his silence is a deliberate tactic to lure the witness into saying something else.

"Does Savine Laroche often give you things?"

"Yes . . . She helps me. She takes care of me and Tom. She deals with the stuff that's too complicated. Bank accounts, bills . . . all the paperwork, you know. When I can't make ends meet, she finds solutions. I mean, she's a social worker . . . That's her job, right?"

"Yes," Lespinasse says, nodding. "And . . . how long has Savine Laroche been helping you like that?"

"Well . . . I mean, always."

The lieutenant refrains from scratching his beard or frowning. The slightest gesture might break the flow of confidences.

"What do you mean, 'always'? Could you be more precise?"

"I mean, since she came to Murol. Tom must have been four or five."

What? Lespinasse thinks. *Savine Laroche isn't from Auvergne?* He manages not to cry out or stand up or shake Paturin. Instead, turning slowly toward the mayor's office secretary, he whispers, "Nectaire, how long have you known Savine?"

Nectaire is still staring out at the farmyard, at the rectangle of shallow snow where the Koleos was parked earlier. He replies automatically, as if someone had injected him with a truth serum.

"Since she moved to Murol five or six years ago. But she adapted so well, and she's made herself so useful, that anyone would think she's lived here forever. She knows more people around here than I do."

For God's sake . . . Lespinasse feels as though he's sitting on pins. His beard itches. So does his nose. But he forces himself to make as few movements as possible, and to look at Amandine as calmly as he can. Her porcelain features are tired and drawn. The paramedics will be back any minute. But he has to press on, and he mustn't rush her.

"Tell me more, Amandine. How would you describe the relationship between Savine and Tom?"

"What do you mean? I don't understand."

Amandine's back is sliding slowly down the pillows. She no longer has the strength to sit up. Her eyelids fall shut, open for an instant, then close for a longer time, like a doll when it is laid flat.

"I mean, would you say that Savine is like a . . . like a second mother for Tom?"

Lespinasse dreads Amandine's reaction, but strangely this question seems to revive her. Her tired smile grows wider.

"Oh, I see now. I see what you mean . . . Savine often says that I'm her favorite, out of all the families she looks after, because I was the first one she cared for here. Thinking back, I was so young. Jonas was never there. I don't know how I'd have coped without her. I shouldn't say this, especially now that I'm older and I can look after Tom on my own, but I think she raised him better than I did . . . She was with him more than I was, anyway."

Amandine's smile has frozen. Her eyes remain open, gazing at images from that happy past. As Lespinasse prepares to stand up, she finds just enough strength left to murmur another observation.

"She spent all her time at La Souille back then. Thinking back on it now, at the time, Tom was practically her kid."

74

Gagged.

Bound.

Like a worm crawling through dust.

And yet I look up at the cave's skylight, finding hope in the faint glimmer of light.

Only the faintest glimmer, but it illuminates everything.

I knew it. I always knew it.

A monster was lurking in the shadows all along.

Esteban didn't disobey me. Esteban hadn't wanted to die. Esteban was not running away from a bee when he disappeared. Esteban had wanted to live, but the monster got him anyway.

The monster kidnapped him.

And she murdered him.

I look up at Savine, standing over me. Her wrinkled face, her plump body, her unkempt gray hair. Who would ever have believed that a demon could be hiding behind such an ordinary appearance?

An ordinary woman dragged into increasing madness, like a snowball becoming an avalanche, her mental illness growing and gathering speed through the years.

"You see, Maddi, there are no coincidences in this story. None at all. I had lost a son. I had been given only a few seconds to hold him in my arms. A few seconds! Do you think that was enough to carry me through a lifetime? Do you think any mother could be content with that? Can you imagine the chasm in my life left by his absence? Can you imagine the precipice yawning beneath my feet, and nothing—nothing at all—for me to cling to?

"First, I looked for an image—a photograph, anything—that resembled my son. There were hundreds, thousands, hundreds of thousands, on social media. All those radiant young mothers showing off their children, at one month, two months, three months, one year, two years, three years old . . . I had nothing else to do. I spent my evenings, sometimes the whole night, searching. It took me years. Did I even know what I was looking for? I probably only admitted it to myself when I found it.

"A doppelganger! The one child, out of them all, who looked most like him.

"His name was Tom Fontaine, and he was four years and three months old. He was posing on a wooden sled in front of his dad, and he lived in a village I had never heard of—Murol—in a region, Auvergne, where I'd never set foot. There was nothing holding me back, so I didn't even hesitate. You understand this, Maddi; I know you do . . . I moved here.

"It was all quite simple. My son had been stolen from me, so I wanted another one, but not just any boy: I wanted one who looked like him. So much so that I could almost believe it *was* him. So much so that he could replace the first one. You must think I'm crazy. Maybe I am, but isn't that what everyone does when they lose what they love? Try to find what was lost? Preferably the exact same thing.

"Much later, I realized what I had become while searching the internet for his face: a casting director. Except I auditioned thousands of children for the role. The role of a lifetime. You see, Maddi, there's nothing strange or magical about that stunning resemblance: all of us have someone, somewhere, who looks just like us—you simply have to search for them. And it's especially easy if it's a young child, whom you can mold.

"The rest was much easier. Tom's mother was young, almost constantly alone, impressionable. She trusted me. The most delicate part, and the most painful, was the birthmark. One weekend, Amandine took a trip to Cap d'Agde with Jonas—it took me ages to persuade her to leave Tom behind with me, but eventually she agreed. He was still only four. I dripped some boiling oil onto his skin while he was asleep. Does that strike you as cruel, Maddi? Don't worry, I consoled him while he cried, and he didn't cry for very long. He had only a vague memory of the incident afterward, or maybe he forgot it completely; I don't know. The only thing that remained was that mark, a slightly darker brown than Esteban's after it healed, but identical in every other way. Birthmarks are common in children, but they change . . . Well, I don't need to tell you that, do I? After a few years, it's pretty hard to tell them apart from a mark left by a burn. Maybe you felt a slight doubt when you examined him, though?

"Listen. That drop of oil, that mark, was his baptism. Was doing that really worse than submerging a newborn baby's head in a basin of holy water? Our fates were linked from then on. He was mine and I was his. Amandine didn't matter anymore.

"Children are what we make them. All it takes is a little patience and a lot of perseverance. My son had loved music and swimming, so Tom would love music and swimming too.

"Amandine listened to me, without ever questioning my choices. I taught Tom some basic Basque, too, on the pretext that it would make his dad happy, even though that conceited surfer didn't know more than a few words of it.

"I have only one regret from that whole period, Maddi. Once, and only once, I felt ashamed of myself. One morning, Tom noticed that a bee had flown into his room. He was too small to reach the window to let it out, too small to open his door. He cried for help, and his wails made me feel sick with remorse. I'd decided to wait an hour before going up there, but I couldn't hold out that long. I went to rescue him after thirty minutes. Was it useful for me to have instilled that fear in him? I don't know. I just thought that shared phobia had to seem meaningful, like all the rest. Tom had to be able to believe in the whole reincarnation thing. I told him so often about this boy who had died of drowning before he was born, who looked so much like him. It was our secret. I didn't want him to merely resemble Esteban . . . I wanted him to *become* Esteban. Two days ago, though, when he fell down the Wolf's Leap waterfall, I really thought that I had lost him.

"To lose him when I was so close to my objective . . .

"You're probably wondering what role you play in this story, Maddi . . . Don't worry; I'll get to that. You understand, though, that Tom was my son now; I had completely tamed him, without having spilled even a single drop of blood. Only a drop of oil. Admit it, Maddi: my plan was perfectly innocent.

"But I didn't want Tom to grow up, or Amandine to become more mature and independent and maternal, to show more interest every day in a boy who would become a teenager. Because if that happened, sooner or later Tom would escape me. Once again, he would be stolen from me.

"So that is how I came up with my plan . . .

"To kill two birds with one stone.

"To get my son back, all to myself.

"And to take my revenge on you."

75

Amandine's eyes close softly. Lespinasse wonders whether he should ask her another question. He has enough already to add Savine Laroche's name to the arrest warrant he's put out for Maddi Libéri and her son Gabriel . . . even if he really has no clear idea what happened at La Souille, the Moulin de Chaudefour, or Lac Pavin. Maybe Maddi and Savine were in on it together? The arrest warrant, though, is nearly useless in this weather, as all vehicles without four-wheel drive—in other words, most of the police's vehicles—cannot go anywhere. There's not much hope of finding them until the roads have been cleared.

Amandine, dozing, turns peacefully onto her side.

"Just one last question, Madame Fontaine," the lieutenant says, "and then I'll let you rest."

Lespinasse hears footsteps on the stairs. Boots thumping upon wood. The paramedics, presumably. They'd told him fifteen minutes, and it's been more than twenty.

"Amandine, your vacation in Saint-Jean-de-Luz, eight months ago . . . whose idea was that?"

The boots stop outside the closed bedroom door. Nectaire, with surprising rapidity, has left his observation post by the window and is now standing beside the gendarme.

"Was it Jonas's?" the lieutenant asks in a whisper. "Please tell me it was Jonas's . . ."

Amandine reacts to Jonas's name. Or perhaps to the sound of the paramedics knocking on the door. She smiles sadly at Lespinasse and Nectaire.

"Jonas? No . . . Family vacations weren't really his thing. He wasn't there. He went off to the Pyrenees on his motorcycle. It was Savine who suggested the destination. She organized the whole thing, in fact: the date, the hotel, even what we did every day. That's how she is, you know. She likes"—one last drowsy sigh escapes her lips—"to plan everything."

76

"My plan was simple, Maddi. Simple and precise. I could live in peace with Tom only on two conditions: that the police were certain he was dead, and that someone else was accused of killing him. Basically, I needed a fall guy, and it didn't take me long to find one: you, of course! You were the reason I had failed ten years before. Back then, Esteban had known me only a few months, and our escape was partly improvised.

"This time, I would leave nothing to chance. Tom had known me for as long as he could remember. I wouldn't need to convince him; he would follow me. He'd be fine without Amandine, and after a few weeks, he would forget all about her. It would be like a big vacation. First, we'd hide in Spain, then in Morocco, then . . . anywhere in the world, changing our identity each time. When you work in a mayor's office, it's not difficult to falsify identity papers.

"I was very careful, Maddi. Much more careful than you were.

"All I had to do was look at your Facebook page, and I could learn every detail of your life. Once I discovered that you were going back to Saint-Jean-de-Luz, everything fell into place.

"I sent Amandine and Tom to the same beach, the same day, with him dressed in the same indigo trunks. I didn't even need to be there. The results were even better than I expected: you rose to the bait instantly. I never expected you to give up everything as quickly as you did to find that boy. But even if you hadn't moved down here, I knew you wouldn't be able to get that ten-year-old boy who looked so much like Esteban out of your head, knew that you would find out more about him, maybe spy on him, and that to justify it, you would have no choice but to cling to a tall tale about the migration of souls, reincarnation, and a drowned village.

"It wasn't difficult to convince Nectaire Paturin to investigate you either. Piece by piece, he gathered all the evidence that suggested you were crazy, that you were guilty. What better detective could I hope for than an ex-policeman whose instinct is always wrong?

"I stayed in the shadows. Nobody could suspect me. I felt no guilt. You see, Maddi, there was nothing evil about my plan. No one would have to die; not a drop of blood would be spilled. It was just about getting my child back, after all those years, and going somewhere where no one would bother us.

"Was that too much to ask? And yet, once again, you ruined everything!

"You started scaring Tom and Amandine. Martin Sainfoin, the local policeman, was the first one to become concerned. He knew Tom, because they were both keen cyclists, and they often rode together between Besse and Murol. First, Martin was intrigued by the strange way you were acting, and then—after he did some digging—by all those even stranger coincidences between the story of your dead son and Tom. I had no idea that he would work so quickly, that he would question Tom, that Tom would confide in him, and that he would then want to question me. He arranged to meet me in Besse, at La Poterne, that evening, so I could explain myself. Everyone in the mayor's office heard him, yet strangely nobody suspected me.

"I was stuck. If Martin Sainfoin exposed my role in all of this, my plan would fail. I had no choice; I had to act fast, while he still saw me as nothing more dangerous than a social worker filling a kid's head with her bizarre theories about reincarnation and a drowned village. That day at the mayor's office, when I carried the cups over, I dropped the digitalis in his tea.

"With Martin Sainfoin out of the way, I thought I'd be in the clear, that he would be the only adult Tom would confide in. But then Jonas suddenly reappeared! He suspected you, as I'd hoped. But he also bullied Tom into telling him the truth. How could I abandon that poor kid in such a terrible family? At least you agree with me on that point, right, Maddi? Thankfully, Jonas was one of those men so sure of their own strength that they insist on dealing with their problems single-handedly. He called me when I was at the mayor's office with Nectaire. I arranged to meet him in the Chaudefour Valley, leaving Nectaire to make his herbal tea. I went there and was back barely an hour later. In my pocket I had the Thiers Gentleman knife I'd borrowed from Aster's store; that wasn't difficult, because I spend a lot of time with her and Nectaire anyway. I had no idea your son Gabriel would take one, too, but it worked out perfectly: two stolen knives . . . that really muddied the waters.

"Everything was now in place.

"Now it was your turn to take center stage, Maddi. And you did, repeating loud and clear, to me, to Nectaire, to anyone who would listen, that something bad was going to happen on Tom's tenth birthday. Remember our dinner at La Potagerie? I think all the other customers must have heard you talking about that underwater world and the mysteries of reincarnation. You kept shouting, 'Someone kidnapped Esteban! Someone's going to do the same to Tom tomorrow . . . on his tenth birthday.'

"You were the screen behind which I hid, Maddi, and you fell completely into my trap: coming across like a madwoman, obsessed with the idea that the tragedy was about to be repeated and that you alone could prevent it. That was my plan: everyone had to be convinced that you had lost your mind. Everyone . . . including you! And it worked, didn't it? You can admit it now. You must have thought you were going crazy.

"Yes, everything was in place. The curtain was about to be raised. Every actor knew their lines. Now they just had to play their roles . . ."

77

"She needs to rest, Lieutenant."

Lespinasse does not argue the point. He doesn't like it when anyone questions his authority, so he's not about to do the same to the paramedic standing in the bedroom doorway. He goes out into the corridor. He had plenty of other questions he'd wanted to ask Amandine Fontaine, but they can wait; he has other fish in more urgent need of frying. Two women and a ten-year-old kid have gone missing, and no one has a clue where they could be. They need to dredge a lake to find the drowned body of another ten-year-old kid. He has to call his police colleagues in Clermont and in Saint-Jean-de-Luz, and that psychiatrist, Wayan Balik Kuning. And he should question Aster Paturin again too. This case contains so many mysteries, he is almost prepared to put his trust in that witch.

◆ ◆ ◆

"Monsieur, you must leave now."

Nectaire is still sitting at Amandine's bedside, but the paramedic is insistent.

"You have to let her rest."

Instead of getting up, however, Nectaire leans down even closer, as if he wanted to kiss Amandine goodbye. Surely the paramedic won't mind waiting a little longer for such a natural, harmless action.

With one arm, he rocks Amandine, not enough to wake her, the movement small enough not to disrupt her sleep. With his other hand, he discreetly reaches into his pocket and fishes out the glass vial that Aster gave him when they hugged at the bottom of the stairs. *Your turn, Nicky,* she whispered to him. *Even if you don't believe in it, do it for me.*

"Monsieur, please . . ."

The paramedic is still standing in the doorway. Nectaire turns his back to him and leans even closer to Amandine, drawing her into a long hug, his hands hidden from the paramedic's sight. Using his thumbnail, he removes the cork, then raises the vial to the woman's half-open mouth. The red water pours over her pale lips, and a trickle of spit runs down Amandine's chin. *Come on; at least try to swallow it,* Nectaire thinks.

"Monsieur, if you don't leave now, I'll have to call for backup."

Nectaire lifts the bottom of the vial even higher. This time, like an abandoned kitten, Amandine starts to suckle. A few drops. A few drops are all it will take.

Nectaire just has time to put the vial away before the paramedic comes over to him.

"It's okay; I'm leaving."

78

"The play began, Maddi. We each had a role to play. Yours was a minor part, I admit. I hope you're not mad at me for that. There was no time for rehearsal, and there would only be one performance. But the script had been written. And I was in the wings, directing the action.

"The most difficult actor to direct was Nectaire, without a doubt. His instinct told him you were lying, but experience had taught him not to trust his own instincts, so he was tempted to believe you. He was like a weather vane—you never knew which direction he would end up pointing.

"That was when I had the idea of which I am most proud: the DNA test. Obviously, it was impossible that the comparison between Tom and Esteban would be a match, because only identical twins have exactly the same genes. So, in Nectaire's mind, if the result was positive, that meant you must have rigged the test. And that you had been trying to manipulate us from the very beginning.

"Never could he have suspected that *I* was the one manipulating him. It was easy enough . . . I just gave you my baby's stuffed whale, the only souvenir I didn't leave with him in that baby hatch along with a few pacifiers and a packet of too-big diapers. I'd never thrown it away, of course. Does anyone throw away their child's first cuddly toy? Naturally, I gave a similar toy to Tom; in fact, Monstro was the first present I gave him when I arrived in Murol. Monstro was a whale, like the one sewn onto Esteban's trunks, and Tom slept in bed with him every night.

"With those trunks, too, there was nothing supernatural going on. Back when I was spending time with Esteban in Saint-Jean-de-Luz, I'd pointed out those indigo trunks to him at a store. He asked you to buy them, and you bought them, simple as that. Two pairs, even! Imagine my surprise the first time I saw Gabriel wearing the pair you gave him, which had once been Esteban's!

"Having said that, Maddi, if you've been paying attention, you will notice that there is one coincidence in this story. Just one! I chose that stuffed whale purely by chance, when I was pregnant; it was the biggest cuddly I could afford. Never could I have guessed that Tom's father would be called Jonas, like these caves . . . and like the boy in the Bible who was swallowed by a whale. But I'm sure that if I'd bought a stuffed rabbit or a teddy bear instead, we'd still have found something in common, wouldn't we? Don't you think so, Maddi? You don't have an opinion? Maybe you'd just like to know what happened next, after the test? It's true; you missed a big part of the play, when you were unconscious . . . Well, I can sum it up in a few words: *I go away with Tom and make everyone think you were the one who kidnapped him.*

"I knew I could get Tom to come with me, even in the middle of the night. I wasn't going to make the same mistake again; this time, I spent more than five years earning his trust before I acted. The second part of the play, however, called for a more sophisticated form of stagecraft.

"First, I had to lure you to Lac Pavin, alone. I felt sure that your discovery of the model of the drowned village under Tom's bed would be enough to do that. I'd scattered a few clues before that, of course. Then I had to send Nectaire in pursuit of you, in his old Renault 5, while I pretended that I was going to stay at La Souille to watch over Amandine and tell the cops what was happening. As soon as Nectaire left Froidefond, though, I drove to Lac Pavin, too, on the Fraux road, a detour of about three kilometers. But Nectaire is such a cautious driver that—in a snowstorm, in my 4x4—I knew I'd get there long before he did. All I had to do then, Maddi, was look out for you, knock you out with the first stone I could find, drive you in my Koleos to the top of the climbing wall, leave you unconscious in the trunk, and then call the police.

"When Nectaire finally arrived at the lake, I was ready to start the second act. It took him even longer than I'd expected: almost two hours to cover ten kilometers. I'd put on your ski jacket, your scarf, and your mauve hat, and I rowed across the lake in a boat, accompanied by two simple mannequins, one of them on the floor of the boat—you can buy them online for a few euros—which I dressed in Tom's hoodie. Orange, obviously. My favorite color! Thankfully, nobody made that connection. I was the one who bought most of his clothes, so it wasn't difficult to order a couple extras of each item.

"I rowed so far out, and there was so much snow falling, that the illusion worked perfectly. Nectaire was the ideal actor for that role, because he was incapable of running around the lake to catch me. I had plenty of time to stop rowing and throw the first mannequin—weighed down by a lump of obsidian—into the water, then put my hands into two small boots and crawl a few meters along the shore to leave two rows of footprints, one adult and one child, before starting the climb up that beginners' wall with the second mannequin on my back.

"I waited until I could see the flashing lights of the police cars, and then the exhausted figure of Nectaire, to begin the third and final act. I thought that Nectaire would stay on the shore; he surprised me by climbing into the boat and rowing farther out to get a better view. Not that it made any difference . . . He saw me at the top of the wall, letting go of the second mannequin's hand; I'd weighted it with obsidian too. And he saw it fall like a stone. I chose Lac Pavin over the other lakes because it's the deepest in Auvergne. It's practically bottomless, so the police would hardly be surprised when they didn't find a body. When they reached the platform above the climbing wall, all they found was you, lying there unconscious. I was long gone by then, and the snow had already covered my tracks.

"You see, Maddi, my play wasn't difficult to act. I'd had years to prepare it, and there were only three final things I needed to make it a success: first, I needed to wait for ideal weather; second, I needed to find an investigator who was slow enough not to solve the mystery; and, third, I needed a culprit who everyone believed was completely crazy.

"After that, all I had to do was raise the curtain.

"The perfect plan, or so I thought.

"Unfortunately, there was a fly in the ointment.

"And that fly, I'm afraid, is going to cost you your life.

"The fly's name? Oh, I'm sure you can guess . . . No?

"He's called Gabriel."

79

"I'm falling asleep, Gabriel."

Is it fatigue that's weighing down on Tom's eyelids? Is it all the emotion? Or just the heat?

The fire in the hearth, built up log by log, has finally warmed up the dying room, despite the cold air coming through the barred window. Stick your nose through those bars—Tom thinks—and your skin will freeze, but at the back of the cave it's pleasantly warm. He and Gabriel, curled up together near the fireplace, might easily take off their jackets and sweaters. If only they could . . .

"I'm sorry," Tom says. "I just can't keep my eyes open."

"It's fine," Gabriel tells him gently, moving even closer. "You can lean on me. I'm more comfortable than a ghost, you know."

Tom still has enough energy to joke. "You might be more comfortable than a ghost, but you're almost as skinny as a skeleton."

Even so, he lets his head fall onto the other boy's shoulder.

"I'm scared of falling asleep, Gaby. I'm scared I'll never wake up again."

Gabriel sits up a little.

"Don't say things like that! I'll be on guard duty while you sleep. I'll protect you."

"Thanks, but I'm not sure how you'll manage that. You're trussed up like a chicken!"

Gabriel wriggles as much as he can, but his arms are tied tightly to his torso, and he is barely able to loosen the ropes around his ankles. Tom, too, has tried to untie himself, without success.

"Just give me some time," says Gabriel. "I have a knife."

Tom yawns. The fire is so hot, it feels like his cheek is burning.

"But even if you could free yourself, what then? We can't get past the bars on the window. I've tried."

Gabriel continues pulling at his ankles and his wrists, but the knots are too tight, and neither he nor Tom can reach into his pocket to grab the knife. All he accomplishes with his wriggling is to push his back farther down the wall. With its white walls, the dying room looks like a hospital room dug into the rock, a clinic for cave dwellers, subsequently forgotten for five thousand years . . .

Someone knows that they are here, though.

"Anyway, my mom will come and save us," Gabriel says. "You heard her calling earlier. You answered her. And I saw her."

"She must have failed, though. Otherwise, she'd already be here."

Tom leans more heavily on him. He's right; Gabriel knows that. His mother must have been captured too.

"All right, then . . . I've got another idea."

Tom yawns again. He's too weak to struggle anymore.

"I appreciate that," he says in a murmur, "but don't stress out about it. I'm just going to take a nap. Can you get some cookies from the local supermarket, and wake me up when it's teatime?"

All Tom's muscles suddenly relax.

"Don't fall asleep," Gabriel shouts, shaking him. "Not here. We're in the dying room. If you fall asleep, you'll die."

Tom lets himself fall in the other direction, next to the fireplace.

"It's okay, Gabriel," he says. "You made me drink some of the red water from the Fountain of Souls. When I wake up, I'll be a baby."

Gabriel stares in horror at his friend.

"No, that'll only work if your mother drinks the other half. And how can she do that while we're imprisoned here?"

Seeing Gabriel's expression, Tom draws on his last reserves of strength. He leans against the hot edge of the fireplace.

"I was joking, Gaby. I guess you're even crazier than me. Do you really believe in that legend of the red water from hell?"

"I . . . I don't know. I just got to Auvergne. I listen to what people say. Just like I listened to all the crazy stuff that Esteban told his shrink on that USB key of my mother's."

Tom puts a hand on Gabriel's tied-up legs.

"You know," he says, "I never believed in any of that stuff. The drowned village, reincarnation, ghosts, the water from hell . . . They're just stories, like *Harry Potter* or *Star Wars*. I only pretended to believe it, the way all kids pretend to believe stories. There aren't any elves or goblins or witches in real life."

Gabriel smiles sadly.

"Witches are real," he answers.

"They're not, Gaby."

Tom rests his head on Gabriel's thighs, as if they've been tied together to make him a bolster pillow. Gabriel doesn't dare move his legs.

"Gaby, I wanted to tell you . . . before I fall asleep . . ."

"Tell me what?"

Tom makes one last effort to keep his eyes open. Lying horizontal like that, all he can see is the white ceiling, the flames . . . and the face of the boy leaning over him.

"Thank you."

"It's okay, I . . ."

"Thank you for helping me celebrate my birthday last night. Thank you for following me here. Thank you for trying to save me. Thank you . . . for being my only real friend."

80

The blood around my eye has clotted. At least, it's no longer bleeding, although the bandage around my head is still drenched. Every time I lift up my bound wrists to touch my head, my fingertips feel something sticky and spongelike, and when I look at them afterward, they're bright red. The wound doesn't hurt, though. And my brain is working normally: I can see, feel, hear, understand.

I have given up trying to crawl through the dust on the floor of the cave. I have given up imagining I may pull myself upright on the sharp walls. I have given up trying to spit out the spit-soaked gag. I have even given up staring at Savine with my one functioning eye; doing so is no more useful than aiming an unloaded gun.

I am saving my strength.

A moment will come, I feel sure.

I have to get one last chance.

◆ ◆ ◆

"You should have taken better care of your son, Maddi; you should have protected Gabriel. All this stuff has nothing to do with him. You had a son who replaced Esteban—what more could you want? Was it really so difficult to shelter him from all of this?

"I don't know how he found out. I'm guessing you left paperwork within his reach, files undeleted on your computer, maybe even videos, police reports, psychiatrist sessions . . .

"Somehow, anyway, Gabriel figured it all out. And of course, he wanted to meet this Tom, the doppelganger of his dead older brother, the one who was driving his mother so crazy.

"They're the same age. They're both only children, sensitive, solitary . . . It was natural that they would become friends. Tom was already obsessed with Esteban, the child reincarnated inside his head that I'd told him so much about. Gabriel knew Esteban too: he seemed almost able to enter his thoughts; he'd probably even tried on old clothes you kept. My guess is that, inspired by all those ghost stories, Tom and Gabriel decided to play along with the conceit, just for fun. I mean, they're ten, right? It's normal that they still believe in the fantastical, in magic. Or pretend to believe, at least.

"It was all supposed to be so simple last night. I was just going to slip inside Amandine's house. The door is never locked, and there was no way she'd hear me: Amandine always drinks three cups of valerian tea before she goes to bed. Just to be sure, though, I was planning to give her an injection of oxycodone, then to wake Tom and take him with me.

"I drugged Amandine. I may have given her too much: my hand was shaking, and she kept moving in her sleep. I left the syringe on the floor—I knew they would suspect a doctor as soon as they saw it—and then went into Tom's bedroom.

"It was empty.

"I saw his footprints in the snow covering the farmyard. They went out to the road. I thought history was repeating itself, that Tom was running away from me just like Esteban did ten years ago, that yet again I hadn't been patient enough, hadn't shown him enough love. I thought he was afraid of me.

"I believed that, Maddi, really believed it, for several minutes of absolute panic, as I drove away from the farm in my 4x4, the headlights illuminating the fountain, Froidefond, the bridge . . .

"And then there he was, shivering, a terrified little rabbit in the headlights.

"As soon as he recognized me, he smiled and ran toward me. When I opened the car door, he didn't hesitate for a second. He jumped straight in. I had rescued him again, just as I did at Wolf's Leap, just as I've done so many times through the years.

"At that moment, Maddi, I felt so proud. I could see it in his eyes: I was his real mother.

"While I rubbed his back and dried his hair, trying to warm him up, he told me that Esteban had come to help him celebrate his birthday. *Esteban?* Yes, Esteban, his imaginary friend who he said seemed so real. Of course, I realized immediately that he was talking about Gabriel. There was no other child who could possibly know the story of Esteban. But I wasn't concerned. Tom said that Esteban had gone home, or, he supposed, back into his head.

"I drove slowly for more than a kilometer. I had plenty of time. Mine was the only vehicle on the road that night, and more than anything, I wanted to avoid having an accident. Tom kept coughing. He was surprised when we didn't stop at La Souille. After another coughing fit, I gave him a pill to swallow. A sleeping tablet. He fell asleep less than a kilometer later, his body curled up, held in place by his safety belt, his poor neck twisted, his back bent double. I stopped the car to settle him into a more comfortable position, savoring each motherly gesture. I was free at last to protect him, to love him.

"Everything was going to plan. I was too happy to feel wary. I don't think I looked behind me once, not even when I parked in front of the Jonas Caves. It never crossed my mind that Gabriel had ducked out of sight as soon as he saw the headlights of my Koleos from the Froidefond bridge. And I certainly couldn't have imagined that he would follow me, over a distance of almost three kilometers, watching my taillights fade through the night, walking in the ruts of my tire tracks not yet covered up by the snow, shortening the distance between us whenever I stopped. Three kilometers, downhill—less than a thirty-minute walk.

Even though I was driving slowly, Gabriel ended up losing sight of me. The snowfall was too dense, visibility too limited. He searched for a long time before finding my 4x4.

"Have you been listening, Maddi? Do you understand what that means?

"Gabriel should have hated Tom, his rival, this kid who had appeared out of nowhere, for whose sake you had made him move to a different part of the country. Whom you were favoring, to the point of neglecting him. And yet he wanted to meet him. To offer him his friendship. And when Tom needed him, Gabriel came to his aid. Do you realize, Maddi, what a generous and courageous son you have? Don't you see that, by taking care of Tom, he hoped to prove to you that he loves you?

"You don't deserve him, Maddi. I wasn't lying when I told you in the car, on the way here, that you are not worthy of him.

"I felt my first twinge of alarm when Deputy Salomon went to the Moulin de Chaudefour and called Lespinasse to tell him that your son was not at home. You confirmed I should worry an hour ago, in my 4x4, when you pointed out the red dot on the screen of your phone.

"I was lucky, Maddi. I was really lucky that you're such a terrible mother.

"Don't you see? If Gabriel had had a phone, you would have called and saved him—and I would have been totally screwed. But you preferred instead to sew a tracking device into his jacket, without telling him.

"And in doing so, you doomed him."

81

Lespinasse stands in the snow—back straight, legs parted, like a statue—in the middle of the farmyard, his ankles swallowed up by what looks like a block of white concrete. A statue to the glory of the cell phone, frozen to his ear. A statue that is now bellowing loud enough to crack its pedestal.

"Did you hear me, Moreno? I want helicopters. And drones. I want tanks if necessary. Anything that can fly or drive over snow."

The answer is lost in a blizzard of static. Jennifer Louchadière, hopping about in the snow next to the lieutenant, trying to warm herself up, does not catch a single word.

"What's the weather got to do with it?" Lespinasse demands. "The storm's over. There's a kid out there somewhere, Moreno, and two women have set off in pursuit of him. At least one of them is crazy, and the other one might be too."

The lieutenant continues to negotiate for a while before hanging up, then turns to Jennifer. He points at the tire tracks of the Koleos, easily identifiable in the snow.

"Shit, what am I thinking? All we have to do is follow those tracks! Why haven't we gone and found them already?"

Salomon comes over. The antenna of a walkie-talkie sways above his ear. Perched atop ten centimeters of snow, the deputy looks like a giant.

"I just got some bad news, boss. The snowplow has cleared the road between Murol and La Bourboule. All the tracks have been erased."

The three police officers exchange devastated looks. After a brief silence, Lespinasse peers up at the white mountaintops of the Massif du Sancy, the pine forests receding into the horizon.

"Jesus, they could be anywhere! It could take us hours, even days, to find them."

His gaze descends to the second-floor window of the farmhouse, the window of Amandine's bedroom, where he sees Nectaire shaking Aster's hand, while with her other hand the witch is gripping her copper pendant.

What volcanic angels is she praying to? What infernal monster? Behind them, three paramedics stand guard like Cerberus.

82

Savine has untied my ankles so I can walk. She has taken a revolver from her bag, and now she is aiming it at me.

"I'm not going to lie to you, Maddi," she says of the gun. "I've never used it. I may be a terrible shot. I'll leave it up to you to gauge the risk . . . But maybe, instead of making me shoot you, you'd prefer to see your son again?"

I don't argue. How can I, anyway, given that there's still a gag in my mouth? My wrists are still tied too.

I go first, following her instructions: the corridor to the right, then to the left, left again, a room, another room, both of them cold and dark, their lava walls flesh-colored with bloodred stripes, the rocks jutting sharply. My head aches. As soon as I stood up, I felt dizzy. I couldn't tell if my head was spinning, or only the thoughts inside it. I need to concentrate, empty my mind. I need to rid my memory of the poisonous words this monster has injected into it. *I was really lucky that you're such a terrible mother.*

"Turn right; then go to the end."

Savine pushes me into a narrow tunnel that appears to be a dead end. As I advance, the tunnel's end grows increasingly bright. It opens onto the cliff face. Unless I've lost all sense of direction in this maze, we ought to be close to where I heard Tom's voice, before Savine knocked me out.

As I come out into the light, I spot the rocky overhang sheltering the cliff. The snow is not as deep here, and now I can see the crude steps that lead up to one last cell, separate from all the others, its window barred.

"Go!" Savine shouts at me.

Clinging to the wall, I climb along the cliff. The tuff is damp, and it crumbles with each step. I tell myself not to look down, not to let the cold air intoxicate me; urge myself to keep my head in this icy gale, to forget the haunting thought that this monster could, at any moment, shoot me in the back.

I am not a terrible mother.

And I will have the opportunity to prove it. I have to get one last chance.

I reach the platform and fall to my knees before the barred window, exhausted.

My right eye opens for the first time: through a tiny crack, a few millimeters wide, between my pupil and my eyelid, the light filters through. It burns my retina like a flash of lightning.

Without lowering her gun, Savine takes a bunch of keys from her pocket. She opens the padlock that holds the two sections of the iron grill together and pulls them apart. They make a sinister creak.

"Go inside. You'll be warmer there."

I obey. She wasn't lying. The heat is almost stifling in this strange, square, white-walled room. It must be seventy degrees in here, a shock after the frigid air outside. And the room grows ever warmer the farther in I go.

I stagger.

They're here. Oh God, they're here.

The two boys are leaning against a pile of firewood near the wide hearth.

I swallow. My gag is soaked with the ebb and flow of my trapped words.

Tom is asleep. Gabriel is shivering. With fear, I imagine.

Whom should I look at first?

Oh God . . .

Tom is so vulnerable. Gabriel lowers his eyes.

Tom is breathing softly. Gabriel holds his breath, too afraid to speak. Maybe he's waiting for me to speak first. Maybe he hasn't noticed that I've been gagged.

"Aren't you going to say hello to your mommy, Gaby?"

Gabriel's ankles, arms, and wrists are all tied up. Savine is still pointing her gun at me.

"Don't be shy! I've been very complimentary about you. And— good news—you're finally going to have your mother all to yourself. Tom is going to disappear from your life, and so am I. I'm sorry you won't get to say goodbye to him. I had to give him some sleeping pills, so he won't remember anything. Or not much, anyway. You'll always be his favorite ghost, though."

I wish I could gnaw through this gag with my teeth, so that I could scream, spit, bite, say, *I love you; I'm here; don't be scared.*

Don't be scared . . .

Even though Savine cannot possibly let us live, after all this. It would ruin her plan.

She moves closer to the boys, her hand still tight around the butt of her revolver, and leans tenderly over Tom's sleeping body. Is she really going to put a bullet in our heads? Can she really pass so quickly from her love for Tom to her hate for anyone who gets in her way? Is she really that—

Just then, Gabriel leaps up.

Just when Savine is so close to him, when she is least expecting it. Gabriel's feet are still tied, but his hands are miraculously free. He is holding a knife. Without a moment's hesitation, he thrusts it at Savine's shoulder.

She spins to the side, struck by the blade. Gabriel climbs to his knees and stabs her again. I run there as fast as I can, but it's hard without the use of my arms. I am proud of my son, so proud, but he has to stop now before he kills her. *That's enough, Gaby, you'll regret it forever if you—*

The blade strikes Savine's chest once more.

No, Gabriel!

I am almost there. The monster is surely dying, but I am wary of what she might still do.

Not wary enough, though . . .

Savine is lying on the ground. Her body suddenly relaxes, and her feet kick out at my tibias. I collapse as Savine clambers to her feet.

There are no bloodstains on her clothes.

Not a single rip.

I feel as if I have just watched a fight scene in a movie, not a real fight. Savine grabs the knife from Gabriel's hand and shoves him violently into the pile of firewood. His head hits the white wall, leaving a streak of blood, before his body drops like an abandoned puppet onto the logs. He closes his eyes.

Gaby!

His eyes open again, and he lifts his hand to his chest. I discover, to my horror, that his jacket is soaked with a pool of crimson.

No, Gaby, no.

I have never seen an expression of such pain, such terror, on my son's face. He opens his jacket and, looking as despairing as if he were tearing out his own heart, pulls out a small, broken glass vial containing the remnants of some red liquid.

Oh, thank God . . .

Savine observes the smashed bottle and smiles. She is holding her revolver again. She takes a second to examine the knife with which Gabriel attacked her, then turns back toward him.

"You're a very brave boy, Gabriel. It must have taken an enormous effort to cut through your ropes with such a dull little blade . . . Aster's smart enough not to leave dangerous weapons within reach of children in her store. That way, they can only steal toys."

Gabriel's eyes are wet with tears. Tom is still asleep, knocked out by the drug Savine gave him. I am still lying on the ground, with grazed knees and a throbbing head.

"This time," Savine says, "I really do have to go. I don't want Tom to wake up and see all this. Shall I leave you the fire?"

She puts the penknife in her pocket and tosses three more logs into the fireplace.

"Gabriel, you're a smart boy. Do you know what this room is called?"

Gabriel wipes the tears from his cheeks. He's still stunned from his head hitting the wall, dazed by his fall, and exhausted, but I am impressed by the wild animal glare that he still manages to shoot at her.

"The dying room," he says, without looking away.

"Exactly. This is where they used to put the corpses. That's why they painted the walls with lime—it stopped the spread of disease. At least, some of the time . . . As you can see, they needed a big fireplace, so they could burn the bodies when there were too many of them. Thankfully, it didn't have to be used all the time."

Gabriel collapses back onto the woodpile, still reeling from his fall. He fought as hard as he could. I want to convince myself that he's okay. I must examine him, heal him. I must take this chance, this last opportunity, to save him . . .

Savine moves to the right of the fireplace and reaches up to a hidden chain that runs alongside the chimney. If one didn't know it was there, it would be almost impossible to see it.

"That's why," she explains, "most of the time, the chimney of the dying room was kept closed. They could just shut the trapdoor, and it would keep out snow, birds, and anything else that might block it."

Her hand closes around the chain.

"Obviously, you should never close the trapdoor when the fire is lit. Because then the smoke wouldn't be able to escape, and you would soon die of suffocation."

She pulls hard.

The trapdoor closes with a sharp cracking noise. The smoke vainly seeks an exit and, finding no opening, starts to spread through the dying room.

Savine aims her gun at Gabriel's slumped body, but she speaks to me.

"Don't try anything while I take Tom outside. I would hate to have to shoot such a brave boy."

I have managed to get to my feet. Gabriel's expressionless face is already blurring beyond the black clouds that are now rising in wreaths of smoke toward the ceiling. I stand in front of the monster, blocking her path, my legs parted, wrists tied. She aims the barrel of her revolver at my forehead.

"Out of the way, Maddi. I can't risk my son suffocating."

I don't move. I stare at her, determined to make her understand that I need to speak.

"Sorry, Maddi, I don't have time."

I lift my bound hands in a gesture of supplication. Her index finger tightens around the trigger. Still, I don't move. Exasperated, she tears the gag from my mouth.

I take a second to swallow, gulping down my saliva; then I yell.

"Please, just one question."

"Get out of the way. Or I'll shoot."

The smoke is rising up to the ceiling of the dying room and gathering there in thick clouds. Below, the air is still breathable, at least for now. I speak as fast as I can.

"There's something you're missing here, Savine. Who found Jonas's body? Who made the connection between the murder weapon and the stolen knife? It was Aster."

I gesture with my bound hands, causing them to rise and fall as I speak.

"I know that," Savine roars. "I already told you I stole the knife."

She moves even closer, but I can tell she doesn't want to shoot me. She would rather leave us here to die so she doesn't have to watch our death throes. But the smoke is already crowning our heads. She won't risk waiting much longer. She will kill me as soon as the ashes make her eyes water. The words spill from my mouth in a flood.

"But remember, when Aster called the farm earlier, she accused Gabriel of stealing it."

For the first time, Savine looks me in the eye. There's a hint of intrigue in her face, then a frown. The blackness continues to gather and roll down toward us.

"Think about it, Savine. Aster wouldn't have called the police just because a little penknife was stolen."

My hands have continued to move up and down, and now they come to a halt in front of my chest. The smoke is getting into our eyes. My vision blurs. I see the revolver barrel shaking, a finger tensing. A flash of memory: *the gift on my kitchen table last night.* I pour the words out in a rush before she decides to shoot.

"Gabriel did steal a real knife from Aster's store, but he gave it to me."

A look of surprise flashes in Savine's eyes; a second of stupefaction that is enough to slow her reaction. Just as the fog envelops us, I blindly push my bound hands forward and stab her in the heart with the Thiers Gentleman concealed between my palms.

She collapses instantly, a look of bewilderment on her face. All day long, nobody bothered searching me; when it's folded, the Auvergne flick-knife is no bigger than a pen. It took me endless minutes and painstaking care, in the cave, to retrieve it from the bottom of my pocket without Savine noticing my desperate contortions.

I crouch down to escape the smoke. Beneath the black fog, I see the two inanimate bodies of Tom and Gabriel. I have to cut the ties that bind me. I have to get the boys out of here as quickly as possible. The barred window stands open, twenty meters away: the gate to our salvation. All the smoke is trapped at the back of the cave.

Using both hands, I pull the knife from Savine's chest. Her body spasms, but I pay no attention to that.

In a few seconds, we will all suffocate to death.

434

I turn the blade to my wrists to saw through the rope, not caring whether I draw blood.

The black veil is upon us now. It envelops Savine's corpse, as if to take it down to hell.

The ropes give way, along with a long strip of my flesh. I don't care. I crawl, since it's the only way I can move. There are less than thirty centimeters of breathable air above the ground. The two little bodies are lying in front of me.

Tom, to my right, has still not woken. He is deeply asleep. He won't even notice when his blood is poisoned, when his muscles stiffen and his brain is paralyzed.

Gabriel, to my left, has also lost consciousness, but his body shakes and shivers; his entire being is fighting against the toxins now entering his lungs, his bloodstream.

The mist is growing ever denser, its black wings touching the ground. Nothing and nobody can escape it now.

I hold my breath as long as I can.

Petrified.

Tom. Gabriel.

All of these thoughts pass through me in an instant.

I may still have time to get out, but I won't have time to come back again.

A one-way trip. I don't have time to hesitate.

I must choose.

I must choose which child I will save.

83

Time has stopped. All is smoke.

It has entered my throat, my stomach, my head. My heart is still beating, but only to spread the poison through my body, to asphyxiate my lungs, to turn everything black.

I can't choose.

How could I possibly abandon Gabriel? He is my flesh and blood, and I owe him so much: so many apologies, so much love. *Did you really have to look death in the eye, Gaby, before I understood?*

I watch in a panic, amid this unreal black maelstrom, as his little body convulses, and I am incapable of moving a muscle.

Forgive me. Understand me. How could I abandon Tom? He looks so much like Esteban. As if this calmly sleeping boy has come back to me, after I waited so long. How could I not reach out to him? Look; he's like a baby, so trusting, so peaceful. I know you understand me, Gaby, because you loved him immediately too; you wanted to protect him, to save him . . .

I am reaching out to Esteban, crazed once again, cursed forever, when a voice behind me coughs, then whispers imploringly, at once clear and muffled, as if from the bottom of a well, "Mommy."

Time has stopped again. My arms trace a new circle, this time around Gabriel.

Oh, Esteban, I have to abandon you for the second time. You're dead, Esteban, you understand that, don't you? You drowned. Tom . . .

Tom is nothing to me . . . Must I kill him for the curse to finally be lifted? Must I sacrifice him? Must I . . .

Impossible! I already know that I will not be able to choose. I already know that it is too late. I already know that the three of us will die together, that none of us will survive.

Forgive me, Gabriel.

Forgive me, Tom.

I had no choice.

I cease to struggle. I let the black veil descend upon me.

84

"Grab the kid!"

A gust of air stirs the smoke. It whirls like a woken shadow.

A black figure in the fog, rapid, determined.

"For God's sake, Maddi, grab that kid! Quick! I'll take care of Gaby . . ."

I don't think. I drag Tom's sleeping body toward the window. I cough; I spit, but with each meter the air becomes less thick, at first more breathable, and then, as soon as we are out beyond the gates of hell, the darkness opens up to reveal a bright paradise. The smoke from the fireplace in the dying room is now nothing more than a slender thread that is vanquished by an ocean of snow.

The two of us stand on the platform, facing the white horizon, each of us holding a child.

Tom breathes softly, regularly against my heart. I lick my finger and erase some of the black dust from the corners of his mouth. He is saved.

Gabriel opens his eyes, as if returning from a long voyage. He wipes the soot from his face, and his face lights up with a chimney sweep's eyes.

"Mommy?"

"It's over, Gaby. Everything's okay."

Reassured, he clings to the shoulders of the man who has saved him.

I think again about that little green dot I saw on the screen of my cell phone not long after I decided to share the GPS SafetyTrace tracker application with Wayan: the dot I noticed the moment just before I entered the Jonas Caves.

He was the only man I felt duty bound to warn if you were in danger, Gabriel.

A handsome, strong, intelligent man. So handsome, strong, and intelligent that it's frankly annoying.

The only man to whom I gave myself—once—during that period nine months before you were born.

A man too clever not to have guessed, too respectful ever to have mentioned it.

The man who had dropped everything to follow me.

The wind covers us with white powder. We are angels now. As if by magic, the clouds part, and a patch of blue sky appears and then begins to grow.

Wayan Balik Kuning, with his salt-and-pepper beard and his snow-and-ashes hair, looks at me. And smiles.

Hold him tight, Gabriel. Never let him go.

You are safe in the arms of this man who has saved you.

You are safe in your daddy's arms.

XIII

Reincarnation

Angel Dust

85

Four months later

Nectaire parks the car as soon as he sees the sign reading "Col de la Croix-Saint-Robert." The snow melted long ago, and all that remains of it now are a few patches hidden away in shady corners, some tiny puddles of ice that shiver in the June sunlight, and several white streaks piled up at the foot of embankments, offering the few visitors who stop by the roadside one last opportunity to make a snowball or two.

Winter, that year, disappeared just as quickly as it appeared.

There are three bouquets of flowers in the passenger seat. Nectaire picks up the first, a bunch of autumn crocuses, wild chicory, common mallow, and broom gathered in the undergrowth just below. The marker indicating the summit of the col is only about ten meters away: a small block of granite by the side of the road, at exactly 1,451 meters above sea level. Nectaire walks past it. The wooden cross has been planted one meter beyond it. Just a simple wooden cross—two planks of chestnut joined by a single nail—with a few words engraved on it.

Martin Sainfoin. He was no Poulidor.

Nectaire bends down and places the bouquet next to the cross. Martin would have liked this inscription. He'd often joked, with his cycling buddies and Nectaire, that it should be his epitaph one day. Looking down a few bends below, he catches sight of the multicolored outfits worn by a group of cyclists attacking the last stretch of the ascent. How many people will reach this summit today? How many will stop here? How many will spare a thought for Martin Sainfoin?

Nectaire recently learned that Martin's grandson, Julien, won the Auvergne youth championship last weekend. He flew away from his rivals on the pass below this one, the Col de la Croix-Morand. Unstoppable, according to his coaches, who believe he is a future champion. Nectaire imagines that his grandfather's ghost was helping him pedal during that ascent. Maybe, ten years from now, when little Julien Sainfoin is a man, and the Tour de France passes along this route, the two of them—grandson and ghost—will leave the whole peloton behind on the Col de la Croix-Saint-Robert . . .

◆ ◆ ◆

Nectaire drives back from the col. He puts an old tape of Ravel's *Boléro* into the car's cassette player. The oboes, clarinets, and other woodwinds patiently accompany his careful driving. He takes the time to observe the wooded slopes of the Chaudefour Valley, the volcanic dikes of the Dent de la Rancune and the Crête du Coq, rising above the trees like petrified forest rangers. He slows down as he drives past the empty parking lot of the Moulin, observing the old steel pylons left behind by the ski resort, and imagining other ghosts crossing the road in front of him, entire families carrying skis over their shoulders or snowboards under their arms.

The road continues to bend and curve, playing peek-a-boo with the Couze Chambon, and soon he can see the Froidefond bridge, the gray houses, the Fountain of Souls.

As he parks his Renault in the farmyard at La Souille and opens the car door, Ravel's flute and oboe d'amore fall silent, and he is shocked to hear another kind of music altogether. Tom and Gabriel have made a stage in front of the farmhouse from a few wooden pallets and are playing a concert to an audience of three sleepy cats and ten overexcited hens.

They are, as far as Nectaire can tell, playing a mix of rap and rock.

"That's too loud!" shouts the mayor's office secretary. "You'll wake the volcano . . ."

"Hope so!" Gabriel yells into his microphone.

Tom plays a riff on his electric guitar that perfectly imitates a volcanic eruption.

"I'm just trying out my birthday present! Have you heard it, Nicky? This lyre-guitar sounds like a bat out of hell, doesn't it?"

Nectaire smiles. He's never seen Tom looking so happy. When Maddi gave him the guitar, he was practically speechless with gratitude. The instrument was the most beautiful gift Tom had ever received, even if he's using it to make the most infernal racket now.

"So, what is that terrible noise you're making?" Nectaire asks. "Does it have a title?"

"It's 'Hegoak,'" Gabriel proudly announces. "You know, the Basque hymn? But we've rearranged it in our own way, using the score that Esteban wrote."

"He was a real pioneer," agrees Tom. "Everyone thinks the lyre belongs in the past, but Esteban knew the lyre-guitar was the future."

And the two of them start playing again, Tom strumming the strings and Gaby screaming into the microphone, as the hens run around looking scandalized.

"*Hegoak ebaki banizikio,*" Gabriel yells.

If I had cut his wings . . .

86

I watch from the foot of the stairs as Nectaire closes the farmhouse door
behind him. Catching sight of the two bouquets he's holding, I speak
to him in the authoritative tones of the village doctor.

"That's kind of you, Nicky, but now is not a good time. Amandine
is upstairs; the contractions have started, and she's in labor. And you
know her—there's no way she's going to give birth anywhere but here."

"Dr. Libéri is right," says Wayan, standing three steps above me.
He's wearing an apron over his impeccable white shirt. "Now really isn't
a good time."

I turn toward my favorite psychiatrist.

"Wayan's on guard duty for now. I've been invited to the concert."

He groans obligingly, raising his eyebrows at Nectaire.

"I obviously didn't read the small print in the job description,
because I don't remember agreeing to become a midwife."

"Don't be so modest! You did study medicine for ten years . . ."

We smile at each other like two hospital interns joking at the end
of a shift. I climb the steps that separate us and kiss him on the lips.
Just a quick kiss; I've promised to step outside in a minute and listen
to Gabriel sing.

Nectaire has put one of the bouquets in the vase on the dresser, but
he is still holding the other, standing there like a third wheel.

"Don't you have something to do, Nicky?"

"Um, yes . . . of course . . ."

He doesn't move, though. I go back down the stairs and walk over to him.

"Who is that one for?"

"Well . . . for Aster . . ."

I open the door to the kitchen.

"So what are you waiting for? Go give it to her!"

He does, but just before I slam the door in his face, Nectaire has time to ask, "Um, would you like some tea?"

Leaving Nectaire in the kitchen, I head toward the front door. I'll be just outside—Wayan will shout for me if her labor speeds up. But right now, Gabriel is expecting me. I promised him I would listen to their new song.

"Maddi?"

I turn and look. Wayan still hasn't gone back upstairs to Amandine's room.

"Maddi," he repeats. "You don't happen to have a spare DNA test, do you?"

A DNA test? My heart speeds up as I start to panic. Is this whole thing going to start up again?

Wayan looks at the closed kitchen door behind me and whispers, "We could test strands of hair from Aster and from Nectaire." He stares after them in amazement. "Honestly, sometimes it's hard to believe those two are only brother and sister!"

I step out into the farmyard. Gabriel is facing away from me. He hasn't seen me yet. I watch him as he stands, playing music, on the makeshift stage with Tom.

Gaby . . .

I am so proud.

Proud that he's here, proud that he's him, proud of what he did, because I can't imagine any other child risking their life that way. I'm proud that he's as stubborn as me. And I'm proud to hear him singing, laughing, playing. Proud that he's found a friend in Tom. Proud to have found him a father. Oh yes, I'm a very proud mother . . .

Suddenly Gaby stops singing, as if he's sensed my presence. He turns around and smiles at me. *You don't look like Esteban, Gaby—you look far less like him than Tom, his doppelganger, does—and yet . . .*

I love the two of you equally, you and Esteban. I am sure of that now.

Esteban will always remain alive in my memory. But you, Gaby, are my present. And my future.

You hold out your little microphone, your face eager with excitement.

"Come on, Mom. Come and sing with us!"

87

"Here you go, Astic. This is for you. The only woman in my life."

"Thank you, Nicky."

Aster gives her brother a fond look, takes the bouquet, and buries her nose in the wild angelicas and wild pansies, breathing in their scent, before locating a jug on the kitchen shelf so she can prolong the lives of the cut flowers for as long as possible. As she's putting them in water, she speaks to every stem, every petal in the bouquet, while Nectaire opens drawers and jars in search of an ingredient he can use to make some herbal tea.

The subtle art of taking one's time. An ancient tradition.

From upstairs, through the thin ceiling and walls, they hear Amandine screaming with increasing intensity. They hear the front door open, hear Maddi's footsteps as she runs up the stairs.

Nectaire has found some stale cinnamon sticks and wrinkled mulberry leaves at the bottom of a jar.

"Do you think it'll work?"

Aster breaks off the conversation she's having with a blueweed flower.

"Do I think what will work?"

"You know—the red water, the migration of souls. Do you think the few drops that Amandine swallowed will be enough?"

"Oh, so you believe in that now?"

Nectaire slowly crumbles the cinnamon in his hand, then sniffs.

"I believe . . . um, what I believe, ultimately, is that there are two kinds of people in the world. Those, like me, who are content with what they can see, feel, taste, hear, touch, and those for whom that is not enough. Those, like you, who need to believe there is something else, invisible, indefinable, that exists before life or after death. Hence all the world's religions and superstitions—heaven and hell, reincarnation . . ."

He is interrupted by a scream, more terrifying than any that have come before, a scream loud enough to make the kitchen walls shake.

"The baby's coming," Aster murmurs.

Nectaire steps toward her. He stares at the copper necklace hanging from his sister's neck. The spirals of a unalome spinning endlessly.

"You didn't answer my question, Astie. Do you think it worked, the migration of souls? Do you believe that the baby will have Jonas's steel-blue eyes?"

"Of course," says Aster as she kisses the petals of a purple columbine. "And he'll start speaking Basque as soon as he's born!"

Amused, Nectaire blows on the cinnamon powder and, amid almost constant screaming from above, goes on. "So he'll be a surfer too? Very handsome and a little bit stupid?"

"He will break the hearts of many women," Aster replies sadly. "He will fly away like a bird."

Nectaire nods, then pulls a face.

"Was it really a good idea, then, to make her drink that stuff?"

For a long moment they don't say a word; they just stand there listening to the silence, breathing in the blend of spicy, floral aromas. And then Amandine gives one last yell—of happiness this time—and the baby cries for the first time in its life.

"I could swear that was Basque," Nectaire says.

Aster leans down to whisper a secret to a valerian.

"Don't mock me, Nicky. I'll answer your question. Yes, I believe the migration of souls worked. And even if you can't bring yourself to admit that I trapped an invisible little ghost in my bottle, taken straight from Jonas's mouth, so that it could live within Amandine's body, you could at least be happy about one thing: if Amandine sees the man she loved in that newborn child, then the migration of souls has worked."

"Autosuggestion, you mean? That's exactly what I meant when I said that there are two kinds of people in the—"

Aster presses one finger over her brother's lips, silencing him—its tip resting in the place the old myth calls the mark of the angel.

Looking through the kitchen window, they watch as the blazing sun paints the volcanoes primrose yellow, setting fire to the dark facades of the houses of Froidefond, glinting from the red water that flows for eternity, illuminating Tom and Gabriel as they play deafening rock music on their makeshift stage. Maddi is still upstairs in Amandine's room, where she ran the moment Wayan called her.

Aster draws her face close to her brother's ear.

"Listen, Nicky," she says quietly. "When we're born, we don't fall from the stars. We're not delivered by a stork. We're expected, welcomed, and as soon as we open our eyes, we need a thousand markers to guide us. A voice, a smell, a warm blanket, a bottle of warm formula brought to us by a nurse, a onesie bought by the excited mother—a onesie that someone sold to her, that someone else made, that another person designed—and all of the familiar objects that surround us: the stuffed animals and rattles we play with, the music we hear, every detail of the room where we sleep, the stories we listen to, the stranger on the street who smiles at us. We are, always, the result of the thousands of traces we encounter, the thousands of little white stones that others have left for us on our path. We pick them up . . . or we don't. Every person leaves little white stones when they pass through life. Everyone. Call it reincarnation if you like; it doesn't really matter. You see, Nectaire, we are born as dust, and to dust we will return. But that dust is part of the life of every new being on this earth."

About the Author

Photo © Philippe Quaisse

With over thirteen million copies of his books sold in France, Michel Bussi is one of the most successful French authors of all time. His books have been sold internationally in thirty-eight countries and have been translated into thirty-four languages. Known as "the master of the plot twist," he has published seventeen suspense novels with Presses de la Cité. Three of his books have already been adapted for French TV. He lives in France.

About the Translator

Photo © 2019 Kathy Taylor

Sam Taylor is an award-winning literary translator and author. His novels have been translated into a dozen languages, and he has translated more than sixty books from French, including Laurent Binet's *HHhH*, Leïla Slimani's *The Perfect Nanny*, Joël Dicker's *The Truth About the Harry Quebert Affair*, and Marcel Proust's *The Seventy-Five Folios*. He grew up in England, spent a decade in France, and now lives in the United States.